PENGUIN BOOKS

Between the Crosses

Matthew Frank lives in Kent with his wife and three young sons. Between family life and work as an architect he tries to squeeze in a bit of mountain biking, scuba-diving and midnight writing. *Between the Crosses* is his second novel, following on fror

Between the Crosses

MATTHEW FRANK

PENGUIN BOOKS

PENGUIN BOOKS

UK | USA | Canada | Ireland | Australia
India | New Zealand | South Africa

Penguin Books is part of the Penguin Random House group of companies
whose addresses can be found at global.penguinrandomhouse.com.

First published 2016
001

Copyright © Matthew Frank, 2016

The moral right of the author has been asserted

Set in 12.5/14.75 pt Garamond MT Std
Typeset by Jouve (UK), Milton Keynes
Printed in Great Britain by Clays Ltd, St Ives plc

A CIP catalogue record for this book is available from the British Library

ISBN: 978-1-405-91383-6

www.greenpenguin.co.uk

To Sid and Christine, beloved parents,
for everything.

They shall not grow old, as we that are left grow old
Age shall not weary them, nor the years condemn
At the going down of the sun and in the morning
We will remember them.

The 'Ode of Remembrance' from Laurence
Binyon's poem *For the Fallen*, 1914

Prologue

Sunday, 11 November 1984

Foul mud sucked at Neville's boots as he slipped and squelched from the rusty old ladder towards the shape rapidly being reclaimed by the inky waters of Deptford Creek – a corpse; that much was obvious, even from yards away in the dark, half submerged. London's latest flotsam.

River police were on their way but Inspector Smith wanted this one for Greenwich, and the tide was rising fast. So Sergeant Darlington's best boots and uniform were getting ruined. He doubted the smell would ever come out. But he could hardly ask Constable Cartwright to do this on his first week on the job, his first body. The rope bit into his waist and dragged more with every step. Cartwright's police-issue torch shone weakly from the embankment above, barely reaching. Neville's own had been plunged elbow-deep into the mire with his first slip and promptly died of shame.

At times like this, Neville could see the appeal of the investigative branch and a nice warm desk.

He waded into the icy water with a sharp intake of breath, and rolled the body on to its back.

A man. Twenties. Face water-swollen and filthy. Forehead bullet wound.

Christ knew where he'd gone in: it could have been here in the creek, but more likely somewhere up the

Ravensbourne or one of its tributaries. The rivers were high and fast with the heavy rains but the creek was low with the tidal Thames. If the damn thing had snagged on the opposite silt bank some unlucky sod from Lewisham station would be down here instead of offering cheerful advice from their side of the creek.

Breathing through his mouth, telling himself it was the reek that made him want to vomit, Neville searched pockets for ID. Nothing. No wallet, wristwatch, rings or chain.

There was something on the neck. Neville rubbed at the dirt.

A tattoo. Crude. Self-administered, prison job perhaps. One word . . . *Billie*.

Sunday, 12 November 1989

The rotating patrol car lights blurred and flared in the lancing rain, illuminating the street with their eerie blue pulse. There could be little hope of finding anything useful in such a downpour. The scene-of-crime officers had already given it up as a bad job but the two CID detectives stalked back and forth with their torches, perhaps just for the show of the thing.

A girl was missing.

Michael didn't know her name. No one had bothered to tell him and a police constable's job was to pound their beat, not to ask questions of serious detectives. He'd tried eavesdropping but the hissing roar of the rain was like a badly tuned radio. All he knew was that a sixteen-year-old had left her friend's house after dark but not arrived home. Her home was in the next road.

The elderly couple from the nearest house had heard screaming and peeped out into the dark to see two figures struggling. One dragged the other away. The wife phoned the police while the husband ran outside; he'd found nothing but the girl's handbag in the street. He was one of the stubborn onlookers huddled around the perimeter, residents drawn from their warm suburban homes by the spectacle. Now that he knew a girl was missing, the husband was rebounding between guilt and anger, between how he'd done what he could and what he'd do to the thug responsible, harping on at anyone who'd listen. He seemed convinced a thug was responsible. Thugs were definitely a pet topic of his. His wife had furnished him with an umbrella and steaming mug of tea so he was in it for the long haul. Still, you had to hand it to him; he'd run out into the rain in his slippers to help; he was a game old codger.

Michael tried to keep that in mind as the old boy embarked on a fresh tirade – the youth of today not knowing they're born and how he hadn't fought the Japanese so this sort of thing could happen in his street on Remembrance Sunday of all days. Michael tried to keep in mind that preserving the scene of a crime and keeping order was a vital task, imperative to the investigation. He tried not to think that he was wasting time here when he should be helping to search the woodland at the end of the road with Tony and the other PCs. He tried to ignore the water running off the front peak of his custodian helmet in a constant stream and the fact that it had long since seeped through his clothes.

Suddenly the rain stepped up from steady torrent to biblical deluge and the assorted onlookers finally dissolved back into their warm, cosy homes, their warm, cosy lives. Not to mention their warm dinners. Michael's stomach growled. Sergeant Cooper had his Thermos and Tupperware in the car, courtesy of Mrs C. Thirty years of corned beef sandwiches and wincingly sweet tea had left the old sergeant as rotund as he was cheerful. Michael had nothing but the distant prospect of dry toast and beef Cup-a-Soup when he eventually made it back to Shooters Hill nick.

The old boy was the last to admit defeat. His wife, to whom Michael couldn't help appending the words long-suffering, stood silhouetted in their front doorway, beckoning him to march his silly old bones inside before he caught his death. 'Thugs, the lot of them!' he sounded in retreat.

Sheltering beneath the meagre leaves still clinging to a nearby tree, shielding his cigarette from the rain, Sergeant Cooper finally took pity on his bedraggled constable and beckoned him over.

'Nice weather for ducks,' commented Cooper cheerfully. Droplets rattled off his new plastic police poncho with a lively popping noise. They struck Michael's sodden greatcoat with no discernible sound at all. 'Cheer up, lad,' chuckled Cooper, offering the fag.

Cupping it in his hands, Michael took a long, blessed drag.

Cooper retrieved his pack from under his helmet, lit another, and set about coughing profusely. 'Mrs C says I should give up, says they'll be the death of me.' He frowned at the warning message on the pack. '*Warning, by H. M. Government, smoking can damage your health.* "*Can*," I says to Mrs C, "*can* damage your health"; not *does*. "Scientists say they do," she replies. Killjoys. Still, always nice to

4

know she cares.' He glanced at Michael. 'Not married, are you, Mickey?'

'No, Sarge.' He wasn't fond of the name Mickey and worried it might catch on.

'You should, lad your age. Get yourself a nice chubby wife like my Beryl. Always a hot meal waiting in the oven when you get home, whatever ungodly hour.' Cooper's grin and girth spoke to the truth of that. 'And always a hot welcome waiting in the bed,' he added with a filthy chuckle that turned into another bout of coughing.

Michael shook his head to dispel any mental image of that and thought instead about Alison. She wasn't in the least chubby, Michael knew nothing of her culinary prowess and with only one tentative night out so far it was too soon to hope for anything hotter than a snog in a Vauxhall Nova. Not that he didn't hope quite fervently.

Cooper laughed and slapped him hard on the back. 'Got a lucky girl in mind, I see. Well, don't hang about, Mickey lad; with a face like yours best bag her while she's amenable!'

An ill-timed droplet did for what remained of Michael's fag with a hiss and he flicked the sodden butt out into the rain with a sigh. 'D'you know the girl's name, Sarge?'

'Kimberly Bates.'

'Will they find her, do you think?'

Cooper's cheer dimmed. 'One way or another, lad. One way or another.'

Michael stared back towards the woods, imagining his fellow constables walking in a line ten paces apart, torches scanning back and forth like lighthouses long after the ship has foundered.

Cooper stared that way too. The look in his eyes said

what they were both thinking. There was a chance the girl was sheltering from the rain in a phone box, her emergency ten-pence gone towards cigarettes or lipstick. There was a chance she was hiding out at a girlfriend's house, mooning over the latest pop heartthrob in *Just Seventeen* while neglecting to call her mother, wilfully or otherwise. There was a chance she was huddled under a bus shelter snogging a boyfriend, forgetting their quarrel and lost handbag the way only teenagers could. But there was a chance she lay dead under a bush, and on a night like this it was hard to imagine any of the happier endings.

The detectives got in their car and drove away. DI Grove and DS Darlington. Michael didn't envy them. Their work began at unhappy endings. At least on the beat you had a chance of preventing them. There were ugly rumours that CID had their eye on him, that he was being 'considered'. Michael was determined to evade them. Uniform had been good enough for his dad and his granddad and it was good enough for him.

Cooper was watching him. 'There's more to policing than helping old biddies across the road and chasing shoplifters,' he said, strangely. There were times when Michael wondered if Cooper wasn't a good deal more perceptive than he appeared. He couldn't recall seeing the fat old sergeant running after anyone, ever, but *could* recall occasions when Cooper happened to be hovering in just the right place to be run *into*.

Cooper's smile crept back and he slapped Michael on the shoulder. 'Right, that's enough loafing, Constable Groombridge . . . back out on parade!'

PART ONE

I

Sunday, 14 November 2010

A stiff northerly breeze whipped down Whitehall, biting through the back of Stark's damp uniform coat as he stood between the Women Of World War II monument and the Cenotaph trying not to lean on his cane. He'd been standing here an hour and the cold was seeping into his hip. Behind him over eight thousand veterans, relatives and representatives of other organizations and associations stretched all the way up to Trafalgar Square. Army, Navy and RAF service personnel in immaculate ceremonial uniform lined the road either side of the Cenotaph, with the massed band on the far side forming the Hollow Square.

As the Blackwatch bagpipes laced the air with lament Stark read for the hundredth time the words chiselled into the Cenotaph's Portland stone – THE GLORIOUS DEAD. Had Rudyard Kipling come to regret those words after his only son joined their ranks? The stone wreath carved above them stood out in sharp relief accentuated by the dark staining of the rain.

The poppy wreath in Stark's free hand hung like a dead weight, as though it too was carved from stone. It bore no name – commemorating the death, just days earlier, of the last combat veteran of World War One and all those gone before. Stark had intended to take part in the veterans' march past, of course, as he had the previous year, but the ancient mariner's quiet passing had prompted a call from Stark's personal albatross, Major Pierson. Who better to lay the wreath, she insisted, than Sergeant Joseph Stark of Her Majesty's Territorial Reserve, recipient of the nation's highest military award for valour? So here he stood, plucked from the inconspicuous ranks and thrust front and centre once more.

The final note of music faded away and the world stood still, waiting for the tolling of the bell.

Stark's phone chose that moment to vibrate in his pocket. He closed his eyes, thanking the stars that he'd put it on silent. He wasn't on call, but the Murder Investigation Team were chronically shorthanded and DCI Groombridge had decreed that phones must be switched on at all times. He wouldn't have meant this, but orders were orders.

From the Foreign and Commonwealth Office off to Stark's right, the Cross Bearer led out the Chapel Royal party and the Bishop of London. Next came the Major General of the Household Division, then the politicians, service and civilian chiefs, Commonwealth High Commissioners and the other religious leaders, each taking up station around three sides of the Cenotaph.

At two minutes to eleven the parade was brought to attention. The Queen and Duke of Edinburgh led the military royals out to line up with their backs to Stark, each with their equerry behind holding their wreath, enclosing the Inner Square.

Stark's phone vibrated again. Surely no one he knew, no one who knew him, would call him at this time on this day. If it was another bloody cold call . . .

On cue the Palace of Westminster clock-tower quarter bells struck the familiar full-hour chimes of Westminster Quarters and then, in perfect time with the single boom and echo from the field gun in Horse Guards, the Great Bell, Big Ben itself, began the eleven sonorous chimes to mark the hour.

A detonation of silence expanded across London.

Across the land those that remembered, those not caught up in life or disinterested, replaced speech with thought for two long, poignant minutes, perhaps glancing surreptitiously at their watches, perhaps embarrassed before colleagues and friends, perhaps moved near to tears for people they'd never met.

It began to drizzle again.

The gun fired once more on the one hundred and twentieth second and the Royal Marine Buglers sounded the Last Post.

The Queen's equerry presented her wreath, which she placed on the base of the Cenotaph. Then the other royals, one by one, and assembled dignitaries in turn. And then Stark. He limped forward to the base of the monument and bent low to place the wreath, stepped back, stood to attention, saluted and returned to his spot at the head of the march.

The massed bands began a moving piece Stark ought to know but couldn't name. The Bishop led a short service, interspersed with hymns and culminating in the 'Ode of Remembrance' and its final line – *we will remember them*.

'We will remember them,' those assembled repeated, a solemn drum-roll murmur on a dim, cold, wet, blustery morn.

The bands played the national anthem; then the royals departed followed by all the others as they had come, and the Hollow Square were stood at ease.

Stark's hip was singing its own hymn now. He was never sure whether standing was worse than walking. Rain dripped from the peak of his cap.

The Trustees of the Royal British Legion and other service charities laid their wreaths. The band struck up with 'A Long Way to Tipperary' and Stark joined the procession of veterans in their march, eyes left as they passed the monument, maintaining a steady stride as best he could all the way round to Horse Guards Parade, where the Princess Royal received their salute.

His hip had not ached this much in a year, the march adding fire to the earlier ice. As they disbanded he felt drained and energized in equal measure.

Major Pierson met him beneath the barracks portico with her customary Cheshire Cat timing, minus the grin. She stamped to attention and snapped off a vicious salute, which he returned with equally good-natured venom. She outranked him, but not the medal on his chest.

Her sour expression said she hadn't forgiven him for wearing police uniform rather than his army regimentals. She had probably received a dressing down for it, but there had to be give and take and the MoD were too used to taking.

He wasn't theirs any more. He was a copper now.

'How did I do?' he asked.

'Bloody shambles. I'll face a court martial for sure.' Their habitual exchange.

'And so soon after your promotion – shame.' The

crown on her epaulettes had not long replaced captain's pips.

She made a face and jerked her head for him to follow. His civilian suit was waiting for him in the solitary little room where he'd changed earlier. Wishing he'd had the foresight to bring spare socks and shoes, he placed both on the huge iron heating pipes while he changed. They were still damp when he pulled them back on but deliciously hot.

With a perfunctory knock Pierson entered with a bottle and two glasses. 'Courtesy of you-know-who,' she said, cracking open the seal. Royal Lochnagar Selected Reserve – single malt distilled near Balmoral Castle, the Queen's Highland retreat. 'Not that you deserve such lofty favour. I trust you're taking care of that,' she indicated the cane leaning against a chair. It was she who'd scrounged it on his behalf on the day of his medal award to save him hobbling before his Queen on crutches; an elegant masterpiece, the arched silver handle a leaping tiger, and the snakewood shaft with its tiger-like variegated grain and secret sting. Property of the Duke of Edinburgh before he'd insisted Stark keep it. Lofty favour, as she'd alluded. She meant was he looking after himself, of course, but would never say as much.

'I am,' he smiled. 'Sweet of you to ask.'

She pulled a face. Their relationship had begun with intense friction and settled into a kind of sibling détente, with her the disapproving older sister. Sometimes Stark thought back with a tinge of nostalgia to the days when everything he did or said left her spittingly angry. But you could say one thing for Pierson, she never poured short measure and she knew how to enjoy a good whisky in comfortable silence. Today though she looked uncharacteristically pensive. 'Have you given more thought to the events schedule?'

'No more than the last time you asked.' The Ministry of Defence were constantly trying to trot him out on parade and he was constantly refusing. 'Today was remembrance. The rest is PR.'

'You really are consistently irksome.'

'A message that doesn't seem to get through.'

'We're not done talking about this.'

'We are today,' he replied flatly.

The Major bit down her frustration, and nodded. Today wasn't the day. Another skirmish. Another ceasefire. 'Still seeing that girl, Kelly?' she asked. An unusual topic. Stark shook his head, eliciting a disapproving tut. 'Pillock.' Stark shrugged. 'Her decision or yours?'

'Mine.' Not his proudest moment. Pierson arched an eyebrow, waiting for him to expand, but Stark had nothing more to say. If he closed his eyes he could still see Kelly's frustration, her tears. It was seven weeks now. He missed her. That was that.

Pierson turned back to the window. 'Was it the future that spooked you, or the past?'

Stark searched for a way out of the conversation. 'Both.'

She shook her head. 'Always the throwaway truth, the one-word dodge.'

Stark said nothing and she continued to stare out at the leaden sky. 'Would you go back?' she asked quietly. 'If you could?'

It was clear what she meant. Another topic usually skirted. 'Yes.'

'Unfinished business?'

'I suppose.' It wasn't that simple. War never was.

She nodded. 'What if you could go back in time too, would you do things differently?'

'Yes.'

'What would you change?'

'Everything I could,' he answered honestly. But there was no time machine. He'd taken lives, saved lives and failed to save others; there was no way now to alter the tally. Grasping at if-onlys gave no comfort. He looked at her, struck by this atypical conversation, but she offered no explanation.

She turned to look at him, her expression unreadable, then smiled faintly and raised her glass. 'Life is for the living.'

'If you say so,' replied Stark, chinking crystal.

They both drank, then she turned back to the window and they lapsed into silence again.

Stark took a long swig and closed his eyes at the delicious burning, tasting the rich aroma in the back of his nose, feeling himself relax for the first time that day.

'I think your phone's buzzing somewhere,' commented Pierson.

The damn thing had slipped his mind. Muttering a curse, he fumbled for it in his coat but it stopped before he could fish it out. Seven missed calls, Stark read with a sinking feeling. Not a cold caller – the office. No messages. Fran despised voicemail. And she never called with good news.

Giving Pierson an apologetic look, he took a deep breath and called back. 'Sarge?'

'Where the *bloody* hell have you been?' she demanded.

'Seriously?' he asked, deadpan.

He could almost imagine her checking her watch and rolling her eyes. 'Yeah, all right ... but where are you *now*?'

'Dimly lit room with a bottle of single malt and a dangerous dame.'

'Hilarious. How soon can you get here?'

'Why?' There could only be one reason. There was little use reminding her that he was on leave, but he wasn't going to make it easy for her.

'Just get your arse in. We've got a grisly double murder to pin on someone.'

2

'About bloody time,' Fran pronounced by way of greeting, hovering inside the tape in ill-fitting blue overalls. She scowled over his shoulder at the departing cab, taking in his holdall and frowning at his cane. 'What's with the face? No medals from Madge this time?'

'Sarge,' replied Stark stoically. It was always best to play it safe until you were sure of her mood. Smart, funny, fiercely loyal but famously prickly, Detective Sergeant Francine Millhaven was a force of nature. As she was his immediate superior, Stark's level of happiness on any given day was proportional to how far the world had got under her skin. And yet, of his colleagues, she was the one he felt closest to. Another sister figure, the most disapproving of all, worse than his actual sister, and Louise took some beating. Add his overbearing mother to the list and Stark often felt his life was ruled by strong-willed women whose only consensus on what constituted his best interests was that they each knew best.

'Where were you, anyway? Surely your thing finished *ages* ago.'

His thing. She was also indecently nosey, but Stark wasn't going to give her anything for that.

'Wendy displeased with you as ever?' Fran made no attempt to mask her smile at the thought.

Stark could not imagine a day when hearing the

indomitable Major Pierson referred to as *Wendy* didn't jar. 'It's our default position.'

Fran set her jaw. 'You're a copper now. You wear *blue*.'

Stark made no comment. Outside in the road, the usual crowd hovered. Concerned residents. Curious passers-by. Speculative paparazzi. A TV crew had plucked one animated man from obscurity to vent his ill-informed opinion to camera at the behest of a blonde reporter in a tailored red coat and matching lipstick.

Stark turned away to inspect the house. New mock-Tudor, large and ostentatious, in the Blackheath Cator Estate, a series of private roads for private money, tucked away south of the village itself. The house had a Disney feel; mock-perfection. It would hardly have surprised Stark to find the manicured garden was entirely plastic and the building itself moulded in fibreglass. The only incongruity was the police tape across the gate and the harsh glare of the crime-scene lighting dotted around the drive and garden, already bright in the wintry afternoon gloom. 'What have we got then?'

'Thomas and Mary Chase. Husband and wife. Fifty-four and thirty-six,' said Fran. 'No kids. Owned and ran a security firm.' She glanced at Stark. 'The legit kind, apparently.'

Stark's first case after joining the Murder Investigation Team had involved the other kind. 'Non-crime pays, from the looks,' he commented, nodding at the shiny grey Range Rover on the gravel drive and lipstick-red convertible Merc in the open garage, both new.

'Right up until crime finds out and shoots you dead in your home,' Fran said. 'State-of-the-art intruder alarm, not set, of course. Cleaner found the husband just after ten, uniform found the wife upstairs. Neighbour says he heard something just after midnight, maybe shots, but put it down to fireworks this time of year. Might've heard a motorbike in the distance after. Williams and Hammed are already canvassing the area with uniform.'

'Guv'nor inside?' asked Stark.

Fran shook her head. 'Spinning plates for the super.' Her tone added the unspoken word, *again*. Superintendent Cox had been making ever-greater demands on DCI Groombridge's time of late. Upper-echelon wrangling of some kind. Optimists thought Cox was vying for promotion and grooming Groombridge as his replacement, pessimists that the latest round of cuts was about to break the Greenwich Murder Investigation Team up or merge them with Lewisham, or, worse, Bexley. Groombridge would not or could not comment, but neither could he fully mask his frustration. Fran was left to take up the slack and made no secret of hers. They were already short-handed. They'd been without a DI for two years. DS Harper had transferred away and DC Bidden emigrated, neither replaced. Post-crash austerity in action – *make do and bend to breaking*. 'Bloody SOCO are still pissing about,' said Fran, shivering. 'I've been freezing my tits off out here over an hour!'

Security firm? Stark peered again at the house. There were discreet pairs of infrared CCTV cameras on each corner, another over the front door and over the automatic gate intercom. 'What about those?'

'First thing I asked,' sighed Fran. 'The boys in white say the DVR is missing.'

Stark raised his eyebrows. The digital video recorder would have been locked in a cupboard out of sight somewhere. The killer knew what he or she was doing. He stepped into the transition area, a flimsy plastic pergola with cheap plastic crates for shoes and coats, and ripped the plastic off a set of blue disposable overalls and boots.

A few minutes later they were beckoned inside.

Scene-of-crime officers in uniform white overalls were crawling over the wide hallway and paid the blue inter-lopers scant attention.

Oak flooring, pristine white walls, ornate mirror and silk flowers in a crystal vase. Discreet alarm key-panel recessed flush into the wall, PIR sensor in the corner where walls met ceiling, alarm contacts on the front door and stairway window. SOCO checkerplate stepping stones.

And at the foot of the stairs . . . a man in a business suit and raincoat staring up at the ceiling, two bullet holes in his chest, congealed blood pooled beneath him. No expression of surprise or pain, nothing of life; just the cold, glazed eyes of fish on ice. The bodies changed, but the eyes . . .

The best one could say was that at least they weren't staring at you, cursing you. Stark had seen too many dead to be . . . he nearly thought *disturbed*, but really, he'd just seen too many dead. However inured experience left you, the urge to close those eyes, or avert your own, rose in your throat like bile. He swallowed both with a dose of obstinate detachment. But out there beyond the firelight, the same old outrage and guilt stirred, pacing, waiting for dark. The eyes saved their blame for your dreams.

'The wife's upstairs, apparently,' said Fran.

'In equally poor health,' announced a voice from the

stairs. Marcus Turner, forensic pathologist; a slightly portly, greying man in his mid-forties with a perversely cheerful manner, who Stark thought an amusing match for Fran – a notion she rebuffed forcibly every time he teased her with it. 'I'll try to expedite the autopsies, but barring any surprises both look like plain old *plumbum intolerantia*. First shot from around here, wouldn't you say, Geoff?'

One of the anonymous white shapes stood up and pulled down his mask. Geoff Culpepper, Crime Scene Manager. Marcus pointed a finger pistol towards the corpse from the lower flight of the stairs, and the CSM nodded. Marcus plodded down to the floor and stood over the body, pointing down at the chest. 'Second from here to make sure.'

'Weapon?' asked Fran.

'No shell casings,' said Culpepper. 'Either removed or still in the gun.'

'Revolver?'

'Thirty-eight if I had to guess,' said Marcus, nodding at the corpse. 'Won't know for sure until I pull one out.'

'Old school,' Fran remarked.

'No phone or watch. Wallet stripped of any cash and dumped there,' said Culpepper, pointing.

'Robbery then,' said Fran.

'Or a greedy assassin,' suggested Marcus, smiling. 'A little too soon for assumptions, Detective Sergeant.' Fran rolled her eyes at him.

'Photographer just finished there if you fancy a nose,' said Culpepper.

Fran wrinkled her nose. Not squeamish, just impatient. She liked headlines – means, motive, opportunity. An investigation might hang on the 'nerd work', as she called it, but couldn't wait for it.

Stark crouched to peer at the discarded brown leather wallet beside its numbered plastic evidence photo marker. Fat, worn and stretched with too many cards, which the killer had sensibly ignored. Use them and get tracked, sell them on and create loose ends. Plastic was for amateurs. Missing watch tan mark indicated late autumn sun. No wedding band, but a heavy gold signet on the right hand. Valuable, but the victim's fingers were too thick to remove it easily and the killer too skittish or squeamish to go and find a knife. There was a world of difference between shooting someone and taking a blade to them.

Stark sighed faintly, pointing it out to Fran. The signet was inlaid with a silver compass-and-square symbol on blue enamel with the letter 'G' picked out in tiny diamonds. Great Architect.

Fran kissed her teeth in displeasure. Her feelings on the subject were no secret. Open disapproval of Freemasonry was unlikely to boost one's career in the force, but Fran wasn't one to let that stand in the way of a decent rant. Besides, for someone who believed she always knew best, Stark suspected she would be more than content to stay a sergeant forever.

'All right,' she sighed, 'let's have a look at the wife then.'

3

Mary Chase lay face down on the deep, blood-soaked shag-pile, sprawled before an empty wall safe concealed in the back of a walk-in wardrobe crammed with couture and killer heels. Shot through the back of the head – a crime-noir tableau in silk pyjamas, platinum-blonde hair and gore, her pretty face marred by a grotesque exit wound, the forensic photographer strobing the scene with flash-light indifference.

The bedroom itself had been turned over violently, more search than a struggle from the look of it. Jewellery boxes emptied. 'This room was searched *after*,' said Stark. There were items scattered over the top of blood spatter. A wedding photo, the couple tanned and happy, white sand and turquoise sea, glass smashed.

'Maybe they didn't find what they were looking for in the safe,' suggested Fran.

'Or they did, but didn't want us to think so.'

'Or, it's just easier to take the jewellery after your hysterical hostage is dead,' suggested Marcus helpfully. 'And on that note . . . Time of death between ten p.m. and three a.m. I'll narrow that down later. Shot point-blank in the back of the head, kneeling, then twice more in the back to be sure. No early indications of blood or skin under the fingernails or defensive wounds to suggest she fought the killer. No sign of her phone. Watch and wedding rings missing. Marks on her neck hint that a necklace might've been ripped off, probably just post-mortem. Earrings gone too. Early indications suggest this killing was first, and the husband shortly after.'

The bedroom faced the rear, thought Stark. 'The killer may not have heard the husband's car arrive home.'

'So he forces her to open the safe,' said Fran, 'kills her, and her husband arrives home at just the wrong time to interrupt his escape.'

'Supposition is your department.' Marcus shrugged. 'And there are no indications yet as to the killer's gender.'

Fran waved a hand dismissively. 'This sort of thing is always a man.'

'Indeed?' Marcus smiled faintly at the sweeping generalization. 'Only men can tolerate loud noises?'

'Guns are just another form of penis extension,' replied Fran, deadpan.

Marcus huffed in amusement. 'While women put poison in your tea?'

'Or an axe in your head,' she riposted, smiling sweetly.

Stark stared down at the woman's corpse. Lives shouldn't be ranked according to value, but obstinate detachment had its limits. Men had always fought and died; but women and children paid the price. Old-fashioned views, perhaps. Soldier thinking. At least there were no children this time. Stark had never worked a child case, but he'd seen the cost of war in their eyes, living and dead.

His fists bunched so tight the fingernails stung his palms. Better that than shaking hands.

A strand of hair hung over her mouth. Stark wished he could sweep it behind her ear for her.

Had she known what was coming? What had the killer

thought, standing over her, aiming the gun? Stark knew what it meant to kill and what it took, though no longer how it felt – except in dreams. The ones that chased him awake. How such a thing could fade was a mystery. He sometimes wondered if it was only this unlikely ability, to forget, that allowed the human spirit to persevere. Pain. Rage. Love. If only people paused to recall how past certainties faded with time, perhaps they might stop at the brink of acts such as this.

Regret was the only feeling one could never outwait.

Marcus stayed to supervise the removal of the bodies while Culpepper showed them round the rest of the house, culminating in the downstairs loo. The small top-light window was ajar. 'Jemmied open from outside.'

'Tracks?' asked Stark.

'Patio all round, and rain.'

Stark stared at the window. Tight for a grown man. Skinny. And lucky; like all the openable windows and doors, this one had alarm contacts.

Culpepper showed them the under-stairs cupboard, lock broken. The DVR tower inside lay smashed on the floor, hard drive extracted.

'You're doing the frowning thing,' said Fran. 'Out with it.'

Stark replayed the scene in his head. In uniform, he'd served on a three-months' anti-burglary push and first impressions said this was burglary-gone-bad. But the downstairs office hadn't been tossed; portable electrics hadn't been taken; then there was the safe, and the gun . . . Burglars usually preferred a blade or cosh – lighter sentence. 'Sophisticated alarm systems like this have night-settings; activating ground-floor window and door contacts only, limited PIR . . .'

'This one does,' agreed Culpepper.

'Which wasn't on,' said Fran impatiently.

'When the cleaner arrived,' said Stark. 'What about when the killer arrived?'

Culpepper nodded, understanding. 'The data would be logged on the missing DVR hard drive along with the CCTV.'

Fran shrugged. 'Professional burglar.'

'Or someone who knew the system,' said Stark, pointing at the label on the tower, the same as the alarm sounder outside, *Chase Security*. 'Maybe the killer got lucky and jemmied his way in on a night the alarm wasn't set . . . Or maybe they knew how to disable it and remove the evidence. Maybe they thought the house was empty . . . Or maybe they deliberately hit it when Mary Chase was home alone, knowing there was a safe and maybe even what was in it.'

'Or *maybe*,' suggested Fran pointedly, 'you just like winding me up.'

4

The families had already been informed by uniform and Family Liaison officers. Now came the questions.

Fran and Stark collected DCI Groombridge on the way. It might be okay for the DCI to duck out of the crime scene, but victim's families expected to see the slaying of their loved ones taken seriously.

This was the part of the job Stark hated most. Thankfully his role was that of silent observer. Blessed are the low in rank when the time comes to say those dreadful words – *We're sorry for your loss.* Tom's family first, such as it was. The father was long dead, the mother in a home with early-stage dementia. The poor old woman looked bereft, struggling to comprehend the loss of her only offspring, and there was a discernible vagueness to her eyes that made questioning her all the more obtrusive.

I know this is the most difficult time but I'm afraid I must ask you . . . Can you think of any reason . . . ? Anyone who'd wish to harm . . . ? Any recent troubles . . . ? What they kept in their safe . . . ? Own a gun . . . ? Et cetera, et cetera. *No, no* and *no*; as predictable as it was painful.

It went much the same at Mary's mother's home. The poor woman even uttered the classic – *I'm just glad her father didn't live to see this* – before collapsing in tears and being comforted by Mary's sister. The Liaison put a brew on.

It was only as they were about to get back in the car that the sister followed them out and spoke in hushed tones.

'I didn't like to say anything inside. Mum gets anxious about money, and she was always on at Mary about grandchildren . . .' She looked distractedly back at the house. Groombridge stood patiently waiting for her to explain. 'Mary said something about money, you see. In the safe. Tom had . . . Well, he wanted a baby, an heir, I suppose. But they couldn't. Tom looked into adoption, but he was too old. So he'd been talking to someone in China. It was going to be expensive. Fifty thousand. In cash.'

'In the safe?'

'That's what she said. She was . . .' She trailed off, wiping tears from her eyes.

'She was what?'

'Worried about it, I suppose . . .' Mumbling an apology, she turned back to the house.

'Fifty grand,' muttered Groombridge thoughtfully, watching the sister depart. 'Tidy haul for a robbery.'

'Makes you wonder if anyone knew it was there,' said Stark.

'You don't think this was a simple burglary-gone-bad?'

'Stark has an alternative theory,' replied Fran, rolling her eyes, her tone highlighting that this was ever thus. Stark's 'sideways' observations had a habit of generating extra work, and Fran always hid enjoyment of her teaching role behind a thick veil of impatience.

'I wouldn't call it a theory,' said Stark.

Groombridge eyed the young DC. Despite working hard from the beginning to get the measure of Stark, the best he could claim was that he was one of the few who could long endure the lad's gaze. He had an eye-watering solidity. Where Fran was a force of nature, Stark was like a singularity; the metaphoric lead ball on physics' rubber mat – no matter how inconspicuous he tried to remain, he attracted or perturbed all around him.

Stark explained, reluctantly.

Groombridge sighed. 'All right, you'd better get over to their offices and look for likely candidates with knowledge of the Chases' alarm system. And find out where Thomas Chase was out so late.'

Fran stiffened, then jerked her head for Stark to take himself out of earshot. Groombridge braced himself. Things between them had grown fractious of late. Everyone was feeling the pressure but Fran made little allowance for his difficulties. But then she didn't know the half of them. 'You're not coming?' she asked.

'I have a meeting at Division.'

'Guv.'

On most people a poker-face meant keeping your expression even. On Fran, that in itself was a screaming tell. 'Problem?'

She made an isn't-it-obvious face. 'Double homicide, Guv.'

He nodded. 'I know. I'll ask DI Graham if he can spare a DC or two.'

'And he'll say no, again.'

'Probably.' The main CID team were just as stretched as the Murder Squad. The station was wearing perilously thin. Groombridge was hoarse from singing the same song to Cox, and Cox upward. But every super in the force was pleading the same, and getting the same answer – there's no money.

Gone were the competitive announcements of more

bobbies on the beat. Now politicians queued up to promise further efficiencies with ring-fenced frontline services, before passing responsibility for delivery of this oxymoronic conundrum down to their nearest sacrificial lamb. Do more with less or make room. *Austerity* – the byword for impossible decisions, corner cutting and backbiting. Fran's limited patience was clearly wearing thin. But so was his. 'Something else on your mind?' he asked, knowing precisely what it was.

She took a deep breath and let it out, glancing around to make sure Stark wasn't eavesdropping. 'This team can't function headless, Guv.'

There . . . She'd said it. He was amazed she'd held it in this long. 'You're doing fine,' he replied evenly, knowing it wasn't the answer she wanted, or deserved. She waited for more but he was all out of ways to placate her. She was right, and they both knew it. He sighed silently. 'I'll keep my head in the game.'

'Will you?'

'Don't look at me like that, Fran. I'm doing what I can, but I can't fight on *two* fronts.'

She pursed her lips in frustration. 'Perhaps if you told me what's going on I could help.'

He half-smiled and shook his head sadly, knowing that being kept out of the loop was driving her as nuts as the lack of leadership. 'I'm trying to put something in place, I just need a little more time.'

5

Fran resisted the temptation to flick on the lights and siren. London traffic was almost as good for venting frustration on as underlings. Stark was often good for a punchbag, but just like the real thing, his stoic absorption soon sapped your strength.

Today wasn't the day anyway. The morning's commemorations had left him humourless. A pair of corpses didn't help. She shivered, trying to dislodge the images, wishing she could maintain his crime-scene coolness. Brusque gallows humour was the closest she could manage. You'd think she'd be used to it by now, but death never got easier.

Stark, she reminded herself, had seen more than she had.

Chase Security Ltd was run from a small warehouse in the unfashionable end of Woolwich Riverside. They provided alarm installation, private security patrols and guards, as well as temp staff for events and venues, and small-scale retail cash transport. Liveried vans sat idle, while liveried guards did likewise. The news had reached the shop floor.

DC Dixon was talking with a man in a suit whom he introduced as Clive Tilly, Operations Manager. The man looked badly shaken, eyes red-rimmed and harassed.

He led them to his office and closed the door. 'Ops manager is bit of a fancy title for my role. Tom had the charm for all the front-of-house crap, schmoozing clients, winning work. I dealt with the nitty-gritty and all those feckless donkeys out there.'

'And Mary?'

'Did the books. Head for numbers. Really helped turn this place around.' Tilly shook his head miserably. 'Christ knows what I'm supposed to do now. What'll happen to the business?'

'I'm sorry,' said Fran. Sympathetic, non-committal. 'How long have you known them?'

'Tom and I have been sinking beers and locking horns since school, he's . . . he *was*, my oldest friend,' replied Tilly sadly. 'And Mary . . . Who'd do a thing like this?'

Bad people, thought Fran. The world had no shortage. 'Do you know where Tom was yesterday evening? We think he arrived home late.'

'Hotel in Birmingham. Business meeting. Piss-up, usually. Alcohol lubrication. He had a room booked, to stay up there. Don't know why he didn't. I'll get you the name of the hotel and the guy he was meeting.'

'Can you think of anyone with a grudge against the Chases? Ex-employee, business contact? Were there any financial problems that you're aware of?'

'I thought this was a burglary?' Tilly looked confused. 'Your colleague said . . . '

The bereaved grasped for answers, but baulked at questions. 'We have to explore all avenues.'

Tilly shook his head. 'Mary kept the books close to her chest. I know we've had our share of disgruntled creditors; perhaps more than our share. I'll get you a list. Times have been lean since the crash. We've made lay-offs. But you can't seriously think . . . '

'My inspector does the thinking.' Fran smiled evenly. 'I just do the asking.'

'The culprit did a number on the security system,' added Stark. 'We have to look into the possibility that they had prior knowledge.'

'Of the system? Someone here?' Tilly frowned. 'Mike Parsons installed that one, I think. Old school. Proper craftsman. Retired a couple of years back just in time to drop dead – poor sod. There's no justice. Wish we had more like him.'

'Including the safe?'

Tilly shook his head. 'Didn't know they had one. Must've come with the house.'

'Who else would have knowledge of the system?' asked Stark.

'No one specific. Mike wouldn't let any of the youngsters near his jobs. But any of the fitters. And half the idiots here have helped out on installations at one time or another . . . It's not rocket science.'

'Would anyone here know the alarm code?'

'No. Tom's been in the business long enough to set a new code the moment Mike walked out the door.' Tilly shrugged. 'Family, maybe?'

'We're going to need a full list of your employees, including who was working last night and where,' said Fran. Tilly nodded. 'And can you confirm your whereabouts last night?'

'Me?' Tilly looked predictably affronted. They always did. 'I was here until nine-ish, then out on a job.'

'A job?'

'On a round. In one of the patrol vans.'

'You?'

'One of the donkeys didn't show and I had to do their round. It happens.'

'Can anyone corroborate that?'

'Not really. Most patrols are single drivers. But . . .' He glanced at the door to make sure it was shut. 'Look,' he sighed, annoyed, channelling grief into anger, 'the staff don't know this, but the vehicles are all fitted with GPS trackers. We've had problems in the past with drivers skiving, or worse, using the vans for their own ends. We use the tracker logs in our customer billing to demonstrate service, and in disciplinary procedures against staff who take the piss. I can get you the logs.'

'That would be useful, thank you. Do you own a gun, Mr Tilly?'

Tilly blinked in surprise. 'No, of course not.'

'What about your staff? Any rumours, bragging?'

'No,' Tilly replied earnestly. 'Tom had an old gun . . . back in the day. Gave me the willies.'

'Back in the day?'

'When we were young, if we ever were. His grandfather's, from the war. A revolver.'

Fran kept her face straight. 'Calibre?' Tilly shrugged. 'Did he still have it?'

Another shrug. 'It was twenty years ago, *at least*.'

'What do you think?' asked Fran after he'd shown them out.

Stark shrugged. 'Looks like a man staring into the abyss.'

'Doesn't mean he's not our killer.'

6

Midnight seemed the appropriate time to call it a day.

The initial investigation had achieved little more than preliminary background checks and tracking the victims' movements leading up to their deaths.

Tomorrow they'd start turning over stones.

Stark hung the cane on the hook inside his front door and stared at it. He only took it down if he expected to be on his feet all day or he'd overdone it the day before. His hip recovered quicker these days and troubled him less than it had, but he'd got used to the thing. It had a certain comfort in his hand. Odd that he should think so – Mr Stubbornly Independent.

Unpacking, he placed the leather cases on the side: two campaign medals, Iraq and Afghanistan, and the VC. It was supposed to go back into the bank safety deposit box first thing in the morning. Fat chance of that now. The powers that be, not to mention the insurance company, would have a fit if they knew. They would prefer he used the replica. But that wouldn't have felt right; not today. Aside from the inscription on the rear they were identical, and yet the real one always felt heavier in the hand. Both were bronze, but maybe the bronze of that Sebastopol cannon was indeed denser. One was worth over a million, the other a few hundred pounds. What a world. Value had little to do with cost in this case. Cursing his Army OCD, he took them out, polished them, again, and stowed them in the back of the sock drawer.

He showered the day off and pulled on baggies, then took the Royal Lochnagar and one of his pair of lead-crystal glasses, collapsed on to the sofa and poured himself a triple.

One for the present, future and past, perhaps.

Time was he'd have tossed down a pair of OxyContin too. Relic of the bad old days, they called out to him from the bathroom cabinet. He hadn't used them for over a year, for pain physical or mental, yet it was rare he enjoyed a whisky without thinking of those innocent-looking little pills. Tonight, though, darker thoughts tugged harder.

Thomas and Mary Chase, slaughtered in their own home; lives, loves and laughter stolen. The bitter truth that, blue uniform or green, he couldn't protect everyone.

Pierson's strange questions still rang in his ears, and her toast. Life *was* for the living. But where did that leave Stark, forced to acknowledge that some portion of him remained *outside* that definition? His shrink, Doc Hazel, would have words of wisdom, or scorn, to pour over him on that point, but she still thought this was all about grief and he hadn't corrected her.

All certainty was fragile. The black-and-white world of his youth was a fading comfort, a thinning conceit beyond which the greater issue grew harder to ignore. A thing was in him that must come out. But for the first time in his life he doubted his strength. Doubt bred caution, hesitation, fear. Perhaps that was growing up. It couldn't be before time. But it felt like growing old.

As we that are left grow old . . . The words from that

morning's service echoed in Stark's mind like the boom of the gun, and the tolling bell.

Closing his eyes, he sipped the whisky gifted him by Her Majesty the Queen.

'Joe.' The whisper echoed around the bare concrete room but Stark didn't recognize it. He looked around but saw no one. His eyes strained to see into the dimness but had not yet adjusted from the searing sunlight outside. The sweat on his face seemed strangely cold. He wiped at it but could not feel. His fingers were numb. He stared at them, pale skin, nails tinged blue. Cyanosis? Rigor mortis. Cold, lifeless as the two corpses in the corner; a woman and small boy. The blood from their bullet-ridden cadavers, black with time, black as the flies buzzing around their withered flesh.

His breath froze in the meat-locker air. The desert heat from the doorway rippled like a mirage but could not enter this place. Major Collins lay dead on the floor, lips snarled back with decay, the index finger on his outstretched hand pointing, pointing at the woman and child.

'Joe?' Stark spun round. The mother and child stared at him. Collins shooed them to their feet and out the back way . . . but he was dead on the floor, finger pointing at Stark now, blood leaching into the sand like mascara weeping into white cotton.

The rifle felt heavy in Stark's hands, pulling, dragging, tearing at his shoulders. He was too tired to hold it any more. Too tired. Its blue-black anodizing was blistered with rust, blood-red rust. His hands too, blue-black and bloody, morphing into the gun; he shook his arms in horror, trying to drop it, but he didn't have hands any more, just the gun.

'Joe!' He looked up. Sergeant Tyler crawled towards him, blood spewing from his neck in a gush of blue-black flies, lifting up his desiccated arm and pointing, his mouth snarling, screaming. Not pointing, aiming, aiming his rifle at Stark, and not Tyler, Stark, his own face shrunken, lips peeled back over blue-black teeth, skin cracked with death – aiming at himself.

Screaming, he pulled the trigger, but it wouldn't budge, wouldn't, congealed with rust. He thrust the bayonet instead, the mirror shattering into a thousand splintered Starks.

'JOE!' The room shook with it, the *boom* of it. Every window and door, faces crowded in, death faces, calling his name. Stark laughed, trapped in a George A. Romero movie. But he wasn't laughing, he was screaming, screaming himself hoarse, screaming without sound, drowned out by the booming call, 'PLEASE, *JOE*!'

Stark jumped out of his skin. His eyes burned open in horror, icy hands grasping at him in the darkness.

'*Joe!* It's all right, it's just a dream. It's all right! It was just a *dream*!'

Kelly? Her eyes running with tears, brimming with fear, stroking his face, soothing his brow. 'It's *all right*, Joe. It's *me*. You're *okay*. It was just a dream.'

Stark's body was still clamped with horror, cold with sweat. He swallowed hard, trying to shake it off. She rested her head on his shoulder, her hand over his thudding heart. 'Shhh . . .' she whispered. 'It's all gone now, Joe.' He could hear the pain in her voice, the desperate

38

sorrow. He raised his hand to stroke her hair, but it passed through as though she was naught but midnight mist.

Stark shuddered awake.

Cold pre-dawn light filled the room corner to corner, crystal clear and pitiless. There was no mist, no Kelly, no groping dead.

He was alone.

7

'Right,' Groombridge said with theatrical purpose, 'let's make this quick so I can update the super before the tap dance begins.' He tapped the incident board, as yet with little on it but before-and-after photos of the deceased and rudimentary timelines from former to latter. 'Thomas and Mary Chase were model citizens; happily married, entrepreneurial go-getters, job creators, tax contributors, pillars of the community; they had it all and someone took it away. So what have we got?'

Six-a.m. faces blinked back in the fluorescent glare. Out there in the dark, press hounds were salivating for a statement for their early news cycle.

Stark went first. 'Thomas spent every Saturday morning coaching kids' football on Blackheath. Chase Security sponsors the team, and the mini-league. He spent the afternoon in the office and evening in Birmingham, schmoozing a prospective client. But the client was called away and dinner abandoned. He cancelled the hotel room and returned home early.'

'To find a killer descending the stairs,' said Groombridge.

'He had a regular Sunday morning golf round,' added Stark. 'Hated to miss it, according to his club.'

'Mary spent the morning at home,' said Hammed. 'Lunch with friends, shopping in Knightsbridge, then the gym, masseuse and home around seven.'

'I spoke with the pathologist last night,' said Fran. 'The Chases died within an hour of each other sometime between eleven and one, making the neighbour's suggestion of shots fired around midnight more likely. He agreed to rush autopsies overnight.'

Groombridge smiled. 'Your charm lessons are paying off.' Marcus Turner would always give an extra inch, and Fran would always take a mile.

'And hot off the press . . .' She waved some paper, ignoring him. 'Preliminary forensics. Numerous different fingerprints to check . . .' she read, 'blah, blah, bl . . . oh . . . no fibre evidence from the point of entry? Squeezing in? Bit odd . . .' She glanced at Stark. 'Ah, here's the headline . . . point thirty-eight calibre two-hundred-grain bullet . . . bullets in this calibre no longer made . . . most commonly used World War Two . . . UK military use until 1969. Bullet markings don't match anything on the National Ballistics Intelligence Service database. No sign of the weapon at the scene or surrounding area so far.'

'We've checked back with Thomas's mum,' added DC Williams. 'She doesn't remember a gun in the family, but she doesn't remember much at all to be fair.'

'So,' said Groombridge, 'we have old bullets and a clean gun, possibly the victim's grandfather's. What else? Possible motorbike?'

'Nothing so far on nearby cameras, Guv,' said Hammed. 'Nothing useful from the neighbourhood canvass or incident number.'

Fran looked at Williams. 'Victim background checks?'

'No form,' he said. 'The usual parking tickets and speeding points. Both left previous marriages to be together.'

'Jealous ex-spouses?'

'Karen Chase, formerly Karen Baker, forty-six, winters at her villa in Spain, been there since last week. Family Liaison say she's been contacted. Not planning to fly back. Mary started life as Ms Stubbs; did a six-year stint as Mrs Murphy, before becoming Mrs Chase. Her ex, Colin Murphy, moved back to Ireland after the divorce. Hasn't been in the UK in two years. Border agency confirmed.'

'Solid alibis all round then,' said Groombridge.

'Especially if you've ordered a hit,' replied Fran.

Groombridge ignored her. 'No children from either marriage. Who's looking at the Chinese adoption?'

'Nothing yet, Guv,' answered Williams. 'Hopefully we'll find something on their emails.'

'Okay. Anything else?'

'Uniform were called to a disturbance six months ago,' added Hammed. 'Row between Thomas Chase and his neighbour over leylandii trees blocking out the sun. Got quite heated.'

'Have you looked at the neighbour?'

'He's eighty-two, Guv, and not too steady on his feet according to the report. Still had some choice words to say about the Chases.'

Groombridge nodded. 'All right, keep digging. I'll request warrants for the accounts, computers, emails and phone data. We'll reconvene this afternoon.'

Fran's phone beeped and she opened an email. 'Autopsies are done . . .' She scanned the content. 'Cause of deaths confirmed as lead poisoning; no anomalies. Mary Chase had been struck hard in the face before her death, a punch, Marcus thinks. Two points of interest . . . She had engaged in sex some hours earlier. Semen residue recovered. Pubic hair too.' She looked to Groombridge. 'DNA?'

Pressure to limit expensive forensic testing was higher than ever, and there was nothing to suggest the husband hadn't popped home for a quickie before heading off to Birmingham. He shook his head. 'And the second . . . ?'

Fran sighed, gravely. 'Mary was pregnant. Approximately ten weeks.'

Groombridge winced. He wasn't the only one. Stark could see the same angry questions in everyone's eyes. Had the killer known when he pulled the trigger? Had Mary pleaded for the life of her unborn child? 'Let's keep that away from the media while we can,' said the DCI.

No argument from Fran on that one.

As the meeting broke up, Williams, the team's only parent, was first in expressing sentiments they all felt.

Stark kept his own bound tight. In the eyes of the law this remained a double homicide, but a third life had been robbed of its future. The most innocent of all. His first child case after all.

He tried to concentrate, but the darkness crowded in. Memories. Fearful, suspicious eyes of the young ones as you passed on patrol, Satan among them, come to kill and defile. Blank eyes of hunger, abandonment, bereavement; of childhoods lost. Tears, and terror. He could still barely bring himself to enter Greenwich's famous covered market. All it took was a child's laugh to set him back in the marketplace in Basra, bustling one moment, car-bombed the next. The little hand in the rubble . . .

Standing quietly, he left the room.

He only just made it to the toilets in time to be sick,

retching over and over until there was nothing left but eye-watering convulsions and vertigo.

'You okay?' asked a voice over the cubicle door.

'Will be,' managed Stark. 'Something I ate.'

'Canteen's a death-trap,' muttered the voice, leaving.

Stark sat in the stall, eyes closed, head in hands, until the coast was clear. Until his heart slowed, and his hands stopped shaking.

8

'Nasty business, this,' said Cox, packing papers into his briefcase. 'Bound to draw attention.'

'Sir.' Groombridge had known Cox long enough to spot an opening gambit.

'The residents' group are making a fuss. Thomas Chase was chairman of their Neighbourhood Watch. Want to know what we're doing to protect them.'

Live on TV, no less, outside the Chases' home; speculating wildly about whether this was the start of a new scourge of deadly home invasions. 'Yes, sir.'

'They ran a charity, did you know? Aid to the Maldives, apparently. Something to do with football. Visited every year.'

'Pillars of the community, sir,' agreed Groombridge, still wondering where this was heading.

'Deputy Assistant Commissioner Stevens called to make sure we were giving it our full attention,' continued Cox, innocently. 'Thomas Chase was an acquaintance.'

So that was it. 'I'm sorry to hear that, sir. Like brothers, were they?'

Cox gave him a dry look. 'I know you don't approve.'

Groombridge did not. They had long ago agreed to disagree on the topic of Freemasonry. Maybe it *was* the '*beautiful system of morality, veiled in allegory*' it claimed to be, but how were the unaffiliated supposed to judge? Any secret society was to be distrusted on principle. What was to prevent innocent fraternal networking edging into nepotism, and nepotism into collusion or coercion? Bad enough in business; much, much worse in positions of power. *Without fear or favour*, his dad had taught him – otherwise what was the point of being police at all? Cox was on the side of the angels, but angels could fall.

'I used the opportunity to mention recruitment, of course,' said Cox. 'No go, as usual. But I do think I might swing something temporary.'

Things that sounded too good to be true . . . 'DI Graham says he can spare a DC to help,' said Groombridge, 'probably towards the end of next week.' Cox's expression said it all. They both knew even that lame offer was unlikely to materialize. 'But a body or two from elsewhere would help, sir.'

Not much, though. Any detective free to be loaned out would inevitably be that CID team's lukewarm, their least valued member. Cox's face said he remembered that all too well. 'I'll ask around again, of course, but I was actually thinking of the alternative we discussed . . .'

Ah . . . This again . . . 'I don't think it's come to that, sir,' Groombridge replied, keeping his voice even. 'DS Millhaven has everything under control and I'm managing to keep a foot in both camps – as we agreed.'

'And you'd rather advance your own plans,' added Cox shrewdly.

Groombridge stuck with diplomacy. 'Let's see how the initial stages of the case unfold, sir.'

Cox nodded. 'Very well. But keep an eye on things. The press are all over this already. We can't afford any slip-ups with a Deputy Assistant Commissioner watching.'

*

'There you are . . .' Fran smiled sweetly. 'You were out of the room so we saved the short straw for you.' She handed him an address. 'Mary's sister, from yesterday. She's agreed to ID both bodies.'

No one's favourite job. Fran had given up sending Dixon, whose incurable squeamishness undermined the requisite tone. Hammed and Williams kept their eyes down. Stark sighed.

The Family Liaison officer met him downstairs. It should've been the same one as yesterday, but wasn't. The system was stretched at every level. This one was experienced enough to pick up on Stark's mood and cut the chatter short.

The sister, Jenny, was ready and waiting, anxious to see this through, to put it behind her. The Liaison nodded Stark to sit with her in the back. It seemed impertinent, but the man insisted with his eyes.

'You're him,' she said, eyeing Stark while the Liaison drove. 'The soldier on TV yesterday, at the Cenotaph?'

Stark nodded.

'You were on the front page of this morning's paper,' she said quietly, turning her gaze to the passing traffic. 'Mary was on page eleven.'

There wasn't much to say to that.

Marcus Turner met them at the mortuary reception. 'Short straw, was it?' whispered the pathologist genially, while the Liaison talked Jenny through the procedure.

'DS Millhaven sends her regards.'

Marcus smiled at the lie, but the banter was forced. He blew out a tired sigh, another long night of thankless endeavour weighing him down. 'I wish I could say this got easier.'

'What would it say about us if it did?' replied Stark.

Marcus nodded sombrely, and slipped through the side door into the next room.

The viewing suite was not dissimilar from the police line-up suite. But instead of a row of shifty characters through the glass, there was a pair of sheet-draped cadavers. By agreement, Marcus folded the sheet from Thomas Chase's face first.

Jenny swallowed, and nodded. 'That's Tom.'

Marcus moved to Mary. Jenny's hand was already at her mouth, but a quiet gasp still escaped.

Marcus had done his best, but the cosmetic tricks of the undertaker were not available to him. Careful not to expose the ruination of the right side, there was still no escaping the wretched pallor of death on a face she'd loved in life.

Tears sprang immediately.

Jenny turned from death to clasp at life. Perhaps Stark was just nearest. Her weeping face buried in his chest, he had little choice but to hold her sobbing form. The Liaison watched helplessly. This was his job; to comfort and reassure, to provide a conduit between the bereaved and the investigation, and the necessary distance.

Stark eschewed meaningless condolences, but returned the embrace until the sobbing subsided and Jenny stepped away, apologizing, avoiding his eyes. The Liaison passed the tissues.

Paperwork signed, they drove her home.

Before going in, she turned to Stark. 'You will find them, won't you? Whoever did this?' Her red eyes watched his, earnest, pleading. 'Mary . . . had her faults. But she didn't deserve this.'

48

'No one does.' That was as far as Stark was willing to go. Innocents died. Killers went uncaught. Promises were empty. Jenny nodded all the same, forcing the faintest smile, and let the Liaison walk her to her door.

Stark frowned. 'What faults?' he called out.

'This is hardly the time, Detective Constable.'

The Liaison was right. But Jenny lifted her chin. 'It's okay.' She looked at Stark. 'No one's asked. What she was like. I suppose it doesn't matter, in a burglary.'

Stark met her gaze. 'It matters.'

'Personally? Or professionally?'

'Both.'

'Aren't you supposed to stay . . . detached?' She glanced at the Liaison, meaningfully.

'We're not machines.'

'No . . .' She sighed quietly. 'You lost people? In the war?'

Her eyes searched his. Not for the first time, Stark wished he'd kept his questions to himself. 'Yes.'

'Was this a burglary or not?'

The Liaison stiffened, but Stark knew better than to overstep. 'I don't know,' he replied honestly. 'But if there's anything about Mary or Thomas that we should know . . .'

Jenny appeared to come to a decision. 'Look . . . Mary was never . . . quite the angel people believed.'

'In what way?'

Jenny looked around guiltily. 'She was . . . never faithful. To Tom, or her first husband, or boyfriends. It wasn't her fault really; she was always the pretty one, always got what she wanted. She never learned how not to. I loved my sister. She could be warm and generous and carefree . . . but she was selfish.'

Stark weighed this up. Jenny might have mentioned it yesterday but reluctance was understandable. A good ten years younger but unconfident, mousy, unmarried, Jenny might have worshipped her glamorous sister. But growing up in Mary's shadow must have taken a toll. Jenny hid intelligence behind diffidence. For a moment Stark wondered if she were capable of murder. On the face of it, not; but wouldn't one say that of most? 'Mary was having an affair?'

'She told me about it last week. With someone at work, I don't know who. She'd usually tell me these things to try and shock me, get a reaction, but this time she was worried.'

'She said that?'

'Not consciously. It wasn't her way. She laughed about always getting herself into trouble. But Mary always had everything under control.'

In trouble? The pregnancy? Stark glanced at the Liaison, whose job it would be to share that particular snippet of news. 'And she didn't give *any* clue who this affair was with? The smallest thing might help.'

Jenny shook her head mournfully. 'All she would say was that she had a plan. Mary always had a plan. It was the last thing she said to me.'

9

Clive Tilly was heading out the door of Chase Security as they arrived.

'I've got meetings with the solicitors and the bank,' he explained. 'See if we can salvage this mess.'

Fran smiled apologetically. 'I'm sorry, I can see you've enough on your plate, but we'll need help organizing interviews with your staff.'

Tilly looked appalled. 'Why?'

'It's been suggested that Mary might have been conducting an affair with one of them.' She glanced at Stark, as if daring him to be wasting her time again.

'One of that lot?' Tilly scoffed. 'You must be joking. Mary wouldn't dirty her designer heels stepping over them.'

'Perhaps you were less abhorrent to her?'

Tilly huffed, shaking his head. 'Do I look her type?' He was fit enough for a man in his fifties, but didn't enjoy Thomas Chase's chiselled looks.

'Tastes vary,' Fran replied genially.

Stark suppressed a smile at Fran's brand of diplomacy – saying *nice doggie* with a steak in one hand and a rock in the other.

Tilly eyed her uncertainly. 'Mary wasn't above batting her eyelids or waving a bit of cleavage my way, that was her solution to everything, but she wouldn't risk anything more.'

'Did you wish she would?'

Tilly shook his head. 'A shark is a beautiful creature, but only a fool jumps in the water.'

'You didn't like her.'

'I wouldn't go that far. But I didn't trust her. She was good for the business, and Tom adored her, but the Marys of this world never want for much. But now she's dead, along with my best friend. Do you have to go muck-raking?'

'Never for pleasure, Mr Tilly.'

'I've got enough problems here without you bringing that lot to my door.' He nodded past them to a figure that had just pulled up on a moped beyond the fence and held up a mobile to film them.

Fran clicked her tongue in irritation and stepped towards them, but the figure pocketed the mobile and drove off, engine buzzing like a gnat.

Tilly sighed. 'Ask for Mark inside. He'll help you herd the donkeys if you must. He doesn't say much but he has a knack for logistics; helps out around the office when he isn't on donkey-work. Ask him for anything you need, names, information, tea or coffee. I'll be back later if you need more.'

On first impressions Mark White looked more security guard than logistician; fortyish with balding head shaved to stubble and a bushy brown beard, big-framed and paunchy. Tattoos showed where his company polo-T rode up his triceps. He kept his eyes low and spoke only when necessary. A gentle giant, perhaps just shy; though one of the tattoos was a tornado, Stark noted. He worked efficiently enough with them at organizing the interviews and personnel files, and kept them topped up with caffeine and biscuits, so he scored points.

Fran, Stark and DC Dixon divided the interviews between them and kept the questions simple.

When White's turn came he answered Stark's questions with slow, chosen words, clearly uncomfortable under scrutiny. He'd been with the company five years, didn't know Thomas or Mary Chase personally, home alone Saturday all day and night. He looked uncomfortable, but answering police questions could do that.

'You called in sick yesterday?' asked Stark.

'Tummy bug.'

'Better now?'

'Peachy.'

Stark thought he looked a little pale, but police questioning could do that too. He put him down as maybe but unlikely, and moved on.

Tilly might have been a bit harsh about the rest of the staff, but not by much. Most were sullen or wary, some openly hostile, some shy and awkward. Few had a good word to say about Thomas and Mary Chase, Tilly or indeed each other. Chase Security was not a happy workplace. Blazing rows between Tom Chase and Tilly were apparently commonplace. None confessed to fraternizing with Mary, some seemed appalled at the thought, some amused, others openly titillated, but none leapt out as a suspect, leaving the detectives with nothing more than boxes of personnel files and financial records to cart away for their troubles.

Stark knew whose desk they'd end up on. It had taken only the slightest proficiency to become the 'office whizz' on tedious tasks no one else wanted. He wasn't sure exactly when he'd made this metamorphosis, but it was an improvement on 'smartarse'.

*

Groombridge brought the team together again at the end of a long afternoon. 'So, do we think the sister was right?'

'No one seemed overly surprised, including Clive Tilly,' replied Fran.

'But no one put their hand up either.' Groombridge nodded. 'Unsurprising.'

Stark handed out copies of his notes. 'The company appears to be in the black. They employ thirty-one full-time staff, eleven part-time, and have dozens on their books as agency resource for events. Of those directly employed, nine have written warnings on file for misconduct or underperformance, of which five have ongoing disciplinary procedures. I've drawn up a list of all whose age and appearance might put them on Mary Chase's radar for an affair, of which three appear on both lists. Also listed are seven people sacked for misconduct or underperformance in the past five years, and eleven more made redundant since the 2008 crash.'

'Any favourites?'

'Not really,' admitted Stark, knowing what that meant for his days ahead.

Groombridge rubbed his chin, in thought. 'Okay, draw up a shortlist and follow up: fingerprints, DNA swabs and background checks. At least we've got an excuse to get the semen and hair tested now.'

'And the foetus?' asked Stark. Knowing it needed saying didn't make it any easier. The team's silence said it wasn't easy hearing either. But paternity – *unwilling* paternity – was as lousy a reason for murder as any.

10

Stark stuck at it, but it wasn't diligence that kept him at his desk long after the others drifted away. Distilling his paper mountain into salient foothills was easier than confronting his empty flat. Last night's dream had rattled him. The worst in a while.

When he could put it off no longer he walked home via the kebab shop.

As he approached his building he felt a shiver. Every nerve ending was suddenly screaming at him to *beware, take cover, raise the gun!*

But scanning round, heart scudding, he saw no threat.

Not the first time his mind had played tricks.

Not the first time it had saved his life, it hissed back.

No. This was just more phantoms, night terrors reaching into waking hours again.

Gritting his teeth, he let himself in – but couldn't stop himself leaving the lights off and stepping into the dark corner within.

Nothing came at him from inside. Nothing stirred in the street outside.

His heart slowed. His kebab cooled.

Cursing, he took the stairs up to his flat, collapsed on to the sofa and saluted the lands of the living and the dead with two fingers of whisky, a cold beer and congealing calories. Sleep tugged, and terrified. Pills were off the menu, so he poured another double and stepped out on to his tiny balcony.

Through misted breath and a gap in the buildings his 'Thames View' was a sliver of oil-black sparkling with reflected lights of the Dockland towers beyond. The number of lights reflecting the number of souls still selling themselves to the mighty dollar, or was it the rouble now? Or the yuan? The blinking lights atop the towers mirrored those of the passenger jets lining up forty seconds apart for their final approach over the city to Heathrow. Traffic throbbed through the choked arteries, trains clattered and sparked somewhere to the south, and somewhere to the east a siren wailed.

Light pollution, air pollution, noise pollution, soul pollution; London had it all.

He recalled Kelly saying, when he was still new here, that London was too big to describe, too complex. She preferred to compartmentalize. Most Londoners Stark had met thought likewise. They described, eulogized, decried and lamented their pocket of London, their village. But if you took them anywhere else in the country, the world, and asked where they were from they'd say London, not Greenwich, Lewisham or Tower Hamlets, not the East End or West nor even North or South of the river. They were Londoners, proud bubbles in the mighty melting pot.

Fran would say pressure cooker. Or cesspit.

Back then Stark had been the outsider. Slowly since, he'd come to realize he wasn't alone. London was a crazed interlocution of layers, social strata, language, culture, age, purpose; crammed in, overlapping but separate. London was coexistence. Regardless of origin everyone was an outsider, outside the lives of those around them. And everyone was a Londoner, welcomed, despised or ignored. The only requirement was to come and to be. No one would notice your arrival or departure, but while you were there you were part, one among the huddled mass.

Cops were supposed to enjoy a love-hate relationship with their city, to know its mean streets like the back of their hand, to feel its pulse through the soles of their boots after years of pounding the beat. All Stark could feel was the overwhelming indifference of the place. It went on beyond sight without meaning, sentiment or constraint, the weaving river drunk on countless lost creeks and subsumed tributaries. There was nothing to hold on to and little reason to care. Better to forget the city altogether, forget the streets and focus on the meanness.

Mary Chase, dead on the carpet, a dead life within her. Loving husband, cuckolded or otherwise, staring lifeless.

If only it stopped there.

Every time he closed his eyes, death, present and past, groped for him. Unless he could learn to disentwine the two, he would soon have to abandon this extended experiment; find some other way to live the life luck had gifted him; something that didn't continually stoke the dark fires within. Whatever that might be.

Kelly's light had helped hold the darkness at bay, for the most part. But Kelly was gone.

Life was for the living.

He shivered in the chill night air, and stared up at the stars glittering coldly against the ink-black void.

11

'Right.' Groombridge clapped his hands together. 'Mary's mystery man?'

'Nothing yet, Guv,' confirmed Stark. The previous evening's background checks on Chase Security staff had not proved simple. Several had pasts one might call unclear and Fran would dub murky. Stark's shortlist was still on the long side.

'Follow-up interviews?'

'This morning.'

'Good. Test alibis and any other connections to the Chases. Personal lives and finances – sex and money.'

'Tom and Clive started out together in business,' said Stark. 'Before 1994 Chase Security was known as T&C Security, owned jointly. Thomas bought Tilly out. Could be hard feelings. Staff at Chase Security say they rowed as much as they laughed, and that Tilly and Mary Chase didn't get on at all.'

'Who's on Tilly?'

'Guv.' Dixon, youngest member of the team, raised his hand. 'Same age as our vic, Thomas Chase, fifty-four – they went to school together. Divorced in 1994 from Sandra Tilly, née Wiggins. Thomas Chase was best man at their wedding. Tilly was best man at Thomas's wedding to his first wife Karen but not for his wedding to Mary.'

'Beach wedding,' added Stark, remembering the smashed photo. 'Maldives, probably.'

'Any form?'

'Nothing relevant,' replied Dixon. 'Tom and Clive were involved in a fatal car collision as teenagers. They were both cautioned for underage drinking. Their mate, Billy Forester, got four years for causing death by dangerous driving.'

'Thirty years ago. What about Saturday night?'

'CCTV covering their yard shows Tilly getting into van twelve at nine p.m.,' said Dixon. 'GPS tracker log shows him driving to Greenwich Peninsula and doing circuits of five customer premises until four a.m.'

'No deviations?'

'Just a petrol station.'

Groombridge nodded, looking around and frowning at the empty chair. Hammed hadn't turned up for work today and wasn't answering his phone, adding a little angle to Fran's scowl. 'Okay. Get to it.'

Leaving the others following up on those recently sacked or laid off, Stark went to find more coffee and a uniform car to take him to Chase Security, in that order. He'd sold his old car in Gosport after his injury and given the cash to his mum. He'd intended to replace it when he started back at work but never got around to it. He told himself it was cheaper and easier in London, that his flat didn't have allocated parking and there were pool cars at work. But in truth he resented the fact that clutch pedals still hurt his hip and wasn't ready to buy an automatic or accept a disabled parking badge. It also helped him visit home less often.

Sergeant Ptolemy willingly agreed to drive him and waved to PC Peters, who was deep in conversation with some colleagues. She extracted herself among laughter and greeted Stark with a smile. During his first days in this nick they'd given him guided tours so he could familiarize himself with the borough and Stark enjoyed their easy-going rapport.

'Mind if our rookie tags along?' asked Peters, beckoning to one of the crowd. 'Joe, this is PC Pensol, two months into her probation and already showing precocious promise. Pensol, this is DC Stark, as I'm sure you know.'

Pensol smiled awkwardly. She had to be little older than eighteen, with fine blonde hair cut with a straight fringe and ponytail, wide almond eyes, dainty ski-jump nose, petite pointy chin and immaculate uniform – Met Police Barbie incarnate.

For some reason Peters looked amused. Pensol glanced over her shoulder at some of her peers, who were watching from a distance. Stark had the distinct impression they were watching him – an all too familiar sensation. Most of the station had tired of gawping, but every now and then he caught a surreptitious glance, usually from new faces. 'Just so long as I don't have to change my name to fit in,' he joked.

Pensol sat beside him in the back of the car, listening to her experienced colleagues' banter. A timid thing, she spoke only when spoken to and looked his way only in stolen glances, as if frightened of him. Stark sighed inwardly.

Clive Tilly looked like he'd passed through flustered into a state of resigned exhaustion, but vans came and went and fewer people milled about. He also looked increasingly displeased to see police at his door. He offered them the meeting room again and went first to show willing, or get them off his back; providing fingerprints and DNA swab, reiterating his alibi for the record, with nothing new.

'Last question, Mr Tilly,' said Stark, placing a printout on the desk. 'Company House records show Chase Security Ltd started life as T&C Security Ltd, owned equally between you and Thomas Chase. How did he end up owning the business outright?'

'I needed cash. My wife took the house in the divorce.'

'Can't have been easy.'

'Tom bailed me out when I needed it. Had to dig deep, too.'

'No hard feelings then?'

'None,' said Tilly flatly. 'Now, if we're done? I'll have Mark help you with anything you need, I have clients to reassure.'

Stark had phoned ahead to make sure his shortlist were available. They followed one by one with varying degrees of enthusiasm, while Ptolemy and Peters witnessed and logged everything and Pensol kept herself out of the way.

Last came Carlton Savage, on Stark's list because there was a written warning on his file and he was both young and handsome. It was immediately obvious why he had the first and that he knew the rest. Tall, lean but muscular, hair cropped to the same length as the designer-clipped facial hair with zig-zag patterns trimmed around the back of his scalp, diamond earrings too large to be real. He swaggered in, cocksure and insolent, looking them up and down as he listened. 'You're joking, right?'

'Just to eliminate you from our enquiries, Mr Savage.'

'I'm not a suspect?'

'Not at this time.'

'Then you can't make me.'

'No,' said Stark patiently. 'We can only ask for your help. And you will receive written confirmation that your DNA and fingerprints have been destroyed and deleted from the database when the case is resolved or closed.'

'Says you . . .' scoffed Savage, unconvinced.

White stiffened, staring crossly at Savage. 'We're supposed to assist them.'

Savage ignored him, looking Pensol up and down with a smile. 'I'm sorry, but I haven't done anything wrong and I know my rights, and I've got a van waiting.'

Stark nodded. Reluctance had become more common on this score. Well-publicized cases regarding failure to destroy innocent people's biometrics had soured public trust. Savage was within his rights to refuse. Just as Stark was within his to run Savage's name through the system for anything in his past to explain his reticence.

Savage left, and Stark began to pack the fingerprint scanner into its case.

'What about me?' asked White.

Stark looked up at the man, surprised. 'You want to give prints and a swab?'

'I want to be eliminated from your enquiries.'

Stark frowned. 'We've no reason to think that's necessary at this time, Mr White.'

The big man sat down all the same.

Shrugging, Stark took the prints and swab and Peters logged them. White inspected his digits, as if expecting to see ink. 'I got the impression you don't much like Carlton Savage,' Stark commented.

White shrugged. 'He's an arrogant little prick.'

'Seems like a fair assessment,' agreed Ptolemy. 'Rest assured, Mr White, the world has a way of taking such people down a peg or three.'

Stark's phone bleeped cheery accord with that sentiment. Unfortunately the text from DC Williams wasn't so cheery.

12

'Thanks for letting me know,' sighed Groombridge. 'Keep me posted.'

Fran waited expectantly. Her first thought on receiving the news that Hammed's mother was in intensive care with a heart attack, was for her DC. But close second was whether they could now shake a lukewarm or three out of DI Graham or another borough, and, more importantly, whether Groombridge would now have to commit to the investigation. 'So you'll talk to Cox?'

'Of course. But don't get your hopes up.' Groombridge stood and began sorting files into his briefcase from the mountains littering his desk.

Fran frowned. 'You're heading out?'

'Meetings at Division.'

She could hardly believe her ears. Didn't he even want to talk to the team? Offer some encouragement? Or was there really no message to impart but *You're on your own and don't hold your breath for reinforcements*?

'You're hovering,' he said, snapping his case shut.

Fran was almost lost for words. He'd promised to keep his head in the game and here he was, off to reinsert it up Cox's arse! 'We can't carry on like this. Things will get missed.'

'Will, or have?'

'Have, for all I know. Will for certain. Half-staffed and . . .' She hesitated, knowing she was in danger of letting her mouth get the better of her.

'And what? Headless?'

'Running a murder squad investigation is for *inspectors*, not *sergeants*.'

'I have every faith in you, Fran.'

'Fat lot of good that'll do either of us when we're explaining to the victims' families and press that the killer walked free because we were "a bit stretched". Does Cox even know how exposed we are?'

Groombridge stared back at the accusation. 'What do you think I'm doing all day long?'

I wish I knew, she stopped herself saying, but the sentiment must have been clear on her face.

His eyes narrowed. 'Look ... I've recommended a solution, but I'm struggling to get it ratified.'

'By Cox?'

'Higher.'

'And will I like it?' she asked, sensing not.

'More than the alternatives.' A typical Groombridge answer.

'And in the meantime ... '

'Keep calm and carry on.'

She stared at him, incredulous, all her fears confirmed. No one was doing *anything*! 'Why aren't you taking this seriously?'

'I am –'

'No, you're not,' she interrupted hotly, her mouth winning out as usual. 'If you were, you'd have sorted this *months* ago!'

Now he bristled. 'You think you can do better?'

'It's not my job,' she railed. 'And it's not *yours*.'

'The super is doing all he can.'

'And we can expect new staff any day now?' she scoffed.

His pained silence was all the answer she expected. 'Something has to *happen*.'

Groombridge held up a hand. 'I agree. But there is a delicate balance to be struck here.'

'*Balance?*' she spat angrily. 'Can you even *hear* yourself? You sound more *brass* than *copper* every day!'

Groombridge's face flushed with anger. Jaw clenched, he glared at her for several seconds as if searching for words, then snatched up his coat and stalked out.

Fran had crossed the line with him many times, but never so far. Scowling at his departing back, her pang of regret only stoked her resentment. Maybe he hadn't deserved that, but something had to be done!

It had become common practice of late to avoid Fran's eyes when she emerged from Groombridge's office. Their conversations were held more and more often behind a closed door, the blinds on the glass wall closed.

Unfortunately Stark arrived back just too late to pick up the vibe and just in time to see that door open to eject Groombridge past him like a fast-moving thunderhead, followed by Fran looking around as if daring anyone to speak and spotting Stark marooned mid-office like an idiot. 'What are you gawping at?' she demanded.

'Nothing, Sarge.'

'Arrest anyone yet?'

'No, Sarge.'

'Then get your bloody coat off and get to work!' she snapped, storming off in Groombridge's wake, though probably not in the same direction.

Stark looked around. 'That about Hammed? Any more news?'

Dixon looked anxious. Williams just puffed out his cheeks and shrugged. 'Only what I texted you. Fingers crossed, I guess.'

Neither of them had come up with much in his absence. So far, ex-employees with hard feelings had hard alibis to match. So before the end of the day Stark moved on to the business itself, cross-checking the list of creditors Tilly had given them.

The picture that emerged was less benign than Clive Tilly's shrugs had suggested. Behind the scenes, Chase Security had been nothing short of ruthless with cash flow management. Aggressive invoicing, delayed payments. Several cases settled through the Small Claims Court, a few others never paid out with a wad of shitty letters filed with the invoice.

'Quicker to *chase* money than pay it,' Williams commented wryly, when Stark showed him.

'Doesn't quite sit with their reputation for charitable giving,' mused Stark.

'You can only give if you've got,' said Fran, materializing in the doorway, a habit of Groombridge's which she was adopting more and more of late. She looked over his results. 'And you don't get rich being nice. Get this lot over to Economic Crimes, see if there's any proper dirt. Dixon, you're on late duty. The rest of you clear off home. The victims aren't getting any deader.'

She looked at Stark, no doubt expecting him to protest or volunteer, but he didn't. They'd all been running on fumes lately and she had to rotate her team as she thought best. A non-com's duty was to see the men and horses sheltered and fed. Dogged endurance gave diminishing returns without kip and rations.

He could feel her eyes on his back as he left; an all too common sensation of late. She was worried about him. Probably with good reason, but any effort to deflect her concern or curiosity only ever made matters worse.

13

Stark arrived at the gym later than usual. A hard workout had become a dependable antidote to his darker moods, more so since the split with Kelly. Pain, endorphins and hard, fast music were just what he needed. Tonight, though, an additional distraction materialized when a gorgeous, petite, raven-haired girl with dark eyes and olive skin got on the cross trainer next to his.

They puffed along side by side, facing the wall mirror, raising a healthy sheen of sweat free in the rhythm of their iPods. Stark inevitably pushed himself a little harder than normal, the way chaps do in the presence of the fairer sex, making sure he trained faster and longer than she did. Their paths crossed a number of times around the resistance machines and free weights and they exchanged eye contact and a smile before she left, which Stark chalked up as solid groundwork.

When he'd finished stretching down he sauntered up to Andy, the Aussie personal trainer who in the early days had helped translate Stark's physio regime into a training programme that addressed his limitations. He'd just finished showing a cute redhead around the gym for the membership team and clocked Stark's appreciative glance at her departing form. 'Out of your league, I reckon.'

'Aren't they all?' replied Stark.

'So's the other one you've been eyeing up for the last hour.'

Stark smiled sheepishly. 'That obvious?'

'Like you didn't want it to be,' commented Andy dryly. 'Attends one of my spinning classes if you want me to put in a word? Selena. Spanish.'

'I'm not treading on your toes?'

Andy laughed. 'Nah, mate. Not my type.'

Stark frowned for a second, before catching on. A macho, sporty, thorough-going Aussie bloke, Andy fitted a different stereotype. 'I'd never have guessed.'

'I don't need to advertise.'

'Fair enough.'

'Besides,' chuckled Andy. 'No point coming on to the straightest fella I ever met.'

Stark smiled. 'My sergeant used to think I might bat for your side.'

Andy gave a wry smile. 'Nah, you play your cards close to your chest, mate, but not that close. So what about it, want me to put in a word?'

Stark declined with thanks. He did, though, ask the time of the spinning class.

He stepped out into the cold wind feeling positively refreshed, but as he unlocked his bike a different chill made him glance around, like the night before, certain he was being watched. But there were no guns trained on him, no hate-filled enemy; just the cute redhead, done with her gym tour, texting on her phone.

More tricks.

He shook it off and cycled home.

'The police are keeping us in the dark,' insisted the man to camera on the evening news. 'While we lock our doors at night not knowing if we'll be murdered in our beds!' Fran recognized him – an overbearing oaf who'd made his presence felt outside the Chases' home on the morning after. President of the neighbourhood committee, self-anointed king of his little enclave of private wealth. He'd had his face in a camera then too; spouting the ever-helpful theory that there was a psychopathic burglar about to embark on a house-to-house killing spree.

Fran half wished he was right. Theft left a trail, and thieves didn't stop thieving. Whereas a deliberate murder was more likely a one-off. One set of clues, one chance to piece them together. Every chance you'd be left staring at a jigsaw puzzle with nothing but edge pieces.

The TV cut to DCI Groombridge, who calmly countered rabid hyper-bile with anodyne bullshit.

Oh good, thought Fran, so we're 'collecting evidence, conducting a detailed investigation, keeping an open mind and asking for witnesses to come forward' . . . that's nice. No doubt we'll soon be 'following multiple leads and vigorously pursuing several lines of enquiry' too. *With half a team and no chief half the bloody time!*

She loathed this stage of an investigation; heads down, reviewing, cross-checking, summarizing, fumbling in the dark . . . getting nowhere slow. And with Groombridge consistently busy elsewhere, an irritation that soured everything. She had left her old nick in Bromley to escape the dictatorship of one toxic DI. By comparison Groombridge had seemed golden, the atmosphere here a breath of fresh air. What she wouldn't give now for a touch of dictatorship.

She clicked the TV off and rubbed her eyes.

A text vibrated her phone on the table next to the wine.

She allowed herself a smile, but it wasn't who she'd hoped. It was Groombridge.

My office, 7 a.m. sharp.

Curt. One might even say *dictatorial*, thought Fran with a sigh.

14

Groombridge rubbed his eyes. He'd been up half the night reading divisional reports, and had little to look forward to but a day spent shadowing Cox in meetings and another dance for the TV cameras. And before that . . .

'Thanks for coming in so early . . .' He waited for Fran to close the door and waved her to the opposite chair.

She waited, stiffly, for him to go first; for the bollocking she had coming. He was still angry, but mostly with himself. A team without trust between its sergeant and inspector was diseased. The cancer had to be excised, and quickly. But right now neither of them knew how to apologize or felt it was they who should, which wouldn't make the following conversation any easier. The only way out of this was to press ahead with his plan, if he could; and before Cox gave overdue credence to the 'alternative'. DAC Stevens had been on the phone again last night, apparently, with Hammed's absence adding further pressure. It was now or never. 'Tell me about Stark.'

Fran answered warily. 'What do you mean?'

'It hasn't escaped my attention that he's lost his usual sparkle. What's going on?'

Fran looked taken aback, and justly so; it was inappropriate to put her on the spot like this. She would draw his attention to anything affecting performance, but otherwise you stood by your own. 'He's okay.'

'He's sound?'

'As he ever was.'

Dark humour was in poor taste, in his view. Fran had learned to respect Stark's privacy regarding his physical and emotional injuries, grudgingly, but she kept watch. Groombridge no longer had time to do likewise. 'I need to know.'

'He's just a little lovesick, Guv,' she admitted reluctantly.

'Kelly? They broke up?'

Fran nodded, clearly uncomfortable.

'I didn't know.' He rubbed his eyes again. Fran watched him carefully. She kept watch on him too, of course, and God knew she had reason of late.

'Tell me this isn't about "*reorientation*",' she said. The rumour mill was aware of Cox's pet word for their predicament, then. Groombridge hesitated, and Fran's face betrayed alarm. 'For Christ's sake, we can't take any *more* cuts! Bidden was a good copper. Even Harper knew which end of a truncheon to hold. And now Hammed's off. How are we supposed to go on like this? You can't be thinking about losing anyone else!'

Groombridge had blundered, again. 'I never said that, Fran. I just need to know who I can rely on.'

Her eyes bulged with indignation. 'Me! You can rely on *me*, and every member of my team until I say otherwise! We need *more* staff, not less!'

He held up his palms. 'Nothing's been decided –'

'But things are being *discussed*,' she interrupted hotly, 'above my pay grade. Meanwhile I'm rotating DCs through midnight shifts despite the sodding overtime cap. I'm warning you . . . Unless this team gets help, somebody is going to end up on the news spouting grovelling apologies or tap-dancing in front of a select committee, and it won't be me. You need to *do* something!'

'There is no quick fix for this, Fran. At least none you would like.'

'What does *that* mean?' she cried. 'What could possibly be worse? This team is falling apart. If you won't tell Cox, I will!'

Groombridge bristled. 'Don't push me on this, Fran.'

'Or what? Are you threatening *me* now? I'm sure Cox would be delighted to see the back of me.'

'*Superintendent* Cox is on our side, *Detective Sergeant*.'

'Superintendent Cox is kissing arse for promotion and standing on *your* shoulders to do it. But if he thinks this station needs to lose even more weight, tell him I suggested *decapitation*!' She stood and stormed out.

Groombridge let her go, speechless at his own ineptitude.

At least she didn't slam the door.

Fran was forced to abort a good door-slamming by the sight of Stark sitting at his desk.

'What time do you call this?' she demanded, ignoring the fact that he was almost as stupidly early as she was. A selective conscience was essential when indulging in good old-fashioned cathartic nastiness.

'Sarge,' he replied with dull indifference. Not even a sigh – *killjoy*. Probably keeping his head down after overhearing raised voices. Anathema as it was to her, she could be fairly certain he'd resisted listening at the door; but what would he say if he had? Probably retreat even further into his shell, saying nothing to defend himself.

Groombridge was right in one thing. Stark had been more withdrawn than reserved of late, but this went deeper.

She'd studied him for a year and a half, determined to

peek beneath his hard shell, caustic retorts, sly sarcasm and the occasional blunt truths he dropped to trip her. But when she did catch the occasional glimpse of his workings it was like looking into the blurred gears and springs of a well-oiled, complex machine of unfathomable purpose – no place for curious fingers. Groombridge had always understood Stark better than she did, a truth that irked her beyond reason.

It was easier to form a lazy opinion. *Goldenboy*, DS Harper had labelled him from the start: a bit too clever, a bit too righteous and a bit too prone to piping up with insights, oblivious to who he made look foolish in the process – something a fool like Harper took to heart. Stark had trained himself to suppress the instinct but Fran kept an eye out for that tell-tale tic in meetings. She'd learned Stark's value, which Groombridge had known all along. He wasn't a natural copper but he was, she would admit under torture, a natural detective.

Watching that spark fade from his eyes was maddening.

He looked tired the last few days, too, like in the bad old days. And something had chased him from his bed. The last thing she needed was him regressing down *that* road. Not long after joining the station he'd confessed uncertainty as to whether police life was still for him. After the dramatic events of those first weeks he'd not mentioned it again. Over time he'd slotted in and she'd got used to him, but every now and then something in his expression caused her to wonder if his thoughts weren't only one step ahead, but right over the horizon. Where once she would have been indifferent if he'd left, now she would feel it keenly. She was fond of Dixon, Hammed and Williams – like younger brothers. It was different with Stark. Perhaps because he'd been harder to like, perhaps because he'd come to her broken and in her small way she'd helped put him back together. Perhaps because he didn't expect anything from her, or fear her disapproval – he just was – and there was something oddly comforting in that. She felt no closer to under-standing him, but closer to him all the same. Losing him would be the last straw.

She sat in her chair and stewed. Her threat to bypass Groombridge and speak with Cox directly had been empty frustration. It would be the grossest violation of trust. But Groombridge wasn't making himself heard, and she *so* wanted to *shout*!

There was a courier envelope on her desk. Fran ripped it open, scanned the contents, and dumped it on Stark's desk, but with none of the ill-concealed delight she would normally have revelled in.

The last bloody straw. She stomped off to the canteen.

15

Dixon and Williams entered as Fran left, spun briefly in her wake and took their seats, perturbed.

Williams caught Stark's eye, gesturing to Groombridge's closed door. 'Trouble at t'mill?'

Stark didn't deny it.

Williams nodded, resigned. 'They've been at each other a lot lately.'

Too true. Stark nodded but added nothing.

'Reorientation?' asked Dixon.

Stark shrugged. 'Impossible to tell.' He wished he could offer something to alleviate the anxiety in Dixon's eyes, but speculation was useless. Fran and Groombridge enjoyed a certain level of friction, but things had been different for a while now. Cuts, break-up or merger aside, the worst threat the team could face would be a breakdown in trust between its DS and DCI. And right now he wasn't much in the mood for positivity.

The nightmares had kept away, but pain of a physical nature had curtailed sleep instead. He might have left the gym feeling like a new man, but he was still the old one; a sore hip and aching muscles, penance for his apish chest-beating.

He picked up Fran's parting gift. The ping on the Chases' missing phones had provided no activity or location – switched off. Now the service provider had sent over a DVD with all the previous activity data. Both

Mary and Thomas had backed up their contacts in case of handset loss, so they had names to go with numbers.

The last call Mary had made was to her husband just after seven p.m. Triangulation placed her phone at home, his at the hotel in Birmingham. The last call he had made was from his car to his golf club just before nine thirty p.m., no doubt to notify them he'd play in the morning after all. Stark worked his way back in time, searching for a needle in the haystack, that might not even be there. The morning meeting should have come as a relief, but Groombridge emerged from his office with a scowl.

Groombridge stared at his team: Williams solid, Dixon expectant, Stark . . . Stark. Fran avoiding his eyes, the yawning gulf between them unbridgeable for now. All of them tired. One notable absence.

Hammed's mother was undergoing surgery and he couldn't say when he'd be back. Further strain on the other DCs. They took the news stoically. It was his job to motivate them but he hardly knew where to start, other than to launch into the round-up. At least he was here for once. However briefly.

'So,' he tapped the suspect photos pinned to the board. 'Clive Tilly – GPS alibi would seem to put him in the clear but he might've pulled a fast one somehow or, as Detective Sergeant Millhaven loves to point out, he may have orchestrated their deaths via a third party.'

'I'll be right one day,' she muttered unsmilingly. Her breakfast of beating enemy's heart washed down with coffee had clearly done little to improve her mood.

'No doubt. But what have we really for motive?'

Williams spoke up. 'The company's solicitor tells us that

Tilly takes over as managing director with responsibility for recruiting a new financial director to replace Mary Chase. But ownership of the company goes with the estate, split evenly between Tom and Mary's families. No favouritism, no obvious motives for murder. The first Mrs Chase gets nothing, but she already has the house in Malaga and a generous divorce settlement. They all have reasonable alibis and we haven't uncovered any hidden connections to Tilly.'

'So,' Groombridge concluded. 'That leaves us with the jealous lover, thus far unidentified. Stark?'

'Nothing on ex-employees so far, Guv,' said Stark. 'Biometrics taken on Tilly, plus five employees. One other refused.'

'This one?' Groombridge tapped the photo of Carlton Savage.

'Juvenile record sealed,' said Stark. 'Mostly shoplifting according to uniform. No adult convictions. Uniform attended a call in May this year to A&E, girlfriend accusing Savage of beating her, but no charges brought.'

'So why refuse bio?' asked Dixon.

'Exactly.' Groombridge stared at the photo. DNA results on the semen, hair and foetus weren't back yet. The lover might have known about all three. 'Gut feeling?'

Stark shrugged. 'Arrogant. Distrustful. Hard to like.'

Groombridge noticed Fran's half-smile. The same description might apply to Stark, on first impressions at least. 'So far all their alibis check out, Guv,' she put in. 'None of the others have form. Full forensics from the scene is due this morning.'

Groombridge bit his lip. Two persons of interest. But with the psychopathic home-breaker angle gaining uncomfortable traction with the media and DAC Stevens breathing down their necks, they needed a suspect. Much longer without one and Cox's Plan B was going to bob to the surface again like a turd that just won't flush. 'Right, forward it on to me when it comes in. I'll be up at the Yard for the rest of the day.'

They kept at the background checks, but something kept nagging at the back of Stark's mind. Something someone had said. Hours later, it came to him. Jenny, Mary's sister. She'd said Mary 'had a plan'. The Chinese adoption agency had proved legit, as far as these things can be when they'd charged Tom an upfront fee of two thousand US dollars. But Mary had a plan . . .

It took a while to get her GP on the phone between patients. If anything, the news was worse than Stark's guess. The doctor had confirmed the pregnancy to Mary a week earlier. Mary had appeared shocked. Not least because she'd been on the contraceptive pill for years.

'But they were trying to adopt?' said Dixon.

'More his idea than hers, then . . .' mused Williams.

Stark felt somehow deflated by the discovery. Mary had deceived her husband in more ways than one. Marriages had secrets, like relationships of all kinds. Only the magnitude varied. And the motive. The doctor had also confirmed Stark's nagging theory. Mary had been unequivocal: she wanted an abortion.

16

'Where do you think *you're* going?' demanded Fran, seeing Stark pulling on his coat at the end of the day.

He shrugged apologetically. 'Shrink.' She rolled her eyes. 'I can cancel,' he offered, hoping she'd say yes.

'No. You should go. Why the hell not?' She threw up her hands despairingly and waved him away, turning her attention to a text on her mobile.

You should go.

As in, you *should* go.

The leaden skies matched his mood during the stop-start cab ride. London looked shabby, tired and muddled, its faceless denizens scurrying along beneath clutched hoods and wind-bent umbrellas. As he exited the cab a car swept wide to avoid a wayward moped, sending a wide arc of cold puddle over his shoes. Stark just shook his head. A day at his desk had added stiffness to soreness, and he limped into the hospital in pretty much the perfect frame of mind for the task ahead.

Doctor Hazel McDonald kept him waiting, as was customary. His appointments were monthly instead of weekly now, more top-up than oil change, yet still as uncomfortable as they were necessary. There had been a time when he was so assured of her obtuseness that he resented the waste of time, but he'd learned otherwise a long while ago. Now he disliked going because she cut through his crap in a way that was too incisive even for Stark, who liked forthright women. He was better for attending, but it was like sitting in a room without shadows.

Their conversation about Remembrance Sunday went much along the lines of the previous year, though perhaps less raw. They talked about why feeling old before his time might be a perfectly rational response to the events of his life. Similarly, his latest paranoid episodes of being watched or followed. She had no comment on Selena, and Stark's consequently stiff muscles; perhaps letting the dust settle on that side of his life for the moment; this being only their second session since the split with Kelly. A pity he had to spoil it by mentioning the dream.

Hazel looked up from her notes. 'Care to elaborate?'

He didn't care to, but did.

She listened without expression, then retracted her pen nib with a snap – never a good sign. Hazel saw him tense, and smiled. 'At ease, soldier; you're not on a charge.' She pursed her lips thoughtfully. 'A bad one, though.'

'A bad one,' he conceded flatly. They were rarer now, but common enough that falling asleep still felt like lying down on train tracks. Hazel said they may never go away, not completely.

'Interesting,' she commented, 'the decay.'

'Are we doing the Freud thing now?' She rarely picked apart the symbolism, preferring to focus on triggers and feelings.

'I do find the imagery interesting – time having passed.'

'A sign I'm putting things behind me?' he offered, more in humour than hope.

She shrugged. 'Do you have thoughts of death when you're awake?'

'Suicidal thoughts?'

Hazel tilted her head. 'That's not actually what I asked.'

'But it's what you meant.'

'If you say so.'

'Nicely played.'

Hazel pursed her lips. 'Even so; you used the S word.'

'And you think that's significant?'

'Such thoughts aren't uncommon around this stage in recovery.'

'What stage is that?'

Hazel arched her eyebrows, unimpressed. He'd been drilled in the signs, symptoms and protocols since the early days recovering in Selly Oak. One tool, the Kübler-Ross model, postulated five stages of grief: denial, anger, bargaining, depression and acceptance; in that order or sometimes not. When he'd first come to her he'd been stuck between denial and anger. It had taken her patience and guile to demonstrate this to him. The bargaining urge, she suggested, was somehow missing from his character – like so many other things. Hazel obviously thought he was in the depression stage now. Stark couldn't see much difference between that and acceptance, so maybe she was right.

'The gun wouldn't fire,' he offered. 'Surely that's encouraging?'

'And the dead, beckoning?'

'They were pointing.'

'Accusation rather than invitation, you think? And when they called to you?'

'Kelly's voice forcing its way in.'

'That part was dream too, remember,' she pointed out.

'This time.' That part was as much memory as dream, of a plethora of awakenings, Kelly's hidden tears, forced smiles and hollow assurances.

'Have you spoken with her?'

Hazel had steered the questions this way. 'I've no intention of doing so.'

'As you've said. And she hasn't called you?'

'I asked her not to.'

'As you've said.' Hazel looked thoughtful. 'I still wonder if you gave her too little credit –'

'I gave her *every* credit,' interrupted Stark. 'She would have stuck with it, accepting the little I could offer no matter how it hurt her, thinking, *hoping* she could heal me. She gave *me* too much credit.'

'So you hurt her to spare her – I understand. But where does that leave you?'

'You're asking if I've given up?'

'Exactly.'

Stark mulled this over. 'On that aspect of life, for now, but not on life itself.'

They overran. That hadn't happened in a while. Time flies when you're facing excruciatingly personal questions about your emotional wellbeing. Worse, Hazel suggested he come back the following week to pick up where they left off.

Fran hustled towards the restaurant, late as ever. Never one to worry about keeping a man waiting, she couldn't help smiling at her unseemly haste. More than one cautious date had been scuppered by his workload or hers, but only she was ever late.

Fishing out her phone, she reread the last text mocking her tardiness. She started a brusque response, but the damn thing rang in her hand. *Groombridge*.

She cursed aloud.

'Guv,' she answered, but could barely make out his voice as a bus passed. 'Hang on, I'm outside.' She turned her back on the street and covered her other ear. 'Okay, go ahead.'

She listened with a falling heart. *Damn.* 'Yeah, okay.' She sighed. 'We'll announce tomorrow morning?'

Groombridge started to say something else but two people came out of a nearby pub to spark up in the frigid evening, letting noise spill out. 'Sorry, Guv, say that again.' She moved away as the smokers began chatting raucously.

Then she nearly dropped the phone.

'You're not serious?' Groombridge carried on talking but she cut him off. 'No, Guv. *No!* You've got to be *fucking joking*!'

17

It was quickly clear that something was wrong in the office this morning.

Fran had arrived, dumped her coat without looking anyone in the eye and gone straight up to Cox's office without explanation.

Dixon looked anxiously between Williams and Stark. 'Reorientation?'

Williams deferred to Stark. 'She say anything to you?'

Stark shook his head. It was uncomfortable hearing them openly suggest that Fran might confide in him when they'd known her longer. But in this case, he was in the dark.

She reappeared half an hour later, but made no move to instigate the morning meeting. Minutes later Groombridge came out but passed through the office like a ghost.

Bad news, thought Stark. Someone had died, someone had screwed up so badly that neither Fran nor Groombridge were high enough to drop the requisite ton of bricks, or the axe had finally dropped on the team. Or something else completely, it was anyone's guess.

Fran said nothing. Minutes later she took a call, simply thanked the caller and knocked on Groombridge's door. 'He's finished with HR, Guv. On his way up now.'

He's finished with Human Resources? Cox? The axe, then? Closure or merger? Stark could not decide on the worst scenario.

Groombridge appeared in the door to his office. 'Okay.

Listen up. I have some bad news. Detective Constable Hammed's mother passed away yesterday afternoon. I have offered condolences and sent flowers on all our behalves. I leave you to make what contact you consider respectful.'

There were nods and shared looks, but little to be said. Stark thought of his father and the intangible, all-encircling loss Hammed must be feeling. The question was settled – this was the worst scenario.

Groombridge waited for the news to sink in. 'DC Hammed has of course been granted compassionate leave, and this brings me to my second announcement . . .' He nodded past them.

Standing, grinning inappropriately, in the door to the corridor, was the last person Stark had ever expected to see again, or wished to.

The detective constables stared at the smirking new-comer, agog. Fran stared with a face like winter.

Groombridge broke the silence. 'All right, you all know each other. With our shortfall in personnel and other duties taking up so much of my time, Superintendent Cox has seconded Detective Inspector Harper to run the team for as long as required.'

Cox had raised the idea during a busy spell several weeks earlier but Groombridge had managed to park it, or so he thought. Then Hammed's news, and another call from DAC Stevens, had forced the issue. Fait accompli. The answer to all their problems – a low-pay-band DI who knew the team and the beat.

Groombridge might have pleaded for anyone else. Owen Harper was a good man deep down, a solid copper with his heart in the right place. He'd been an effective Detective Sergeant. But his alpha-male over-confidence and sense of entitlement were frequently undermined by his own limitations. Fran's arrival on the team three years ago exposed his weaknesses and sparked an unhealthy rivalry. Stark's arrival a year later, with his obvious abilities and military notoriety, stoked smouldering insecurity. Combined with his wife's resurgent drinking, it brought out the worst in Harper. Stark's credit for wrapping up a major case proved too much. Harper had pushed himself forward for the inspectors' exam, failed, and soon after taken a regional job 'nearer to his wife's family'.

He must have squeezed through his exam on the second try and seemed to have got his life back on track. Maybe he'd lost the chip off his shoulder with it, but Groombridge wasn't hopeful. More likely they'd just been lumped with a recently enfranchised bully ready and happy to gloat over Fran and make Stark's life a misery.

Stark's head swivelled to look at Groombridge. Most of the time you had to read his emotions by minutiae. Less so today.

'All right, numpties.' Harper grinned. 'Save the gushing welcome for later. I've read the headlines. Now show me the board so we can collar the killer and get down the pub.'

Fran got slowly to her feet and ran through the board in meticulous detail and with zero humour. Harper nodded sagely throughout. Groombridge left. Stark felt sick.

Harper hated him.

Stark had slept within bullet and mortar range of men intent on killing him, but to have someone actually hate you, personally, was a sleep stealer. Dislike from one's boss was never good; outright enmity was a disaster. And how would Fran cope, with this arsehole lording it over her?

'Okay,' said Harper. 'Looks like I got here just in time. Someone get me coffee. I'll be in my office. Detective Sergeant Millhaven . . .' He jerked his head and strode into Groombridge's office. Fran followed him in and closed the door. The others exchanged looks. Stark just stared at his tiny desk.

When she emerged a while later Fran looked no happier. 'Your turn,' she said to Stark. As he stood to go in she caught his arm and whispered, 'Bite your tongue.'

Stark entered the lion's usurped den. There was a cardboard filing box on the floor in the corner. Groombridge's family photos and personal items were gone. So was the legendary in-box. The desk was clear, aside from one file. A personnel file. Stark's.

Groombridge's careworn leather office chair creaked as Harper looked up. Stark was not invited to sit. Harper opened the file and perused it. 'Detective Constable,' he mused aloud. 'Made it through, then. Congratulations.'

'Sir.' Stark kept his tone civil, waiting for Harper to ladle on the sarcasm. He was well used to showing deference. If Harper wanted to get a rise out of him he was in for a long wait.

'You can call me Detective Inspector, or Guv,' said Harper levelly.

Stark swallowed that one.

Harper stared at him. 'There's no mention of insubordination on your file . . . Or assaulting a senior officer.'

Stark said nothing.

'I'm glad now, that I didn't report you,' continued the big DI, nodding.

Unsure what Harper expected, Stark returned his gaze evenly. Harper had not reported the incident for two good reasons – because he'd started it, and because Stark had ended it without breaking sweat.

Harper closed the file. 'Clearly we got off on the wrong foot.' He smiled, a little self-consciously. 'I take my share of the blame. I'd like to put all that behind us; start over. What do you say?'

Stark didn't know what to say. He'd endured similar conversations with superiors in his other uniform. The pragmatic détente of two people who knew they needed to crack on more than get on. He doubted Harper's sincerity, but they had to work together. Perhaps the promotion he'd lusted after had eased the man's insecurities.

'I'd like that too.' He couldn't quite bring himself to add Guv, and waited for a rebuke.

Instead, Harper stood smiling and held out a hand.

Stark shook it uncertainly.

'Good.' Harper looked pleased, possibly even relieved. 'Good. Right then. I've got to prep for a press release. Go catch me a killer.'

18

The forensics report arrived. The pubic hair and semen were from the same Caucasian male, that male was father to the foetus, and it wasn't Thomas Chase; perhaps one reason Mary had planned the termination.

Fresh fingerprints that didn't match either victim, the cleaner or any of the relatives. But no hits for any of it on the offenders' database, and none was a match for Clive Tilly or the shortlist of employees. None of them was Mary's lover.

That left Carlton Savage. But unless they could cast doubt on his alibi they had no way of compelling him to provide samples. They'd spoken with his battered ex-girlfriend, still pissed at the police for swallowing Carlton's 'bullshit' alibi, but with nothing to contradict his current one.

Stark helped Dixon copy photos and printouts and pin them to the board.

He found himself staring at the police report on the Chases' neighbourly spat. They were even greedy about trees. He remembered those trees. They weren't that high. They'd been lopped, neatly halved. Perhaps the Chases were more conciliatory than they seemed. He frowned at a photo of the front of the house. 'Who does the outside?' he wondered aloud.

'What?' Dixon looked over his shoulder.

They'd talked to the cleaner, who had keys to the house,

a solid alibi. But who kept the outside so fastidiously neat? Thomas Chase spent his weekends in the office, coaching football or on the golf course, and Mary Chase spent hers in shops and restaurants. 'Who does the gardening? We haven't found invoices from gardening companies.'

'Must've been paying someone cash,' commented Williams. 'Tax contributors when they couldn't avoid it, I reckon.'

'All right, we haven't got time for you three to stand around chatting,' Fran cut in. 'If you think a question needs answering, ask it. Dixon, call Tilly to see if he knows who did the garden, or ask the cleaner. You two go talk to the neighbours.'

Williams drove, glancing at Stark from time to time. Of the other detective constables Williams was the most at ease around Stark. A family man, older, experienced and comfortable in his skin, as happy to pass the time in silence as chat. 'Cheer up, Joe,' he chuckled suddenly. 'It can't get any worse.'

'It can always get worse,' replied Stark automatically. The infantryman's mantra.

'Oh, I don't know. At least if we're all made redundant next week we might find work at Chase Security. Life in the real world might be nice.' Williams sighed. 'Your parents both alive, Joe?'

'Just my mum,' replied Stark.

Williams nodded. 'I was thinking about Hammed. Christ knows what I'd do without my parents.' He shifted in his seat. 'Bloody childcare costs would go through the roof!'

Williams never seemed to let any of this get to him. Dixon and Hammed grew quiet in the dark times.

93

Williams found the funny side, went home and kissed his wife and kids. Perhaps that was the difference. Stark envied him. For every reminder of why you did the job there were a dozen reminders of why no one else would. The poverty and greed, the fear and loathing, the banality and spite, the death. Perhaps the worst impact was the way it made you look at the world. Fran let it erode her faith in people. Stark preferred to give people the benefit of the doubt. He'd witnessed the extremes they might endure. Most people made the best of a bad lot. And for the rest, there were people like him.

The octogenarian neighbour was every inch the retired RAF squadron leader, right down to the pencil moustache and prints of aircraft on every wall. His wife waved cheerily from her wheelchair but she was, he told them, 'a bit doolally'. Looking after her and the garden kept him fit and occupied, and the third great love of his life was his two-seater Cherokee that he flew out of Biggin Hill every week, weather permitting.

He liked to talk and before they knew it they were ensconced in a shady nook in the garden with a pot of tea listening to his stories. Stark could have stayed all day. Eventually the conversation made it to the disputed leylandii. 'Yes, they had a gardener,' he said. 'Quiet chap. Offered him a cuppa when he lopped this lot but he had one of those energy drink thingies; fancy pop with caffeine. Rot your guts, I reckon. Don't know his name. Works here most Saturdays.'

'Could you describe him?' asked Williams.

'Young.' The old man shrugged. 'Everyone looks young when you get to my age. Thirty? Forty? I can't tell any more. About your height,' he said, nodding at Williams, who edged over six feet. 'But then I'm shrinking year on year, so the police get taller as well as younger.' He chuckled and wheezed as if he was powered by steam. Stark would defy anyone not to like him.

'Anything else?' asked Williams.

'Muscular, but not like one of those pumped-up body builders. Short hair, like one of those skinhead types, but with a beard. Tattoos on both arms.'

'Of what?'

'Oh, I don't know.'

'Like a fleur-de-lis,' announced his wife suddenly, 'but on a circle.'

Stark frowned and took out his notebook. 'Like this?' he asked, producing a hasty sketch.

'That's it.' The wife nodded. 'He's nice. Always waves hello.'

'And the other arm; was that a tornado?'

She smiled, but glazed over slightly.

Her husband patted her hand, with a sad smile. 'Gone again.'

The chair creaked as Mark White lowered himself into it. His eyes looked back and forth between Stark and Williams but he waited for them to explain why they were here.

Stark cocked his head. '*Honneur et Fidélité?*'

White twitched, his eyes flashed with alarm. Stark pointed to his right upper arm. 'May I see?' White used his left hand to slide up his T-shirt sleeve to reveal the tattoo. At first glance it did look like a fleur-de-lis, but was in fact flames rising from a circle representing a grenade.

Stark had noticed the base of the circle when they first met but the whole image told the tale. He had seen one like this before, on one of his instructors during special-forces training, the insignia of the Légion Étrangère, the French Foreign Legion. Their motto – Honour and Fidelity. 'How long were you in?'

White shifted uncomfortably. 'Two terms.'

Ten years, then. 'Rank?'

'Sergeant.'

'See the sights?'

White nodded. 'My share. Enough not to want to talk about it.'

Stark knew that sentiment all too well and changed the subject, pointing at White's other arm. 'The tornado?'

White shrugged. 'Nickname.'

Stark paused. 'You garden for Thomas and Mary Chase.'

White looked cagey; perhaps he had been expecting this. 'So?'

'You didn't think to mention it?'

'You didn't ask.'

'I asked your colleagues one by one if they had any relationship with the victims outside of work, while you stood in that corner and watched. You asked to be eliminated from the investigation. But you didn't think it relevant?'

White hesitated. 'I knew it wouldn't look good.'

'Not telling me looks worse,' said Stark. 'How well did you know them? What were they like at home?'

White shrugged. 'Didn't see them much.'

'How did you get the job?'

'She asked me. Too cheap to bring in a firm. She read in my CV I'd done some landscaping.'

'You gardened for them on Saturdays?'

'Mostly.'

'Were you there the day they died?' White nodded and looked down. Not just an omission this time; he'd been asked for his whereabouts and lied. 'For how long?'

'I got there at nine, knocked off at four when it started getting dark.'

'Did you see the Chases?' asked Stark.

'He's always gone by the time I get there. Football.'

'But Mary was there?'

White's face flushed. With anger or embarrassment? Stark ducked his head, trying to catch the man's eyes. 'If you saw someone or something out of the ordinary, you must tell me.'

The big man looked up. 'I didn't see anything "out of the ordinary". He was there most Saturdays.'

'Who?'

'They thought they were being *clandestine*. The husband's away and rats will play. Didn't think I'd notice, or didn't care.'

'Notice what?' demanded Williams. 'Who did you see?'

19

Carlton Savage.

Stark had summed him up well – instantly unlikable. Some people summoned to police interview went to pieces, some turned to stone, some blabbed like children, others thought they could bluff it out. Savage slid into his chair, oozing. Not oozing confidence or insolence, just oozing.

Harper settled into the seat beside her. Fran would have given an arm to have Groombridge instead. The fact that Harper had proposed the very game plan she'd have expected from Groombridge somehow made it all the more humiliating.

Fran swore silently.

Why had she forced Groombridge's hand? He'd warned her she wouldn't like the options. Having any DI brought in over her was the last thing she'd wanted, or so she'd thought; but *Harper* . . .

He'd sat behind Groombridge's desk and been nice as *bloody* pie. That cat that got the cream. Christ knew what the smug bastard had said to Stark. The irksome DC remained characteristically tight-lipped, stoically taking life's latest joke on the chin.

This was a *disaster*.

One of the big ones, only cockroaches survived.

Savage listened as she went through the spiel, confirming his name, address, employment, all with the same ill-masked sneer. He kept glancing at Harper, wondering why he wasn't talking. They were banking on his being the type that wouldn't like being questioned by a woman, or a woman of mixed race, or the less senior officer.

Fran smiled. 'How well did you know Thomas and Mary Chase?'

Savage made a show of frustration. 'You brought me down here to ask me the same questions as before?'

'Plus some new ones. How well?'

Savage rolled his eyes. 'Not well.'

Fran pretended to look at her notes. 'You've worked there . . . three years.'

He shrugged.

'You were working on the night of the killings?'

'Yes.'

'Were you called in on your day off? Clive Tilly said he was short-handed that night.'

Savage shrugged. 'Don't know anything about that. It was my shift.'

'What time did you start and finish?'

'I've already answered all this,' insisted Savage, losing patience. He looked to Harper but the DI stared back dispassionately.

Fran consulted the file. 'You clocked in at nine and went straight out in van seven, returned at six a.m. and clocked off.'

'If you're answering as well as asking, I'll be down the pub,' said Savage.

Fran looked up from the paperwork. 'And earlier in the day?'

'What?'

99

'Where were you before work on the day of the killings?' For the first time Savage looked uncertain. 'It's been suggested Mary Chase was having an affair with someone at work. Would you know anything about that?'

Savage looked to Harper again, probably trying to assess if they already knew.

'More than one person has suggested it was you.' Technically true, if you counted Williams and Stark.

Savage's face darkened. 'Who? That freak White? He's just jealous!'

'Of what?'

'I've seen the way he watches her. He's like a ghost, always watching. He wanted her. They all did. Couldn't hack the fact that she wanted me.'

'She wanted you?'

Savage shrugged modestly, perhaps trying to cover his slip. But the sneer was there, in his eyes, the girl-beater showing through. 'Look,' he sighed. 'I didn't want to say anything before. Ain't right to speak ill of the dead and all that. She weren't even my type. Stuck up, and well . . . a bit of a bitch. But she came on strong. Practically begged . . .'

'So, what? You threw her a bone?' He didn't leap to deny it. 'And once she'd had a taste she wanted more?'

Savage searched her smile uncertainly. 'That's about it. And it was a laugh . . . to start with. Doing the boss's wife, listening to the rest yapping about her while I was busy getting what they all wanted. She started off as his secretary, did they tell you that? Shagged her way in, then shagged her way up. She was still married to some other bloke then but she changed horses quickly enough; gold-digging tart. She was happy to flounce around in her bling and convertible, but she never lost her taste for slumming it below stairs, if you know what I mean.'

'Were you with her in her house that morning?'

Savage nodded. It was out now, but he didn't seem overly concerned; confident in his alibi. 'It was getting boring. She'd started calling me all hours. I went round that day to sack her off but she was stressing out about something so I gave her one for the road.'

'I suppose she was lucky you didn't knock her teeth out,' said Harper, speaking for the first time.

Savage's smile faded.

'What was she stressing out about?' asked Fran.

'I didn't ask. I was going to bin her next day but . . .'

'But she was dead by then,' Harper finished the sentence.

Savage's face tightened. 'You can't pin that on me.'

'There's something off about that one, Guv,' said Fran.

'Specifically?' asked Groombridge, who'd been watching the interview through the mirrored glass with Williams and Stark.

'He's an arsehole,' said Harper.

'But hardly uncommon in that,' Groombridge countered. 'Alibi?'

'GPS from the security van,' replied Harper. 'Doing laps of the Abbey Wood commercial park all night.'

Groombridge looked back at Savage through the glass. Things were looking up on the motive front, but opportunity was still lacking. 'You didn't mention the pregnancy. Probably best. Rattle him with that one when we have more. Still refuses to provide samples?'

'What about a warrant, compelling him?' asked Harper, but he knew the answer.

'Not unless his alibi spontaneously implodes.'

'We could lift prints and sweat off the table in there,' suggested Williams, half-jokingly. Savage and a hundred others; useless without a comparison set – consented or compelled.

'Does accidentally bleeding on your cell floor count as consent?' growled Harper, making a show of his frustration.

'Afraid not,' replied Groombridge. 'Still, good work you two.' He nodded to Williams and Stark. 'Have uniform drop him off. Then go grab a pint, you lot; you've earned it.'

Harper was certainly on good form, dragging them all to Rosie's to celebrate his triumphant return, buying the first round with ostentatious largesse. There was no disparaging comment when Stark requested a soft drink, nor when he finished it and made his farewells. Judging by the look of the rest, he wouldn't be the only one trotting out midweek excuses.

There was just time to get to the gym. Stark had been cycling more since the split with Kelly and felt no shame in turning up for an advanced spinning class. Andy chuckled when he saw him. 'Sure you're up for this, mate?' he asked.

Selena was already perched atop her bike in black cycling shorts and a pink singlet, looking perfectly at home. 'Still out of your league,' offered Andy with a smirk.

Stark shrugged. 'I'm just here for the exercise.'

'Fair go. But let's see if we can't work your muscles while you're working your eyes.'

Stark had used exercise bikes during post-op rehab and they all worked on similar principles. He copied other people adjusting their seats and bars, while Andy started the music. 'Everyone, this is Joe, don't mind his ugly mug, he's all right underneath. We'll start off easy and work up. Joe, just follow what I say and go as hard or easy as you feel. Right, let's go!'

The bikes had the usual adjustable tension to simulate hill climbs or sprints, and Andy called the pace to suit the speeded-up dance music. Ten minutes in and Stark was considering the merits of a beginners' class. Ten minutes later and his legs and chest were on fire, ten more and he had a stitch. Selena was making it look easy enough, while others whizzed along like maniacs. Andy worked them up to a sadistic, endless climb, always promising the summit, always laughing and demanding another minute, and then into a final lunatic sprint, a full minute and a half of tearing pain, leaving the whole class gasping during the cool-down. Stark saw himself in the mirror, dripping, ruddy, limp. Selena was glistening, sweat moulding her singlet to her sports bra, her small bosom heaving and her eyes alive. One of the maniacs said something to Andy about the pace.

Andy laughed. 'Yeah, sorry about that, everyone. But Joe there ripped the piss about the rugby so I had to pay the Pom back a bit.'

There were groans, and Stark's classmates all looked at him with good-natured accusation, Selena among them. *Bastard*, thought Stark, exhausted. He shrugged and smiled apologetically. 'Sorry, everyone. I guess some countries breed sore losers.'

'See you next week?' asked one of the obvious regulars.

'Work permitting.' Stark nodded, ignoring Andy's amused expression.

Selena smiled at him, and Stark decided the evening could be considered a success. Even so, it was a slow, painful ride home.

20

'Look at these two . . .' Fran waved a hand at the board in disgust. 'A rich businessman who took advantage of his best friend's divorce to take over the business, and his gold-digging trophy blonde who steals him from his first wife, spends his money like it's going out of fashion and cheats right under his nose.'

Or a regular couple with problems, who gave to charity, coached kids' football, provided employment for dozens and didn't deserve to be gunned down before their time, thought Stark.

'Seriously,' she continued, undeterred by his silence. 'We've been at this all week. I can't be the only one thinking – who cares?'

Stark suppressed a smile. She didn't mean it for a second, but a night out with Harper might well leave a person doubting the point of it all. And Fran commonly got the hump if an investigation refused to wrap itself up neatly within a week. 'And yet the flame of righteous justice burns strong in our hearts, Sarge,' he mused dryly.

'Don't you start. That crap's bad enough from the Guv'nor.'

Which one? thought Stark despondently. Harper had always been wont to mimic Groombridge, though from his lips it usually sounded as pompous as it was hollow.

'Morning, troops,' sang the man in question, walking

in and clapping his hands together with vulgar cheer. 'Right, let's bust some alibis!'

The meeting eventually broke up with tasks allotted. You had to hand it to Harper, he had energy. This was his big chance. A juicy double homicide to put a shine on his freshly minted DI pips, and perhaps seal his occupation of Groombridge's office with the stamp of permanence.

On that gloomy note, Stark opened the GPS log from Carlton Savage's night-time vehicular vigil of the Abbey Wood commercial park. Dixon had been through them all but Harper wanted everything rechecked.

CCTV showed Savage arriving at work, getting into van seven shortly after. Stark traced the route on the map, noting the short cuts Savage used to bypass traffic. At no point did he stop for more than a minute. He then settled into laps of the business park, stopping every now and then, once for over an hour, but well after the time of the killings. Shortly before six in the morning the van returned to Chase Security, Savage went inside, then left minutes later. So that was that. The Guv'nor was building a case for a generic mobile phone data map in a radius around the Chases' home, to pick up all the numbers used in the location within the window, but it was a laborious long shot – it only triangulated a handset in use, and only a fool would keep his phone switched on when he was off to commit murder.

The hour-long stoppage niggled, though. The night-shift lunch break, he assumed. He opened some of the other logs and saw that it was almost universal, a stationary period or diversion to the nearest drive-thru fast food. Even Clive Tilly had taken a break. Stark stared at the time. And then the location. 'Shit.'

'What is?' asked Fran from the doorway.

Stark glanced about for Dixon but everyone else was out and about. 'Sarge?'

Fran shook her head. 'Don't give me the innocent look. Spill.' She peered at his screen to see what he was reading. 'GPS logs. Savage?' She looked closer. 'Tilly? What did you spot?'

'Just something I wanted to ask Dixon about, Sarge.'

'What?' she asked firmly. She wouldn't be fobbed off.

He glanced again at Dixon's empty chair and cursed his timing. 'I noticed Savage was stationary for a while so I checked to see if that was normal. They all take breaks of an hour or so some time during their shifts. Even Tilly. Van twelve was stationary at the petrol station for over an hour.' Dixon had identified the deviation but failed to flag the duration. Stark pointed at the time on the screen. And then the location.

It took a moment to sink in. 'But that's . . .'

'Barely half a mile from the crime scene.' Stark nodded. 'Smack in the middle of the time-of-death window.'

Fran straightened up, a thoughtful expression on her face. 'I'm going to kill Dixon.'

'It was easy to miss.'

'*You* spotted it.'

'It's probably nothing,' Stark said quickly. 'Let me check it out before you go off on one.'

'I do not "*go off on one*"!' Fran bristled indignantly.

'Please. If it turns out to be nothing I'll have a quiet word with John myself, let him bring it to you.'

'Bollocks to that,' Fran scoffed. 'If you're getting out of this hellhole, I'm driving!'

*

It wasn't far but the journey passed in uncomfortable silence. Where Fran would once have used the time to pester and pry, silence had gradually crept in and squatted. She'd been under a lot of stress recently, but the rest was down to him. Yesterday's bombshell wasn't going to help.

The petrol station had CCTV cameras up under the high flat canopy over the pumps, one angled to the entry, one towards the exit, with a third over the out-of-hours security window used at night when it wasn't safe to let customers inside the shop. There were more inside. The manager was friendly and helpful, allowing them free rein of the back office to replay the footage from six nights earlier.

At 23.27, Chase Security van twelve pulled up on the forecourt. Clive Tilly got out, filled up and went into the shop. The camera inside showed him buying a sandwich, drink and tabloid, paying by card and leaving. But instead of driving out on to the road he reversed away from the pumps to a small parking area at the rear corner of the forecourt. The lights went out. Then . . . Nothing.

The only camera that could see the van was the one above the out-of-hours window. The driver's side faced away and it was impossible to see Tilly sitting inside. Over an hour later the interior light came on as Tilly climbed out and walked back into the petrol station. He spoke to the cashier, used the toilet, bought a coffee and went on his way. The times on the screen matched with the GPS tracker. Van twelve continued its rounds until four in the morning before parking up outside Tilly's house until eight. It was back at Chase Security before nine, where their camera had shown Tilly climb out yawning and walk inside, to all outward appearances oblivious to the fate of his bosses and the 999 call soon to be placed by the Chases' cleaner.

Stark left Fran to pester the manager for a copy of the footage and wandered out to where the van had been parked. Vent pipes poked out of the ground by some kind of storage tank; low greenery filled the space before a standard wooden fence with concrete posts and a buff brick wall. The wall was seven feet high but the timber fence only five, simple enough to scale. Just the other side was a driveway and en-bloc garages behind some houses.

In the footage the bright lights of the forecourt threw the planted area into dark contrast. All Tilly had to do was switch off the van's interior light so it didn't operate when he opened the door, slip out and hop over the back fence, then sneak back the same way and turn the interior light back on. Simple, but unlikely. More likely he'd just been eating his poor-man's dinner, reading his paper, taking a well-earned break. Only he hadn't read the paper; the interior light had never come on.

Back inside Fran was hovering and the manager's accommodating smile had wilted into anxious haste to comply. He was just taking the DVD out of the drive when Stark noticed what had been staring him in the face all along. The computer and monitor each had a sticky label, matching the branding on the cameras outside and the signs on the pumps and shop window – the security firm's name.

Twenty minutes later they were standing in Clive Tilly's office. 'I don't understand,' he said, frowning.

'What were you doing, for over an hour?' Fran asked again.

'Eating a limp sandwich and admiring the tits on page three.'

'But the interior light was off,' said Stark.

Tilly waved a hand. 'She was too skinny, so I was checking my eyelids for holes.'

'You were asleep?' asked Fran doubtfully.

'Our drivers get an hour break, health and safety. They all stop off somewhere; check the logs. I've stopped there before; at my age it's useful to know places with a toilet. What's this about?'

'You knew it had a toilet and more,' Fran said. 'Chase Security provides and maintains their security systems.'

'That's how I knew they had a toilet. I supervised the system installation.'

'Meaning you knew exactly where to park the van so you could get out unseen, climb over the back fence and go kill your oldest friend and his wife.'

'*What?*' Tilly looked panicked. 'You're not serious? Why would I do that?'

'Sex, money or both,' replied Fran. 'I'm sure I'll find out soon enough. You booked the hotel for Tom that night.'

'So?'

'We spoke with the client Tom met for dinner. He told us you set up the meeting, and called him twice that day to check it was still on.'

'He has a habit of cancelling last minute.'

'You texted Tom to make sure he'd shown up. Checking that the coast was clear. Must've been a shock when Tom came home after all.'

'This is *rubbish*!' Tilly insisted.

'What were the grounds for your divorce?'

'What the hell has that got to do with anything?'

'Time will tell.'

Tilly looked exasperated. 'Irreconcilable differences.'

'Lousy timing for you, though. Must've been hard for a proud man,' said Fran, 'going from partner to minion.'

'That was nearly twenty years ago . . . Would I have stuck around working for Tom if I harboured a grudge? We were mates, we grew up together. Tom, me and Billy, we were family!'

'Families fall out,' said Fran.

They put Tilly in the back of the car, white as a sheet and silent, though they could see the pleading taking place behind his darting eyes.

They left him in interview room one to wait for Harper.

'I'm not convinced,' said Stark.

'Oh? Okay . . . We'd best let him go then,' said Fran dryly.

'I'm not convinced,' said Groombridge.

Fran rolled her eyes but said nothing. Harper's frustration looked more convincing this time.

She and Harper had grilled Tilly for an hour, going over and over the same ground, the same questions, the same anxious responses, exasperated pleading, the same interruptions from the lawyer friend he'd called. 'He doesn't strike me as the cold-blooded type,' added Groombridge, 'but it wouldn't be the first time I've been wrong.'

'We'll find out, sir,' said Harper. 'Leave it to us.'

Was that a slight dig? She'd noted Harper's flicker of displeasure to find Groombridge hovering outside the interview room again.

Groombridge glanced at his watch. 'All right, spring him on police bail. I'll request a warrant for his bank and mobile phone records. See if you can speak with his ex-wife.'

Harper nodded and left, but his face betrayed some impatience at still being subject to orders.

Groombridge stood staring in at Tilly, so Fran hovered. She was still awaiting some quiet reprimand for her recent behaviour. Groombridge could be cutting when pressed and she had pressed hard. But he didn't look at her. She bit her lip, determined to keep her temper. She wanted to scream – *I told you so!* But it was way too late. 'What about Dixon?' she asked, trying to provoke the conversation.

'What about him?'

'Will you want to speak with him?'

'I'll leave that to you. Go easy. They'd all worked late and it won't be the last time we ask them to.' He sighed. 'Well then . . .'

Fran watched in disbelief as the door closed behind him. Nothing about their cross words, nothing about the seriousness of Dixon's oversight or the implications, or how to stop it happening again. Surely he hadn't stooped so low that he would brush this under the carpet, just to cover his arse, or Cox's? No. He wouldn't. She was less certain about Cox. For all his bumbling bluster he was a copper, started from the beat unlike so many of the recent influx of brass, but he'd been on the pay grade between police and politics a long time. Hearing could get selective up there in the thin hot air.

Barking at the custody sergeant to bail Tilly, she took the lift back up to the MIT and beckoned Dixon aside for a private bollocking. Having set the team's plates spinning, she swept off to the canteen to stew over a coffee.

21

Friday night at Rosie's.

Station custom. No midweek excuses. But a bigger crowd to avoid Harper in.

Stark bought Dixon a drink. No hard feelings. Dixon didn't blame him. The youngest DC had more metal than people thought. But things like this only ever highlighted the disconnect between Stark and his peers, and that *was* his fault. It was a shame, but it was what it was. He got on with them all, shared a drink and a laugh, but they were colleagues, not mates.

The same had been true in his old nick in Gosport, his home town worn with memories and landmarks that merged and faded more with each return and old school friends that grew more alien by the year, living lives so different from his that he hardly knew how to speak to them any longer. In the TA he'd had comrades rather than mates, and he'd deliberately dropped out of touch with them all since his injury – analgesic necessity. In London the only friends he'd made were Kelly's, and friendly no longer.

It wasn't something to dwell upon but he didn't make friends, not close ones. Doc Hazel thought it stemmed from the loss of his father, but it went back further. He'd always been aware of his otherness. But it wasn't until he was wounded that he really faced the truth of it, the hesitancy in their eyes and how little it hurt him.

Perhaps he shared something with his adopted city after all . . . Indifference. He cared about very few people specifically, beyond immediate family; as few as possible. Beyond that he cared about concepts, freedoms, rights, law and justice and people; all the people. What a hollow-sounding conceit.

Hazel was his only confidante – his confessor. Pierson was his conscience. Bizarrely, worryingly, Fran was the closest thing to a friend he had in the world and she would howl with horrified laughter to hear it.

He ordered himself a double, cheap blend, no ice and a lager chaser. Harvey the landlord shrugged and put the good stuff back on the high shelf without comment. Bringing Fran's traditional large Chardonnay and two packets of crisps, Stark deposited the lot on the table stained from decades of slops and cigarette burns – the Compass Rose wasn't about to rush into anything as taste-less as refurbishment – necked his scotch in one and took a slug of lager.

'What's with you?' demanded Fran.

'Just washing the dust of despair from my throat, Sarge,' replied Stark flatly.

'If you're still moping after that girl you can piss off and sit somewhere else.'

That girl. Fran and Kelly had in fact got on just fine. When they weren't pissed off with him, the women in his life took pleasure in ganging up on him. But since the break-up, Kelly had been reduced to *that girl*, and Fran seemed determined to interpret any anomaly in his mood as latent pining.

He stayed put anyway. Better than propping up the bar with Harper. The new-minted DI was still acting friendly.

But Stark had spent time in enough bars with bombastic braggarts to know that nothing spoiled the former quicker than the latter.

Fran glanced at Stark as they drank.

If Hammed had been there Dixon and Williams might have invited him to make up doubles at pool, but they asked less often these days. It wasn't just Groombridge who'd noticed the change in Stark. Whatever he said, Kelly *had* to be the problem. Men were such twits, and good-looking boys the worst. They never knew a good thing when they had it, sulked when they'd lost it, then clammed up and let it gnaw at them from the inside.

Mind you, girls weren't much better – deluding themselves that ice cream, a good blub and a night out with gal-pals would make everything right. Fran favoured the first item on that list, disdained the second and was woefully short of the third. Maybe it was growing up with older brothers, but she'd never really understood the girl-power thing. She had mates, not BFFs, and a good blub just gave her a headache, puffy eyes and snot.

Stark looked like he could use a mate about now, but Fran prodded more out of habit than hope these days, and that was getting boring.

Perhaps he was saving it all up for that insufferable shrink, as he sat there sipping his lager with a face like a bulldog chewing a wasp. At least that was the face he might have had if he were anyone else, anyone normal. Instead he was like a bulldog stoically holding an angry wasp in his mouth while it stung him repeatedly. Where was his bite?

Groombridge was right, and her conscience on that

score gave way to temper. 'Oh, for God's sake!' she blurted out. 'I'm not sitting here with you like this. Either pick up the phone to Kelly or go out and get laid!'

Stark winced and shook his head. 'You're barking up the wrong tree.'

That was it. Ever the impenetrable sod. She shook her head, drained her white wine and plonked the glass in front of him with a clunk. 'Oh, get them in, then. If neither of us is going to cheer up, let's at least get *plastered*.'

He trudged off to the bar.

Some people vied for service by bobbing on tiptoe, displaying a crisp note, leaning forward or even calling out. Stark simply waited, with eye-watering stillness, a fixed point in the peripheral vision, un-ignorable. Harvey quickly turned his way.

A similar effect could be observed around him. The regular uniforms loitered, shadowed by the latest intake of timid rookies; the government's 'new bobbies-on-the-beat' – low-pay-grade replacements for all the experienced officers squeezed out through carefully applied 'efficiencies'. Fewer each year, though, whatever the politicos claimed. The latest batch included a gaggle of girls, and the old lags circled like vultures, Harper included. But more than one pair of their prey's eyes flitted towards Stark.

Nice looks, visible scars and notoriety made him an object of constant speculation on the lower floors. The fool had no idea how easily he could take her advice tonight, if he only chose. He shared a nod and words with a few, Ptolemy and Peters and others. Those that were used to him found it easier.

A peal of laughter erupted around the girls and one, a

petite blonde with beautiful eyes, blushed deeply and glanced anxiously across at Stark as he carried the drinks back through the crowd with no outward awareness of the turbulence in his wake.

Oh dear, sighed Fran.

There was another girl at the bar following Stark with her eyes. A pretty redhead, alone, un-circled by vultures, so not a copper. Fran frowned, realizing she had no idea whether Stark liked redheads *or* blondes. Kelly's hair had been the kind of glossy brunette that was just plain unfair outside a shampoo ad.

Red was holding her phone in an odd way, not texting or surfing . . . It looked for all the world as if the brazen floozy was taking Stark's picture, probably to post online for her BFFs! If only his 'reputation' was restricted to the station. One of the old lags turned to her with a drink. Chancing his luck. Wasting his time. And Stark . . . sat down to drink, oblivious.

22

Fran's was not the only hangover in evidence, but she was certain it was the worst.

Her pact with Stark had accelerated after Harper collared him on one of his trips to the bar, forcing Fran to join them and endure Harper *harping* on; regaling them all against their will with tales – some old, some new, few credible and all of crushing disinterest to Fran. A miracle she'd held her tongue. If she had. Most of the evening was now a blur. Little wonder the man's wife drank.

He was on a call when she'd crawled into the office; someone important from his body language. He liked to keep the blinds open but the door closed. So far, he'd maintained the act – start over, work together, best of bloody friends. Fran wasn't fooled for a second. When he eventually emerged he peered around the office. 'Where's Stark?' he demanded, over-loudly.

'Getting the coffees,' replied Fran, hiding a wince.

Harper looked displeased, his own headache showing, maybe. He announced that he wanted to re-conduct the interviews. He'd had the pleasure of Clive Tilly and Carlton Savage, but not Mark White. He wanted all three in. He handed her a copy of the work roster – complete with alterations. DI prerogative, but a treading on Fran's toes that felt deliberate. A new broom had a brush on one end, but a stick at the other.

Perhaps she hadn't held her tongue last night.

She broke the news to Stark when he returned with the caffeine. He'd been down for Sunday off.

'Plans?' she asked at his faint frown. Only she knew that he used any free Sunday morning to visit his pal in prison. *Boys'-only war stories and medal-polishing club.* He didn't know she knew.

'Nothing urgent.'

She could offer to cover for him but if he insisted on secrets . . . Any decent person would just lie. 'You could say you've got church.'

He huffed the tiniest laugh. 'Or confession.'

'Talking of penance,' she said, nodding to the fresh stack of files on his desk. Harper's other roster tweak and evidence, were it required, that underneath the 'Mr Nice DI' act he was still the same petty shit he'd always been. 'You get the Longshits.'

Otherwise known as the Longshots – the tedious cross-referencing of modus operandi and forensics with the database, looking for any links with known killers, burglars, armed robbers and general low-lifes. The list had to be collated and sorted by match indices, geography, age, psychological profile, et cetera. It had all been done, but in light of Dixon's slip, Harper wanted it redone and had been at pains to point out Stark's prowess in that sort of thing. The job was usually divvied up to prevent any- one jumping from the roof. Perhaps Stark hadn't held his tongue last night either.

Williams and Dixon were dispatched to fetch the lucky contestants in Harper's *I'm On Secondment, But Try Getting Me Out Of Here* show.

Clive Tilly, Carlton Savage and Mark White were all found at work, so at least it wasn't just coppers working weekends,

Williams pointed out with his usual glass-half-full. Nevertheless, it took all day and persuasion-bordering-on-threat to get them in and interviewed.

Clive Tilly's ex-wife had been tracked down, but had nothing of interest to say, on the divorce or anything else they could use to trip Tilly. Records showed his phone hadn't been used in the time window, and so failed to place him conveniently at the scene. They had nothing new on the others either, but Harper wanted his go on the merry-go-round.

He gave all three a grilling, spending most time on Mark White, shortly thereafter promoting him to favourite for having no alibi whatever and lying to conceal his relationship with the victims outside work. Fran found his style heavy-handed and predictable compared to Groombridge, but White left suitably rattled and maybe that was worth something.

Harper had certainly enjoyed himself.

The DCs had been invited to observe, but Stark had stuck at his menial task. His backwards brand of defiance.

Both Williams and Dixon offered to stay and help Stark that evening, but he declined with thanks. He was schooled in the army way. Good officers would turn a blind eye to short cuts if you gave them a good enough excuse, because they knew you probably had a better way of getting things done than the way they'd told you, particularly with TA soldiers who usually arrived with a more worldly pragmatism. Harper was the other kind of officer, and fretting wouldn't alter that.

Stark was sure he saw Harper glance back with a

satisfied smirk, but he knew how to frustrate this kind of officer. He kept at it past midnight and placed his bullet-proof report front-and-centre on Harper's desk before leaving.

No doubt the DI would find him something equally tedious to do the next morning, but if there was one thing an infantryman didn't mind, it was boredom. If it became a battle of wills, Stark could out-stubborn a mule like Harper.

Unfortunately, the following morning he walked straight into every infantryman's nightmare, an improvised explosion.

23

'What the *fuck* is this?' demanded Harper, storming in waving the *News of the World*, Britain's favourite sensationalist Sunday red-top. On the front page was a picture of Mary Chase at her most angelic beneath the headline, **SLAIN WOMAN PREGNANT!**

Beneath were three long-lens photos – Tilly, Savage and White. And underneath ... **POLICE INTERVIEW SUSPECTS**. All three stills were of the men climbing in or out of police cars in the rear yard to the station the day before.

'Someone tipped off the *paps*,' spat the big DI as if the word were poison. He glanced at Stark, who'd been up here alone during the interviews.

'Oh, for God's sake, Owen!' cried Fran. 'No one here tipped anyone off!'

Harper rounded on her, and for a moment Stark thought he would rebuke her informality, but perhaps he knew better than to belittle her openly, or lacked the courage. Instead he waved the tabloid angrily at the whole team. 'This isn't the local rag. This is a *national*. It'll be all over the TV as well by now.' He eyed each of them in turn, lingering longest on Stark. 'If I find out any of you is tipping the press, you're finished. While I'm in charge this team will be the squeakiest it's ever been. We stand together. Otherwise what's the point?'

An hour after that he was standing on the front steps

of the station taking questions from the press. The team gathered round the TV to watch his performance.

You had to hand it to him, thought Stark grudgingly, Harper looked the part. Tall, solid, handsome in a weather-beaten way, confident. He played down the significance of the three 'suspects', saying they were merely helping with enquiries, et cetera, et cetera. He didn't carry it off as well as Groombridge would have, but better than Stark ever would. Harper revelled in the theatre of it; Stark had endured quite enough time in the spotlight for one life.

'Think we have a leak?' asked Cox, switching off the sound as the news anchor moved on to the next story.

Groombridge pursed his lips. 'Maybe.'

'You're supposed to say no.'

Groombridge shrugged. 'It wouldn't be the first time.'

'It would be the first time in *this* station,' insisted Cox.

Wishful thinking, thought Groombridge. 'Could just be a lucky freelance photographer peddling snaps to a half-decent investigative reporter.' More wishful thinking.

'I've already had Deputy Assistant Commissioner Stevens on the phone, furious.'

Groombridge kept his counsel on that news. By reputation, DAC Stevens had never been slow to make hay out of other people's misfortune. 'Could be the other thing.'

'Phone hacking?' Cox made a face. 'Celebrity tittle-tattle is one thing, but a murder investigation . . . they wouldn't dare.'

Groombridge didn't necessarily agree. Rumour of a broader investigation was being tightly controlled for obvious reasons, but if true, he had a feeling his sentiments about the tabloids might prove more justified than even he would wish. Everyone had been told never to leave case-explicit voicemails, but standards slipped. Phone PINs were changed regularly, but as a result they were often written down. It only took one rotten apple.

'They'll have a field day with this, though,' Cox said bitterly. 'Demanding to know if it's true, how long we've known, why we're not offering any progress.'

'We don't comment on investigative detail.' Line one in the unwritten handbook.

'Quite.' Cox nodded.

It was a losing battle either way. The press loved questions every bit as much as answers. And tomorrow's headline was writing itself: *Where Will the Baby-Slaying Blackheath Fiend Strike Next?*

'DI Harper handled it well, though,' added Cox, fishing for an opinion from Groombridge.

'That he did.'

'One would hardly think he was freshly promoted.'

'No.' It was indeed hard to credit. But they were where they were . . . Groombridge would not undermine Harper now. The man deserved a chance.

'I'm sure you'll be wanting to maintain some discreet oversight,' said Cox. 'Make sure the team is comfortable with the adjustment.'

More fishing. Probably wondering about Fran. Groombridge bit his tongue. He'd made such a mess of this; and just when the demands on his attention were dragging him ever further away. If only he'd advanced his plans quicker. He wanted to blame Fran, but this was on him. He'd procrastinated, waiting for the opportune moment, and now his plans for the team hung by a thread.

'No time for regrets, Michael,' said Cox, perhaps mistaking his silence for wistful reminiscence.

'No indeed.'

'Well then.' Cox picked up his leather document wallet. 'Best not keep the bigwigs waiting.'

Predictably, Stark was rewarded for the thoroughness of his Longshots report with the task of following up – checking names off the list he'd generated, one by one.

Harper stayed out with Fran for most of the day, 'following up on other things' – throwing his weight around and no doubt enjoying every second of having Fran as his 2IC and Dixon and Williams as his minions.

Stark took solace in solitude, more than happy to enjoy a silent office, interrupted only by occasional calls.

'MIT. DC Stark speaking.'

'Hi, this is the switchboard. I have a call for DCI Groombridge but he's not answering. I don't know whether you'll want to take it either, to be honest. Says he knows the DCI but he's quite rude and he sounds more like a heavy breather than anything else.'

'Put him through, I'll take a message.' Stark waited for the click. 'Hello, this is Detective Constable Stark. Can I help?'

For several seconds the only other sound was wheezing. 'Yes. You can put Mickey Groombridge on. I need to speak . . .' Anything further was lost in a desperate coughing fit.

Stark waited until the caller could breathe. 'I'm afraid DCI Groombridge is unavailable –'

'Don't give me the run-around, lad. I knew Mickey when he was a green, snot-nosed constable like you and I –'

'*Ronald!*' cut in another voice angrily. 'What've I said about sneaking in here? Now give me that . . .'

'Tell Mickey . . .' More coughing erupted. There were sounds of a brief tussle and the line went dead. Stark dialled the switchboard and asked if the caller's number could be traced, but it hadn't come in via 999 so hadn't been picked up automatically. Stark emailed a quick note of the few facts he had to Groombridge.

He spent the rest of that day and most of the next with the main CID team, checking names off his list of database longshots. Burglary-murders were usually a tragic case of unfortunate timing, the intruder mistaking the house for empty, someone returning home at just the wrong moment, one person or the other panicking or overestimating their chances. Breaking into an occupied house, forcing your victim to pop the safe before killing them . . . That was something else. Stark's list was dwindling nicely.

A good portion of the names were reassuringly incarcerated. Several were dead. Some had emigrated. Of those left, some had already been questioned by their local CID. Stark hadn't unearthed any new names. It was worth taking a second run at it, though. Only Harper's motive added a hint of bitterness to the boredom.

As a trainee investigator and then freshly minted detective constable, Stark had enjoyed unusual access. Groombridge had taken him under his wing. Fran had mentored his training as if his swift progress reflected on her, which it did, in her mind. Stark had been spoiled. Now he was being benched. To let it irritate him was childish vanity. Time his fellow DCs enjoyed some preferential treatment.

Now they were off with Harper and Fran, enacting warrants to sweep-search the homes and the workplace of the three suspects. Harper's energetic approach would suit Fran, were it not led by Harper. Perhaps she had been guilty of waiting for Groombridge to lead. Harper had no such hesitation. However long he was here, he would use every moment to make himself look potent.

Towards the end of the day Stark had his list down to three names. He was back at his desk making arrangements with three regional forces to sweep up the individuals for re-questioning when the news reached him: he'd been wasting his time.

24

Carlton Savage had been arrested on suspicion of murder. A diamond necklace, matching that habitually worn by Mary Chase, had been found in Savage's coat in his work locker. One pocket had a small hole. The necklace was found in the jacket lining. It was being checked for DNA, but Harper had slapped the cuffs on Savage on the spot.

'Kids these days!' Harper grinned, basking in the glory. 'Should've learned to sew!'

'Obviously never got his cub-scout darning badge,' added Williams.

'The look on his face,' laughed Harper. 'I thought his eyes were going to pop out!'

Fran sat at her desk, trying to appear gracious. Admittedly, it had been satisfying watching Savage shocked, cuffed and bleating the usual denials as giant Sergeant Dearing tucked his head safely into the back of the uniform car; but Christ, Harper was pleased with himself. Cox had popped down to congratulate him personally. A press conference to announce an arrest was being set up. Groombridge, presumably, was busy. That was the only explanation for letting Harper hog the limelight. Now he had his feet under Groombridge's desk he would do everything in his power to keep them there. And, damn his luck, he was off to a flying start.

Fran watched him, on a high as he was now, ebullient and charming. Sadly, the rest of the time he was petty, jealous and mean. A classic dictator, thought Fran, reminding herself to be careful what she wished for. If Harper's appointment became permanent, she would have to move stations again. It was a shame. This had been a good team, for a while. Then the bankers had pissed the economy up the wall and here they were, stuck with the likes of DI Harper, the true price of austerity.

Groombridge entered the station via the tradesmen's entrance. The press were milling out front, waiting for the DI Harper show.

He went straight up to Cox's office to watch on TV. Harper came out and waved down the sea of raised hands so he could read the short statement. An arrest had been made. No name would be released at this time. Enquiries were continuing.

He took questions but gave sterile non-answers as he had been trained. He seemed to grow in confidence with every turn in front of the cameras. A collar like this could make his career. Barely three days in charge of the MIT and Harper was shaping up to make the position his permanently, while Groombridge rattled around, office-less, doing donkey work for Cox, his photo of Alice in a cardboard box in the storeroom. All his hard work, his team, his plans, still hung on the thinnest thread and Owen Harper, of all people, held the scissors.

As he was watching, the news anchor went live to his reporter on the steps of the station. The reporter, wrapped tightly in her flattering scarlet coat with glittering remembrance poppy brooch on her lapel, summed up Harper's statement succinctly: 'And while the police are not willing to identify the man in custody, sources are reporting that his name is Carlton Savage, an employee of the two victims. These images were taken earlier today outside the business premises of Chase Security . . .'

Groombridge and Cox sat up straight at the photo on the screen. Carlton Savage being led out in handcuffs, between two uniforms, under the satisfied supervision of Detective Inspector Harper.

The anchor and reporter batted the next-to-nothing they knew about Savage back and forth to each other for the requisite allotted seconds of air time and then the anchor moved on.

Cox hit mute.

Groombridge let out a sigh.

Cox looked at him, less sanguine. 'Look into it.'

'Yes, sir.'

'Stark!'

Stark turned to find Groombridge bearing down on him across the station's small car park. 'Guv?'

'Where are you going?'

'Crystal Palace, Guv. Following up one of the longshots.'

Groombridge frowned. 'When we have a suspect in custody?'

'Detective Inspector Harper wants to make sure we're shiny, Guv.'

'By wasting valuable time covering old ground?' Groombridge rolled his eyes. 'Okay, well, do as he says and keep your nose clean. I've something I want you to do for me.'

Stark's heart sank as Groombridge explained. His unhappiness must have been obvious. 'I'm sorry to ask you to do this,' added Groombridge. 'I'm far from happy about it myself. But two press scoops in as many days can't be ignored.'

'Guv.'

Groombridge looked at him appraisingly. 'There are many people in this building I trust, Joseph, but few as much as you in this instance. This requires delicacy. Far better no one knows you're digging. Just keep your ear to the ground and your eyes open. Find out who knew what when.'

'But Harp . . . DI Harper . . . has me out of the loop. I hardly know what *is* known, let alone who knew it when.'

Groombridge bit his lip, openly vexed. 'I understand. I'm sorry, Joe. But DI Harper is in charge. Swallow your pride and get on with it. I'm not expecting miracles, but whatever snippets you can glean. What's the mood?'

'DI Harper wasn't happy when he saw the TV, Guv.'

'No. He was generous with his displeasure when he saw the paper yesterday.'

'Could just be some freelance pap getting lucky, Guv.'

Groombridge nodded. 'Once is luck, twice is coincidence. A third would be bad news.'

It already was in Stark's book. 'Did you get my email about that call, Guv? Ronald somebody . . . '

Groombridge raised his chin, squinting into his own memory. 'Oh yes. Buried among all the rest. I only caught up last night.' His lower lip jutted out as he thought. 'Can't say I know many Ronalds. If it's important they'll call back, I suppose.'

Stark's interview with the name at the top of his list produced no new information. The local uniform and CID had nothing more to add. Greenwich was seven miles from Crystal Palace – in London terms another town; they had nothing linking their recidivist to the area or the victims and the man himself was saying nothing.

Stark drove back to Royal Hill in the pool car. The radio was on but he didn't hear it. His mind was rolling around the unsettling idea of a leak. If they had one, distilling the crime to MMO got you almost nowhere. Means was a mobile phone. Motive had to be money; they weren't in any kind of investigative cul-de-sac where frustration at seeing someone getting away with a crime might tempt coppers to instigate trial by tabloid. No one joined the police for the pay, but the recent overtime restrictions hurt people's bank accounts. And opportunity? Again, half the building would've known about the interviews, the raids and the arrest, and they'd have told the other half soon enough. If they had a leak, *if*, then Stark would never find it alone.

When he got back he went to find Ptolemy.

'Are you lost?'

Stark turned to find PC Pensol looking up at him from where she was working. 'I was looking for Sergeant Ptolemy.'

'He's off today.'

'Constable Peters?'

'Out on patrol. Can I help?'

'Thank you, no. I'll catch up with them tomorrow.' He turned to leave.

'Is it true that you took on a gun-wielding killer with just your walking stick?'

Stark looked at her. 'Is that what you've heard?'

She smiled. 'That, and more.'

Stark sighed inside. A reputation was a tiresome thing.

For the first time he focused on her properly, seeing the person and not just the latest rookie, and suddenly the scales fell from his eyes – Peters' knowing looks, the peer-group giggling. Rumour of his split with Kelly must've reached the ground floor. Constable Pensol, he didn't even know her first name, had a crush on him.

He suddenly felt a hundred years old. What was she, nineteen? Cute as a button, fresh as a flower, sweet as honey, innocent as a lamb gambolling towards a land-mine. 'You shouldn't listen to tall tales.' He tried to keep his voice on the kind side of cold but she still blinked in surprise.

'Yes, of course. I'm sorry, I didn't mean . . .' She looked down, blushing. 'I'll leave a note for Sergeant Ptolemy that you were looking for him.'

Stark nodded silent thanks and left.

Out in the frigid night air he paused and took a deep breath. A few years ago he would have seen this situation as an open goal. Now look at him. He closed his eyes and saw the flash of pained embarrassment on the poor girl's face, and felt ashamed. He told himself it was for her own good, but it was a long, cold walk home that night.

25

Peeping in through the door vision panel, Groombridge waited outside the observation room until Harper and Fran had gone in to begin the interview proper. Savage had declined the opportunity to spontaneously confess and been left to stew overnight. His fingerprints and DNA were finally in the system.

Groombridge slipped in quietly, holding a finger to his lips at Williams and Dixon, unsurprised to see Stark absent. What damn fool errand had Harper cooked up to keep Stark sidelined today? More of the same, most likely. Groombridge set his teeth in frustration. Wanton waste, to score a petty point. He didn't know how bad things had got between Stark and Harper before the latter's departure, not for certain. It was best left that way. If he knew *for certain* that it was Stark who put Harper's arm in that sling he might have been compelled to do something about it. It was a year and a half ago. Best forgotten. Wishful thinking again.

He put that from his mind for now and watched through the one-way glass. Harper let Fran do the pre-liminaries and begin the interview; keeping his powder dry. Savage looked exactly like a man who'd barely slept a wink all night in a police cell facing a murder charge.

Fran placed an evidence bag on the table. 'So,' she said, 'you've never seen this necklace before. At least that's what you said yesterday after it was found in your jacket. Odd, because by all accounts Mary Chase never took it off. So I would've thought you got a pretty good look at it every time you screwed her behind her husband's back.' Savage was straight on the back foot and Fran took full advantage. 'What, no witty quip? No – "You don't look at the mantelpiece when you're stoking the fire"?'

Savage glanced at his court-appointed legal rep, who leant in. 'What my client meant is that he didn't *recognize* the necklace, and doesn't know how it got in his locker.'

'His *locked* locker.'

'A simple three-dial combination. Child's play to a building full of security staff. It must have been placed there by the actual killer or . . .'

'Or what? By us?'

'I never said,' answered the lawyer craftily. 'But your other suspects both work there.'

'Your client's DNA was on the necklace,' said Fran.

Sweat or saliva. Fran had pulled strings to get the samples compared overnight. Groombridge smiled to himself.

'We were shagging,' said Savage, trying to sound confident but not pulling it off.

'So was Mary Chase's blood,' added Fran. 'Which puts you in rather an awkward position.'

'I was there earlier in the day, like I told you . . . but that was the last time I saw her, I swear!'

'Swear all you like, sunshine,' scoffed Harper harshly. 'It won't make anyone believe you. That necklace was ripped from Mary's neck and taken along with all the other loose valuables and contents of the safe, by her killer; by you.'

Savage shook his head. 'No.'

'What was in the safe?' asked Fran.

'How should I know? Didn't even know they had one.'

A lie. He was getting rattled, answering without thinking. Fran was playing this well.

'You'd been in that room many times,' she continued. 'You never had a quiet snoop around while Mary was freshening up?'

There, thought Groombridge. Savage's tell. When trying to decide what to say his eyes flitted between Harper and Fran, attempting to guess what they knew or didn't.

'Your fingerprints were found on the safe door,' explained Fran helpfully.

Savage glanced anxiously at his lawyer. 'Yeah, all right, I had a look. Just curious. Like I said, I was just giving her one for the road. So I had a little look around. I didn't care if she caught me.'

'So you're changing your story?' asked Fran, for the record. Nothing played back quite as badly to a jury as a changed story. 'You were looking for something to steal.'

'No. People in my world don't have safes in their bedroom cupboards. I just wanted to see what was in it. But it was locked.'

'So you came back later and forced her to open it,' growled Harper. 'And then shot her in the back like a coward and helped yourself.'

'No!'

'What happened – did she put up more of a fight than Tracy Mills? Or do you just get a kick out of hurting women?'

Savage looked alarmed. 'No! I . . .'

'But while you were *fleeing the scene*, her husband finally caught you in his house,' continued Harper. 'How ironic. And you shot *him* dead too.'

'*No!*'

'Did she tell you she was carrying your child?' asked Fran.

'*What?*' Savage looked genuinely sideswiped. 'You're lying.'

'DNA confirms it. A girl, apparently. Tell me, did Mary beg for the baby's life as well as hers?'

'Or was getting rid of it a perk of filling your pockets?' added Harper disgustedly. 'But by the time you'd shifted everything else, the necklace had already slipped into the lining of your coat. Bet you wish you'd asked your mum to sew up that hole.'

'No.' Savage looked angry now.

'No? What then, you kept it back on purpose? Thought it would go nicely with your earrings and tiara?'

'First you lie about seeing the necklace before,' explained Fran calmly. 'Then about the safe . . . You're a liar, Carlton.'

Groombridge smiled. It was fascinating to watch Fran playing the calm one for a change. She was surprisingly good at it.

'I was working that night,' insisted Savage, finally remembering his alibi. 'You can check, I was doing my rounds in the works van.'

'We have checked,' replied Fran. 'But every other piece of evidence says you were miles away, busy murdering two people in cold blood. Which makes us wonder if someone else was driving your van . . .'

Suddenly Savage looked scared.

The lawyer held up her hand. 'A minute alone with my client, Detective Inspector?'

Harper looked far from happy, but shut off the recording equipment.

Groombridge cursed silently. Not wishing to scram like a schoolboy, he had to stay and be discovered looking over their shoulders again. Harper definitely looked annoyed, Fran hardly surprised.

Back in the interview room the lawyer was talking and Savage was shaking his head. But his body language said he was losing the argument. After a while the lawyer beckoned to the glass and Harper and Fran went back in.

Groombridge listened intently. A confession would wrap things up nicely, but such gems usually came with some plea offer, and what did Savage have that might mitigate his guilt?

The lawyer did the talking. 'My client wishes to confess . . .'

Harper sat forward eagerly.

'But not to your double murder.'

'So what does he want to confess to?' Harper scowled. 'Telling Mummy he brushed his teeth when he hasn't?'

'To the burglary of ninety-six Cavendish Road, Woolwich,' replied the lawyer. 'He can and will furnish a full description of the house itself, everything stolen, plus the name of his cousin who took over the Chase Security van route while my client was miles from your murder scene busy *not* killing two people.'

In the dim light of the observation room, Groombridge let out a long sigh.

26

Wendell Savage looked terrified. A few years older than his cousin Carlton, severe learning difficulties meant Wendell had to be accompanied by his mother, with whom he still lived. It also meant he had struggled to find employment. When his cousin had offered him regular money to drive his routes the boy and his mother had jumped at the chance. Carlton had told them he was moonlighting at a nightclub. Wendell would meet Carlton at a prearranged spot and they would swap vehicles. Carlton would leave a map of the route and a time to meet back. This had been going on over two years.

You could tell from the mother's eyes that she'd known Carlton was lying.

In the meantime, here was Wendell; the unwitting accomplice. So scared he looked fit to piss himself. CPS would probably not come after him for the burglaries. But he was still guilty of driving without a licence or insurance and and, as his guardian, his mother was guilty of benefit fraud and failing to declare earnings to the revenue. Hardly Fran's finest arrest. No wonder Harper had sent her to pick him up.

'Can I go now?' asked Wendell. His eyes were brimming with tears. 'I want to go now. Please!'

His mother gripped his hand reassuringly, wiping tears from her own eyes.

'Just one more time,' sighed Fran. 'For the record. On

Saturday the thirteenth of November, you are certain that you met your cousin, Carlton, at the corner of Jackson Road. And what time was this?'

Wendell pushed his pocket diary closer to her, his eyes pleading. 'Carlton. Jackson Road. Nine thirty p.m. Don't be late.' He tapped the diary. It was all in there, his desperate life: appointments with his doctor, social services, the day-care centre where he passed most of his time while his mother was out scraping a living cutting hair, charity day trips to rain-lashed seaside towns, and every few weeks or so . . . Carlton, an address, a time, and *don't be late!*

'We will have to keep this. You understand that?'

The boy's hand gripped the diary. His lower lip quivered.

'He's very proud of the diary,' said his mother. 'He's . . . he's worked so hard on it.' She stifled a sob, and Wendell turned round and enveloped her in a reassuring hug.

Fran closed her eyes. Some days this job made you feel so proud.

Carlton swore the burglary of Cavendish Road was a one-off, a desperate rush of blood to the head that left him full of remorse. He was glad to have it out in the open and would cooperate fully. He had panicked afterwards and dumped the loot in a public bin. He was sorry this meant the homeowners would never see their valuables again.

All the other times he'd swapped with Wendell, he said, he'd been sleeping or out clubbing or with some girl, a different one each time, or latterly with Mary Chase who couldn't corroborate. This was what became of perps' right to spend time with their lawyer before you questioned them. He made quite a good show of it; handy dress rehearsal before his command performance for the magistrate.

Fran wasn't buying, but for now that didn't matter. She rubbed her eyes. It had been a long morning. Now she would spend the rest of her day in CID checking the dates from Wendell's diary with local burglaries. She had no doubt each would match one. If only it were just one. Between the boroughs of Greenwich and Lewisham alone there might be a dozen burglaries to choose from each time. And the missing hours on each night in question could put Carlton anywhere in Greater London or beyond.

When he let go of his mother, Wendell was crying too. But there was a fierce look in his eye. Protective.

Fran promised herself that if she ever found herself alone with Carlton Savage she was going to slap his face so hard his ears would ring for a month.

'Where the hell have you been?' barked Harper before Stark had even got his coat off.

'Rechecking the longshots.' Wasting time on the road to talk with the wrong people. Stark nearly added 'like you told me', but it was evident from Harper's expression that this wasn't the time.

Harper's face darkened all the same. 'I want a summary on my desk before you leave the building.' Coat in hand, he strode out of the office like a fury, leaving Stark to wonder what had happened. When he'd left that morning Harper had been all but rubbing his hands together with glee at the prospect of hauling Savage over the coals. The office was empty now, so he went to the canteen to see if anyone was about and spotted Ptolemy and Peters finishing their dinner. Pensol was with them but, seeing him enter, said something and carried her plate and cutlery to the dirty dishes trolley and left with a backward glance.

'You've scared my rookie away,' said Ptolemy, as Stark sat.

Peters was looking at him accusingly. 'What have you said to her?'

'What makes you think I've said something?'

She gave him a look. 'You can't be that dense.'

Stark sat down. 'If it's what I think you're suggesting, it's best nipped in the bud.'

Peters looked crestfallen. She had clearly been indulging in a little matchmaking. 'What's wrong with you?' she demanded. 'She's young, hot and smitten. You could do a *lot* worse.'

'She could do better,' replied Stark in a tone that he hoped might close the topic.

Ptolemy winced. 'You're crushing hopes, Joe. She's been in a mope all day.' He glanced at Peters. 'And poor Pensol too.'

Peters elbowed him.

Stark shrugged. 'I'm sure you'll both get over it.'

Peters tutted in disappointment. 'She was my *favourite*. You should know there's far less sweet girls downstairs talking about you.'

Stark wished with all his heart that she was joking. 'I'm sorry, but I don't have head space for Pensol or any other complication.'

'*Joe*,' Ptolemy chided. 'What kind of attitude is that?'

'A temporary one, let's hope.' Life, after all, was temporary.

Peters grinned. 'So there's still hope for Pensol.'

'Leave the girl alone.' Stark smiled wearily. 'She shouldn't be waiting around for anyone at her time of life.'

'"At *her* time of life",' laughed Ptolemy, who had ten years or more on Stark. 'Get you, oh wise and ancient one.'

Stark chuckled, rubbing his eyes. He was tired, and he had a long report to write.

'You okay, Joe?' Peters' voice held a hint of concern. Ptolemy was sizing him up too.

Stark noted that he may not have close friends, but he did have good ones. 'I'm fine.'

'Harper giving you a hard time?'

A leading question if ever there was one. If it wasn't bad enough having his romantic prospects giggled over, did half the station know about his past confrontations with Harper? 'Did I miss something today?'

'Ah . . .' Ptolemy nodded sagely. 'Now therein lies a tale . . .' He filled Stark in on Savage's reduced charges.

'I heard Harper was steaming after.' Peters smirked. 'Back on TV explaining that he's got the wrong man.'

'One rabbit of negative contentment,' agreed Ptolemy.

Stark chuckled. 'That explains that then.'

'Was there something else you wanted to talk to us about?' asked Ptolemy. 'Pensol said you were looking for us last night.'

Stark sighed. This would not be an easy conversation. He looked about to make sure they weren't overheard, and explained his secret mission from Groombridge.

Perhaps it was the clandestine conversation, but Stark walked home on edge. Clouds covered the moon, and every dark corner or blind spot seemed menacing. The night closed in around him, oppressive, imagined eyes and footfalls herding him towards his door like a foe to an ambush. His heart beat a paranoid flutter as he forced the key into the lock and hastily closed the door behind him, as if he could shut out the fear.

Training cautioned him to leave the light off again. Instinct told him to take the stairs. Weariness made him give in to both and what little sense remained mocked all three, even as he paused in the darkness to scan out the landing window.

He was about to turn away when something glinted in the darkness of the alley across the street.

A puff of breath caught in the lamplight.

Charging downstairs, Stark ripped open the door and ran across the street . . .

But the alley was empty. The breath, a boiler flue, nothing more.

More damn tricks! He kicked the wall in frustration, and shame.

A small engine spluttered into life, away through the buildings, revving its scornful laughter at his madness.

27

Fran walked out of the court into the sharp morning air, confused. It wasn't the first time one of her collars had failed to surrender, but it was unexpected. Pleading guilty to a first offence, Savage was likely to walk – twelve to eighteen months suspended. He should be grinning and slapping arms with his lawyer and family right now. Instead he'd have 'failure to surrender' added to his charge sheet, a breach of trust that meant he'd spend time behind bars for certain.

She'd expected to leave with a bitter taste in her mouth. Now she had a nasty feeling in her gut.

'Sarge?' Dixon hovered, uncertain as ever of her mood.

'Get a car around to his. Ask his mum where he is. Get the photo out to all cars. I want to talk to him.'

'Detective Sergeant?'

Fran turned to find a reporter thrusting a microphone at her. A cameraman hovered, red light on, spotlight glaring in the overcast morning light. 'Detective Sergeant,' barked the reporter again. 'We understand that Carlton Savage has been charged with burglary but not with the murders of Mary and Thomas Chase. Does this mean the killer is still at large?'

Fran took a deep breath. 'I have no formal statement to make at this time. Enquiries are continuing.'

'What do you say to accusations that Greenwich Police are fumbling about in the dark?'

'Whose accusations?' asked Fran levelly. It took effort not to ask *pointedly*.

The reporter ignored her anyway. 'What about the other suspects interviewed last week?'

So it was to be that kind of interview, all about the reporter and not the report. It was the same woman as before. A black coat today but accessorized in red, accentuating the poppy brooch, white teeth smiling through blood-red lipstick, quick, intelligent eyes. 'Those individuals are helping with our enquiries.'

'So you have no suspect. You're at a loss. Where does the investigation go now?'

'Please don't put words in my mouth,' said Fran, knowing it was too late and that her protestations would never make it to air. 'We're not at a loss. The investigation is meticulous, vigorous and broad, and will not be rushed.' Classic Groombridge, dragged from memory she didn't know she had.

The reporter actually rolled her eyes. 'In other words, you're getting nowhere slowly. Are you even aware that one of your non-suspects, Mark White, appears to have little or no past to speak of? My investigations have uncovered evidence suggesting Mark White died as an infant.'

Fran struggled to keep the shock from her face. If this was true someone had dropped a massive clanger. That she had foretold just such a risk was little comfort now. 'We don't comment on investigative detail. Now if you will excuse me.' She stalked away with Dixon in tow. 'Who did the background check on White?' she hissed.

'Not sure, Sarge,' he replied unhappily.

He was lying. It wasn't him, but he knew who it was.

*

146

'What the fuck was that?' barked Harper, jabbing a thick finger at the mute TV as Fran walked in. 'In my office, Detective Sergeant, now.'

Fran followed him in and shut the door.

Stark looked at Dixon. DC Hammed had done the background on White before leaving to look after his mum. If what the reporter said was true, they were going to have to pick over everything from the beginning. Stark already had White's file open and was trying to see what the reporter had seen.

Groombridge strode in and looked about. 'Fran?'

Stark tilted his head towards Harper's door. It still felt abhorrent to call it that, even worse to see Groombridge knock before entering. The door closed again. The three DCs exchanged a look that confirmed they were heartily glad to remain outside.

Doing his best to ignore the sound of raised voices, Stark pored over the information, but his brain just wasn't firing on all cylinders. White's personnel file said he'd worked as a nightclub doorman for two years before joining Chase Security five years ago. His reference from the nightclub manager described him as reliable and hard-working but was typically short on detail. Before that, according to his CV, he'd worked as a landscape gardener for three years. Hammed's notes said the firm had laid White off in lean times, before going bust anyway. There was no personnel file, but Inland Revenue confirmed that White had paid taxes during that time, and confirmed his employer.

Before that his CV dried up. Chase Security obviously hadn't cared enough to delve. That was it for his personnel file, and there was nothing else from Inland Revenue. No list of qualifications on his CV. No school named.

He was forty-three. That left a long gap between school age and first known employment. Ten years of that, he said, were his military service. Why had he not just listed it on his CV? Stark guessed the answer: because people still thought of the French Foreign Legion as the last refuge for those no one wanted – or for those who *were* wanted, for crimes in their own countries. But the days when no questions were asked were long gone. Any fool who rocked up at the Legion with a warrant outstanding would find themselves tossed in the brig and shipped home for trial.

Hammed had satisfied himself that White had no criminal history and, it seemed, left it at that.

Stark called the local register office in hope but they couldn't find a Mark White fitting the profile. Expanding further would take an age. If the reporter was right, they must have tracked down the birth or death certificate, but whether they'd be willing to share was another thing.

The certificates were key.

The classic method for setting up a false identity . . . Move into a new property or bedsit/squat. Visit your local family records centre and look up the name of a person who was born around the same time that you were. Order a copy of their birth certificate. The key point here – no proof of identity was required and you could pay cash over the counter. No 'audit trail', and you could collect the certificate by hand the following day. Now you had a name to clone, contact a suitable utilities provider, gas, electricity or phone, and inform them you'd just moved into your home and wished to open an account. Twiddle fingers for a while and wait until the first utility bill arrived. You now had the two forms of ID required – a birth certificate and a proof of address. Get a passport application form and ask a fellow conspirator to sign your photos declaring that they were a doctor or solicitor. At most, the only check made against them was a phone call. Since 2008, anyone over the age of eighteen applying for their first passport had to attend an interview, but White probably got his earlier. A couple of weeks later your passport would arrive in the post; apply for a National Insurance number, then move out of the property and vanish along with your new fake identity. There were people who'd provide the whole service for you.

A thought occurred to Stark. He picked up his mobile phone and slipped out of the office.

'Make it quick, Sergeant,' answered Pierson curtly, 'and I'll see what I can do.' Conversations with the redoubtable Major began with opening salvos rather than warm greetings. She only ever called him if she wanted something and naturally assumed the reverse. Stark explained what he needed in the fewest words possible, went back to his desk and sent her the email.

When the door finally opened, Groombridge stalked out wordlessly, sparing barely a nod for the three DCs. Fran came out and sat with them as Harper took centre stage. 'Right,' he said gruffly. 'Mistakes have been made. But they didn't happen on my watch so I'm giving you a pass. No more fuck-ups. Fran, find White and bring him in. Whatever he's hiding about his past I'll get to the bottom of it. Williams, go through everything we have on him with a fine-tooth comb. Dixon, recheck everything on Clive Tilly *and* Carlton Savage. I don't care if they didn't do it, I want everything from their first kiss to their inside leg measurement. So where are we on finding Savage?'

'His mum says he didn't come home last night,' said Dixon. 'Not unusual, apparently.'

'He doesn't usually have court in the morning,' said Harper. 'So what's he running from?'

'His car isn't there. I've put out the licence plate and description.'

Harper nodded, then looked round. 'Stark, stay on the Longshits. That should keep you from fucking anything else up.'

Stark blinked. Of course, Harper had pinned the slip on him.

Williams raised a hand. 'Not now,' Harper cut him off. 'Get to it. I've got to go shovel us out of the shit.'

Stark collated the start he'd made on White and handed it wordlessly to Williams.

'It's not fair, Joe,' Williams said. 'Hammed's a big boy, his shoulders are broad enough.'

'He's got enough on his plate. Harper can't hate me any more. Make sure Fran finds the birth certificate and passport, et cetera. I've emailed a friend of sorts in the army, to see if she can get White's military records. The French won't give them up easily.'

'The infamous Captain Pierson?'

'She's a major now.'

Williams grinned. 'Rumour has it she's a hottie.'

'She certainly burns.'

A double act of burglars had been arrested in Richmond and he'd invited himself to observe the interview, glad to get out of the building. But as he walked out into the car park he heard a raised voice.

'– two-way street. This wasn't part of the deal!' Harper, pacing and gesticulating, spotted Stark and froze, eyes narrowing in anger.

Stark kept his own eyes forward and focused on finding the pool car. As he drove away, there was a sick feeling in the pit of his stomach.

28

Fran looked at her watch. Harper had left White to stew for a full hour so far. Fair enough, *if* he'd told her, instead of leaving her twiddling her bloody thumbs! Through the one-way glass White checked his watch for the thousandth time too, perhaps realizing he'd graduated from unlikely to prime suspect, at least as far as Harper was concerned. Fran wasn't so sure. He looked nervous enough, more so than the last time, but innocent people often looked the most nervous. An evident loner with a mysterious past, no alibi, shaved scalp, beard, tattoos, he looked every inch the perp, but . . . there was something wrong with this picture.

The door opened behind her and Harper joined her at the glass. 'Right, let's get to it.'

White looked up nervously as they entered, shifting in his seat and licking his lips repeatedly as they ran through the preambles for the record. Fran offered him water but he declined.

'Please state your name,' she said.

'It hasn't changed,' replied White flatly.

'For the record, please.'

'Mark White.'

Harper leant forward. 'Prove it.'

White frowned. 'You've got my birth certificate, passport and driver's licence. What else d'you want?' Perhaps he hadn't seen the news yet.

'Death certificate?' asked Fran.

'I don't understand.'

'Never mind,' she said, 'I've just been emailed a copy. Says here you died aged three weeks.'

White frowned. 'It's wrong.'

'Perhaps your parents can confirm that?'

White shuffled in his seat. 'Mum died in childbirth.'

Fran kept her face straight. Both certificates were from just outside Manchester. According to the register office there, the mother's death certificate was filed next to the son's. If he'd faked his ID or bought it, the homework had been done.

'Dad?'

'Unknown.' The birth certificate was blank on that side.

'Siblings? Other family?'

'No.'

'There's no record of you in the care system.'

'Mum was a gypsy. When she died I went with them. Got passed around. Some of them might be relatives but none would say. I was dirt to them. Something to do with the mystery father, I guess, or the fact I'd killed my mum. No one would talk about it and I learned not to ask. I grew up in caravans, went to school if we settled anywhere for more than a few weeks. I don't even know where; it wasn't worth learning the names. Stopped bothering when I was thirteen. No one came looking for me. When I was fifteen I left, did any shitty job I could get, cash-in-hand. I never settled anywhere to speak of.' He lifted his other sleeve to show the tornado tattoo.

Fran watched hard, but if he was lying he was well rehearsed.

Harper huffed through his nose, unconvinced.

'Employment records then?' suggested Fran. 'Something to show where you've been.'

'Or *who*,' added Harper.

White shook his head defiantly. 'My name is *Mark White*.'

'Since when?' asked Harper.

White stared at Harper with little love.

'According to the records, a copy of your birth certificate was purchased ten years ago,' Fran stated. 'And your passport shortly after.'

'I'd lost the originals.'

'Or that's when you became Mark White,' Harper put in.

'According to the passport office, that was your original,' added Fran. 'You'd never held a passport before.'

White nodded. 'I had a French one. Service gets you citizenship.'

'How did you get to France without a passport?'

'Fishing boat.'

'Running away from something?'

White shook his head. 'Towards.'

Fran tried a change of tack. 'Tell us about your military service.'

'Ten years, Légion Étrangère.'

'Got anything to prove that?'

White yanked up his sleeve to display his other tattoo. 'You don't get ink unless you can back it up. Not if you want to keep your teeth.'

'I meant paperwork. Discharge papers?'

'Burnt them.'

'*Burnt* them?'

'I've been to some of the worst places in the world. It

isn't holiday snaps and souvenirs. I've all the memories I want.'

'Your French passport then?' asked Fran.

'Lost. Like I said.'

Harper shook his head. 'Sounds fishy to me.'

White shrugged, indicating indifference.

They had already tried to get his records, but the French sidled behind their wall of bureaucracy. Something about a 'declared name' policy. Stark could probably give her chapter and verse, but the short version was they could only release a private soldier's file with that individual's written permission, or via convoluted official channels. Harper had passed the problem upstairs.

'Before the army, then. What jobs did you have?'

'All sorts. Nothing official.'

Harper leant forward again. 'This all sounds like a massive crock of shit. No one has a past *this* invisible. I think you're a liar.'

There . . . Just the briefest flash. More than frustration, more than irritation. White didn't like being called a liar.

Harper saw it too. 'I think Mark White is a *sham*. And I think you killed Thomas and Mary Chase.'

'No,' White stated firmly.

'You called in sick the next morning – guilty conscience?'

'I . . .' White rubbed his temples, frustrated, but added nothing else.

'Were you sick or not?'

'I didn't *do* this.'

'Oh . . . Why didn't you say so before?' asked Harper. 'Oh wait . . . because you're a *liar* and no one believes you. You had a hard-on for Mary, didn't you? I think you watched Carlton Savage show up at her door every weekend and wished it was you. I think you watched through the windows like a pervert.'

White ground his teeth, but didn't answer. Harper was pressing the right buttons.

'Didn't she ever flirt with you like she did with everyone else?' continued the DI, patronizing, scornful. 'Didn't she ever invite *you* inside?'

Nothing.

'Answer the question,' said Fran.

More silence.

'She *did*, didn't she?' scoffed Harper. 'She got bored one day and beckoned you in to scratch her itch.'

White's bitter glance was eloquent, but he was smart enough to keep shtum. The fake ID was little better than speculation as yet, so unless he said something incriminating for the tape there was every chance they'd have to let him walk. They had to keep pushing . . .

'Just the once, was it?' said Harper. 'A passing touch of magic, never repeated. And you're back out in the cold, nose pressed to the glass, watching. Slogging your guts out all week then shovelling shit for them in all weathers every weekend. And all the while he's on the golf course while she's spreading her legs for the likes of *Carlton Savage*. And when you couldn't take the humiliation any more you exacted your revenge.'

'No.'

'Did it give you thrills? Did you get hard?'

'It wasn't *me*!'

'You hated Carlton Savage too, didn't you? Brash and flash; everything you're not. Did you decide to plant that evidence on him when you realized he was in the frame, or was that your plan all along?'

'You're wrong. I didn't do *any* of it.'

'Yes, you did. And I think you've done it before.' Harper stared at White, daring him to deny it. 'I think you became Mark White to cover old tracks, and I'm going to prove it.'

White set his jaw. 'You're wasting your time.'

'You're going to spend the rest of your life behind bars.' Harper smiled nastily.

But White straightened, staring back with unexpected defiance. '*I* think *you're* full of shit. I can see it in your eyes,' he sneered, turning the tables. '*You're* the sham here, *Detective Inspector* Harper. It's you who's hiding who you really are.'

Harper bristled. 'I'm going to take you down,' he said coldly.

White met his glare, unflinching. 'Whoever killed them is out there laughing at you right now.' He grinned darkly. 'It's going to be *your* face on the TV this time, not mine.'

29

Another wasted day, covering old ground, removed from where he should be, from what was important. Much like his next port of call.

Stark dutifully summarized the relevant events of the last week, for Doc Hazel. She made the most notes while he was describing the return of Harper and Stark's consequent frustration at being deliberately kept out of the investigation loop. And his side assignment for Groombridge. Whatever else he might say about her, Hazel was discreet.

In the faint hope of returning to monthly sessions he tried to keep things light.

She opened the batting. 'This spinning class . . . ?'

'My first. Agony. Don't know what I was thinking.'

'About a girl, it seems.'

'I paid the price.'

'Nothing by halves, Joe.'

'It helps.'

'To forget about life for a while?'

'Yes.'

'To forget about Kelly?'

'I suppose.'

'So long as it stays exercise, and not punishment.' She knew him too well. 'You've been busy.'

Statements from Hazel were rarely anything but leading, and best tackled head on. 'You think I'm taking on too much.'

Hazel smiled faintly. 'That's for you to say.'

'You're suggesting I'm overcompensating for the void in my life.'

'Your words.'

'Life doesn't feel empty, it feels ... chaotic,' he conceded.

'It must be hard to plan. Not knowing when a new case might erupt,' she suggested. A lifeline?

'It's easy to go from overstretched to flat out,' said Stark. 'It's not just me, it's the whole station, the whole force.'

'Is your job under threat?'

The best traps presented like lifelines. 'You think I feel insecure?'

She smiled and shook her head. 'No. But I might say, uncertain. You don't appear to doubt your abilities, but you often seem to doubt your suitability.'

Suitability. Stark almost smiled.

'You've always demonstrated a level of indifference about the job,' Hazel continued. 'Has that changed?'

'I'm not sure what else I could do,' he replied honestly.

'Just about anything you put your mind to, I suspect. But that's not what I asked.'

'But it is the answer,' said Stark. 'The job has good days, and for the rest . . .'

'For the rest you man up and crack on,' she smiled, 'to quote the vernacular.'

'Yes.'

'A lot like life, you might say.'

He might. Stark often wondered if one of the reasons he kept coming here was admiration for the attention with which she placed her words; like chess moves, or a string of primary and secondary IEDs.

'I'm confused, though,' she continued, frowning. 'You reject a girl at work, whilst pursuing a girl at your gym?'

Boom. Stark permitted himself a smile. She wasn't in the least confused. And there was no way to gloss his answer. 'The girl at work likes me, or some version of me. It can only end badly. The girl at the gym . . . I'm hoping she's less . . . interested.'

'You're looking for meaningless sex?'

Stark shrugged. 'You think that's wrong?'

Hazel looked thoughtful. 'That's not for me to say. But it's a notable shift from where you were a year ago, I think.' She avoided statements of certainty where possible; professional circumspection. It added a level of amusement to their question tennis. But when she did fire one, it was usually an ace. 'And what of sentiment?' she asked.

'Sentimentality is the indulgence in emotions one hasn't earned,' replied Stark flatly, paraphrasing Oscar Wilde.

Hazel smiled at her mistake. 'Love, then. Another indulgence, to be judged on benefit?'

Wilde also said that life without love was a sunless garden, and Stark couldn't disagree. But too few people pontificated on the dangers, the damage. If the price of love was holding your loved ones a safe distance from you, then Stark could stand some time in the shade. He shrugged. 'I suppose.'

Hazel snapped her pen shut. 'Same time next week, then?'

If Hazel thought he was depressed going in, he was closer coming out. Curry and beer would set things right, he decided, dropping in at his local Indian takeaway on the way home. He had just ordered his usual when his phone rang.

'Sarge?'

'Where are you?' demanded Fran.

'Heading home.'

'Not any more. You're on night duty.'

'No. I'm not. I know this because my sergeant sets the rota and she never lets me forget it.'

'Your sergeant has revised the rota.'

No, she hadn't. But she was too dutiful or proud to admit Harper had. Stark would not put her on the spot. 'Understood. I'll head there now.'

'Stark . . .'

'Sarge?'

Fran sighed. 'Nothing. I've taken you off tomorrow. Get some rest.'

He waited for his food. Harper might cheat him out of some downtime and a cold beer, but not out of dinner. He ate at his desk, updating his report on the Longshots before catching up on the case file. Try as he might, Harper wouldn't cheat him out of that either. Savage was still on the lam; no sightings. No progress on unpicking White's past or true identity. He'd walked. Literally. Impolitely declining the offer of a ride home.

Stark's mobile rang. 'Good evening, Major.'

'For some,' she replied tersely. 'You haven't just spent precious hours of your life on a wild goose chase being stonewalled by one condescending French tit after another. I've never met a more obtuse, bureaucratic, evasive bunch of arseholes in my life and I work for the Ministry of Defence!'

'Ahh . . .'

'Trying to get a straight answer out of them was almost as infuriating as trying to get one out of you,' she continued, on a roll.

'And yet . . . ?'

'And yet I did finally manage to establish two things.

The first, hitherto suspected and now proved, that you are an arse who gets his perverse kicks wasting other people's time. And second, there is not now nor ever has been a French Foreign Legionnaire named Mark White.'

'They checked pseudonyms?'

'Have I done anything, other than agreeing to your fool's errand, to make you think I'm an idiot?'

Stark sighed. Until very recently recruits were still forced to enlist under a 'declared name', one tradition that *had* survived from the days when the Legion was considered a refuge for fugitives and sundry scum. Nowadays they did background checks with Interpol, but Stark had already checked with them.

'You used me to check out a long shot, admit it,' said Pierson.

'Yes.'

There was a pause. 'Are you well?' she asked.

Stark blinked at the question. 'Yes,' he replied cautiously. 'Why?'

'You gave a straight answer to a direct question. And you sound like crap.'

Her roundabout version of concern. Stark smiled.

'Forget it,' she sighed impatiently, 'I don't care enough to ask twice. I've emailed you the confirmation. Don't waste my time again, Sergeant. And get some rest.'

Some time later Stark was watching the White interview when he became aware of someone behind him.

'Don't mind me,' said Groombridge, watching the recording over Stark's shoulder. 'Just catching up too.'

The film finished with White's adamant prediction. He sat back, arms folded tight.

'Not quite what DI Harper hoped for, I would think?' said Groombridge.

'Guv.'

'Still keeping you where you can do little good, is he?'

'It's not my place to second-guess my superiors, Guv.'

Groombridge suppressed a smile. 'As I'm sure I've told you on numerous occasions. Any luck on the problem I set you?'

Stark shook his head. 'Hard to keep one's eyes open and ears to the ground while also keeping one's head down, lip buttoned and nose to the grindstone, Guv.'

Groombridge nodded thoughtfully. 'Enlisted any help?'

Stark couldn't be bothered to lie. 'Sergeant Ptolemy and Constable Peters.'

'Ptolemy? Good choice. Likes a gossip, keeps a secret, knows the job. I don't know Peters.'

'The same, but with a penchant for matchmaking.'

'All right. So what do you think? Have we sprung a leak?'

Stark shrugged. 'I don't like not knowing.'

'That's Fran rubbing off on you.' Groombridge smiled, but when Stark didn't join the joke his eyes sharpened.

He had the most penetrating gaze Stark had ever known. Not unkind but calm, measured and inescapable. A company sergeant major might blush and look away. Stark's walls never felt secure under the assault. Groombridge had always been able to tell when he had something on his mind. 'She's gone quiet, Guv. It's not good.'

Groombridge nodded. 'With me too. Think she's giving up?'

Stark was deeply uncomfortable now. It was bad enough being Groombridge's eyes and ears on the leak. 'Doesn't sound like our Fran.'

'No. Think she's biding her time?'

Now Stark chuckled. 'Neither does that.'

'DI Harper had better tread carefully, I think. Though *that* doesn't sound like *him.*'

'Guv.'

'Don't get caught in the middle. You here all night?'

Stark nodded. Groombridge nodded, and left.

Stark's eyes were drooping by midnight. He needed coffee. He was forcing himself to his feet to visit the canteen when the main phone rang. 'MIT.'

'Is that you, sweetie?' Maggie. The matriarch of the emergency call centre had addressed him this way from their first introduction. Stark's gradual acceptance of it was a testament to his regard for her. Some people in life wore scrupulous honesty as a badge of pride; Maggie just enjoyed reality so much she saw no need to embellish.

'That's a matter of ongoing debate.'

'Poor baby. Better pop your coat on, though. Patrol car just confirmed a floater in the Quaggy.'

30

The waters of the River Quaggy rose near Bromley, where it was called Kydd Brook, and meandered all the way to Lewisham where they debouched into the River Ravensbourne and thence into the Thames via Deptford Creek.

Stark's surname had encouraged him, as a boy, to take an interest in Old English etymology. Quaggy, he guessed, derived from quag, meaning bog or marsh; as in quagmire. As an indication of the places through which it had once flowed it was hard to picture now. London had swallowed up the rivers and creeks that once veined its surrounding countryside. Many were lost forever, dried up and forgotten in all but the idiosyncratic place names they'd deposited along their banks. The rest clung on, squeezed between vertical concrete banks, forced through unnatural turns, culverted beneath streets and buildings. They went largely unnoticed, marked where they passed beneath roads by brick walls or cast-iron railings thick with a hundred years of dull, rust-blistered paint and retrofitted with twentieth-century spikes or razor-wire.

Stark wondered how many such silent markers he'd passed without thought as his ride pulled up next to the uniform cars already blocking off a narrow side loop off Lee Road. It was a bitterly cold, cloudless night, but the assortment of post-booze fast-food establishments on the main road were enough to supply a small gaggle of gawpers. He checked his phone but Fran hadn't called back. He tried again, but had to leave another message. He didn't have Harper's number and wasn't in much of a hurry to ask Control for it.

SOCO were unpacking equipment from their vans. A rookie Stark didn't recognize stood guard on the tape, looking miserable with cold and more. Stark flashed his warrant card and ducked under.

Sergeant Clark stood looking on.

'Evening, Sergeant.'

'I'd say you've been around long enough to call me Tony, Constable Stark.' Clark was part of the bedrock upon which Royal Hill police station was founded. At some time he had assumed responsibility for shepherding rookies through their first few weeks, and as a consequence would accept calls day or night to show the poor newbies their first body. It wasn't cruelty, just necessity.

'What have we got, Tony?'

Clark pointed down into the darkness. A body bobbed face down in the water, its jacket snagged on something, making it loll around in the fast current. 'Reveller stopped to puke over the side. Spotted the body and called it in.'

Stark huffed the barest laugh. 'Two ends of the civic spectrum in one.'

Clark nodded sagely. 'She's sitting in the patrol car when you want to speak with her. Doesn't look like a drowning.'

'No.' Even from a dozen metres away it was obvious the back of the skull was not the shape it should be.

'No blood up here. Old Quaggy's up from the rain, body probably floated from somewhere further up and snagged here.'

Stark glanced around, consulting his mental map of the

illogical, zig-zagging cartography of the borders between the boroughs. 'Shame. If it'd made it under the road there it would've been Lewisham's problem. ID?'

Clark looked around to make sure none of his lads were watching, then pulled out a battered pair of bifocals and put them on. He fumbled with his mobile phone keys until he found what he was looking for. 'One of the lads snapped this when the body flipped over.'

A grainy, low-light zoom shot on a phone from a distance, but good enough. Stark stared at it, unflinching. He'd seen the startled expression of instant death too many times to be shocked, but it always looked surreal on the face of one recently seen full of life.

'Well,' he sighed. 'That makes things more complicated.'

There was no safe way of securing the body. Clark was right; the river was up. What in the summer would've been a muddy trickle overgrown with weeds and brambles was now a dark, churning, unknowable force. No one wanted to explain waving the body away into Lewisham, but if whatever it was snagged upon gave, they'd be sent scampering to the other side of the bridge like some tragic game of Pooh Sticks.

Stark tried Fran again. Still no answer.

Eventually police divers arrived, conducted a rigorous risk assessment, made thorough preparations, and then sent in a bloke on a rope to lash the corpse to a buoyant stretcher. By the time they were ready to winch it out, distant dawn was lightening the sky and everyone was chilled to the bone.

Stark hated the cold. It reminded him of night exercises on Dartmoor and escape and evasion across the Brecon

Beacons. It made you slow and clumsy, sapped your will, seeped into your bones like poison. But he was duty-bound to see the dead man safely into the SOCO van and away. Yawning, he nursed the sweet tea he'd cadged from one of the divers, men who knew the value of a full Thermos. The dive officer circled his finger in the air slowly and the winch-man wound in the steel cable. After several stop-starts the stretcher inched up into view, water running from it. It caught on something and tilted.

Carlton Savage's head lolled over to face his accusers, his ruined visage slack with death, one arm hanging from the bindings like some grotesque parody of Christ being taken from the cross, only with a bullet hole in the forehead for stigmata.

Then it was on the ground lost to view amid the attentions of the SOCO team. Stark had been hoping Marcus Turner would show up and conduct an initial assessment, but his junior was there instead. Even Marcus got the night off occasionally. And cause of death looked like a no-brainer, pardon the pun.

'Haven't I seen you somewhere before?' Groombridge materialized at Stark's shoulder.

'Guv?'

'I was up early when I saw the message.'

'But I didn't call you.'

Groombridge smiled awkwardly. 'Strictly between us, since I've been forced to take my hands off the tiller I've had a little arrangement with Maggie.'

The perfect agent for tip-offs. Stark nodded in admiration. 'Your secret's safe with me, Guv.'

Groombridge looked Stark up and down disapprovingly. 'You should get yourself a thicker coat, lad. Hat, scarf and gloves wouldn't hurt either. Or did the army immunize you to cold?'

'I stopped shivering a couple of hours ago.'

'The latter stage of life-threatening hypothermia, I believe.'

'I have the burning torch of justice to keep me warm, Guv. SOCO are still searching here, and now some areas upstream. The divers are planning a search of the river once the light gets better.'

'Right, well there's sod all we can do here,' said Groombridge brightly. 'There's a cafe just opening round the corner. The burning torch of justice is all very well, but caffeine and calories serve better.'

The traditional cafe was about as far from the cosmopolitan, metro-chic *café* as it was possible to get. Nowhere on the streets of Paris or Milan would you find a home for the greasy spoon, that quintessential great British institution; dispensing mugs of tea and full English to the dawn-trade working man and brunch-time hungover. And to footsore coppers, marking time between night and day in a futile attempt to realign their body clocks with the rest of the world.

'You must be knackered?' suggested Groombridge, as they levered themselves into the fixed plastic seating.

'Nothing hot rations and a brew won't sort, Guv.'

Groombridge sighed. 'Things are about to get busy.' He looked tired too. He may have had a few hours' sleep, but not enough. There was more salt than pepper in his hair these days, and the lines around his eyes had deepened.

Stark nodded. The unsmiling waitress in her pink-and-brown polyester uniform slopped two steaming mugs on the plastic table and returned moments later with plates loaded rim to rim with heart-attack happiness.

Soon Fran would wake and see the missed calls. She would call Harper and the peace would end. But for now two comrades ate in consenting silence, content in the quiet before the storm.

31

'Stark?'

Stark jerked. Three days, three nights, nearly letting him sleep then the blast of lights and white noise like the buzzing of a mosquito. His limbs stiff and aching from the stress positions but the bone-gnawing cold was gone. They thought he was tired but his mind was racing. They thought he was weak but he already had his hands free. The inquisitor coiled behind the lights hissing his lies and venom, whispering honeyed words. 'You're ill,' they said. 'We have a doctor. Just say the word. This is just a test, a simulation . . . Everyone breaks in the end. Why not call it a day?'

'Come closer, snake,' whispered Stark inside his head. 'Come closer and we'll see . . .'

'*Stark.*'

Stark jerked awake, speakers and spotlights morphing into tyre noise and a low, stabbing sun. He squinted at the passing streets. The car was nearly back at the station, miles and years from 'Tactical Questioning' and his disastrous delirium. He took a deep breath and rubbed his eyes. 'Sorry, Guv. Old habits.'

'Your phone was ringing.'

Stark fished it out. 'Missed call from Fran.' He tried to call back. 'Engaged.'

Groombridge stole a glance at him. 'You okay?'

'Nothing a few more hours' kip won't sort,' lied Stark.

Perhaps he'd been twitching or calling out. He hoped not. Kelly would wake him if it got bad. How many times had she lain there wondering what to do, whether the sleep he was getting was worth the dreams he was suffering?

Groombridge took a call on his mobile as he parked the car. Stark stepped out, to offer him privacy. While he waited a budget beamer swung into the car park, and Harper climbed out.

'Stark!' he barked. 'What the fuck? I'm just hearing about this now on my way in?'

'I called DS Millhaven –'

'And left a *message*! This is a murder investigation, not a holiday camp. A senior officer should've been at the scene, not some –'

'Good morning, Owen,' said Groombridge cheerily. 'That was Fran on the phone. Said she'd just spoken with you. Hope you don't mind me jumping in. Thought I'd give Stark a hand with the legwork, let you come at it fresh. Talking of which, let's get inside.'

Harper's face was a picture – an abstract in reds. Forced to swallow any further words, he led the way in silence while Groombridge kept up his cheerful chatter all the way upstairs, but Stark could sense the resurgent resentment radiating from the big man. If Harper's olive branch had ever been genuine, it was wilting fast.

Williams and Dixon weren't in yet. They would have been Fran's next call. 'Get us some coffee, Stark,' suggested Groombridge. The message in his eyes was that Stark should be out of earshot for the next bit. They both understood the impropriety of dressing someone down in front of their subordinates, particularly someone like Harper. It was his job to make sure everyone in his team had his phone number and he knew it. Enough damage had been done outside without adding more.

As he gratefully headed for the stairs, the lift door opened and Fran barrelled out looking flustered. She stopped when she saw Stark, and made, of all things, an apologetic face.

'Coffee, Sarge?' he asked.

'Double espresso.' She nodded and took off to face the music. It was her job to take the call, whatever the hour. She had explaining to do too. Stark had expected his own dressing-down for not trying hard enough. If there was one thing a person could normally rely on, it was to know where they currently stood with Fran. This thing with Harper seemed to have knocked her sideways. Stark felt he should ask how she was, offer help. God knows she butted in quickly enough the other way round. But the mere thought was laughable.

'Well . . . at least we know why he didn't show up to court,' said Harper, as the meeting formed.

'Note from his doctor,' said Williams.

Fran stared at Carlton Savage's face on the board. First the shameless Chases, and now a cuckolding, girlfriend-beating burglar. Really, what was the point in caring? It was a sergeant's job to keep the troops at it, not to let chins drop. At least that's how Stark would put it. But some days motivation was harder to summon.

She made Stark lead off the meeting with an update of the night's events. He looked like shit, but he had every right to. She felt like shit and deserved to. A childish two fingers to Harper in switching her phone to silent, celebrated with too much Chardonnay. She'd left Stark alone to cope with a murder. And to make matters worse, the Guv'nor had mopped up the mess and been nice as pie about it.

She didn't believe in God or karma, but a mixture of Church of England schooling and her father's wild Caribbean bedtime stories and sayings had left her with an understanding that the bill had always to be paid. No good turn went unpunished and warm nights preceded dark days.

Her phone buzzed and she looked down to read a text.

Shame you had to run. Hope all's well. Call me later X.

Fran smiled.

'Something you'd like to share with the class, Fran?' asked Harper.

Dark days, thought Fran, tucking the phone away.

'Dixon,' continued Harper. 'Names and addresses taken at the scene last night – get statements. Fran, call your secret admirer in pathology for their preliminary findings. Then go with family services and see what the weeping mother has to say.'

'You don't want to come?'

Harper shot her a hard glance. 'I'm here to collar killers, not hold hands. I'll get some uniforms to bring Mark White in for another shake.'

Fran nodded. 'We should get Clive Tilly in too.'

'What about me?' asked Stark.

'You can write your report and piss off home,' replied Harper coldly.

'But –'

'Don't whine,' interrupted Harper. 'If the rest of us mere mortals have to get by without overtime, so do you.'

Stark glanced at Fran for support but she silently shook her head. Under normal circumstances a fresh murder trumped a rest day, but every moment Stark and Harper were in the same room was a risk. As crazy as it was to have Stark's skewed brain removed from the investigation, having him under Harper's nose, right now, had a greater potential to get in the way. 'You've done your bit. Get some rest. I want you fresh as a daisy tomorrow morning.'

He opened his mouth to protest, but closed it again. It wasn't often easy to read Stark's feelings, but his silence said it all. Allowing for the unfortunate pun, it stood in stark contrast to Harper's exaggerated man-on-a-mission posturing.

That her team had been reduced to this . . .

She had little choice but to work with it, for now. She couldn't undermine Harper without risking the case and the team. She sighed and called Marcus, knowing he'd chuckle at Harper's 'secret admirer' quip if she told him – which she most definitely wouldn't.

32

Clive Tilly would say nothing until his lawyer arrived, and precious little after. He was a long way from the harassed-but-compliant man Fran had met on day one. They tried the usual tricks to see if he would let slip prior knowledge of Savage's death but his lawyer wasn't about to let that happen. When they finally told him he looked genuinely shocked, but then being the killer gave you time to rehearse. After a private conference he let his lawyer do the talking.

He had been working late in the office, trying to do three people's jobs. The police were welcome to scrutinize the yard CCTV, but otherwise he was all out of ways to tell them he had nothing to do with the murders. He had lost his best friend, the managing and financial directors of the company and two key members of staff. If the police continued to waste his time he would consider a harassment suit.

'*Two* members of staff?'

'Since the sodding press started calling Mark White all sorts he won't leave the house,' said Tilly crossly. 'I need him back at work but you've got him wound up like a spinning top. Surely now Savage is dead you lot can stop chasing your tails. Winding up dead shows he was in this up to his eyeballs. You're probably looking at him for a whole string of burglaries. He obviously had an accomplice, or more than one. They share burglary stories for the night and bingo, Savage has an alibi. The selfish prick probably went back demanding a bigger share and got more than he bargained for; or they just realized he was a liability. There's no honour among thieves. I just hope it's not one of my lot. The last thing Chase Security needs is *another* burglar on the payroll.'

'He may have a point,' said Fran afterwards.

'Which bit?' muttered Harper. 'When he called us thick or when his lawyer told us to fuck off?'

'The accomplice. Two burglaries; the alibi . . .'

Harper didn't look convinced. 'I think Mark White killed them all. Unless he was Savage's accomplice. Either way, he's going down.'

Writing a report and pissing off home were never as closely aligned as the likes of Harper, or Fran for that matter, thought. Luckily they were busy downstairs. Having indulged his pedantry for detail, Stark filed his report and was halfway downstairs when his phone rang. Switchboard. He'd forgotten to cancel the office-number redirect.

'Is this Inspector Groombridge?' asked a woman's voice curtly.

'DCI Groombridge isn't here right now. Can I help?'

'Who are you?'

'Detective Constable Stark. Perhaps I could take a message?'

'This is Karen Wilson, care manager at Dignity Retirement Community, Eltham. One of our residents is adamant that he speak with Inspector Groombridge concerning a murder.'

'He wants to report a murder?'

'I don't think so but he won't discuss it with me. He

keeps babbling on about the television, but he's always deriding some police drama or other. I suppose I should add that he used to be a policeman. He says he knows Inspector Groombridge.'

'What's his name?'

'Ronald Cooper. Not our most cooperative resident and I wouldn't normally give him much credence, but he's got himself rather worked up. We've caught him sneaking into Matron's office twice this week to phone some hotline number he says he got from the TV. But he also had your switchboard number, ripped out of Matron's phone book. Since then he's tried stealing mobile phones from the other residents and we just found him outside trying to flag down a taxi.'

Stark thanked her, hung up and swore, then called by the switchboard to cancel the call redirect and went to see if Groombridge was still in the building.

Since vacating his own office, Groombridge had taken temporary possession of one on the top floor. The door stood open but Stark swallowed his surprise and knocked. It was a storeroom; windowless and uncarpeted, shelving up the walls lined with stationery and boxes of God knows what, dusty desk fans, small electric heaters, redundant desk phones and defunct printers. More boxes had been stacked aside to make space for a tatty old desk.

Groombridge looked up from his paperwork and smiled wryly. 'If my old mum could see how I've come up in the world, eh?'

Stark held out the note wordlessly. Groombridge's mother and father were alive, well and enjoying retired life in the country.

Groombridge read, frowning. '*Ron Cooper?* You sure?'

'Sunday's heavy breather, Guv?'

'And the rest. Christ, I can't believe I forgot I know a Ronald! I thought he was long dead. Right . . . Well, you've got your coat, let's go see an old friend.'

Harper deliberately left White to second. Uniform had all but dragged him from his house, reportedly. The big security guy sat now, arms folded, tired, nervous perhaps, but still defiant.

'Do you now or have you ever owned a gun?' asked Fran, reading through the same questions they'd asked Tilly, the same questions they always asked. The bullet had passed through and was not present in the skull, but first impressions suggested thirty-eight millimetre, the same old-fashioned calibre used to kill the Chases.

'No.'

'Where were you yesterday?' With his usual morbid delight, Marcus had informed her that, allowing for the temperature of the flowing water, the rectal temperature of the body suggested it had been in the river approximately nine hours; if it went in straight away. Unfortunately at this stage there was nothing to establish how long it may have been out of the water beforehand. That uncertainty gave them a time of death window between four thirty a.m. and nine p.m. Dumping bodies in water was a smart move, if you didn't mind them bobbing up. Williams and Dixon were busy trying to establish the last time anyone had seen Savage alive. SOCO were still working with uniform searching likely areas upstream where the body may have gone in.

'Home.'

'Did you leave the house?'

'How can I?' complained White. 'Since you set the paparazzi on me? This is only going to make it worse. Why can't you leave me alone?'

'Because you're a killer,' said Harper, leaning forward and putting his big fists on the table.

'I didn't kill them. How many more times do you want me to say it? It was Savage, it must've been!'

'Why?'

'Because he was a thief, a housebreaker! It was on the news. And he's done a bunk. Why aren't you looking for *him*?'

'And what do you think he'd tell us?' asked Fran.

White looked confused. 'How would I know? Tilly sacked him, that's all I know. He'll be sacking me any day too. I can't go to work because you set the dogs on me. How am I supposed to live like this?'

'I'm sorry for the press intrusion, but that's beyond our control –'

'Bullshit,' interrupted White. 'It's what you do. When you think someone is guilty but can't prove it. You knobble them. Trial by media. Sentencing by mob!'

'Quit your whining, Mark,' said Harper. 'If that's your real name. We've got Carlton Savage and he's talking all right. About you.'

White leant back. 'I'll bet he is, lying bastard. What's he saying?'

Harper leant forward. 'That you killed Tom and Mary Chase and he can prove it.'

Fran didn't approve of this tactic. Flat-out lies too often came back to bite you.

White was shaking his head. 'He's a liar. Bring him in

here and let him say it to my face.' If he knew Savage was dead, he was well rehearsed too.

Harper sat back and began a slow hand clap. 'Bravo. Take a bow. Stop pretending you don't know he's dead.'

'Who?' White frowned. 'Savage?'

'Oh, you remember now, do you?' Harper slid three photos of death on to the desk. Thomas and Mary Chase, and Carlton Savage. 'He's talking all right; his body is telling us he was shot with the same calibre bullet as the Chases, less than a mile from their home. His body is telling me that he didn't kill them but he knew who did. His body is telling me that he knew you were the killer and he could prove it.'

'No.' White couldn't take his eyes from the photos; particularly Mary, face down among the scattered remains of the robbery. His eyes widened, as if in realization – of what he'd done.

Harper nodded, smiling darkly. 'I'm not going to let you get away with it again. I'm going to connect the dots and when I do, I'm going to come knocking. You're going to spend the rest of your life in prison for murder.'

'I'm not a murderer!' insisted White.

Harper terminated the interview and turned off the tape. Fran was half out of the door when she saw Harper lean in and whisper something.

White recoiled, eyes wide with anger, or horror. And then exploded. *'I'm not a murderer!'* he bellowed, bursting out of his chair, eyes wild. He tried to wrench the table aside but it was bolted down. Instead he picked up his chair and threw it against the mirrored glass. It bounced off the laminated polycarbonate facing without a mark. Custody officers were already in the room. Out-numbered, White backed into the corner. '*I'm not a murderer!*' he screamed at them, voice like a wounded animal, eyes wild, his big frame quivering with rage. '*I'M NOT A MURDERER!*'

It took several minutes and the presence of Mick, the custody sergeant, and three additional men, to talk White down. He only became compliant after Harper left the suite.

'What did you say?' Fran asked Harper.

He shrugged, half smiling. 'That I was going to nail him to the wall. Didn't expect him to pop his top.'

White was offered the hospitality of one of the cells until he calmed down and apologized for trying to break Mick's window. He looked more shocked than relieved to learn he would be released without charge, for now. But as Fran drove him out of the gate through a yelling bank of flash photography, his expression was one of ashen-faced horror.

33

The first thing you noticed was the colour scheme – pastel purgatory. Close second was the smell: fire-retardant furniture, disinfectant and the real or imagined hint of stale urine. And finally, the dead-eyed disinterest on the face of the woman in her fifties who glanced up from behind the reception desk. 'Can I help you?' she asked with robot warmth.

Groombridge flashed his warrant card. 'DCI Groombridge and DC Stark, here to see Ronald Cooper.'

'That won't be possible, I'm afraid. Visiting hours are between –'

'If this were a social visit I wouldn't have identified myself as a policeman,' interrupted Groombridge with surprising sharpness. 'Please inform your manager that I received her urgent message and that I am here to interview my old friend Sergeant Ron Cooper, retired officer of the Metropolitan Police Force, and that I don't give a rat's arse about visiting hours.'

The robot blinked, then smiled thinly. 'Of course. Please take a s—'

'I will not take a seat, because you, personally, will take me to Ron Cooper now. I'm a very important man with very little time, but I do have many underlings ready to relay my complaints regarding obstruction to the Deputy Commissioner of the Metropolitan Police Service who, I believe, plays golf with the Chairman of Dignity Retirement Community PLC.'

'Is that true about the golf?' whispered Stark as the woman led them through the pastel labyrinth.

'Quite possibly,' replied Groombridge, straight-faced.

They were marched through a room with a TV in one corner and elderly people arranged around the perimeter who barely acknowledged their passing or, in many cases, the TV or anything much at all. The receptionist stopped outside a door, knocked and entered without pause.

'Clear off!' said the fat old man inside, from his wheelchair. He had one of those clear plastic tubes looped over his ears and under his nostrils, delivering oxygen from a bottle on the small sack-barrow beside him. He glanced away from the television with watery, yellowed eyes and his indignation melted. 'Mickey!' he wheezed, grinning round incongruously white dentures. 'As I barely live and breathe! You took your sodding time! Got a cake with a metal file in it?' he whispered loudly. 'Or a mobile phone? The screws here have rescinded my privileges.'

'You were banned from the communal TV room for hogging the remote and shouting at *Midsomer Murders*,' said the nurse who'd just appeared at the door. The receptionist had evaporated. 'And your phone was confiscated until you promise to stop ordering pizzas.'

'They don't feed me,' muttered Cooper. 'They're trying to cull the prison population.'

'Now, now, don't be like that,' said the nurse, checking the gauge on his oxygen bottle. 'You get the same menu options as everyone else.'

'There's no tick-box for all of the above,' complained Cooper, eyeing her resentfully. 'I'm half the man I was when they wheeled me in here. My clothes are hanging off me, look!'

The nurse ignored him. 'Who are you gentlemen?' she asked. Groombridge told her. 'You mean he really was a policeman? We're never sure what to believe. When he's not making things up, his mind wanders almost as much as his hands.'

Cooper chuckled, and descended into a long bout of gasping coughs. 'Please try not to excite him,' said the nurse, handing Cooper a tissue to mop up his spittle.

'Should've listened to Beryl, Ron,' smiled Groombridge. 'Those cigarette packs say "Smoking Kills" now.'

Cooper grinned sheepishly. 'Good old Mrs C, God rest her soul. Cancer got her first, where's the justice? Least she was spared this place. Dignity Retirement Community, get Dignitas on the bloody phone!' He collapsed into more wheezing coughs.

'I'll leave you gentlemen to talk,' said the nurse brightly.

Groombridge sat on the edge of the bed opposite Cooper and sighed. 'It's good to see you, Ron. It must be fifteen years!'

'If a day.' The jowly old man nodded, smiling.

'I'm sorry.'

'CID kept you busy after they snatched you. Too busy to keep tabs on retired uniforms.'

'I'm ashamed, Ron.'

'Don't fret.' Cooper waved a hand. 'You probably all thought I was long dead. I *am*, too. They just won't stop prodding me.'

'Said the man with the wandering hands.'

Cooper wheezed a faint laugh. 'I was a one-woman man for forty years. And what a woman. She wouldn't begrudge me a little diversion in my dying days. Who's this?' He looked at Stark properly for the first time.

'Wait . . . I know that face. Well, well . . . I don't suppose the force is a patch on the old days but they'll be better for the likes of you, young man. You'll be no good for undercover with that face, but learn from young Mickey here and you'll make a decent copper.' He turned back to Groombridge. 'Funny enough, it's a face off the TV I wanted to talk to you about, Mickey. A face I never thought I'd see again.'

There were press outside White's block of flats.

'Let me out here,' he said urgently.

'No,' said Fran. 'It'll be all right. I'll escort you inside.'

'*Please!*'

She pulled the car around the corner, still disconcerted by White's sudden decline from strong-silent to gibbering wreck. He was out of the door almost before they'd stopped, away up the street in the opposite direction to his besieged home.

She watched him in her mirror, trying to decide what she thought of him, whether she could picture him as a killer. She couldn't decide. A big, powerful man, quiet unless provoked, pent-up feelings, aggression, rage and an odd level of fear – a prime candidate for sudden violence. But the killing of Mary Chase didn't feel like that. It felt more . . . deliberated. Whatever past he was concealing he must believe it was worth all this attention and anxiety, and that made Fran doubly determined to uncover it.

She tapped her fingers on the wheel. White turned the corner and disappeared from view. Tutting, she pulled out and headed back to the station to see what Harper wanted to try next.

34

'Wait!' Cooper held up a hand, eyes fixed on his small TV.

'You're enjoying this, aren't you?' said Groombridge.

'Old men have to get their kicks somehow. Here it comes.'

The news anchor announced the discovery of a man's body in a river in south-east London. The scene cut to police divers entering the Quaggy, in daylight, failing to mention the body was long gone, then SOCO and uniformed officers searching somewhere upstream.

Next came the steps of Royal Hill police station, with Harper holding up his hand for quiet amid the baying press. He made his short, bland statement then called for questions.

'*Detective Inspector! Detective Inspector!*' yelled the loudest reporter. '*Do you have a name for the victim?*'

'The body is yet to be formally identified. Until that time we cannot release the name. Next question.'

'*Detective Inspector, are you any closer to an arrest?*' called another disembodied voice.

Before Harper could answer, a female voice shouted out. '*Is it true you're linking this murder with the double homicide of Mary and Thomas Chase?*'

Harper blinked. 'We have made no such statement . . .'

'*What do you say to unofficial reports that the same gun was used in both cases?*' called the same voice.

Stark shot Groombridge a loaded glance. Once was luck, twice coincidence; third was a leak.

Harper's face was rigid with stifled annoyance. 'I won't comment on rumour and neither should you –'

'*Is Mark White your prime suspect?*' interrupted the voice. The other reporters seemed to have taken a back seat, recognizing that the story was unfolding right here. '*Are you any closer to establishing his real identity?*'

'Get out,' murmured Groombridge to the image of Harper.

Harper held up a hand to stop the questions. 'As I've already stated: this is a complex investigation into a heinous crime. We are pursuing multiple lines of enquiry. Several people are assisting us in this. We are doing everything possible to bring the killer to justice. That's all for now.'

'Killer *or killers*,' Groombridge tutted disapprovingly.

'Keep watching,' murmured Cooper.

The image cut to the on-the-spot reporter, scarlet coat and lipstick, serious expression; same voice as the questions. 'While police remain tight-lipped, we have exclusive information that the latest victim is none other than Carlton Savage, former suspect. And the man named there as "assisting with enquiries", is Mark White, interviewed last week in connection with the double murder of Mary and Thomas Chase, and again this morning following the discovery of the third body.' Footage showed a car pulling out of the station car park past paparazzi, Fran at the wheel, Mark White in the rear holding up a hand to shield his frightened face.

'Several newspapers have focused on the apparent uncertainty surrounding the past of Mark White and whether indeed that is his real name,' added the anchor. 'This footage was taken two days ago at his flat in

Greenwich.' They cut to a reporter banging on White's door and getting a muffled reply that had to be bleeped out.

This was getting out of hand, thought Groombridge. The picture they had on the screen behind the anchor was of White getting into a police car outside the station, flanked by uniforms, looking as disreputable as it was possible to look short of a mugshot. There was no picture of Clive Tilly, the ordinary-looking middle-aged businessman. Mark White was far more interesting; the big, scary enigma.

The anchor had moved on to a brief conversation with her crime correspondent, who reiterated that White, and others, were helping with enquiries and the police were at pains to stress that. Everyone was innocent until proven guilty, added the anchor unhelpfully.

Groombridge had a sick feeling he was watching a man's life being stolen on national television. The story was to be discussed after the headlines in the afternoon round-up of today's papers. He could picture it – the smiling presenter turning on his or her sofa to a pair of B-list commentators who would take turns to hold up that day's front pages. Innocent until proven guilty. The keepers of settee wisdom discussing how the public must not rush to conclusions, citing the salacious speculation of the red-tops, yet all the while waving that same image of White looking as though he was already in custody, where he belonged.

Cooper clicked off the sound and turned to Groombridge, an expectant look on his face. Groombridge stared back blankly. 'Come on . . . Two and two . . .'

'Just tell me,' said Groombridge testily.

'You never did have much patience, Mickey. Could see

it in your eyes. That was why we waved you under CID's nose.'

'You did *what*?' spluttered Groombridge indignantly.

'See? You were always going to be happier demanding answers than waiting for them. Uniform is a patient man's game. How do you think CID got wind of you in the first place?'

Groombridge closed his eyes for a second, years of blind misconception crumbling. 'Bastard.'

'Now, now. We did the right thing. Your old dad was a solid copper, but you got your brains from your mum and you know it. You'd have done a lot of good in uniform, Mickey, but more out. Got a fag on you?'

Groombridge raised his eyebrows at the plastic oxygen tube tucked under Cooper's nose. 'My wife had more influence over me.'

Ron nodded sagely. 'How is Alice? Still on at you to find a nice safe desk?'

'We were fortunate men, to find good women to love us.'

'Fortunate men indeed,' Ron echoed wistfully. He turned his gaze on Stark. 'How about you, young Stark, have you struck lucky as we did?'

Stark smiled. 'My old general once told me I'd used up my share of luck and more.'

'Bah!' Ron waved a hand dismissively. 'Luck is a state of mind, don't let it slip away. Find yourself a nice round woman to remind you every day. Do you smoke?' he asked, more in hope than expectation. 'A man with your past can't be all that risk-averse?' Stark shook his head and Ron sighed. 'Young coppers these days. The only puff I've had since they banged me up in here is when I lifted a pack out of Nurse Ratched's pocket. Still thinks I was copping a feel.' He chuckled breathlessly. 'Only got half-way down one fag before the bloody smoke alarm brought the Fun-Gestapo running. Look at me – reduced to petty larceny and accusations of attempted arson.'

'Ron . . .' Groombridge interrupted the flood of mock melancholia.

'Quite right, Mickey . . . I digress.' He scrabbled around on the table behind him and pulled out a copy of the *Sun*, opened it to an inside page and tapped on a photo – Mark White, some old snap they'd trawled up, looking almost demonic.

'White? You know something about him?'

'Don't you?' Cooper looked disappointed. 'I hoped when you never called back you'd seen it yourself, but the news just kept using the wrong name.'

'Saw *what*?'

'You didn't interview him, did you?' Cooper saw the truth in Groombridge's eyes. 'No. If you had you'd have seen it, plain as day. It's the eyes, Mickey, everything changes but the eyes. You had him in but you let him go.' Cooper descended into another paroxysm of coughing.

Groombridge stared at the picture of White. There *was* something familiar there, but you could say the same for countless people. When you looked properly you noticed it, the same body shapes, gait, facial structure, eyes, end-lessly reappearing throughout the population, the same genealogy dividing and recombining . . . He froze, his mind screeching to a halt like a speeding train with some-one yanking the emergency cord.

'You see it now,' said Cooper, studying him. 'Took me a while too. Thought I was finally losing my marbles till I saw the same news report later. I may not be half the man I was but there's enough copper left to recognize those eyes, even if the face around them is twenty years older.'

Groombridge couldn't take his eyes off the image. They'd had him in, more than once. 'Fuck.' It was all he could think to say.

Cooper chuckled, nodding his head. 'That's exactly what I said.'

35

Stark looked back and forth between Groombridge and Cooper. 'Is someone going to tell me what's going on?' he demanded impatiently.

Cooper wheezed in amusement. 'Cut from the same cloth as you, this one, Mickey.'

'Just tell me, one of you.'

'That man,' said Cooper soberly, 'is Simon Kirsch. And he's killed before.'

'That was never proved,' said Groombridge.

Cooper shrugged. 'He did it, though.'

'Did what?' asked Stark, exasperated.

'Killed Kimberly Bates,' said Cooper. 'Denied it, of course. Sixteen to his eighteen, they'd had a fling. She disappeared walking home from a friend's house one rainy night.'

'Remembrance Sunday, 1989,' said Groombridge. 'We searched and searched, but she was never found.'

'Trail kept leading back to Kirsch,' pitched in Cooper. 'Mickey here was a green young constable back then. Can't be many left who'd remember his face. DI Walhurst ran the case but he's long dead. What happened to Neville Darlington? He was detective sergeant.'

'Retired a DCI,' said Groombridge, still staring at the newspaper. 'I can't believe I didn't see this.'

'Took your eye off the ball,' said Cooper. 'The pitfalls of promotion, Mickey. I always told you. Sergeant, yes, inspector if you can, but no higher. Neville knew the

game. Shine too bright and the brass will use you to fea-
ther their nest; thieving magpies, the lot of them, stealing
talent and wasting it, I always said. If you were the type to
follow advice I'd tell you to use this, Mickey: take some of
the shine off before they stuff you into a super's uniform
where you'll be no damn good to anyone.'

Stark watched Groombridge for any recognition of this
potentially timely advice. 'So what happened?'

'It was the story of the year. Went to trial but the jury
couldn't reach a verdict. Went to retrial but Kirsch walked.
Not guilty. I always thought there should be a middle
result – guilty, not guilty or *pending proof*!' Agitated, Cooper
broke into another bout of coughing.

Stark already had his phone out. 'Come on, come
on . . . Sarge.'

'What is it? I'm driving,' barked Fran. Meaning she was
now driving one-handed. She had never bothered to learn
how to sync her phone with the car and thought rules
were for everyone else.

'Where are you?'

'Nearly at the station – why?'

'Where's Mark White?'

'What's it to you? You're supposed to be sleeping.'

'I'm not at home. I'm with DCI Groombridge –'

'What? Why?'

'I'll explain later, but do we have White?' He put his
phone on speaker so Groombridge and Cooper could hear.

'No. DI Harper gave him a grilling but got nothing. I
just dropped him off.'

Groombridge winced. 'Fran, it's Mike. You dropped
him at home?'

'Sort of . . .'

'Turn around. Have uniform meet you there.'

'Seriously?'

'He's been lying to us. His real name is Simon Kirsch. He walked for murder twenty years ago and I'd say he's got some explaining to do.'

'I'll put the call out to uniform, Guv, but there was press outside his flat. He wouldn't go in. He left on foot in the opposite direction.'

Groombridge looked pained again. 'Okay. Do what you can. Make sure everyone knows to approach with caution. We think he was dangerous twenty years ago. He may still be.'

'Guv.' She rang off.

'This is what you get for not answering your phone,' wheezed Cooper, then bent double, coughing again. Stark called for the nurse when he started to go purple.

Once she finally had Cooper back in the land of the breathing, she looked to his guests apologetically. 'I'm sorry, gentlemen, but I think you should go.'

'Take me with you, Mickey!' Cooper managed to joke, ashen faced after his episode. 'Stark, lad, give her a karate chop across the back of the neck and we'll stuff her in the bed as a decoy.'

The nurse managed a weary smile.

'Don't let him slip away this time, Mickey.' Cooper was serious now. 'Good people worked hard. Make him tell you, Mickey. Make him tell you where she is.'

They nodded farewells and followed the nurse out to reception where the robot glared at them over the counter.

'How bad is it?' asked Groombridge.

The nurse looked apologetic again. 'I'm sorry, I can only discuss that with family.'

'Of which he has precisely none living, as you know,' said Groombridge softly. 'But the uniform he wore for forty years protecting and serving his community makes him family to me and this young man. So I would beg a little flexibility.'

The nurse cast an eye at the watchful receptionist and spoke quietly. 'Chronic emphysema. But it's not just his lungs. His heart could go at any time. That's why we try to stop him getting overexcited. Not that he'll listen. He's bullish enough on the outside, but inside, he's giving up. I know the look.'

Groombridge nodded. 'He loved his wife.'

'The last few days have been different, though. He's come alive.'

'He loved his job too,' said Groombridge. 'Please look after him, he's earned his full measure of respect.' He handed his card across. 'Please call me if his health deteriorates. I'm his family now.'

36

'Right . . .' Groombridge strode to the board, pulled off Mark White's photo and held it up to the team. 'In 1989 the man we know as Mark White was an eighteen-year-old called Simon Kirsch. Although it was never proved, it was believed that he attacked and killed sixteen-year-old Kimberly Bates as she walked home on a wet November evening. I was only a rookie constable back then and can't tell you much; only that he's been lying to us from the start. That doesn't make him our killer but it does make him a person of interest. Not enough to search his flat again, yet, but if he's definitely gone to ground . . . Fran, anything from uniform?'

'Nothing yet, Guv. Everyone has his description.' Stark could see from her face that she was frustrated. Wishing, like him, that he'd got Cooper's full name from that first call.

'Okay. Well, it's usually just a matter of time. Request the original case files from storage; use my name.' Groombridge nodded to Harper. 'You all know what to do. Keep me in the loop.'

No sooner had he gone than Harper turned to Stark. 'I told you to go home.'

'DCI Groombri—'

'Don't hide behind the DCI's skirts, Constable,' interrupted Harper. 'Request the old files and then clear off, understood?'

'Sir.' Harper's eyes narrowed, but Stark would not call him Guv'nor until he earned it.

Stark requested the files, went home, had a shower and some food and set the alarm.

He hardly seemed to have blinked when the clock radio woke him, but it was dark outside and six hours had passed. The newsreader covered foreign policy fears, domestic policy gaffes, the latest celebrity fall from grace and the impending stormy weather the jet stream was bringing their way following heavy snow in North America. Stark let it all roll over him as he summoned the will to get up.

'In the latest development in the recent double murder of a Blackheath businessman and his wife, Metropolitan Police are now describing Mark White, who has been interviewed several times already and is the subject of intense media speculation about his identity, as a "person of interest". White has not been seen at his home. The public have been urged not to approach him, but to report his whereabouts.'

At least the news of White's real identity hadn't leaked yet.

Forcing himself up, he dressed and cycled to the gym. If he wasn't allowed to progress the case he would progress his own.

Andy eyed him curiously as he set up his spinning bike. Stark was disappointed to see Selena wasn't there, but she bustled in with a minute to spare and took a bike opposite Stark. Andy made a comment about taking it easy this week and the class groaned theatrically at the lie. Soon they were blowing hard. Stark felt the weariness and frustrations of the day fall away, heart rate rising, adrenaline stoking him to life. Opposite him, Selena glistened with sweat. A wisp of black hair had escaped her bungee, and in a brief drinks free-wheel she set about resetting the whole ponytail. Elbows high as she reached up, sweat ran down her cleavage, her legs still pumping up and down in neutral. She took a long drink, looked directly at Stark, smiled and leant into Andy's next burst of high-tempo sadism.

Stark felt the inner boy rise to the challenge and push hard. At the end of the session he was dying, gasping, buzzing. They entered the two-minute warm-down amid shared groans, gasps and laughter from the masochists. Selena grinned at Stark, noticeably more flushed and out of breath than the previous week. She had a competitive streak. He liked that.

As they gathered their belongings she stood next to him and quietly slipped him a note, smiled and was gone. Andy was grinning.

Stark glanced at the note and sighed. A Facebook ID. As a policeman he lauded the additional level of first-contact security it gave a girl, but if this was how the dating game had moved on since his last ventures, he was at more of a disadvantage than he'd thought. He had no Facebook profile or Twitter account, nor any form of social media. Aside from his private nature, his public notoriety made it impossible. He kept an email account for family and close friends and another for the day-to-day necessities of online life and commerce, both anonymized.

'Why so glum?' grinned Andy. 'Not a bad end to the day, I reckon.'

Fran stepped on the gas. Harper was en route from his home but she would get there first. She would have preferred to have Stark along. He was handy for this sort of thing. She'd grown accustomed to the security he gave her, his solidity, frankly his unflinching capability. But Harper expressly forbade it. They didn't have time, he said. Arsehole.

She slowed down as she passed the restaurant, if that was the right word for an all-night McDonald's. She craned her neck but could not pick out Mark White, or Simon Kirsch if that was his name. Three uniform cars were waiting around the next corner, two of them armed response.

She spoke briefly with the sergeant in charge. Harper pulled up minutes later.

Kirsch was still inside. Harper entered into a forthright exchange with the ART sergeant. The latter was firmly of the opinion that Kirsch represented an unknown danger and as such they should all wait for the CO19 Specialist Firearms Officers, the Met police equivalent of an American SWAT team. Harper's view was that he and Fran should go in quietly so as not to alarm the suspect or endanger the other diners, and that he held higher rank.

Fran cursed him. Eighteen months ago she'd felt what it was like to have a killer hold a pistol to her head. The Simon Kirsch inside was a lot scarier than the Mark White she'd let out of her car that morning. They had no reason to think he'd be armed. She kept telling herself that, as they crossed the street on foot. She watched Harper's big frame moving with his usual misguided confidence and misdirected purpose. The great lumbering oaf. At least if bullets started flying she could hide behind him.

Kirsch was sitting in the corner looking out, a baseball cap low over his face. He looked up as they entered and clocked them at once.

His eyes shot wide with panic. He dumped his burger and scrambled to his feet.

Harper walked forward, hands out to show they were empty. 'We just want a word, Simon.'

Bloody fool! Fran cursed inside. Why tip Kirsch off that they knew who he really was?

Kirsch looked like he would choke on his mouthful. He forced himself to swallow; but not to speak.

The other customers stared in a mixture of confusion and concern.

Harper took another step.

Kirsch looked panic-stricken. Then he pulled out a gun and shot Harper in the chest.

Harper dropped like a stone, convulsing to the crackling tune of arcing electricity.

It took Fran several horrified seconds to register what she was seeing. Not a real gun. Not a lead bullet but tens of kilovolts – a Taser!

The look on Kirsch's face was one of strange fascination. Then he looked up at Fran and their eyes locked. For a moment she thought she was next. But most Taser guns were one-shot wonders. His face flashed with anger, and with an animal snarl he charged the serving counter and vaulted it, crashing through the kitchen.

Fran was already shouting into her radio.

The responses were abrupt. Barking sitreps, orders and confusion, but Fran wasn't listening. The only words that mattered were hers: '*Man down*'.

The ART boys burst in and found her furiously yanking the two barbed electrodes from Harper's chest and slapping his face. Serve the stupid oaf right if he'd had a heart attack. Kirsch hadn't been holding a police issue X26. It was something bulkier. Some of these illegal imports carried double the power or more and no time limiter.

'Wake up, you stupid prick.' She slapped him again.

He groaned, eyes fluttering open.

Fran slapped him again, for luck, and got to her feet.

One of the ART guys knelt by Harper to check him over. The rest had already disappeared through the kitchens.

Fran saw blue lights outside. More racing up the road under sirens. She snatched up her radio from the floor but couldn't make sense of the overlapping calls. She hurried outside; the ART sergeant had disappeared.

What the hell was happening?

It was ten agonizing minutes before she knew.

Kirsch was gone; dissolved into the night. A helicopter was up, cars out, ART boys running hither and thither, but Kirsch had evaded them. Perhaps he'd scoped out his escape route on the way in. Stark would say something like that. Stark would've anticipated that. Stark would've stopped him. Stark wouldn't have got himself shot with a bloody Taser!

Fran swore viciously, earning wary glances from the chagrined ART man. Mark White, aka Simon Kirsch, had just jumped from person of interest to prime suspect, and he was in the wind.

PART TWO

37

It was dry, hunkered down in the ditch; the autumn rains long bled off. The sun was nearly at its zenith but he could still see his breath. The desert had a purple tint beneath grey clouds. The distant mountains were whiter with snow than they had been a month earlier. And the insurgent sniper still had them pinned down.

Rousseau had sent him forward to try and pinpoint the sniper's location. He had a good eye for reckoning, a reputation for sneaking up, and for killing without hesitation.

He'd worked his way forward three hundred metres along the dried irrigation ditch, barely deeper than his prone shape. The sniper either hadn't seen him or was waiting for the kill shot. One soldier was already in a chopper to the field hospital and a villager was dead, shot at random just after dawn to get this whole sick game underway.

He didn't fancy being next. He was enjoying himself too much. This was what it was to be alive. A battle of wits. A contest of nerve. His heart skipped with the unfettered joy of it.

Removing his helmet he slowly raised his head, using the fallen branch of the nearby tree to mask his dome, scanning for the sniper's position through his own scope, checking the sun's angle to ensure it didn't glint off the glass. He held his breath, lest the faint breeze lift it into sight.

Where are you?

There? Sun glint off something, scope glass? Yes? Yes.

Eyes wide, he took in every detail; then slipped slowly back down, gradually letting his breath escape. He checked his GPS, bought at home with his own money, better than shit military issue; took out his radio and relayed the coordinates. The sniper was in a house up near the top of the hill, packed in among others, each probably full of families huddled together in terror of what the viper in their nest might bring down upon them.

He waited. Impatient. Itching.

There. Finally. The point man of Rousseau's team, then three others, crabbing along the side of a house within a hundred metres of the sniper.

Eyes straining, he meticulously studied the scene again, re-estimating distance, elevation, wind speed, and carefully adjusted his sights accordingly; he'd only get one chance.

Rousseau looked in roughly his direction and gave a thumbs-up. If the sniper wanted a target, they'd oblige.

The point man crept up the edge of the house, poked his head round the corner and withdrew it. Then again, just an edge. Then pulled off his helmet and put it on his rifle butt and tilted it into view.

The muzzle flash lit up the distant window and the helmet spun off the rifle butt.

He squeezed his trigger.

The sniper was down before the helmet hit the ground, limp hand hanging in the air as he slumped against the window frame. Another insurgent appeared and began firing wildly. He took aim again and shot him. A third began climbing awkwardly from another window on to the adjacent roof but fell to a third bullet.

No more movement.

He let out his breath with a low hiss of satisfaction, of monstrous triumph.

In the west a murder of crows took flight, laughing their raucous song of death . . .

Stark woke, swallowing hard at the sudden rush of nausea and imagined taste of bitter blood in his throat, the wild thrill of violence in his scudding heart.

He blinked at the ceiling, letting the past retreat to its proper place. He hadn't thought about that day in a long while. Had forgotten about it in fact. What did that say? Was it better that it was all still locked away in there, or to hope that one day it would be gone for good? Regular dreams morphed between surreal imaginings and twisted recollections but could be relied on to fade after waking. Dreams like this did not. A reminder of what you were. Lest you forget.

He fumbled for the phone vibrating on the nightstand. 'Stark.'

'You're awake,' said Fran.

Stark glanced at the clock. One in the morning. 'Is that enquiry or triumph?'

The station was buzzing. All three choppers were up now and uniform were busy covering a search grid of the borough. Fran stood in the centre of it all, demanding the plates spun themselves to her satisfaction. Stark strode in barely twenty minutes after her call, clean-shaven and neat as a damn pin. How did he do that? she wondered, for the umpteenth time.

'Right,' she jerked her head upward. 'We've a city-wide search on but things are about to go national. I need bodies at desks. Get upstairs and chase archive for the Kimberly Bates case files; wake someone up if you have to. Then dig into Mark White's file and see if there are locations we're not already looking. Get Williams and Dixon to help, they're on their way in.'

'DI Harper?' asked Stark.

'Hospital, getting checked over.' She rolled her eyes. 'Bit his tongue when he was shocked and hit his head on the floor.'

Stark made no comment, but looked at her with those piercing eyes. 'And you?'

'I hid behind Harper.'

'Good thinking,' he smiled, satisfied. You could almost see his mind ticking that off and moving on as he left. He had a sharp intensity in moments like these, she'd learned. A cut-to-the-chase efficiency of movement, thought and purpose; part of the reason she would far rather have entered that burger joint with him than Harper. Harper made a show of things; Stark made short work of things . . . as he had proved more than once, not least the time a perp held a gun to her head.

Fran stayed down on the uniform floor where they were marshalling the search, checking and rechecking with border control, regional police, national crime agency and traffic control. The most likely scenario was that White – or Kirsch, or whatever other names he might have – was hiding in a local hole, but there was no guarantee.

The hospital called to confirm Harper was concussed and staying in for observation. Fran almost felt sorry for him. She'd experienced concussion, and not being allowed to sleep when all you wanted to do was curl up in a ball with your eyes screwed shut till the dizziness and nausea went away. Harper was in for a rotten night, meaning she had maybe twenty-four hours without him in the way. She had every intention of making the most of it.

The search dragged on into the daylight hours.

She didn't even know Groombridge was in the building until she was summoned up to his makeshift office. In the windowless room there was no reference to day or night, and she wondered whether he'd just arrived or been here all night, whether indeed he ever went home any more. She shook her head. Tired thoughts.

He listened, nodding, but adding little. 'Search warrant?'

'Waiting on the wig.' Judges didn't get out of bed for detective sergeants.

'I'll see if I can chivvy things along.'

'Time to release Mark White's real name?' she asked.

'Not yet,' mused Groombridge. 'Our best chance of finding him is still to find out where he's been all this time. Better if he doesn't know we know, for now.'

'DI Harper called him Simon to his face.'

Groombridge's face darkened. 'That's a pity. Nevertheless, it could still prove a distraction.'

'It might help – get the journalists working for us for a change?'

Groombridge considered this but shook his head. 'We've no proof yet.'

'But you're sure it's him?'

'Sure enough. But his DNA and fingerprints didn't flag up a hit on the database.'

'Maybe the old ones weren't logged. Might be copies of his prints in the files when we get them. You'll do the tap dance?' she asked, meaning the press statement.

Groombridge shook his head. 'You need the practice. Keep it bland – unknown aliases, et cetera . . .'

Seriously? *Now?* She wanted to tell him that she couldn't afford to lose a moment before Harper returned to foul everything up, but of course she couldn't. Flagging up your boss's failings to their own boss wasn't the done thing. Groombridge knew already. It was *his* job to do something about it. It was also his job to make the statement, but he had that perverse patriarchal look in his eye again. If he'd had children he would've taught them to swim by throwing them in the deep end and calmly reminding them to pull themselves together and get on with not sinking.

So she wasted precious time drafting a statement, sorting her damn hair and make-up and trying to make it look like she wasn't wearing yesterday's bloody clothes. God, she hated this. Harper's love of the camera was probably his only redeeming feature. She should send Stark out instead, she thought, imagining him stepping up to the mike with his terse one-liners and short-shrift directness. That would be worth seeing. There were far more press today, but Fran was determined to make this the shortest and least satisfying press statement of all time.

She never got as far as 'unknown aliases'. Before she had even opened her mouth the questions came.

'Can you confirm Mark White is indeed Simon Kirsch?'

'How long have you known?'

'Is Simon Kirsch now prime suspect in the Chase double homicide and that of Carlton Savage?'

'Is the Kimberly Bates investigation being reopened? Is there fresh evidence?'

'Detective Sergeant?'

Fran blinked in the strobing camera flashes.

'Detective Sergeant Millhaven?'

She blinked, pulled herself together and got on with not sinking. She raised her hand and waited for the noise to abate, and then winged it.

'We are acting upon information that Mark White may be an alias but cannot comment further at this time. He is known to be in possession of a Taser gun and has shown himself willing to use it. The public should avoid approaching him and report sightings to the police or nearest person of authority. That is all for now.'

She turned and marched back into the station to howls of protest and questions and quietly locked herself into a toilet cubicle until she felt less like punching someone. The best she could say was that it probably *would* go down as mutually the least satisfying statement of all time.

It didn't take long after her serene re-emergence to uncover what had happened.

The *Sun* had the story – Mark White as Simon Kirsch, Kimberly Bates, the old case in lurid detail. Some hack had put two and two together, remembered the face, or taken a call from a pocket copper. Everyone in the station had arrived before the papers came out and no one in the headquarters press office had flagged it up. Fran was furious, to put it mildly, but she had little time to stew.

The fresh search warrant had come through and CO19 had a Specialist Firearms Officers team inbound.

38

Fran kept her foot down all the way. Running the man-hunt was uniform's job, but if there was any way she could make the arrest before Harper got back from the hospital she clearly wasn't about to let piffling speed limits stand in her way. Stark clung on, navigating as best he could.

The SFOs were already there, directing regular uniforms, establishing their perimeter and evacuating any occupied flats. Stark observed with professional interest. It was much like a targeted search op in Helmand, only about a hundred times slower, infinitely less covert and entirely pointless.

Mark White wasn't home.

An unmarked car had been outside the place all night, and the siege team commander had been phoning the flat since he arrived. Stark supposed he'd better start thinking of White as Simon Kirsch, but the flat was rented in White's name.

When they were good and ready the commander sportingly called out one last time in the megaphone just to be sure that if anyone *was* inside, they were good and ready too.

All this because a man who wasn't inside was known to be in possession of a non-lethal firearm. Stark had half a mind to walk up the stairs and kick the sodding door in himself. Fran spotted him yawning and rolled her eyes. He was too tired to care whether she was pissed at him or at the delay. It was almost certainly both.

Her phone beeped and she read a text and replied with

a faint smile. If Stark didn't know better he'd think she was text-flirting, but it was more likely a parent, one of her four brothers or myriad nieces and nephews.

The siege team made their final approach along the open corridor balcony, huddling behind one guy with a bullet shield like a disorganized rugby maul, banging on the door and shouting to give the imaginary occupant one last chance to come out all Tasers blazing. The doorman finally swung his ram and broke a perfectly good door open while his team shuffled inside, shouting even louder in case any doubt remained that they were definitely the police, they were definitely armed and they were definitely coming in, ready or not.

After one last spot of shouting they traipsed out in a cheerful line and proudly pronounced the flat to be *clear.*

Fran had asked him once why he didn't sign up for CO19. This pretty much summed it up. At least a soldier knew when they were in danger. For these guys, even the real thing turned into practice most of the time.

He of all people had respect for anyone who carried a gun in the name of peace, and these guys operated under constraints that made military rules of engagement look like a one-line memo. No shots had been fired. No bombs had gone off. Armed coppers were an indispensable anathema to a force proud of its unarmed heritage, but all save an unlucky few would never discharge their weapon outside the range, and today Stark found it hard to see the protracted proceedings as anything other than a waste of time.

The SOCO team went in next, as if the scene hadn't just been tramped with a dozen pairs of combat boots. One day, thought Stark idly, someone in CO19 was going to figure out that if they timed things right they could commit a violent murder and also be first on the scene to contaminate or excuse any evidence they'd left earlier.

Finally, Fran and Stark were allowed to don blue anti-contamination gear and see if there was anything they could bring late to the party.

Inside it was sparsely furnished, clean and tidy, everything in its place, often indications of a military past – or as Fran would have it, boot-polishing OCD. Similarly there wasn't much fresh food in the fridge, but where it differed from Stark's was that the cupboards were full. White/Kirsch lived largely from cans, jars and dried foods rather than takeaways. The tiny bathroom was clean, the bed was made. The clothes in the drawers were folded and those in the small wardrobe were ironed. There was gym clothing and a set of barbells and fist grips. What there was almost nothing of was life: clutter, dirty washing, dishes, bills yet to be opened, paid or filed – or indeed anywhere to file them. There was a heavy-duty paper shredder with a sprinkling of shreddings around it.

'That's seen some use since last week,' commented Fran. 'Just because you're paranoid, doesn't mean the world isn't out to arrest you.'

'Covering his tracks after his ID came into question,' suggested Stark, flicking on the TV to see what Kirsch had been watching last. News 24.

'Here . . .' One of the SOCO bodies pulled something from the gym bag in the bottom of the wardrobe. A gym membership card.

The gym in question was a small independent; one of those poorly ventilated, man's-man establishments for serious gym bunnies, tucked out of sight behind some low-end shops. The rubber floor matting was worn but the wall mirrors were polished. The equipment looked sturdy but aging, rather like the bulging man behind what stood for a reception counter.

The eponymous Dave, whose name was emblazoned above the door in peeling paintwork. Enlarged but fading photos on the wall behind showed the younger him mahogany-tanned, grotesquely inflated, veined and oiled, striking poses in obscenely small Speedos and clutching rosettes, a tale of past glories, steroid abuse and a warped brand of self-awareness.

The latter-day Dave greeted them with a wide smile and a wink at Fran, which oddly didn't result in his head being bitten off. 'You here about Mark?'

'What makes you think that?' asked Fran, fishing.

'Only the fact that, according to the TV, you and every other flat-foot from Land's End to John o' Groats is looking for him.' Dave laughed, a deep bass boom.

'Any idea where he is?'

'Sorry.'

'What about anyone else here? Who was he friendly with?'

'Most people, I suppose. Everyone spots for everyone else here. He was a quiet sort but he could bench his weight. I don't think anyone knew him outside, though.'

'He keep a locker?' asked Stark.

'Out the back. Want to see?' He showed them the old battleship-grey metal lockers, dented and scratched, with assorted padlocks. White's was a chunky five-dial combination lock.

'Number?' asked Fran.

Dave shook his head. 'Want a peek inside anyway?' He looked around and picked up a five-kilogram dumb-bell weight, indicating the padlock with a hint of mischief.

'You don't mind?'

Dave pointed at the sign on the lockers. *Property is left in the lockers at the individual's risk. The management are not liable for any loss, theft or damage.* 'I never much liked Mark anyway.'

Fran smiled. 'If he wants reimbursement for the padlock, tell him to come find me at Royal Hill nick.'

Dave grinned and broke the lock with one deft clout.

'You don't like Mark?' Stark queried.

'To be honest, not many people do.' Dave made a face. 'He's got some of the younger, impressionable ones in awe of him, but after a while it gets boring. About how he used to ride in a biker gang and be a famous cage fighter in Manchester – The *Tornado*.' Dave did a sarcastic jazz hands to indicate the name in lights. 'And the foreign legion stuff, doing special ops with the SAS, things he's done but wasn't allowed to tell you about . . . He tries to slip it in casual, but once you've heard it a few times . . .'

'You didn't believe him?'

'I've always thought real heroes didn't brag about it, but what would I know?' He grinned, suddenly pulling a pose to show off his still considerable physique. 'I'm a lover, not a fighter.'

He pulled it off with such panache that he even got away with another wink at Fran without paying for it with his testicles.

'Biker gang?' asked Stark to cover the embarrassment Dave clearly didn't feel.

The big man shrugged and packed away the pose, still grinning at Fran. 'Some notorious name or other. Probably different every time. I'd stopped listening. His bike wasn't all that.'

'*His* bike?'

'Noisy off-road type thing. Everything sprayed black. Bit tatty.'

Fran and Stark exchanged a look. There was no bike registered to Mark White, and a bike had been heard at the time of the Chase murders. 'And the tornado stuff,' said Stark. 'The tattoo?'

Dave shrugged again. 'Who knows? Mark always looked like he could handle himself, but once you start to doubt some of it you stop caring what's true and what's not. He's got a temper, though. One of the kids called him on it all once, and Mark got hissy. Could be the pills. That was the other thing I didn't like.'

'That's a problem here?'

Dave pointed at another sign on the wall – *This is a clean gym. If you don't like it – fuck off!*

'Subtle.' Fran chuckled.

'I'm hardly the best person to tell kids not to dabble, I s'pose,' said Dave, nodding to the pictures of his glory days. 'I can't help what they do at home but it's not allowed on the premises. Course, not everyone will listen to an old fart like me.'

'And Mark?'

'Told me he'd packed it in. It's not true, what they say, though; that they shrivel your extremities.' He grinned at Fran. 'In case you were wondering.'

Deadpan, Fran pulled on a pair of anti-contamination gloves with a loaded snap.

Stark held open a large evidence bag as she began pulling items out of the locker: a pair of fingerless gym gloves and talc, a stiff leather support belt, shower gel and deodorant, neatly folded spare clothing, an empty water bottle, a large container of protein drink powder and . . . a bottle of pills with no label.

Dave's smile was gone. 'Lying bastard.'

Fran added the bottle to the evidence bag and slid out a photo that was tucked into the back of the locker door. A pretty blonde in her late thirties – staged, smiling thinly before a neutral backdrop, like a work photo. She held it up to Dave. 'Who's this?'

'Saw him show it around once. Said it was his girlfriend but didn't give a name. All part of his man-of-mystery act. You work out?' Dave asked Stark. 'Fancy a free trial?' He waved a leaflet.

Stark declined.

'How about you, Sweetcheeks?' Dave winked at Fran. 'You look like you enjoy breaking a sweat.'

A howler of a chat-up line. Stark cringed on Dave's behalf. But Fran just rolled her eyes and took the leaflet.

'Well,' said Stark innocently, outside, taking deep breaths in the cold air. 'He was charming, I thought.'

Fran avoided his eyes. 'I'm immune to charm, you know that.'

'Definitely a lover, not a fighter.'

Fran tried to ignore him.

'Who'd've thought beefcake was your type?'

'I don't have types,' growled Fran.

'Fair enough, Sweetcheeks.'

'Piss off!'

'I refute the allegations of incompetence on the part of Greenwich Police,' said Deputy Assistant Commissioner Stevens to the cameras and microphones as his body men cleared a way to his car outside New Scotland Yard.

Whose allegations? thought Groombridge, staring at the TV in Cox's office.

'Increased oversight is a matter for the Metropolitan Police command structure,' continued Stevens, who was either answering questions asked before the report cut to this footage, or was setting the agenda himself. 'We stand together to make London a safer place,' he concluded, aping the words on the prismatic sign behind him as he climbed into the rear seat and was driven away.

Cox turned the sound off. 'You think I've been played for a fool.'

'Now, don't go accusing me of thinking, sir,' replied Groombridge evenly. The illicitly obtained report Cox had just shared with him suggested they were *all* being played.

'All the same; better catch this Simon Kirsch before we face more *allegations* . . .'

Groombridge nodded and left. In his makeshift office he found a message from the archive storage to say the files were ready, but they had no driver to deliver them. It was a private secure-storage company. Theoretically their contract required them to retrieve and deliver any file, any time. This worked okay for files that had been digitized, but that process began with modern files and worked backwards in time with inconsistent speed and success. The Kimberly Bates files were still analogue. The physical evidence was largely stored with the Forensic Science Service, another private service, but their monopoly was being broken up in the name of 'competitive efficiency' and few people in the police had high hopes for that. Such exercises looked logical on budget sheets, until you needed something overnight or the driver pulled a sickie.

Downstairs the station was still busy as an ants' nest.

'Where are you off to?' he asked, spotting Stark at the pool-car desk.

Stark explained that he and Fran had just got back.

'Perfect. I've two birds to kill . . . You can drive.'

'Guv.' Stark led the way to the car and climbed in. 'Where to?'

'Archive first. After that, there's someone you should meet.'

The traffic was already thick and Groombridge held the usual Londoner's disdain for any route recommended by the satnav, directing Stark via circuitous back routes to avoid the clogged arteries.

With several boxes packed in the back he directed Stark back to Greenwich via another maze of turns until they pulled up in a quiet, leafy residential street. Wartime bombs had opened holes in the neat terraces on both sides of the road, later plugged by unsympathetic flats, but the mid-terrace house they pulled up outside was original, well kept, with a neat little garden and checkerboard mosaic footpath.

Groombridge stared at it without getting out. 'Any thoughts on our leak?'

Stark took a breath and puffed it out slowly. 'Other than we have one . . . ?'

Groombridge nodded. 'A busy case gets in the way. But it also tempts the leaker to show his or her hand. This morning was blatant. We must be vigilant.'

'You're assuming it's just *one* leak, Guv.'

'Well, that's a cheering thought.' Groombridge sighed. 'Come on . . . time to visit another old friend.'

39

Stark recruited some friendly faces to help carry in the boxes, but was appalled to find Harper inspecting the incident board with a comedy bandage around his head, a full day early by anyone's reckoning. He supposed he shouldn't be surprised. Harper was too insecure to lie in bed and risk someone else making the collar. Stark was hardly one to criticize anyone for ignoring the advice of their doctors, but when it came to concussion he was content to think Harper a damn fool all the same.

As for the rest, Stark had been Tasered himself during Special Forces training, ostensibly to gain an understanding of the weapon's usefulness and limitations, though he strongly suspected the directing staff got a kick out of zapping recruits. He wouldn't wish it on his worst enemy. And that was one positive thing about post-military life – at least Harper with his misplaced jealousy was the worst enemy Stark had to worry about.

Fran's stony face did little to mask her dismay.

The big man appeared just as annoyed to see Stark. 'What are you doing here?' he demanded, around a swollen tongue.

'I called him in,' said Fran.

'Last night?' Harper's eyes narrowed. 'Then where have you been?'

'Helping me,' announced Groombridge, arriving with the last box. 'All well, Owen? Doctor's said you were fit?'

'As a fiddle, sir,' lied Harper, frowning at the elderly man trailing in Groombridge's wake.

Groombridge put his box down with the rest and tapped the lid. 'Right, this little lot are the Kimberly Bates files. There's enough about the young Simon Kirsch to keep us busy, but in the meantime DCI Darlington here has agreed to step briefly from well-earned retirement to help us with a summary. He was DS on the case. Neville . . .'

Darlington had been DS to Groombridge's DC, DI to his DS and DCI to his DI. Fifteen years side by side on the thin blue coalface. Groombridge had a photo of them together on his desk, or had before Harper's return. Now it was in a box.

Average height but thin and drawn, watery eyed, Darlington looked much older now, as if age had descended on him with retirement. A man not long for this earth, would be Stark's guess. There was little justice in this entropic universe, little but what men like Neville Darlington sought to fashion.

His bony fingers fiddled with the visitor badge hanging from his neck on blue-and-white ribbon. He stared at the photo of White aka Kirsch for several seconds, then shook his head and turned to face the room and cleared his throat.

'Good morning. Right, listen up and don't ask questions unless they're good ones,' he began in a strong voice that belied his appearance. 'Simon Kirsch was an only child, raised by his mother, Miriam, alone. The mother taught him that his father had died but we soon discovered he'd just walked out.

'Simon was a shy boy, big for his age but lacking talent

or interest in sports. Academically above average but socially awkward, he became a target for bullying at school. But he was unpredictable. Most of the time he took his licks in silence, the gentle giant, but every now and then he would explode; not violent, but crazed, all but foaming at the mouth, quoting the bible. It was a Catholic school but his mother's piety was hardcore and alienated her from most of the other parents, adding to Simon's isolation. He gained a reputation for being "a bit mental", to use the vernacular of the time, and the kids learned to leave him alone.

'A year before Kimberly's disappearance Simon had come to the attention of our uniformed brethren. He'd found recognition with a young religious studies teacher called Susan Watts. Fresh out of college, naive, she mistook his attentions as academic while Simon mistook hers for more. When she cottoned on and rebuffed him, he reacted badly. There was a fuss. She narrowly kept her job but Simon left the school. He was seventeen at this point.

'Not long after, she began to complain about a peeping tom and being followed, she claimed, by Simon Kirsch. Uniform had a quiet word with him and the stalking stopped. But then it started up again. Uniform spoke with him again and again it stopped, for a while.

'Simon finished his A-levels from home and joined Greenwich School of Management on a foundation course. His teachers described him as a loner, often inattentive or plain absent. After a year and several more complaints by Susan Watts, there was an incident. A pair of uniform coppers put Simon in the hospital. They claimed it was unrelated, that he'd been lippy in the street, they'd pulled him up for it and he got violent. Because of his history of outbursts they got off with a short suspension, but Kirsch had broken bones. His mother made a stink.

'It may have been this brief notoriety that caused Kimberly Bates to take an interest in him, or perhaps the lingering gossip that he'd been lovers with Miss Watts. Kimberly was two years his junior but far less innocent in the ways of the world. They engaged in a sexual relationship. Not her first, but his.

'On Sunday, the twelfth of November 1989, Kimberly spent the day in Bromley with girlfriends, before returning to best friend Maria Soames's house around four. She was due home for tea at six. Foul weather was closing in and Kimberly's mother called Maria's to say Kimberly's father would pick her up, but Kimberly had already left.'

Darlington stepped up to the huge wall map. 'She left Maria's house, here, at just after four on foot. Her mother didn't start getting worried until after eight. It was far from the first time that Kimberly had taken a diversion on her way home. She called around Kimberly's friends – she knew nothing of Simon – and then called us.

'Just before nine a resident of Dumbreck Road, here . . .' he jabbed a gnarled finger, 'near Kimberly's home, here . . . dialled nine-nine-nine, claiming her husband had witnessed an abduction. He had heard screaming outside in the street and looked out to see two figures struggling. The larger figure appeared to hit the smaller and drag them away. The husband had run outside but found no trace. Uniform were sent round for a look. The husband had found a handbag lying in the street, containing the usual teenage girl's clutter, recently purchased cosmetics, cigarettes and a purse containing a name and address. Kimberly Bates.

'Maria told us Kimberly had been planning to meet Simon in some secret rendezvous. We later established that this was probably Severndroog Castle, the old folly up on Shooter's Hill that had been boarded up the year before. We found both their fingerprints inside, some candles, blankets and a soiled condom. Simon later claimed these were from an earlier tryst. Critically, Maria claimed that Kimberly had been planning to end it, that Simon's affection had become overbearing. Also that Kimberly had been seeing another boy at the same time, James Rawlings; incidentally Simon's chief playground persecutor. Cast-iron alibi.

'A motorist later reported seeing someone carrying someone else over their shoulder on the south side of Rochester Way, right by one entrance into Shepherdleas Woods, so the initial search concentrated there, to no avail.

'A line was quickly drawn from Kimberly to Simon. His house is just a few streets away here, in Crookston Road. A car was dispatched there and he was found all tucked up in bed. He reacted with considerable distress when told Kimberly was missing, and fervently denied involvement. His mother swore he had been there with her all afternoon and evening. The coppers were shown around the house and found nothing suspicious.

'We followed countless leads. Past and potential boy-friends, local trouble-makers and known sexual predators. But we always came back to Simon Kirsch.

'Given his history of emotional instability, the theory was that he reacted badly to being dumped, and/or found out Kimberly was going behind his back with his worst enemy. Or she just told him; anecdotally she could be quite cruel, though you won't find any mention of that in the newspaper cuttings. Once she was missing no one would say a bad word.

'Simon's home backed on to Oxleas Woods just to the north, so we extended the search there, but the bad weather carried on for weeks, making the search a farce. We never found a body and evidence wasn't there. Kimberly's hair, DNA and clothing fibres found in Simon's house were explained away by their recent relationship. It shouldn't have gone to trial, really. Not guilty, seven to five.'

Darlington sighed and looked again at the recent photo, still labelled Mark White. 'It's the unsolveds you remember most vividly,' he said quietly. 'This one stuck in the public craw too. The press went to town, blaming us in equal measure for persecuting an innocent man and failing to convict a killer. Simon received death threats. His mother too. Their house was attacked. He tried to go back to college but the principal asked him to leave for the sake of the other students.

'Once the media lost interest, the brass quietly wound down our numbers until Kimberly Bates became a cold case. Simon Kirsch moved away and we lost track of him.'

Darlington looked slowly around the room, taking in all the faces one by one, as if sizing them up. Whether or not he found them wanting he kept to himself.

Stark raised a hand, keeping his eye on Darlington to avoid Harper. 'Mark White volunteered to be finger-printed and swabbed. What did he know that we don't?'

Darlington studied Stark, making him await judgement on whether his question was 'good' enough. 'He knew that, as Simon Kirsch, after the trial, he'd success-fully sued the Metropolitan Police Service for a hundred thousand pounds, a public apology, the removal of his fingerprints and DNA from the database and proof of their destruction.'

The faces around the room said it all.

'Right,' said Harper sharply. 'Thank you for your help, Neville. Whenever you're ready Detective Constable Stark will drop you off on his way home.'

'Home?' protested Fran. 'We need all hands.'

'We also need someone on tonight, and everyone knows the only thing Stark likes more than questioning his elders and betters is volunteering. Isn't that right, Constable?'

Groombridge could see Stark weighing up the odds of suc-cessful protest and stepped in, offering Neville a coffee and natter in the canteen for old times' sake, and guiding Stark out with them. 'Keep your powder dry,' he whispered.

'I'm needed here,' whispered Stark.

'Yes. You are. Tonight it seems, so get some rest. The investigation needs you alert and so do I.'

Neville made a show of not overhearing but Groom-bridge knew him too well to be fooled. Eavesdropping was just one of the lessons the old man had passed down. The retired copper was greeted warmly in the canteen by several of the older lags. He and Groombridge traded war stories for as long as seemed decent before Groombridge sent Stark to re-sign out the pool car to take Neville home.

'Harper?' said Darlington, his watery eyes suddenly boring into Groombridge. 'What the hell, Mike?'

Groombridge sighed. 'Long story.'

'I never liked him.'

'He was a half-decent DS.'

'You felt *sorry* for him, because his wife drank and laid hands on him,' said Darlington, shaking his head. 'You mistook darkness for depth. That was why you brought in that girl, what's her name?'

'DS Millhaven.'

'To plug the gaps. She's the real deal, right?'

'She is.'

Darlington leant in, keeping his voice low, but no less intent. 'So why the hell isn't *she* running the show? More to the point, why aren't *you*?'

Groombridge sipped his coffee, and told him.

'DAC Stevens?' asked Neville.

'New generation,' explained Groombridge. 'After your time.'

'Thank heaven for small mercies.'

Neville sat back, weighing the facts, as was his way. He looked a shadow of himself. Pancreatic cancer. Inoperable. Six months, tops. Hardly a fitting reward after forty years of public service, thought Groombridge bitterly.

'Well,' sighed Neville. 'And I thought *I* was in bad shape.'

Darlington seemed lost in thoughts of his own, as Stark drove. Understandable; he'd seen a ghost today, of sorts. The journey passed in silence, until they pulled up outside Darlington's immaculately kept mid-terrace in Lime Street. Stark waited for him to get out, but the old boy turned to him instead.

'Well, Detective Constable Joseph Stark, VC ... It would appear the station has a leak, the MIT is over-stretched, this case is a mess and the best copper you'll ever meet is polishing brass in a broom cupboard while one of the worst is flapping about in boots he can't fill. So, what are you going to do about it all?'

'Me, sir?'

'You, sir.'

Darlington studied him intently. Gone was the watery-eyed bag of bones. Now he was fixed by the watchful eyes of an eagle. Stark had withstood the glaring scrutiny of drill sergeants, officers, Special Forces interrogators and Fran, but only in Groombridge had he ever felt someone had so much the measure of him before now. 'My job.'

Darlington's glare cracked into a grudging smile. 'Make sure you do. All it takes for evil to flourish is that good coppers do nothing. Trust your gut, use your eyes, ears and above all your mind, and your heart will do the rest.' He nodded and got out of the car.

'Did he do it?' called Stark. 'Kirsch?'

Darlington turned. 'The jury thought not.'

'Only seven of them. What did you think?'

'That it's our job to build a case, not decide it,' replied Neville flatly, his protégé Groombridge to a tee. But then he looked at Stark and sighed deeply, his shoulders slumping. 'He was guilty all right, you could see it in his eyes; he was riddled with it. But don't take my word for it. Build a case.' He turned and walked up his short garden path without another word, an old man again, to outward appearance.

Stark sat back in his seat and listened to the engine ticking over, not sure what to think. Whatever was expected of him there was little he could accomplish banished to bed.

His phone interrupted that particular cheery thought. 'Where are you?' demanded Fran.

'Sipping cocktails on a tropical island.'

'Fancy some unpaid overtime?'

'Not really.'

'Oh, come on . . .'

'DI Harper ordered me home to sleep.'

'Justice never sleeps. And we both know you sleep even less than you follow orders, especially from Harper. Stop arguing, knock back your Sex-on-the-Beach. Susan Watts just called the incident line.'

40

Fran played Stark the audio file from her phone as he drove. A tremulous voice, but unapologetic, Susan explained who she was, her historic connection to Simon Kirsch. She had been watching the lunchtime news in the staffroom at school when she'd heard his name.

The call receiver at HQ treated her with courtesy, expressing no doubts and patiently making note of the key details. Miles away in Greenwich the incident line feed flagged the call with key words: *subject connection, stalking, potential sighting*. It was nice when things worked. When Fran called her back Susan asked what would be done and quickly grew emotional. She couldn't take the afternoon classes and was too scared to go home. Then she burst into tears.

That was why Fran had called Stark.

She'd be the first to admit, to herself only of course, that she lacked the temperament for hand-holding. And while Stark was buttoned up tighter than a drum, he had on more than one occasion demonstrated an inexplicable calming effect on the distressed. The exact opposite of his effect on Harper, in fact.

Stark listened to the recording without comment, driving like a country bumpkin as usual. He avoided driving when possible; his dodgy hip, she suspected. Consequently he hadn't adjusted to London's make-it-their-problem school of road sharing. Fran tried not to huff or tut.

The receptionist showed them to the school chapel. The woman inside glanced up from prayer as they entered. Fran shared a look with Stark. There was no mistaking the woman from the photograph in Kirsch's gym locker. Not Mark White's girlfriend, but Simon Kirsch's first victim.

She looked slightly older in person, in her early forties perhaps, more worry lines. Pretty, willowy and blonde. No wedding ring or sign of one recently removed. Susan had told the hotline she lived alone. The small gold crucifix around her neck might put some off, but surely there was a nice God-bothering man to sweep this God-bothering woman off her dainty feet?

'Was it you I spoke with on the phone?' she asked.

Fran nodded. 'DS Millhaven. This is DC Stark. Thank you for calling the hotline, Miss Watts. We know who you are. We have reason to think our suspect and Simon Kirsch are one and the same.'

Susan was already nodding firmly. 'I knew the moment I heard his name on the radio. I've felt him, for months now, cold shivers down my spine. I know what it feels like to be followed, watched.'

'You've seen him?'

'Glimpses. Shadows.'

'Nothing concrete, actionable?'

Susan's face tightened. 'He's had a lot of practice.'

'Months, you say?'

She removed a school exercise book from a zipped sub-compartment of her bulging satchel, handling it as if it made her flesh creep. 'They told me to keep a log. Back in 1988, for all the good it did. He was never punished. I think that's why I kept it; because it was never over. I don't know whether he killed poor Kimberly Bates, but he was never punished for what he did to me. And then . . .' She opened the book to show them new entries, dating back half a year.

Stark photographed the recent pages for timings and locations. 'From what I understand he received quite a severe punishment from two of our kind.'

Susan Watts flushed. Shame, perhaps, for unchristian thoughts. 'Constables Oats and Ferry. They were very kind to me, but I didn't ask them to do that. I wish they hadn't.'

'It can't have helped, with bringing charges for stalking,' commented Fran.

'There were never going to be charges,' replied Susan. 'Simon was too careful.'

'What can you tell us about him?' asked Stark.

'Quiet. Slow. Not lacking intelligence, just thoughtful, pensive. Passionate underneath. Kind, at least that's how you think he is. But . . .' She trailed off. 'It was my fault. I should've realized. I felt a fool after, as if everyone could see it but me. What must they have thought . . .' She shook her head. 'I've never lived it down. Even now, twenty years on. It gets passed down year on year, and the kids I taught have kids at the school. I'm the teacher who had sex with a pupil . . . I didn't, of course,' she added hurriedly. 'But that's what they whisper. Did she really? Would she again? The head teacher encouraged me to leave, try another school. He left himself, after a while. I've seen so many come and go. They made me head of department eventually, but no further. I stayed anyway. I felt a duty . . .' Suddenly she broke into sobs. 'Why?' she moaned. 'Why is this happening again? What does he want after all this time?'

Fran had no answers. It was the best she could do not to tap her foot impatiently while the woman pulled herself together. Fran had grown up with four brothers, and learned early to stand her ground and never let them see you cry.

Stark passed Susan a tissue from somewhere and the woman murmured thanks and forced a limp smile. She blew her nose, wetly. 'I'm sorry,' sniffed Susan, then blew her nose again, red-eyed, weary and somewhat less attractive than Fran's initial assessment. 'I just can't believe he's back.'

'Assuming he ever left,' said Fran aloud, immediately regretting it.

'You mentioned a break-in at the school . . . ?' Stark swooped in with a change of subject.

Susan nodded. 'About six months ago. Our tiny collection of sporting silverware was stolen and the school office ransacked, the small cash float stolen. The police wrote it off as a simple burglary.'

'You think otherwise?' asked Stark, not mentioning the stolen staff photo.

'The silverware was found abandoned. I'd already begun getting the creeps, here, catching glimpses. But after the break-in it started outside my flat too. It's exactly what he did before, when all this first began. Simon didn't know where I lived. I used to catch a bus and I saw him trying to follow me home on his bicycle. Then he was caught in the school office, "just looking around", passed off as just another of his odd misbehaviours. But the next day I saw him outside my flat. When things got bad I moved back to my parents'. Not long after, he showed up there too. But the police couldn't prove anything,' she said bitterly.

Fran had seen too many frustrated victims in her career. 'All I can tell you is that Simon is in real trouble now. I can't confirm or deny the media speculation, but when we catch him he'll face firearms and ABH charges. The witnesses don't get more credible. He won't get bail and he *will* go to prison.'

Susan nodded but looked no less miserable. 'I've put my flat on the market. Even if you catch him, I can't bear the fact that he knows where I am again, that he's been there, watching. It doesn't stop. It never stops. Even knowing he was gone, for twenty years. Even if you lock him up. The fear never leaves you. That's what he did. He stole my life.'

'Is there somewhere you might stay for a few days? Just until we catch him?'

Now Susan looked worried. 'You think . . . ? Well, yes, my friend. She's on holiday. I've got the keys to water her plants. I could text her.'

'I'm sure she won't mind,' Fran said soothingly, trying for reassuring. 'How about we take you home for a few things and drop you round there now?'

Susan's modest flat in an unfashionable area seemed a snapshot of her life. Nicely furnished and un-encroached by slovenly male disorder. A single cleaned plate, cutlery and wine glass sat on the drainer. Fran lived alone too, but it wasn't just Susan's overt Christian paraphernalia that marked them apart. There were hardly any family photos, no souvenirs of travel, no knick-knacks or bric-a-brac, little sign of life lived. It reminded Stark too much of his own flat before Kelly, and after.

She packed a large bag and a box of food and they

followed her little red Nissan to her friend's Edwardian terrace a few miles away – a divorcee, rooms a-clutter with remnants of offspring flown the nest. Stark scanned the mirrors all the way. They saw her inside, checked the windows and doors to reassure her it was safe, and then scared the crap out of her by telling her to be on the look-out for a black off-road motorcycle or other signs of being followed.

'What do you think?' asked Fran, staring at the house and surroundings.

'We should sit an unmarked car here.'

Fran nodded. They'd already told Susan they'd ask uniform to patrol the street. 'I'll ask. Keys . . .' She held out her hand, impatience at his passive driving outweighing her dislike of the station's pool cars.

She answered her phone as she drove, one-handed, basking in the glow of Stark's silent disapproval. 'DS Millhaven.'

'Marcus Turner,' said Marcus, who for a man of science held a perversely Luddite view on smartphone technologies like caller ID. 'Bad time? Should I call back?'

'No, go ahead.'

'Are you driving?'

'No comment. How can I help?' she replied tersely.

'Okay, well in that spirit of plausible deniability, by swearing never to repeat anything I'm about to tell you.'

'I'm intrigued.'

'But are you discreet?'

'Depends.'

'Fair enough. Were you aware that Simon Kirsch's biometrics were destroyed after his acquittal?'

'Yes.'

'Good. Then should anyone ever ask you whether a DNA sample was overlooked at the time, retrieved many years later, sequenced anonymously and compared with a recent sample from Mark White, you would be perfectly justified in denying all knowledge?'

Fran let this sink in. 'Entirely.'

'Jolly good. Then, apropos of nothing, were one attempting to prove that Mark White was indeed Simon Kirsch, one would not be wasting one's time. Entirely inadmissible, of course.'

Fran grinned. 'How deliciously unethical of you.'

'Quite the opposite, I'm afraid.'

'Don't spoil it. You're a bad man.'

'Perhaps I've just spent too much time in the wrong company. Till next time . . .' He rang off.

Fran tutted. For someone so laid back, Marcus had an annoying ability to get the last word in.

Stark scratched his stubbly chin. 'Bad man?'

Fran tucked the phone into her pocket. 'Is there any other kind?'

'Oh, I don't know. I thought Beefcake Dave was delightful.'

'Careful . . . I'm having to work quite hard on my not-punching-someone skills today.'

Stark nodded and stifled a yawn.

'Come on, princess, I'll drop you home. Get yourself fresh; you're back on duty at seven.'

He didn't complain. He never did. He hadn't even asked why she wanted him for these little excursions instead of Dixon or Williams. Perhaps he just knew he was better, or perhaps he was past caring. Much as his quiet self-assurance drove her crazy, Fran had a horrible feeling it was more the latter recently, and her attempts to snap him out of it pinged off his armour like bullets off a tank. Christ, even his maddening military metaphors were rubbing off on her.

41

Stark grabbed a late lunch, an even later shower, a few hours' sleep and made it into the office in time for the evening handover. Dixon and Williams had made a start on sifting the case files for information about Simon Kirsch. They now sat in a series of piles on Stark's previously ordered desk. Fran had just received a preliminary report on Chase Security's finances from the forensic accountants and was failing to interest Harper in it. Taking it from her outstretched hand he dropped it on to her desk with a flourish, clapped his hands together in anticipatory satisfaction and launched into a grand show of dragging everyone to the pub for Friday drinks, even offering to buy the first round.

Stark felt sure some of the bonhomie was for his benefit but was more than happy to miss out. If leaving hospital with a concussion was foolish, going out drinking afterwards put that in the shade.

Fran obviously didn't fancy a Friday evening of fun and frivolity with the lording prick either, and mumbled her apologies.

'Got a better offer, have we?' scoffed Harper, for the crowd.

'That wouldn't be too hard,' said Fran.

Harper grinned, thinking he'd struck a nerve. 'Hot date, is it? I hope he knows what he's letting himself in for.'

She didn't rise to the bait, just snatched up her jacket

and left, ignoring his amusement. Stark watched in sadness. Hot date or otherwise, before Harper's promotion she'd have cut him down to size for remarks like that. Both Williams and Dixon gave Stark the looks of condemned men as they filed out after Harper. They'd been at the coalface since the early hours, but neither would feel they could slip off and leave the other.

Alone, Stark felt his tension dissipate. The incident number on the TV was being run from one of the private firms, with live links to the relevant teams. He kept an eye on the feed as he read through the progress made by the others, but in truth the hunt for Simon Kirsch was out of his hands. The moment Kirsch pulled a Taser this became a uniform operation, with CID reduced to intel support. Armed response teams were patrolling sectors, waiting for the call to action. Uniforms, downstairs, were following up calls from all the well-intentioned members of the public who thought Kirsch looked like so-and-so down the street.

This was why Harper and the team could take some R'n'R, and why Stark jumped when he sensed someone enter stealthily behind him. He spun round to find Pensol hovering uncertainly just inside the doorway with a steaming mug, his start making her spill some on her hand with a yelp.

'Sorry,' she said, sucking scalding liquid from her fingers, looking around for somewhere to put the dripping mug. 'I didn't mean to sneak up. You were sitting so still I thought you were . . . asleep, but of course not, sorry.' She offered the mug apologetically. 'Constable Peters said you liked two sugars?' Her uncertainty betrayed either wise rookie scepticism or personal distaste. Two sugars was a hangover from army days where the coffee was crap, or desert hospitality where the tea was strong. He should probably cut down but, as now, more serious issues always took precedence.

He took the mug from her with a simple thank you and smile, hoping she'd take both and withdraw.

Instead, she hesitated. 'She sent me up to see if you needed any help?'

Undoubtedly, but that was Doc Hazel's job, thought Stark, irritated that Peters was trying her hand again.

Pensol was easy on the eye, there was no denying it. There had to be plenty of young lads here who would jump at the chance. Why Peters thought Stark any more suitable was a sign of how poorly she knew him – or how little he'd let her. Stark sighed inside, wishing the world wasn't so. He should send this girl on her way again but he was too tired to do it nicely, and his conscience still pricked him over his recent bluntness. 'Sure, thanks.' He managed a smile.

Pensol flashed pearly whites and sat down. She wore a subtle perfume: roses, sweet and uncomplicated – a world away from Kelly's intoxicating jasmine, but warm, inviting.

Stark shook the thought from his head.

'What are you watching?' she asked.

'Last interview with Mark White aka Simon Kirsch.' Stark reset it to the beginning and pressed play. He'd already watched it twice, curious at Kirsch's sudden explosion. Harper had obviously whispered something incendiary.

'Mind if I . . . ?' Pensol leant in and rewound a little and watched the explosion again. And then again. 'Hmm,' she said, leaning back.

'What?'

She looked hesitant. 'It's what DI Harper says . . .' Stark must have looked confused, so she went on. 'I'm not sure. My sign is good but my lip-reading isn't so hot.'

'You can lip-read?'

'A bit. Not as well as my brother. We practise together for giggles. He's profoundly deaf.'

'You know what DI Harper whispered?'

She looked anxious now, reticent. 'I'm not sure.'

'But you think . . . ?'

'I think he whispers, "I'm going to nail you. Even if I have to . . . *something* . . . the nails . . . make . . . ? *Fabricate.*"'

Well, that might do it, thought Stark, sitting back and letting the implications sink in. Innocent or guilty, Simon Kirsch had suffered overzealous police attentions before. Had Harper triggered old fears?

Up until that moment Mark White had seemed calm, controlled. Now they knew he was really Simon Kirsch that seemed . . . worryingly practised; the unconscious projection of a pathological fantasist or the calculating ease of a chilling psychopath, or both.

'Hope I'm not interrupting,' said Peters, sticking her head round the door with a smile that said the opposite, 'but there's a Mr Bates at the front desk asking for DS Millhaven. I told him she's not here but he's not budging.'

Stark frowned. 'Not *Brian* Bates?'

'You know him?'

Stark sighed. 'I'll come down.'

42

Kimberly Bates' father was older than he looked on the press cutting upstairs; twenty years and a broken heart older. A short man in his sixties, grey, balding and portly; a man worn down and etched with grief.

Stark showed him to the interview room. Not with a one-way mirror and recording equipment, but the one with plastic flowers and pastel furnishings, where they broke the news. This man's news had broken twenty years ago and it was still breaking every morning, those waking moments of blissful forgetfulness followed by crushing remembrance. Stark offered him tea and phoned upstairs. Thankfully Groombridge was also uninvited to Harper's party, or had the authority to decline.

Brian Bates stood as Groombridge entered, jerking his head in a deferential, apologetic nod. If he'd brought a cloth cap he might have wrung it anxiously in his hands.

Groombridge introduced himself.

'You're in charge, then?' asked Bates. 'I saw the girl on the telly, Detective Sergeant Millhaven.'

'She works for me. Won't you sit?'

Bates sized him up. There was a shrewdness in his eyes as he took his seat. 'How old are you, Inspector?'

Groombridge nodded. 'Old enough, Mr Bates, to remember. I was a newly minted constable back then, but I remember.'

Bates shook his head. '*I* remember, Inspector. You may

recall bits and pieces but I remember, day in, day out. I remember the last words she spoke to me as she left the house that morning. I remember the green nail polish and awful make-up she was wearing. I remember that ridiculous perm and the words I didn't say about what she was wearing. I remember the way she laughed like nothing mattered. *I* remember.'

'I'm sorry for your loss,' said Groombridge.

Bates huffed a laugh, bitter and tired. 'I remember the first time one of you lot said that to me too. Days of "don't give up hope", then "prepare yourself for the worst", and then finally "I'm sorry for your loss". They teach you those at police school, I expect.'

'Yes.'

Bates smiled thinly and pulled himself a little straighter in his chair. 'It's him, is it? Simon Kirsch?'

'I think so. I didn't see it at first. It was my old sergeant who spotted the resemblance.'

'I saw it,' said Bates. 'Only today. My sister called to say they were talking about it on the news. I don't watch the news. One tragedy heaped upon another like snow, one bitter blizzard after another. How can a man hold on to his own tragedy in such a world? I don't dare watch it. But Anne called, so I switched it on as soon as I got home from work and saw him, and I knew . . . The boy that took my –'

He stopped. He didn't choke up or break down; he just stopped, looking down with no other outward sign of the torment that rent his insides.

'Took my Kim,' he concluded quietly.

He raised his head and looked them both in the eye. 'No one should have to bury their child. It's not natural, not fair. It's "the worst possible thing", they say.' Bates shook his head solemnly. 'It's not. The worst possible thing in the world . . . is not having your child to bury.'

He stared at them, expressionless, the fires of hell burning behind his eyes. 'We never held a funeral, did you know that?'

'No.'

'My wife begged me. They all did. A funeral . . .' He shook his head. 'With an empty coffin? I don't understand why people do it.'

Groombridge shrugged with his eyes. What could anyone say?

Stark knew the value of a funeral. He had buried his father when he was just eleven. Comrades had gone into the ground while he was still abroad fighting or on his back in hospital unable to attend, unable to say goodbye, to say sorry. He'd stood to attention as flag-draped coffins were bugled aboard transport planes, many containing less of the occupant than nature had given. But who hadn't seen the funerals of missing children on the news and wondered how anyone could put themselves through it – a coffin containing nothing more than horror and sorrow and the futile hope of closure?

'Don't get me wrong,' said Bates. 'She's gone; I accepted that a long time ago. Hope leaches out of you day by day, thought by treacherous thought, until there's little or nothing left inside. In the end they held a *service of remembrance*,' he said, as if the words were ashes in his mouth. 'Put up a plaque in the cemetery. I went. Didn't speak, but I listened. Listened to my wife's heart dying word by word. Poor Sandra. She went to her own grave five years later. She wished it was sooner. Who can blame her? You can't live without a heart.'

He looked at them. 'But *I* still have a heart. I'm like that bloke in hell having his liver pecked out every day by some giant bird. My heart is ripped out every day but it won't die, *I* won't die. Not before I bury my child.'

The last words came out with a quiet fierceness long in the forging. His eyes were moist, but no tears fell. Stark wondered at the strength of the man. It seemed to be the week for it: Ron Cooper, gasping against the consequences of a lifelong habit but still a copper to his core. Neville Darlington, shrunken by cancer's callous two fingers that would rob him of the retirement with his wife that he'd earned, still giving of his precious time. And now Brian Bates, carrying twenty years of grief in nothing but the bitter hope that his only child would be found long dead. Three old men, defiant of their lot, calling out for justice in the howling storm. Courage incarnate.

'I'm sorry.' Bates stood, suddenly back to the worn-down man who'd entered the room. 'I'm sorry. I don't talk about this any more. Not to anyone. Not for years.'

'Some things are better for talking,' said Stark. He felt compelled to speak, though the words did not come easily. 'Some are not.'

Bates looked at him long and hard, and nodded. 'Make him tell you where my daughter is.' His hands were curled into fists, his quiet voice rigid. 'When you find him. Make him tell you.'

43

Brian Bates refused Stark's offer of a lift home. He'd little left but pride and, as he'd reminded them, they had work to do. The two detectives stood on the station stoop watching him walk slowly away down Royal Hill to catch the first of three buses. He still lived in the same house. The house where he'd raised and lost a daughter, and then a wife.

'Well,' said Groombridge. 'If ever we needed reminding of our triumphs and failures . . .'

'You promised him,' said Stark.

There was no accusation in his voice that Groombridge could discern. 'You think I should've given him some anodyne promise to "try"?'

'You don't think the truth serves best?'

'Sometimes.' Groombridge nodded to the departing figure. 'He knows the truth. He came here to make sure we did.'

'If Kirsch did kill Kimberly Bates, he's unlikely to confess after twenty years.'

'You'll just have to dangle him from the roof,' said Groombridge, glancing at Stark. It was exactly the kind of thing Stark *might* do. Or perhaps it was the kind of thing he would fight to prevent someone doing. After two years Groombridge often felt he was no nearer to understanding the young man. Perhaps he should stop trying. People weren't clockwork, ticking to order; surely he'd been a policeman long enough to know that.

'If DI Harper doesn't first,' replied Stark.

They both smiled at that, but Groombridge couldn't escape the sadness inside. An unsolved murder was like a cancer, eating away at you. Kimberly Bates was his first, but of all those subsequent she remained the only one they'd never even found. Lucky perhaps. He and Alice had tried for children but luck worked both ways. Three miscarriages was enough. If you can't make a life you build yourself a different life. He could only imagine what it must be like to lose a child you've held, raised, but this . . . Bad enough not to know *who* or *why*, but to never even find out *what* had happened – that was the worst. He let out a deep sigh. 'They don't teach us this.'

'No,' agreed Stark and they stood in silence for a moment. 'The *News of the World*?'

An abrupt change of subject. Groombridge pursed his lips. 'Could just be they spotted the resemblance like we did.'

Neither of them believed that. 'There is another possibility . . .' Groombridge told Stark about a broader phone hacking investigation. 'Just high-level rumour. Strictest confidence,' he added needlessly; Stark recognized a need-to-know conversation when he heard one and was smart enough to understand that such an investigation stood little chance if people found out about it.

The young DC nodded thoughtfully, probably weighing up which possibility would be more disturbing: a few bent coppers or a bent press. Groombridge couldn't decide either.

'He wants your office,' Stark said suddenly, as if the words were escaping captivity. 'For keeps.'

'DI Harper?' Groombridge raised his eyebrows. From most people this might be an uncomfortable breach of etiquette; from Stark it was a shocking sign of how desperate he must feel beneath that stone-faced stoicism.

Though surely he could not think it needed saying? Harper had insisted on making a second press statement during the afternoon, having removed the bandage to show off the taped dressing on his bloodied brow. He'd been a lot less circumspect about the possible link between White and Kirsch, and used the word 'suspect' rather than 'person of interest', followed by 'extremely dangerous', 'armed' and 'hunt down'. Grandstanding of the worst kind. Fran thought she was bad at press statements, that Harper was better. She had too little confidence and he too much. 'Are we talking man-to-man now, Joseph?'

Stark winced faintly.

'He can have it,' joked Groombridge. 'I'm getting quite fond of my little room with its lack of view. It's amazing the amount of work you can get done removed from the distractions of actual policing.'

Stark's face creased with amusement, momentarily, then reset to default.

'You look tired,' commented Groombridge, 'since we're talking man-to-man.'

Stark gave a faint shrug. 'Who isn't?'

Who indeed? thought Groombridge. 'I heard about you and Kelly. I hope it wasn't the job.'

'It wasn't.'

'Still, I'm sorry.'

'These things happen.'

Some leaves danced a short-lived merry reel in the street and Stark looked thoughtfully up at the cloudy night sky, as if sniffing the air. 'Storm's coming,' he declared quietly.

Groombridge glanced up. If anything it was an oddly windless night but his weather-sense wasn't what it had been; too many years away from the beat. And now he'd allowed himself to be dragged from investigation too. The storm never really stopped, and he was rapidly becoming less and less use in it.

He could ask if Stark was okay, truly, whether he needed some personal time, but if such questions would be an uncomfortable breach of etiquette man-to-man, to Stark they would be a shocking intrusion. He sensed the moment slipping away. Rare between menfolk, rarer still with those such as Stark – if such there were.

They watched the distant figure of Brian Bates turn the corner from sight. Then words came quietly from Stark as if he were speaking only to himself. 'The woods are lovely, dark and deep, but I have promises to keep, and miles to go before I sleep . . . and miles to go before I sleep.'

Groombridge glanced sideways at him. You grew accustomed to the years in his voice and too easily forgot whence they came; a man in his twenties, honed in ways no man should care to be, scarred and saddened. Groombridge was glad he hadn't asked more. What more, in the end, could one offer? Poetry was not something he had much knowledge of but in the context of the moment the words spoke to him of mourning, duty and peace deferred. Were they for Stark or Brian Bates? he wondered. Or both?

Far to the north, silent lightning lit the sky.

Groombridge bid Stark a good night, with no discernible irony, and left him to his vigil.

There were no credible sightings of Kirsch over the next few hours. CO19 remained on standby and armed response cars were still stopping black motorbikes, but as midnight came and went the incident line feed slowed and little noteworthy disturbed Stark's boredom and solitude.

Pensol had worked on the files in his absence, marking pages with Post-it notes for his attention in neat, feminine handwriting. Stark half expected the I's to be dotted with little hearts. He went back over them, telling himself he was being thorough, and not just patronizing. Christ, he felt old. She'd done a good job. Sharp as well as pretty. He kept at it, propping himself up with coffee and snacks. Taking a break when the headache nagged at him to give in and sleep.

Outside, the rising wind moaned and lightning forked intermittently. Stark automatically counted seconds until thunder rattled the windows, tracking the storm. He'd stood guard in worse but was no less glad to be indoors. Peters and Pensol were out there somewhere. Stark was glad of that too, and barely ashamed of it.

He sighed and closed his eyes.

The warm darkness reached around to fold him in its embrace ... and he snapped his eyes open, shaking off the drowse angrily. Sleeping at his post may no longer result in a court martial, but that wasn't the point.

To distract himself he indulged his curiosity and looked at Brian Bates' house on Street View. A humble mid-terrace in good repair, like Neville Darlington's but with the garden paved over. Stark used the online map to trace the route to Simon Kirsch's childhood home. The houses in Crookston Road were all much of a muchness, except the one Stark was looking for. While the others had cars in the drive, painted front doors and signs of habitation, the old Kirsch house was boarded up. Extensive graffiti, overgrown front garden and general decay suggested it had been so for some time. Strange.

Using the Met Police account, Stark checked the Land

Registry details. The house was owned by one Mrs M. Larson.

Larson? Why did that ring a bell? He frowned at the stack of files, staring through it as if the answer would come into focus. It didn't, and it was several more hours before he found a piece of paper that justified his nagging sense that he knew the name. The transcript of the first police interview of Simon's mother, Miriam Kirsch, maiden name – Larson.

She still owned the house?

It was clear no one lived there. The team had enjoyed no luck tracing her so far. Presumably they'd tried her maiden name? Stark left a note on Fran's desk all the same.

The phone next to Stark rang. More good news, no doubt.

'That you, sweetie?' asked Maggie. Even the indisputable queen of the control room had to pull her share of nights. Her team of civilians hadn't escaped the belt-tightening.

'In the flesh.'

'Ooh,' she made her voice quiver the way only she could.

'And what can I do for you on this dark and lonely night, Maggie?'

'I'll get back to you on that, but right now you need to get downstairs. There's a break-in underway at the Chases' house.'

44

Stark's mind raced all the way there, holding on tight in the back of a uniform car as it forged through the traffic and weather under blues and twos. This could just be some chancer taking advantage of a publicized empty property, but it might also be the killer proving the old adage by returning to the scene.

He found the Chases' home aglow with blue lights for the second time in as many weeks. The house alarm was silent, but a car alarm was sounding from inside the garage, the noise barely audible over the howling wind and lashing rain. The orange hazard lights were visible through the high gable porthole.

Lightning strobed the diagonal rain, momentarily still in the eye, thunder following within a second. Stark's jacket kept his core dry, but his trousers and shoes were soaked within seconds of stepping from the car and he had to grip the edge of his hood to keep it in place. 'Intruder?' he called to the armed response team, emerging from the side of the garage.

'No sign,' barked their sergeant. 'We're patrolling surrounding streets but there's no chance of getting the ghetto birds up in this shit.' His tone suggested that if he was out in it at one in the morning, so should everyone else be. But helicopters, storms and built-up areas were a terrible combination.

Stark looked around for someone more helpful and singled out Ptolemy on the perimeter talking into his radio. 'What have we got?'

'Sod all so far,' replied Ptolemy, raising his voice over the ceaseless hiss of the rain.

'Witnesses? Who called it in?'

'Just trying to get that from control.'

Stark looked around and picked out a diminutive figure standing just beyond the reach of the lights. The intruder? Ptolemy followed his eye, but the figure didn't back away as they approached.

Closer, Stark recognized him. The wing commander. The Chases' neighbour.

'Evening,' said the little man, standing un-hunched in the driving rain in his long coat and flat cap. 'Was wondering when one of you would spare the time.'

'Did you call this in?'

The old man held up a very basic mobile phone. 'Grandson got it for me. Just about induce it to place a call but damned thing goes to gobbledygook if I try one of those text thingies,' he declared in clipped stiff upper lip. 'Anyway, heard the alarm and stepped out for a spot of recon. Gate was open, if you see what I mean; intruder had the code. In and out quickly, not much more than a couple of minutes from triggering the alarm. It was that fella you're after, the gardener.'

'You saw him?'

'Had his helmet on, but you can't fool the old pattern recognition,' replied the old man, tapping beside one eye. 'Recognized the motorcycle too. Noisy brute.'

'You didn't mention a bike when we first talked,' said Stark.

The old man shrugged. 'You were asking about gardening. He'd left it parked round the corner this time, but I followed him.'

Stark nodded. Sound evasion practice – park the vehicle out of sight so you can start it up unobserved after your initial getaway. It would explain how he'd evaded police after Tasering Harper. 'Did you get the licence plate?'

The old boy shook his head. 'Had it blacked out. Can't remember it from before, I'm afraid. Better on aircraft tail numbers.'

Ptolemy turned away to speak into his radio, but it was too late. Over twenty minutes had elapsed since the initial call. If Kirsch was on a bike, he could be halfway across London.

'Sorry I couldn't be more help,' said the wing commander. 'Might've taken him on if I was a year or two younger, but discretion is the better part and all that.' There was a glint in his eye that said he'd have relished the prospect in his time.

Stark thanked him profusely all the same, and sent him off out of the rain with a constable to take his statement.

Waiting for SOCO was interminable. But at least they silenced the alarm.

Stark and Ptolemy were eventually shown inside.

The side gate was open. Not forced. Same for the door from the garden into the spacious double garage. Both hefty locks. As part-time gardener, Kirsch aka Mark White may have had keys.

The Mercedes driver-side window was smashed, the boot open.

The scene-of-crime manager shone his torch inside.

The glove compartment hung open, the fusebox exposed, the same for the fusebox behind the passenger seat. Fuses had been pulled out of both. Stark had no idea whether the alarm could be disabled this way, but the intruder either hadn't known or hadn't bothered. If Stark had to guess, he'd say they'd simply pulled those fuses necessary to open the boot. The boot floor liner was open. The space-saver spare was there, and the pristine tools. Nothing missing. Or nothing obvious.

The SOCM pointed. 'There.'

Stark crouched over something on the floor. A neoprene fabric pouch with a zip, too small for a laptop. There was a logo on it. A common brand of portable USB hard drive. But Stark had seen one like this before, and just as empty . . . among the scattered debris near Mary Chase's body on the night of the killings. Which Harper had shown Kirsch a photo of . . .

'Your phone's ringing,' said Ptolemy.

Stark fished it out. Four missed calls. Stark had asked Maggie to call Fran, but in the car and then rain he'd not heard her call back. 'Sarge.'

'About time!' she cried. 'If you wake someone in the middle of the night, it's only polite to take their bloody call back. Where are you?'

'The Chases' garage.'

'Kirsch?'

'Looks like . . . But long gone.'

'Anyone dead?'

'Nope.'

'Anything missing?'

Stark relayed the little he knew.

'Right then,' replied Fran. 'I'm going back to bed. Leave your report on my desk before you clock off. Are you wet?'

'What?'

'Wet. It's pouring with rain outside.'

'I'm aware of that.'

'So are you wet?'

'Very.'

'And cold?'

'That too.'

'Good.' She hung up. From anyone else it would have sounded caustic, but Stark knew it was her way of monitoring his welfare.

The thought was shattered by the sound of shouting outside. Car doors and engines, sirens and screeching tyres.

'*Sarge!*' A constable beckoned frantically to Ptolemy from the doorway. 'Traffic officer down. Stopped a bike and got Tasered. Ambulance en route but chatter says he's not breathing.'

45

The motorcycle officer didn't make it.

Just before the latest alert had gone out he'd pulled over a speeding bike with blacked-out plates, and got Tasered for his trouble. Fingers would be pointed about why he'd not alerted Armed Response. Perhaps he'd forgotten about the manhunt.

The next vehicle to the scene had found him not breathing. Heart failure, most likely. Or head injury from falling, though he was wearing his helmet. Taser deaths were always the subject of intense scrutiny. Bottom line – a cop was dead and Simon Kirsch was prime suspect.

Stark was back at the station when Fran arrived. The uniform floor was abuzz, seething with muttered anger, as directionless as it was useless. Stark recognized that from operational patrols: when a soldier was killed else-where, it hit the base hard.

He looked around, waiting for someone to take charge. The sergeants were doing their bit, cooling heads, lifting chins, but these situations needed leadership; someone to step up and channel anger into something productive.

Instead, Harper turned up, demanding a briefing, pos-turing and putting backs up.

Dixon and Williams arrived and the MIT team spent the next few hours retracing Kirsch's life for some clue to his current hideout or ownership of a motorbike. Harper spotted Stark flagging and berated him openly.

Stark was tired enough to hate the man. More pointless emotion.

Where the hell was the real guv'nor?

As if his prayer had been heard, the word went round for everyone to gather in the canteen. Groombridge and Cox stood at one end with Harper, DI Graham from CID and the uniform inspector, Cartwright. Everyone else waited in hushed impatience. Harper opened his mouth to speak but Groombridge gently touched his arm and Cox stepped up.

'Right. As you all know, Constable Butler, a long-serving officer of the motorbike section, was fatally injured a few hours ago. His family are being informed as we speak. We'll give a press conference at eight. A Taser deployment tag recovered from the scene matches that found after the Tasering of DI Harper two nights ago, by Simon Kirsch, aka Mark White.'

A ripple of muttered curses rose and Cox held up a hand for silence.

'This of course raises Simon Kirsch from person of interest to prime suspect –'

'To cop-killer,' called out an angry voice and the muttering rose again. The station was tinder dry and sparking.

Cox nodded, but his firm gaze soon brought about quiet. For all his projected demeanour of moustache-puffing bluster, Stark had long suspected Cox was a proper officer. 'A cop-killer is still an innocent man until the courts have proved otherwise. I expect every person here to exercise steely determination and professionalism in bringing that about. I want Kirsch in a cell without a mark on him a barrister could use to get him off . . . understand?'

There were nods and muttered assent.

'Good. Now do Royal Hill nick proud for Butler's sake.'

As the gathering broke up, Groombridge picked out Stark and beckoned him aside. 'Another long night.'

'Guv.'

'You should get some rest.'

'Yes, Guv.'

Groombridge smiled faintly at his error. 'That's an *order*, Detective Constable. Go home. Get some sleep.' He held up a hand to head off Stark's protest. 'I'm sure Fran will call you if we get a lead, or the whim takes her.'

Stark clamped his jaw shut, picked up his coat and left, conscious of Groombridge's eyes following him.

In the corridor he passed Harper. 'Where are you going?'

'DCI Groombridge told me to get some kip.'

Harper nodded approvingly. 'Good. The roster still says you're off all weekend. See you Monday.'

The word *but* was almost out of Stark's mouth, but he swallowed it.

Harper paused, as if daring him, then turned away.

On his way out of the building Stark passed a Deputy Assistant Commissioner with a cold expression striding in. For an officer that senior to be way out here in the early hours, toys were about to leave the pram, and Stark was suddenly glad to be leaving.

Ptolemy dropped Stark off on his way home to his family.

Stark was pulling out keys when footsteps hurried up behind him in the dim pre-dawn light.

He swung around, fists curled, freezing his attacker in their tracks.

A girl, pretty despite sharp features. Not nearly as scared as she should be.

She regained her composure first, thrusting her phone at him, flash-on for filming, shielding it from the rain with her other hand. 'Detective Constable Stark. Is it true that the killing of your fellow police officer is linked to the recent murders of Thomas and Mary Chase and Carlton Savage?'

Stark was still fighting for control, scanning beyond her – vehicles, windows, rooftops; eyes darting, the adrenaline-crazed creature inside writhing for release. Gritting teeth, he turned away, fumbling his key into the lock.

'Do the police suspect Simon Kirsch for all *four* killings and will you pursue him all the harder now a cop has been slain?'

Stark froze. 'The police in this country don't place higher value on our own lives than those of the public,' he growled, unable to keep this most basic point behind his teeth.

'Did you know Traffic Officer Butler personally?'

He turned on her sharply, plucked the phone from her hand and switched it off. 'Where did you get that name?' he demanded, his intensity causing her to flinch. She was young, a junior reporter sent to doorstep a junior cop, for all he knew on her first assignment, but that was no excuse. 'Who told you?'

'No one,' she protested, confused. 'It's online. The news channels have had it for twenty minutes,' she explained, as if amazed he didn't know; as if twenty minutes didn't make it old news in *her* century.

That didn't mean there was no leak. Only that whoever it was wasn't stupid enough to divulge Butler's name before his family was informed, or their paymaster wasn't stupid enough to run it.

The reporter took her phone back, disapprovingly.

Suddenly everything fell into place.

Stark could scarcely believe his eyes.

Her phone cover. Her face. Her sturdy coat, waterproof, shaped for biking. Red curls whipping in the wind. There was a dark-blue moped parked up the street. The cute girl from the gym tour, and outside. And outside Chase Security on day two!

'You've been following me!' He didn't wait for her to deny it. 'Was it you? Taking shots of suspects, crucifying them in the media?'

The girl looked appalled. 'That's not me –'

'What about Mary Chase's pregnancy? Was that fair game too?'

'I wouldn't –'

'Wouldn't what?' Stark interrupted again. 'Follow me? Film me through fences? Blag your way into my gym? Hide in the shadows across the street,' he growled, pointing to the alley. She flushed guiltily. Shit, he thought, suddenly remembering the moped outside the hospital. Dark blue. Had she trailed him to his shrink too?

'It's a personal piece; that's all,' she insisted. 'I'm not really on the criminal case. I'm on you.'

'Me?'

'A follow-up piece, to Remembrance Sunday. But it just took off. The war hero, plunging straight from the Cenotaph into a bloody double murder. The public will love it!'

She fished out a card. Gwen Maddox. Freelance.

Stark ignored it. 'This isn't some second-rate docudrama. These are real people.'

'And so are you,' she replied. 'That's the point.'

'I am. *And it is,*' he stated, pointedly.

The point made no visible impression on her dense-ness. '*Right.* And real people in the street want to know who you really are. How you do it. What makes you face danger and death and how you cope, live, unwind.'

'And what if I want all those people, you included, to mind their own business . . . ?'

Her face displayed a total failure in comprehension. She probably had hordes of online friends and followers and thought 'likes' lent her puerile utterances meaning. She thought opinions mattered more than deeds. 'But this is your chance to tell your side of everything,' she ploughed on, oblivious, pulling a tattered notepad from her jacket. 'If you'll just give me half an hour, just a few questions . . .'

'My side of things is mine,' he said coldly. 'My life is not a "public interest issue". Everything I say, or have said, is *off* the record. I do *not* give you permission to use any image or audio of me. If you say one word that under-mines the hard work of the police on this case or any other, I'll make you regret it. And if I catch you stalking me again I'll smash that phone into a thousand pieces.'

Finally, he seemed to have got through. 'You wouldn't dare.'

'Try me.'

'I'm *trying* to write your true story,' she insisted.

'What would you know about truth? You think you can sum up my life with some stolen snaps and a half-hour Q and A? The only truth you're interested in is sales.'

'Not true,' she said hotly. 'I could've sold this a week ago on the pictures alone.'

Stark's temper finally snapped. 'And taken your place among the rest of the bottom-feeding parasites, scraping a living off slime and decay.' The cold fury in his voice sent her two steps back. 'The bins are over there, in case you haven't finished sucking through my life for shit.'

Her face flushed again, but more from anger than embarrassment, he was sure. 'Isn't that more *your* line of work?' she riposted.

'For *justice*. Not salacious tittle-tattle.' He cut off her retort with a raised palm. 'So . . . just in case I've been in any way unclear . . . *Fuck off!* And no, you can't quote me on that!'

Turning his back, he let himself in and slammed the door, pausing in the dark stairwell to close his eyes and slow his breathing, heart drumming, fists bunched against the shaking, chastising himself for giving vent to frustration, yet again.

The letter box rattled. A business card poked through the brushes. Her silhouette and sharp voice through the glass. 'For when you change your mind!'

Plodding angrily up to his flat he poured himself a measure of the cheap stuff and stared at it.

What was the point?

He tipped it down the sink with gritted teeth, left the glass unwashed, slid open the balcony door to listen to the storm and collapsed on the sofa with a grunt, hip and muscles mocking him for his spinning class hubris and everything since.

Dreams took him almost at once; to places he had been or never been, had no wish to return to or go, places where dreams hid their nature behind reality and vice versa. The tolling bell shifted . . . and cut through the confusion. Gulping, dry-mouthed, he fumbled for his phone and stared at the caller ID until his eyes focused.

Unknown.

The time: 10:04 a.m.

Not for the first time, or likely the last, he cursed himself for a career choice where silencing one's phone to sleep was frowned upon. Few people had this number and his standard policy with unknown callers was to let them go to voicemail; but if voicemails *were* being hacked . . . And if it *was* just a cold caller he was too angry at being woken to leave it. 'Yes?'

'Is that Joe?' asked an accented female voice.

Cold caller, he thought coldly. Or worse, another reporter. 'That depends on who you are and how you got this number.'

'Andy gave it to me. Andy at the gym. It's Selena . . . you know? From spinning?'

'Selena . . .' Stark sat up, rubbing the drowse from his eyes.

'Maybe I shouldn't have called?' she asked, uncertain.

'No,' he said hurriedly. 'I'm sorry, I'm still waking up. I was working last night. Andy gave you my number?'

'He said you didn't have Facebook. He said you wouldn't mind?'

'No, that's fine. I'm sorry . . . the Facebook thing . . . it's complicated.'

'Yes?'

Andy knew Stark's past, but Stark trusted him to have restricted his indiscretion to the phone number. He changed the subject. 'I'm glad you called.'

'Good.' He heard a little relief in her voice.

'I was hoping you might want to meet up.'

'Yes, I was hoping that too.'

'Hang on a sec . . .' He checked the phone for messages, more than half expecting a text from Fran calling him back in; but there was nothing. With Harper waving the overtime joker, Fran had little choice, and Groombridge seemed to be allowing Harper some rope . . . 'Sorry about that. How about tonight? Seems like I'm off duty.'

Playing the short-notice card sometimes offered an insight into how keen, or over-keen, a girl might be.

'Yes, okay. Do you like tapas? There is a good bar near the covered market. Il Palio.'

'Great. What time?'

'Spanish time, ten. But there is a pub around the corner, the Bosun's Mate. Shall we meet there? At eight?'

'Eight o'clock. I'll see you there,' said Stark.

'Good. See you tonight then.'

'Okay, bye-bye.' Stark winced at the lame farewell, but Selena rang off.

He tried to sleep again but his body clock was all over the place. His damp clothes lay in a heap beside the sofa and the blanket was too thin with the balcony door left ajar when he'd fallen asleep. The storm had moved away, leaving a rippled grey-tarpaulin sky behind.

Shivering, he pulled on baggies and warmed up with grudging exercises, hip and muscles now set like concrete, cursing every step.

Two days off. The term weekend no longer held much significance to Stark since joining the police and army. Selena's timely call offered the tantalizing hope of a pleasant pastime, but the *meantime* stretched out before him like a yawning chasm. What the hell was he supposed to do for two days, apart from shopping online to restock his depressingly bare fridge?

He fixed himself a makeshift breakfast and sat on the sofa to watch the latest news report.

MOTORBIKE COP SLAIN!

Butler's picture.

Left out of a live manhunt felt like sitting out a combat patrol. Orders were orders, but a colleague was dead.

He couldn't just sit on his arse.

46

The first half-mile always hurt; damage and scars, rusty limbs. But soon Stark's legs were turning over in smooth rhythm, heart and lungs burning. Road cycling was so much more invigorating than the static gym bike, no need for dance tracks and tongue-lashing with the 360-degree threat that was London traffic. Endorphin and adrenaline, Mother Nature's gifts, blasting away the cobwebs.

Where he might normally head south out of London for a few hours, today he powered up the hill and over Blackheath, following the map in his head, searching for landmarks in the unfamiliar streets of north Eltham. If he couldn't contribute to the hunt directly, he'd do so on the quiet.

The best way to win a battle was to walk the ground ahead of time, like Wellington scouting the terrain around Waterloo a year before the battle. And the best way to understand how one had played out was walk the ground after.

He found Dumbreck Road and stood over the crossbar catching his breath and steaming in the frigid air. Last night's thunder and lightning had passed over, but he'd had to fight the wind all the way here and the air was thick with the threat of further rain. He looked about him, the scene half-familiar from online Street View.

Harper's whispered threat may have been a trigger, and naming Kirsch to his face couldn't have helped, but the source of all this death was twenty years earlier, in these streets.

This was the spot the elderly couple reported the altercation in the street back in November 1989. An ordinary street like any other. How could such a thing happen here? people always thought. The elderly couple was gone, him to his grave, her to a home.

The wind shifted and Stark shivered in his rain shell. He needed to keep moving. He followed Dumbreck Road to where it curved north to a footpath emerging by the Rochester Way, a short section of east–west dual carriageway linking somewhere to somewhere for some reason.

Here a motorist had reported seeing one figure carrying another, according to Darlington's notes; barely a glimpse between streetlights through wiper-smeared rain, a figure emerging from the footpath on the south side as Stark had just done, freezing in the headlights and retreating back, exactly where paths led up into Shepherdleas Woods.

Hoisting the bike's crossbar over one shoulder, Stark walked a short way in. The main paths were slippery but the ancient woodland off them was thick. A killer need not have gone far in to dump a body. But to hide one . . .

Crossing the carriageway to the northern side, Stark followed the cracked tarmac path uphill beside Oxleas Meadow, a broad slope of grass topped by a solitary cafe located for the view, bordered by the much larger Oxleas Woods.

Both woods had been searched by officers with dogs and local volunteers but it had rained for three days straight, and then on and off for weeks, and no trace of

Kimberly Bates had been found then or since. Somewhere uphill to the east stood Severndroog Castle, Simon and Kimberly's secret love nest, all locked up tight now according to uniform. Stark would check for himself, but first . . . A track of sorts led along the back of the houses of Crookston Road, too rarely trod to be free of brambles, but often enough to be churned with mud.

Using his phone map, Stark approached the old Kirsch house. Like most, it had a back gate on to the woods – bolted from the inside. The rear garden was paved but cracked and strewn with weed and loops of bramble. The back door wore a heavy padlock. The plywood nailed over the windows was grey and blistered. Time or historic elbow grease had faded most of the graffiti. But Stark could just make out one word, writ large – *KILLER*.

He was about to climb in for a closer look when he clocked the old lady and her dog approaching. She stopped, regarding him thoughtfully beneath her clear plastic dome umbrella, pink wellingtons splattered with mud. The elderly, overweight Jack Russell terrier in its tartan doggie coat paused, wheezing, at her feet, fixing Stark with a baleful stare.

'Bit conspicuous for a daylight burglary,' she announced, with a hint of amusement, eyeing the bike for its impractical getaway capabilities.

Stark fished out his warrant card.

The dog growled but she silenced the sorry hound with a gentle tug on his lead. 'Don't mind Binky. He was a decent yapper in his time but an arthritic hip takes the fun out of life.'

Being saddled with a name like Binky probably hadn't helped, thought Stark.

She glanced at Stark's ID. 'You're a bit late to the party. You might've found Simon Kirsch skulking around here twenty years ago but he's long gone, and good riddance.'

'You remember him?'

'Oh, I remember Simon; and his fool of a mother. What sort of policeman are you, then, dressed like that?'

'The off-duty over-curious kind.'

'Ah.' She tapped the side of her nose and winked. 'A busybody. Expect that comes in handy in your line of work. I'm not averse to a spot of gossip myself.' The old lady broke into a grin. 'You look in need of a hot cup of something. This is me,' she said, opening the back gate of the house next door. 'Come in out of the rain for tea and a natter; I'll tell you about the boy if you tell me about the fugitive.'

Stark looked down at his splattered cycle gear.

'Don't worry about that,' she told him. 'Binky's in a worse state and I'm sure I can find you an old blanket too.' Without waiting for agreement she set off towards her back door, leaving him to follow or appear rude.

A good soldier never shuns the offer of a hot brew and a dry place to drink it. And winning the trust of the locals over a brew was page one of the hearts-and-minds handbook.

47

Denise Albright was her name. In her seventies or more, Stark guessed. Twice widowed, she announced, as if it were perfectly normal to share such a thing with a stranger. She gave him a towel, a blanket, a pair of dead husband number two's old carpet slippers, tea with two sugars and a plateful of chocolate Hobnobs in the cause of putting some meat on his bones. Photos of the last husband had, since his passing, been joined on the mantel by photos of the first. There was a fine candidate for number three at the local over-sixties dance, but she feared her reputation as the Black Widow might put him off. 'Couldn't blame him, I suppose,' she mused.

Stark sipped his steaming tea gingerly.

'Don't worry. It's not poisoned,' she chuckled, a devilish twinkle in her eye. 'So while your lot are chasing Simon Kirsch again, you're here on your day off snooping round his old house – why's that then?'

'Curiosity.'

Her eyes narrowed shrewdly. 'He had a family, your motorcycle man?' She nodded to her morning newspaper.

'Wife and daughter.'

'Then I'm twice as sorry. And you think Simon did it.'

'Thinking isn't knowing.'

'Hmm.' She pursed her lips at the dodge. 'Won't find much next door; place has been boarded up for years. I can't blame Miriam for up and leaving, with broken windows and paint daubed on her door. She came into some money from somewhere. Some said they sued the police – was that true?'

Stark would have liked to indulge her, but he just shrugged. Denise looked disappointed. 'Anyway, she moved away somewhere, no forwarding address. The place went up for sale but no one would have it. Stood empty for years. Eventually the story died down and some tenants moved in, nice people, there for a while. But the next lot made a nuisance of themselves, had to be evicted in the end. Then came the squatters, left the place in a state. Took everything that wasn't nailed down and most of what was. The place got boarded up soon after. Figure Miriam still owns it, wherever she is. I hoped someone else would buy it to do up but they never did. It's a crying shame. This is a nice road; there's better folk than me living here. That house is as much a stain on the present as it is on the past.'

'The past . . . ?' asked Stark invitingly.

Denise nodded. 'I can't say whether young Simon did for that girl or not. I think he was capable of it, but I think more people are capable than would care to think it. But I can see why folk would believe he did. He was a skulker, hiding in the shadows. Old dame Farley who lived the other side back then wasn't much of a sleeper; used to say she'd see him sneaking out back into the woods late at night, or sneaking back in at dawn. I'd see him too, out and about, off the paths, creeping through the trees. Used to dress himself up in that camouflage get-up but he wasn't in the cadets or anything, he just liked sneaking about. Still, can't blame him over-much . . . Not with a mother like that.'

Binky growled in his sleep, sprawled on a filthy blanket

beside the electric fire and giving off smells that weren't all wet fur.

'Like what?' asked Stark.

Denise's face wrinkled in displeasure. 'Pious past the point of politeness, that one. Never bothered with church much myself, but I've no issue with those as do, so long as it makes 'em happy. But Miriam Kirsch . . . She was never happy. She'd give you that pitying look and say she'd pray for you, say it right to your face like she could see the flames of hell licking at your heels. Cut it any way you like, that's just plain rude. I've put two good husbands in the ground and here's me, a flirty old baggage with little good to say about anyone, fit as a flea – where is the all-powerful benevolence in that, I ask you?'

Stark nodded politely. 'What about Simon? Did he share her beliefs?'

Denise shrugged. 'Didn't get much say in the matter, I should think. She was going to church every day by the end. Perhaps she had a lot to confess.'

'She was a nurse at the local care home?' asked Stark, recalling the old case notes.

'St Luke's. Run by the nuns for the aged congregation. A good place by all accounts. Lots of dotty old ladies ready to share a prayer with Miriam. Closed now. But Miriam's public face was nothing to the Old Testament scorn she saved for behind closed doors. I could hear it through the walls. Least I buried my husbands instead of chasing them off. She got worse after that and poor Simon copped the lot; can't have been more'n a toddler. She was putting out his mattress to dry in the sun for years, probably blaming the devil for the poor boy's sins. I could hear him crying himself to sleep some nights.'

'Did she hurt him, physically?'

'More than his share of smacking, that was for sure, but it's the mental whipping that scars a child. Church to the eyeballs, told day and night you're a sinner, no friends round, no music or television, threadbare clothes . . . I ask you, guilty before he'd done a thing . . . hardly any wonder if he turned out wrong.'

She sipped her tea noisily, staring into the past. 'Used to see him in the library, nose in books,' she said as if just remembering. 'But he never took 'em home. Miriam probably disapproved of anything that wasn't the bible. I think he lived in his head, if you know what I mean. Never spoke much, but busy behind the eyes. Still,' she added, snapping into the present with a wistful smile, 'which of us isn't? You married?' she asked. 'You don't wear a ring but that's all the fashion these days.'

Stark shook his head.

'You've a nice young lady in tow, then,' Denise fished. 'Or is it a young fella? That's all the fashion these days too now, of course. Miriam Kirsch would've been quick to call names; too many things were sin in her eyes. But I've nothing against it. We are what we are and those as say otherwise are fools or worse. A person should do and be as makes 'em happy, harming no other, that's what I feel. Least it's legal now. Too many perfectly nice young men back in my day, forced to live a lie.' She shook her head angrily. 'You pay heed, mind, there's good laws and bad laws and a young policeman like yourself should know where he stands.'

Stark nodded again.

She sighed, then brightened. 'How about a snifter? You being off duty, after all.' She pulled open a drinks cabinet, one of the old-fashioned ones with a door swinging down into a leather-topped tray to reveal serried ranks of spirit bottles. 'What's your poison?' she cackled, turning round with whisky in one hand and gin in the other.

Stark's phone rang and he fished it out apologetically. It was Fran. 'Excuse me,' he said to Denise. 'Work.'

'Don't mind me. You're a man in demand, I'm sure.'

'Sarge?' he answered.

'How soon can you get in?'

Stark wondered why it was that the women in his life hardly ever concerned themselves with greetings. 'A while.'

'Why, where are you?'

Stark looked around. 'I'm not sure you'd believe me.'

'Den of iniquity with some chick you picked up on the street?'

Stark glanced down at the tartan slippers on his feet. 'Close.'

'Well, give her a kiss and get on your way.'

'Kirsch?'

'The mother.'

48

'Thank you for fitting me in at short notice,' said Groombridge, as Doctor McDonald gestured him to the chair opposite hers. Designed to put people at their ease, the layout had the exact opposite effect on him. No desk; just the two chairs. He was used to accuser and accused having something solid between them. And to knowing which he was. Decorated in white and pastel yellow, her office was lined with weighty tomes and professional certification. There was a framed photograph of a man in his forties, but no children, no wedding ring.

'How can I help you, Detective Chief Inspector?'

'Call me Michael,' said Groombridge, feeling it was appropriate, and then feeling it wasn't.

She nodded but said nothing.

He shouldn't be here. Butler was downstairs in the mortuary and the station was a powder keg. But the miserable truth was that Groombridge was a spare wheel. Cox was acting as figurehead, Inspector Cartwright was directing the uniforms' anger into a city-wide search and beyond, Family Liaison were comforting Butler's family, and Harper was running the investigation with Fran. Groombridge had used the excuse of speaking with the doctors and collecting Butler's personal effects, but it was as much about getting out from underfoot ... And, if possible, scratching a different itch.

He sized Hazel up, but with no more success than the

last time they'd met, well over a year ago now. He knew her to be efficient, confident and careful, but also inscrutable. In his line of work inscrutable people were the most interesting, and dangerous.

But of course that, after all, was why he was here.

She waited. She was good at it. She knew the efficacy of a loaded silence.

'Doctor McDonald –'

'Call me Hazel.'

He looked for sarcasm in her smile but saw only patience. He tried to imagine the conversations that had taken place in this room between her and Stark, between her open-faced calmness and his damned defiance. 'It's a matter of some delicacy . . .'

'Concerning?' She expressed interest, encouragement. He suspected she was enjoying this. But then how could one not, and carry on? He wondered if he should just come out with it, but if she was enjoying herself, why shouldn't he? 'I have this . . . *friend* . . .'

Yes. There it was again. The faint twinkle of amusement in the corner of her eye at his choice of cliché. 'Go on . . .'

'He's a loner. He's been through a lot. He keeps people at a distance, but those close enough have noticed a change, a . . . deterioration.'

'You're concerned he may be suffering from depression.'

Groombridge pursed his lips. 'That's a strong word.'

'To the wrong ears, perhaps.'

Groombridge nodded, conceding that point. During his time in uniform words like 'depression' or 'stress' were synonymous with words like 'desk' and 'duties', or 'temporary suspension'. He'd faced down many threats during a twenty-year career, but never the police counsellor. How many officers had he since sentenced to time in a room just like this? He stifled a shiver.

Hazel put aside her pen and unblemished notepad. 'Why don't we put the charades aside?' she said, a shrewd intelligence showing through. 'You're here about Joseph?'

He nodded slowly.

'And what exactly did you hope I would tell you, bound as I am by doctor/patient confidentiality?'

Groombridge had expected this but come anyway. 'To be honest, I'm not sure what I hoped for. I've been guilty of taking my eye off the ball. I didn't realize how serious things were until last night.'

'Last night?'

He opened his mouth to explain about Brian Bates' visit, about Stark's odd detachment and poetic utterance, but of course he could not.

Hazel raised her eyebrows in shared understanding. 'And here we are; two people bound to confidence.'

'With shared concerns?'

She shrugged politely. 'Who can say?'

Indeed. Here they were; two people with the interests of a third at heart, hamstrung by integrity. He wanted to ask her if she was as worried about Stark as he was, but couldn't. Something in Stark's demeanour, speech and attitude had kept Groombridge awake most of the night. He'd sounded . . . weary. Not just exhausted but resigned to it, lacking hope. That couldn't be good. Groombridge had seen a fair few self-murders in his time, with many different causes, but essentially they all boiled down to a failure of hope. Suicide wasn't something that fit with what he knew of Stark, but then what did he really know?

After everything Stark had been through, everything he'd seen. This woman knew more. But the only hope she had of helping Stark was to keep his confidence. Groombridge could get a warrant for her files or force Stark to undergo a psych evaluation, but both would do more harm than good. Perhaps the best he hoped to achieve by coming here was simply to bring his concerns to her attention, and leave her to her job. He sighed deeply.

She nodded empathetically. She was good at that too. 'In your capacity as his boss, all I will say is that it's not my job to comment on his fitness for work. In your capacity as his friend, all I can say is stick with it, and good luck.'

'Great.' He huffed a tired laugh.

'If there's anything you'd like to get off your chest while you're here?' she offered, knowing the answer. 'A man of your responsibilities might benefit from an impartial ear?'

There was a shrewd look in her eye now. Groombridge had the disconcerting feeling she had been studying his tells just as hard as he had hers. She enjoyed her job all right. They were in the same game, essentially – unravelling puzzles, teasing out truths. She was more than a match for him, he suspected. She may even be a match for Stark. The mere fact the young man still came here, after all this time, spoke volumes. And for now, Groombridge would have to content himself with that.

'You did make an appointment after all,' she continued. 'And you have fifty minutes left.'

She had seen the news, no doubt. 'Too little by far, I fear,' he sighed wearily. 'And too long by half.'

Fran's car pulled up with a minor screech of tyres – an open display of her impatience at having to wait for him to race home and shower. 'You drive,' she barked, climbing out to walk around the passenger side with her phone pressed to her ear. 'Address . . .' She handed him a barely decipherable Post-it.

There was a half-drunk takeaway coffee in the cup holder and a half-eaten Danish on the dash.

Fran cursed and hung up. 'We got a warrant for White's bank account. Empty. Records show rent and bills going out each month and everything else withdrawn in cash, regular as clockwork.'

'An escape plan.'

'No sign of the hundred grand he weaselled out of us, either, but that was twenty years and at least one identity ago. We heard back from Manchester; their gangs unit didn't recognize him from any of their biker mobs. There was a Steve Tornado Thompson on the local cage-fighting circuit but not a match, and they've no hits on his photo. Whatever he was, wherever he was, he wasn't famous.' She yawned expansively and set about texting someone.

Stark knew she found his driving style pedestrian, but she was clearly too preoccupied for the normal digs. She sent her text and leant her head back on the rest, shutting her eyes for a moment, while he told her what he'd learned about the Kirsch family dynamic.

She sniffed, either dismissing it as irrelevant garden-fence gossip, or rejecting it as mitigation for Simon's actions, before filling him in some more. The rush of potential sightings had petered out. The traffic stops had found nothing. Armed response patrols were being scaled down. Details of stolen motorbikes were being checked and traffic CCTV pored over.

In the meantime, Simon Kirsch had gone to ground or

escaped. Ports were on alert, other forces were up to speed and the media was all over it. They'd been sifting the Kimberly Bates files, but added nothing so far to off-set the frustration that they'd let Simon Kirsch walk to kill a copper. The only useful thing recovered was this address for Miriam Kirsch. 'Everyone's flagging, I'm strung out on coffee, I need a level head and yours will have to do. Have you had any sleep?'

'Tons.'

It suited her latest theft of his R'n'R to let the lie pass.

49

The address was for Miriam Larson. Kirsch's mother had reverted to her maiden name, no doubt in an effort to shake off the stigma that followed her son's name. It was a shabby high-rise in Charlton. There were graffiti tags everywhere and the lift stank of piss.

Miriam lived halfway up. They made their way along the open-air corridor with its bare concrete balustrade. Her door was half-glazed but security bars had been fitted behind the frosted glass, and two additional locks.

Fran knocked and waited. Through net curtains on the living room window Stark could see the blue flicker of a television. Fran knocked again, impatiently.

'All right, all right . . . I'm not deaf!' A silhouette appeared in the hallway through the glass. 'Who is it?'

'Police.'

There was a pause. 'Got ID?'

Fran held her warrant card up and the figure inside leant in to the spyhole to inspect it. Evidently satisfied, she began laboriously unlocking and unbolting the door. It opened to reveal a careworn woman in her sixties or older, looking them both up and down with little enthusiasm. Stark could only just make out the resemblance with the photo in the case files. 'Can't be too careful,' she said. 'The last lot tricked me into opening the door.'

'The last lot?' asked Fran.

'Journalists,' said Miriam, with the same tone one

might use to describe shit on one's shoe, peering past them to make sure they were alone. 'One of the red-tops, though he more than hinted he was one of your lot till his foot was in the door and his photographer started snapping away.'

'When was this?' demanded Fran.

'This morning. Should've known they'd beat you lot to the punch. Nothing changes. Come on then, close the door before you let all the heat out. And wipe your feet!'

She jerked her head for them to follow and wandered back into the living room. A shabby little flat like so many of its kind, barely big enough for its furniture, old-fashioned ornaments, lamps and mirrors. A cathode ray TV that took up too much space sat on mute with a game show fronted by some B-list celebrity Stark couldn't name.

There was just one family photo, a school portrait – Simon, pre-pubescent and smiling, unaware of what he might become. And draped over it, a faux-bronze medal on a blue ribbon – Long Distance Under 13s.

'What did the journalist ask you?' said Fran, taking a seat on the sofa opposite, clearly piqued. If someone in the station *was* tipping them off it clearly wasn't a two-way street.

Two-way street . . . Stark frowned, trying to drag something from his memory.

'The same things they always ask. What's it like being mother to a monster.' Miriam glanced at the photo, her face unreadable. 'My response earned me a few extra Hail Marys. You'd think I'd remember. They hated me as much as Simon. They'll have their headline photo for tomorrow, but Satan will stack their pyres with their sinful lies.'

Fran looked momentarily taken aback, but stayed on message. 'Have you seen Simon?'

'They asked that too,' sighed Miriam. 'No. And I don't know where he is. Haven't seen him since he took off to France, nineteen years ago.' She glanced at the photo again, a hint of anguish. 'They did this, the press, and you lot – turned him against the world, against his own mother, against God . . .' Now the anguish came out. 'Condemned my beautiful boy to hell . . . You'll all burn,' she muttered.

'He took off for France, you say?' asked Fran, ignoring the slur on her immortal soul.

Miriam was still staring at the boy in the picture as if she could see satanic flames consuming him. Stark wondered if her torment was anything approaching that of Brian Bates. Perhaps they had *both* lost their only offspring that same night back in 1989, though only Miriam had got to say goodbye.

'I begged him not to go, but he'd long since stopped listening to anything I had to say. After everything I'd done for him!' She glanced at them as if shocked to hear herself talk so, and Stark thought he saw more than a touch of madness in her pain. 'He wanted to start over, leave everything that had happened behind. He'd read about the Foreign Legion of all things. I said he was better off sticking it out here, finding a new college to get his exams, but he said it wouldn't be any different – the way people looked at him, talked about him, as if he was guilty.' She looked at them fiercely. 'But he wasn't! He was just a boy. He wasn't capable of murder. He swore with his hand on the holy bible! He was tried and found innocent.'

After three days of deliberation and by the narrowest majority, thought Stark. The crown thought they had their man but the evidence wasn't quite there. That was justice. That was the whole point of the courts, the essence of jurisprudence. Simon, as any other, was entitled to the benefit of reasonable doubt. Stark could guess what Fran might say to that, of course.

'That was a long time ago, Mrs Kirsch –'

'Larson,' interrupted Miriam sharply.

Fran appeared to weigh that up. 'There's no legal record of you changing your name.'

'There's legal record of him divorcing me, but that means nothing in the eyes of the lord,' replied Miriam, as if her words made sense. 'He's dead to me, dead in the eyes of Jesus. The last thing I want is his name. The only thing he left me other than a child to raise was the house, and that's been nothing but a millstone around my neck.'

'You still own the house?' Fran asked.

This topic did little to brighten the woman's mood. 'Tried to sell it. D'you know who came round to view? Damned newspaper with some clairvoyant claiming that wicked girl's ghost was in the walls.' She made the sign of the cross and glanced at the crucifix dominating one wall; a deep wooden cross with its tortured brass figurine pinned with real little nails.

Stark shivered. He didn't begrudge faith, he just found it baffling.

'I thought things might get better after Simon had gone,' continued Miriam, 'but the graffiti, the vandalism . . . I had to stop work with stress. Moved in here with my mum but she died ten years ago now. I'm surprised you took so long to find me.'

'Did Simon take the name Larson too?' asked Stark.

Miriam shook her head. 'He wanted to leave me behind as well. He made that quite clear.' She grew upset again. 'The first time I've seen my son in twenty years is on the television, looking like some biker thug with that beard, and his hair all shaved, using a made-up name!'

'Does Simon have any connection to Manchester, family history?'

'No. For all I knew he was still in France. Now I find out he's living right here, in Greenwich. Right here! And he never let me know!'

She was becoming hysterical and Stark could see Fran had no idea how to calm her.

'Might've been *dead* for all I know!' wailed Miriam. 'After everything I did for him!'

Stark crouched down in front of her. If this had been on patrol he'd have removed his sunglasses and taken his hand off his weapon, but here all he had were calming words. 'Sons never stop loving their mums,' he said softly, 'whatever they might say, whatever passes between them in the heat of the moment. It's hardwired. That might even be why Simon came back to Greenwich, to be near you.'

The words appeared to have some impact, and her sobbing decreased. 'Do you think so?' she asked, looking pleadingly into his eyes through her tears.

'The other thing about boys is we find it hard to know who is supposed to say sorry, and even harder to ask.' Miriam smiled a little at the truth of it. 'He may even have watched you from afar. Are you sure you haven't seen him?' asked Stark, showing her the photo of her son as he was now.

It was clear she wished she had. Her eyes filled with tears again. 'He didn't kill those people,' she said earnestly. 'He's not a murderer, whatever they say, he's a sensitive boy. Satan won't have him. He'll repent his sins and join hands with Jesus. Jesus knows,' she insisted, staring at the crucifix with a faraway look in her eyes.

'Do you mind if I look around, Miriam?' Stark smiled apologetically. 'I'm sorry, but we have to report that we checked thoroughly.'

The conversation seemed to have exhausted her. She numbly showed them around the flat and then saw them out. Fran called control to request an unmarked car to sit on the place before dropping him home. She didn't invite him to 'help' write up the report or thank him for giving up two hours of his first day off in forever, hours after an all-night shift. Clearly she didn't have Harper's permission to enlist Stark in this little outing. Perhaps she was keeping an eye on him or keeping him busy to stop him 'moping'.

50

If there was any voice Stark was more horrified to wake to than Harper's, he couldn't name it. It took several seconds to realize he'd fallen asleep with the TV on and wasn't in the grip of a nightmare.

'– net is closing in,' declared Harper sternly. Stark unpeeled his face from the sofa leather to face the screen, forcing his eyes open. Harper wasn't in front of Royal Hill station, but was standing in front of the iconic rotating sign of New Scotland Yard. Superintendent Cox hovered in the background but there was no sign of DCI Groombridge.

'How?' demanded one of the reporters who crowded round.

'Obviously we can't comment on details of our ongoing investigation, but rest assured, no stone is being left unturned.'

'Reports suggest there've been no further failed raids overnight . . .' another voice taunted.

'There is no such thing as a failed raid,' said Harper in his best patrician manner. 'Every false lead we run down only narrows our search.'

'Has Simon Kirsch fled abroad?' shouted another.

'We have no reason to believe that. Border staff have been on high alert since Friday, Simon Kirsch's picture is everywhere, and with the vigilance of the public we are sure he will be apprehended very soon. It's only a matter of time.' Harper stared straight into camera. 'I say to you, Simon Kirsch . . . Hand yourself in. Armed officers are scouring every dark corner and hiding place. Hand yourself in, while you still can.' The report ended on that threat, Harper's honest, determined face with the rotating sign behind him declaring that they were *Working together for a safer London.*

Pompous windbag, thought Stark, fumbling for the remote and switching it off. He clamped his eyes shut again but as he feared, sleep would not return. His blanket had slipped on to the floor and he was cold.

Stark sat up rubbing his eyes and rotating his sore shoulder with a grunt.

He got up and reluctantly worked through his physio exercises. As both his hydrotherapist and girlfriend, Kelly had made it her business to keep him up to the mark, but since she'd gone it had become harder and harder to motivate himself. The bike and the gym were for heart and mind, and lungs, but the physio workout was specific to his injuries and all the more painful for it. In the early days he'd attacked the mountain, but the plateau he'd reached since sapped his will. He'd long passed the point where he relished the penance of it.

Perhaps it was some nod to Kelly that made him attack it now, given his evening plans.

Selena was late. Stark wasn't surprised, attributing it to the casual habit of beautiful people, passing through life with everything falling at their feet, oblivious to the labours of mere mortals. Selena was very beautiful, so Stark patiently sipped his whisky. Not as smooth as 'the good stuff' secreted behind the bar of the Prince of Wales, but that was Kelly's local, the staff *her* friends, and his no longer. The Bosun's Mate was more of a locals' pub, smaller, dingier and arguably more authentic. Stark had drunk in places that made this a palace, but wouldn't have chosen it for a first date.

'Oi, you're 'im, aren't ya?'

Stark turned to face his accuser, a slim lad, probably old enough to be served but not by much, trendy white trainers, thin jeans, England football shirt, short back and sides, over-gelled curls on top, tattoos on both arms, thick gold-plated chain and sovereign rings. He smelled of lager, cigarettes and over-applied aftershave.

Yob. Could be a perfectly personable young man but he presented like a yob.

'It *is* you!' cried the yob, delighted, clearly a few pints into his evening. 'Here, lads, I told you it was 'im! Fuckin'ell, 'e's famous! Fucked them Taliban right up!'

His mates, different shapes and sizes but from the same mould, joined him in pestering Stark for handshakes and phone selfies, but fortunately had oozed back into their corner before Selena finally arrived.

She smiled, kissed him on both cheeks and gave no mention of her lateness.

'Aye, aye!' called the yob, followed by a wolf whistle and raucous laughter.

Selena's smile dimmed momentarily, a cloud passing before the sun. They should move on after one drink, Stark decided.

He asked what she wanted and turned to catch the barman's eye, but the man was fiddling with the TV remote, flicking channels. He settled on a sports channel. There was a football match beginning shortly, but for now it was on the news so he left the sound down. Stark sighed to see Harper's face on the screen, mouth moving wordlessly, a repeat of his earlier hollow threat. The barman came to take Stark's order.

Stark was about to speak when the next story caught his eye – a still photo of a soldier smiling in Dress Twos. *British soldier killed in Helmand named* . . . declared the banner line, scrolling across the bottom of the screen. Stark didn't need the sound up. His heart had already fallen through the floor.

'All right, Doris! You wiv my mate the hero, are ya?'

Stark turned, mind floundering between the here and now and the over-there. The yob was back, a pint further into his evening, standing too close to Selena. She was leaning away, expression wrinkled with thinly disguised disgust.

'I know 'e's got a medal an' all, but I've got a bigger gun!' gurned the yob, to the uproarious appreciation of his mates.

'Thanks but no thanks,' replied Selena coldly.

'Wassat? Foreign, are ya? Where you from, babe? I like a nice Brazilian.' Laughter from his audience. Selena tried to ignore him.

Stark tried to shake off the buzzing in his head. He needed to intervene but felt intoxicated in the worst possible way.

'Got any English in ya?' asked the yob suggestively. Anticipatory laughter from the mob. 'Would you like so—'

'Go away,' managed Stark.

The yob looked angry at having his punchline interrupted. 'You what?'

'We're just here for a quiet drink. Please leave us alone.' Not diplomatic enough. The words sounded like they were coming from someone else's mouth and failing to defuse the situation, but Stark couldn't order his thoughts to find better.

'I'm just talking to the girl, no 'arm in that. She likes me, ain't that right, babe?'

'Please. Just leave us alone,' said Selena. She looked to Stark to do more.

'We should go,' he said to her.

'Na, don't go!' protested the yob. 'Babe and me are just getting to know one annuva.'

Stark stood. 'Thanks, but we need to be somewhere.' He placed himself partially between the yob and Selena so she could slip off her barstool.

'*Oi!* Soldier boy!' A hand on Stark's shoulder. 'I *said* I'm talking to the . . .'

Stark spun and stepped right into the guy's space, nose to nose, murder in his eyes, fists itching. '*Walk away . . .*' he hissed.

The yob flinched back but Stark followed, staying right in his face until he back-pedalled into a chair, stumbling over. A couple of his mates were on their feet, laughter gone.

Stark checked himself, fists uncurling, leaving the yob to scramble up into the safety of his crowd. He shouldn't have let this happen but the face on the screen still swam before his eyes. He took Selena's arm and led her from the pub.

The cold night air could not wash away that face. His head was buzzing.

He should've heard the door open again behind them, heard the footsteps sooner. As it was he turned barely in time to see the fear in Selena's eyes and feel the bottle smash over his head.

51

Fran winced, watching the figure on her laptop screen stumble, clutching his head. Blows followed and he went down, curled in a ball as the six lads laid into him with fists and feet. The girl backed away screaming soundlessly. It looked to be all over.

But then the prone figure stood.

How was that even possible? Like a robot, seemingly oblivious, impervious to the raining blows, he climbed to his feet. His attackers stepped back momentarily. It almost appeared sporting but was probably just group bafflement. Then, with hesitancy, they renewed their assault.

'Jesus!' Fran hissed, wincing again, earning more than one sideways glance from the waiting wounded and pasty-faced ghosts of the A&E waiting room. The CCTV footage was like a horror film; awful, spellbinding. It wasn't balletic or choreographed like one of those ridiculous martial arts films where the bad guys wait turns so the good guy has time to deal with them one by one with stylish efficiency. Stark applied himself to whatever opening or weakness presented itself, certainly, but with ugly, relentless aggression.

The key to violence is the readiness to act without hesitation or restraint, she'd once been told. Stark had nodded. She'd rolled her eyes. But if ever there was a demonstration in action, this was it. It was the critical distinction between the one and the six against him.

Fran shuddered.

She'd learned to like Stark. He hadn't made it easy; he still didn't. He was the younger brother who saw everything too clearly, dug his heels in at the most annoying times, asked why when you were still wondering how. She didn't notice his scars any more. Then every now and then he did or said something that reminded you they were there. This was very definitely one of those times. A reminder that for all his boyish, stubborn charm, for all his quiet stillness, he was a very dangerous man indeed.

Fortunately only one attacker had been seriously hurt, the instigator with the pre-emptive bottle. Bruises to more than their pride for the others – a black eye, a sprained wrist or three, they lay about winded, gasping like fish out of water. But the first guy was out cold and departed in an ambulance; broken nose, wrist, three fingers and concussion. He was already making noises about a complaint. It would not be the first levelled at Stark.

Excessive force.

Not from where Fran was sitting. Any reasonable person could see this was self-defence. Unfortunately an IPCC panel wasn't necessarily a reasonable body. And Stark's public history would send this stratospheric with the press. This fire needed snuffing out before it could roar.

No one else had seen this footage, not even the manager of the pub whose camera it had come from or the uniform who'd recognized Stark and called her. She'd made certain this was the only copy. All she had to do was hit delete.

On screen, the girl turned and ran out of shot as Stark stood panting in the centre of his own whirlwind, last man standing. Fists curled, shoulders back, he threw his face to the sky howling like a wolf at the moon. It sent a chill down Fran's spine. She was never so grateful for silent CCTV.

She'd caught up with Stark at A&E as he sat glumly receiving five stitches to the back of his head. His face was bloody but otherwise unmarked. He'd defended his head. That came with a cost. His arms, legs and ribs were badly bruised, apparently, but nothing broken, Stark assured her. The knuckles on both hands were bruised and split. He'd explained himself eloquently enough but she'd seen those vacant eyes, heard that flat intonation before. Shock, she'd assumed last time, though subsequent reading into combat stress had led her to wonder if it was more of a dissociative state.

This could go wrong in so many ways.

Her finger hovered over the delete key.

'Ready?'

Stark stood over her, bandaged and bruised. Fran knew him too well to bother with sympathy. She closed the laptop and they followed a nurse out through a back way, far from prying eyes.

He said nothing on the journey home. She took his keys from his bruised hands and let them into his building, up the lift and into the flat. The last time she'd been here was for dinner with Stark and Kelly. A happier time, though looking back the cracks had begun to show. The flat was as tidy as ever, nothing out of place, nothing waiting to be washed, a place for everything and everything in its place. Fran shook her head, wondering how anyone lived like this. No wonder Kelly had never quite moved in.

Stark sat wordlessly on the sofa and flicked on the

television while she found the coffee. The fridge was all but empty bar essentials, takeaway leftovers, beers and a bottle of Sauvignon Blanc; Kelly's, thought Fran. She itched to open it. There was a single plate, knife, fork and whisky tumbler on the drainer. Nothing in the slim-line dishwasher, probably unused since Kelly left.

The report behind her announced the name of the latest British soldier killed in Afghanistan. Fran glanced over. Stark stared at it blankly. How did he stand it, she wondered, the relentless news of the war he was no longer part of? The report finished and he put the TV on mute.

Fran finished making him a mug of sweet tea and coffee for herself. She brought them over and found him fast asleep on the sofa, a grey, institutional-looking blanket over him.

She stood there, steaming mugs in her hands, wondering what to do. The doctor had said there was no concussion but to keep an eye on him all the same. How was it possible to go from sitting upright watching TV to horizontal and asleep in less than two minutes? She placed his mug on the coffee table and shook his shoulder gently. 'Stark.'

A minor grunt. Fists pulled the blanket in tight. It would probably take a bugle to rouse him.

Shrugging, she retreated to the kitchen area. The TV flickered silently in the corner.

The blanket worried her. Curious, she wandered into the bedroom. The bed was made, the room pristine. How long since he'd slept in it? she wondered. Since Kelly left? Surely not.

He'd been on a date tonight; disastrous, but nevertheless . . . Like most people, Fran saw advice as something to be passed on rather than embraced. Stark was seemingly impervious to it. More likely the date had been his perversely direct way of moving forward, putting Kelly behind him. How very male.

There was a stack of books on the nightstand. Fran sat on the bed and inspected the uppermost. War poetry? Vaguely revolted, she opened it at the ribbon bookmark and read the short poem there. Poppies and crosses. Death and duty. Very Stark.

Flipping through the pages, she sampled a few more, trying to piece together the wilful obscurities, to comprehend any purpose in this deliberate wallowing in horror, writing it or reading it. She gave up and picked up the next book, non-fiction, a journalist tracking down the surviving men who'd walked on the moon. More pointless endeavour. She sighed, thinking of the wine in the fridge, kicked off her shoes, sat back and read on.

The next thing she was aware of, was screaming.

Larks fled the sky, brave-song forgotten, before the mobbing crows, as the guns stuttered silent.

Mourners huddled around the grave, heart-lost and broken.

Stark ached to join them but shadows held him – too weak to break free or speak as the funeral party faded from sight.

Now he stood before the open grave alone, the bottomless darkness within . . . whispering.

And the stench . . . ever-present and all-pervading.

Night-black birds pecked at the nearest corpse, twitching off scraps and tossing them into their snapping maws like a party trick. Flies filled the air with their despotic buzz, sending shivers down the spine like nails on a blackboard. Dozens of dead. Countless. Littering the broken ground.

Blood sprang between them, blooming up through cracks and craters, blood-red poppies blowing between the crosses in the desert heat; white stone, row on row, unblemished, uncarved, unnamed; stretching beyond sight . . . to Flanders, Sebastopol, and beyond . . .

And one, empty grave . . . waiting.

Turning, he wandered among the dead, trying to place them, recognize them, kicking at the crows as they fluttered a few metres away and settled on another carcass. Kicking, then chasing, till he was running through the killing field like a man possessed, leaping over the dead, raving, screaming at the birds till he was hoarse, wailing until his heart burst.

His foot caught and he fell, but the hand grasped his ankle. Kicking out in horror, Stark looked into the lifeless eyes, staring from the blackened, burnt face. The Velcro name tape on the fatigues – LOVELACE. Hating, accusing eyes, Stark's own eyes, the bleak, desolate eyes of the carrion crow.

Screaming, he kicked free and tumbled from the sofa, catching his temple on the corner of the coffee table, staring around in panic.

His living room. His flat. His reality.

Stark felt tears welling in his eyes.

'No!' he shouted, shoving the table away and scrambling to his feet in fury. Movement in the corner of his eye. On the balcony outside the window perched a big, black crow. Stark stared back, not daring to blink in case it wasn't there afterwards. Was true life entering his dreams or the other way around?

299

The crow cocked its head and fixed him with one bale-ful, flint-black eye, then slowly, deliberately, unfolded huge dark wings and leapt into the sky.

Stark stared at where it had been, or hadn't, until his knees buckled beneath him and he collapsed back on to the sofa, sheathed in cold sweat and shaking like a leaf.

'Joe?'

He jumped at the sound, twitching round to face it, fight or flight, fists curled . . .

Fran stood in the door to his room, the same look on her face he'd seen so many times on Kelly's – too many times – that confusion of fear and pity.

52

Fran saw little of the traffic as she drove home. She'd only seen Stark, normally so impassive, give in to fury once before the footage last night, but this was the first time she'd ever seen him frightened; literally terrified.

She knew he'd suffered from nightmares in the past, or she'd hoped it was in the past. He'd told her once, to get her off his back, to curtail her questions. It hadn't worked, of course. But today she'd made her excuses and left as quickly as she dared, to escape their mutual discomfort. It was his weekend off, and she wouldn't be calling him again.

Was this what it was like for him – sleeping on his sofa and waking in terror? And what was he eating? He normally ate like a horse, but now she thought about it, she couldn't remember seeing that lately. Just like before. He was slipping away again.

Something had to be done.

She showered at home and grabbed coffee and Danish from the café around the corner on her way to work, trying to ignore the *Times* newspaper being read by the guy in the corner.

HE'S NOT HERE! *– **Mother denies contact with killer!*** Mad Miriam Kirsch's face frozen in ugliness, beside an equally damning image of Simon. Fran ground her teeth.

It took her a while to find the number, scribbled on one

of the full notepads she kept in her desk. For privacy she used Groombridge's office to make the call. She refused to think of it as Harper's. Her fingers tapped impatiently on the desk while it rang.

'Hello?'

'Doctor McDonald?'

'This is my private mobile number,' replied the woman, irritation in her voice. 'Who else would it be?'

'This is DS Millhaven.'

'I'd guessed that, Sergeant,' replied Hazel. 'Though I don't recall giving you this number.'

Fran remembered how much she disliked this woman for her curt, superior demeanour. She gave the impression of being constantly ahead of you in the conversation, waiting for you to catch up. How Stark could bear her was a mystery, although he often gave the exact same impression, if less consciously. 'I'm calling about Stark.'

'Yes?'

'I'm worried about him.'

'Yes?'

'There was an incident last night . . .'

'Oh yes?'

Fran ground her teeth and explained, and about the morning.

The woman listened without interrupting. 'Yes. I was informed that he'd been in A&E last night. Thank you for filling in the details.'

Fran waited. 'Is that it?'

'Is that what?'

'Aren't you going to say something?'

'Such as?'

Fran knew she was being wound up but that just wound

her up more. She was just about to say something quite rude when the shrink spoke first.

'I'm sure you realize that I can't discuss Joseph with you in any professional capacity. Thank you for sharing your concerns with me. I suspect that you don't like me and that this can't have been easy. I will, of course, not tell Joseph that you called.'

Fran blinked, trying desperately to summon the correctly insulting response when the door burst open. Harper stared at her with the amused look of a teacher catching a hated pupil red-handed. 'Trying it on for size, Sergeant?' he mocked. 'Want me to find you a cushion to sit on?'

Fran hung up, stood and left with all the silent dignity she could muster. The alternative would have been ugly and detrimental to her career.

She couldn't bear to be around Harper right now. Making sure everyone had something to do, she scanned her own desk, noticed the forensic accounts report and reluctantly took it to the canteen to read.

Thank God for coffee, she thought a while later. They should send someone over to explain this crap, or include a cyanide pill. But Stark had been right to think something was off. Before Mary took over the finances, Chase Security had been a regular-looking company, ticking along. As far as Fran could make out, the Chases had been on the fiddle ever since.

To the taxman Chase Security presented as barely profitable. This was, the forensics surmised, because it had unusually high outgoings. Chief among these was a company called MCA Agency who provided Chase Security with event staff and agency workers. Its managing director was Mary Chase. Both companies were paying out for all sorts of advertising, mail drops and cold calling to another company, TCA Media, director, Thomas Chase. Another company under Mary's name provided 'Consultancy Services'. Another in Tom's owned the property and leased it to Chase Security. Each was minimizing its tax liability by paying high overheads and outgoings to mystery suppliers and creditors, and running barely a pulse. Every company donated to the Chase Foundation, offsetting every charitable penny against tax. The final cumulative tax bill was minuscule compared to what would have been owed, and the account into which all these savings accumulated belonged to a blandly named shell company conveniently registered offshore in the Cayman Islands, where it turned out another Chase company was buying up holiday homes.

And the charity . . . Tom was chairman, Mary managing director, both drawing decent wages again. More invoices to the various 'agencies' and 'consultancies'. Even their trips out there went through expenses. Money did make it through to the Maldives, a small football ground in their name, grass-roots coaching. But the charity HQ was a beach-front house.

So much for model citizens, thought Fran. The Chases had been rinsing cash for years.

Clive Tilly's problems were just beginning. Fraud Squad would pick this house of cards apart.

There was one more anomaly. A single Chase Security invoice, filed among the rest, almost identical but with a different post-box address and bank details, another offshore account. A shadow company, designed to look like the original? Fran scribbled down the address and finished her coffee.

*

Groombridge nodded in genial greeting and pulled the curtain around the bed.

The patient looked at him from two black eyes, suspicious. 'Who are you?'

Groombridge flashed his warrant card but didn't give his name.

The man sneered. 'Come to beg, have you?' He held up the cast enclosing his arm from elbow to hand, splinted fingers protruding. 'Save your breath, Soldier Boy's going down for this.'

'I have not come to beg, Mr Stratham.' Groombridge pulled the visitor chair around to face the bed and sat down. 'I've come to discern whether you really are as stupid as your actions would have you seem.'

'You can't talk to me like that. I'll make a complaint against you too.'

'That is your prerogative.' Groombridge leant forward and picked up the copy of the *Sun* from the bed. 'Treating you well, are they?' he asked conversationally.

'What do you want?'

'Popular rag, this one.'

He could see Stratham's confused reaction out of the corner of his eye. 'So?'

Defensive. Good. Groombridge kept his eyes on the headline.

ULTIMATE SACRIFICE! The photo of a soldier smiling proudly in dress uniform with a smaller image inset of the same young man lounging in desert fatigues, grinning, gun propped against the earthen wall beside him. Private Nathan Lovelace, killed by an IED on patrol, a secondary device, going to help a comrade injured by the first.

'Patriotic too,' Groombridge mused aloud.

'What is this?'

There was another picture inset – Stark, VC adorning his dress uniform. Had this snivelling little shit even noticed, or simply skipped straight to the tits and football? 'Are you patriotic, Mr Stratham?'

Stratham looked predictably affronted. 'Course I am!' He probably had a Union Jack and three lions tattooed on his scrawny backside.

'Funny you should be reading this. I brought one too,' said Groombridge, pulling a copy of the *Sun* from his inside coat pocket. 'From a year and a half ago but pertinent, in my humble opinion.' He laid the two papers side by side on the bed, Lovelace on one, Stark receiving his VC on the other. 'As a patriot, what do you think the readership of this paper will make of tomorrow's edition? The story of an unemployed nineteen-year-old man drinking at the taxpayer's expense, backed up by five mates, sneaking up behind one man, a war veteran, recipient of this nation's highest decoration for valour, hitting him over the head with a glass bottle and then giving him a right old shoeing as he lay curled on the ground?'

He watched Stratham's face as the question settled into what passed for a brain.

'And on the very day that another British serviceman was reported to have lost his life fighting for the freedoms said nineteen-year-old abuses, and named as one of the men our decorated veteran earned that medal saving. Striking coincidence, that. Tell me, Mr Stratham, do you think your newspaper of choice will paint said youth in a favourable light?' The truth was visibly sinking in. 'It will be a popular story, given the extraordinarily high public opinion of said veteran. It'll be on the front page of every newspaper in the land and the leading story on every television news programme too, I should imagine.'

'He beat the shit out of us!' protested Stratham.

'Yes,' chuckled Groombridge. 'The perfect dénouement. The unpatriotic, cowardly scrounger gets his comeuppance at the hands of the national hero. And all caught on CCTV!'

Fran had confessed her temptation to wipe the file. She would have enjoyed this conversation, but some things were better done with the fewer people in the know the better.

'I've asked my local newsagent to set aside a copy of every paper.' Groombridge used a hand to punctuate the strapline, '"Britain's Most Hated Man!" Stories like that just run and run.'

Stratham had gone slack and pale.

'There's already a sweepstake going round my office on how long it will be between your most recent brawl and your next. I've got twenty says you're back in this hospital in less than a day. One of my sergeants reckons you'll be stabbed before the week is out. You may even need official police protection. Of course I might have trouble staffing that detail, at least staffing it with officers I'd trust not to tip the odds.'

Groombridge smiled at Stratham. A genuine smile. A smile of enjoyment. God knows enough boring, important things would fill his day; it was nice to fit in something worthwhile *and* fun. 'If I were the nineteen-year-old in question I might think twice before I made my delusional grievance public. Particularly as it would land him and his five mates in the dock for aggravated assault. I can't imagine they'd be best pleased.' Indeed all five had spent the night in the cells and had listened most attentively to Groombridge before he let them go.

'All right, all right!' spat Stratham miserably. 'I get the point!'

Groombridge smiled again. 'Good. Not so stupid after all; not quite, at least.' He stood and picked up the old copy of the *Sun*. It hadn't been hard to find. Half the station had one secreted in a drawer. It was probably better that Stark didn't know that. 'You can keep this. You should read it. Perhaps you can get one of the nurses to help with the unfamiliar words . . . duty, honour, valour, et cetera. Get well soon, Mr Stratham, and . . .' he poured ice into his voice and stare, 'don't ever give me cause to look your way again.'

53

Fran stared at the tatty steel doors. There was a tatty letter-box slot in them, the property number hand-painted above it. No reference to Chase Security, legitimate or shadow, but the post-office box was registered to this address.

The doors were large enough for a decent-sized vehicle to pass through, with a person-sized wicket door inset, the only opening along the short road that barely quali-fied as an alley, its ancient concrete so cracked and broken it was mostly mud and aggregate. The building opposite was the blank red-brick rear wall of an old single-storey factory unit, now subdivided into a warehouse selling car-pet off-cuts, a car body-shop and other examples of grimy light industry, all facing the other way, leaving the address unobserved.

'What do you think?' asked Williams.

Fran glanced up. There was just one streetlight, right outside the lock-up. It was smashed, not simply out of order. Shards of its glass lay about the ground, but cleaner than the general crust, more recent.

There were no windows they could claim were broken, no back door with a damaged lock, no plaintive cries from within; nothing they could claim reasonable cause for suspicion to excuse them breaking in. Fran clicked her tongue in irritation and called Groombridge. Harper would be pissed that she'd bypassed him but it served him right for being a tit earlier. Groombridge sounded worryingly cheerful on the phone as he noted down the details for the warrant request.

'Any news from above, Sarge?' asked Williams over his plate of gammon and egg, as they waited in a nearby cafe.

Fran couldn't bring herself to sample the delights of the greasy dive. Everyone thought she subsisted solely on coffee and pastries but the truth was she was a food snob. She loved to cook, and if food was fast she wasn't in a hurry to eat it. Better to get through the day on caffeine and then cook up a storm in the evening, or whenever the day ended. 'I wish I knew.'

An hour later they were watching two hefty lads from SOCO cutting the heavy padlock and drilling out the Yale lock. They had the doors open in under a minute. An inspector from SO6 Fraud Squad had rocked up, declaring both seniority and jurisdiction. Fran didn't much care. If there was a body inside it was hers. If not, the rude bastard was welcome to chase boring numbers till his eyes bled.

Uniform gave the all-clear and SOCO went in.

The SO6 inspector and Fran did the mental equivalent of circling each other like cats, while Williams and the SO6 constable shared a joke.

A shout went up from inside, dulled in the echoey space.

The Crime Scene Manager, Geoff Culpepper, emerged several minutes later. The SO6 inspector stepped forward to meet him but Culpepper held up a hand and turned to Fran.

It was not a pleasant space to be in. Bare, dusty bulbs hung from the old iron truss frames, and the corrugated roof looked like asbestos. There were roof lights at regular intervals, but their glass was so dirty that the only direct light came through two that were broken like spotlights, casting both glare and shadow. The bare brickwork walls were filthy with decades of dust and soot.

The place felt musty and unused, but the SOCO team had cordoned off a small white van parked inside and there was a faint smell of bleach. Fran and Williams, in their SOCO-issue suits, boots and gloves, stood where told to stand.

Through the open door the daylight looked bright and cheerful, despite leaden skies. The SO6 inspector stalked back and forth, talking crossly into his phone. Fran smiled to herself. This was MIT jurisdiction for now.

'Here,' said Culpepper, showing them an area of floor. Dustless. The smell of bleach was stronger and there was a trail showing where the liquid had run off to the nearby drain. Culpepper's pointing finger moved from the floor up the nearby wall, also showing signs of rough cleaning. There was a crazed brick, its face split off, about head height.

'Bullet?' asked Fran.

Culpepper nodded. 'Most likely. See the radiating fracture lines. But if it was in there, someone dug it out. No sign of it, I'm afraid.' He saw Fran's disappointment and moved on. 'But here . . . They had a good go, but getting blood off brickwork is a bastard. And they always underestimate the spread. See . . .'

Fran could see nothing. Old London stock buff brickwork was uneven in colour and pocked with black burn spots at the best of times. Culpepper wafted a mist over it with a spray can and held up a small UV torch, describing an arc, up and down. 'Splatter,' he pronounced. There was no mistaking the pattern.

'Testable?'

'Type this afternoon,' replied Culpepper. 'DNA ... FSS are quoting five days.'

Same old same old, thought Fran. Luckily she knew someone who could get results out of the FSS more quickly. She took in the scene slowly, picturing a bullet passing through someone at head height and burying itself in the wall, the body falling. She looked around, pondering. 'You thinking what I'm thinking?' she asked Williams.

'If you're thinking this is where Carlton Savage departed this life.'

She nodded at the van. 'That's not his.'

'I'll run the licence.' Williams took out his phone and dialled.

'You'd best take a look out back too . . .' said Culpepper. 'Stay on the plates.' He led them across the evenly spaced metal stepping stones through a creaking door in a thin timber and wired-glass partition separating off a rudimentary admin area out the back. The smell of bleach persisted. As well as a couple of desks, most of the area was taken up with the kind of utilitarian metal racking you saw in spare-part depots, littered with empty boxes and discarded, yellowing paperwork. One might easily believe the place hadn't been used in years, were it not for the treasure trove of items best summarized as *portable valuables*.

Jewellery boxes emptied of their precious contents, small electricals, wallets and purses, designer shoes and handbags. Most looked low-value, perhaps what was left after the good stuff had been fenced. Nothing obviously identifiable – they clearly weren't that stupid.

'Sarge.' Williams was looking out through the grubby, cracked glass in a time-warped rotten door at the rear.

Fran's eyes followed his down to the narrow stream flowing fast between the green concrete banks underpinning the rear walls of this building and the back of the one opposite. 'Want to bet that's the Quaggy River?' said Williams.

Fran nodded. Stark would probably know. He'd have memorized the map, synchronized his watch by the sun and secreted a compass where the sun didn't bear thinking about shining. She tutted crossly, trying to push concern for him aside so she could concentrate.

'The way the floor's been scrubbed suggests the body was dragged through and dumped out there,' commented Culpepper. 'And then there's this . . .' He crouched on a plate set out next to an ancient wood burning stove. 'It's cold,' he said, carefully opening the door. 'But someone's burned something in here recently, and we found this underneath . . .' He held out an evidence bag containing a large black glove.

'Boss!'

They turned to find one of the masked SOCOs approaching holding a battered old tin box. 'Wedged in behind a loose brick,' explained the man, laying the tin down and opening it.

Inside was a cloth parcel. There was little mistaking the shape within. He teased it open with tweezers.

Ah, thought Fran, smiling. Maybe they're stupid after all.

'Well, well, well,' said Culpepper, crouching to peer at

the revolver. 'Webley, Mark Four. Don't see so many of them these days.'

There were two small cardboard boxes with the gun, tattered, old-fashioned print. Bullets. Thirty-eight calibre, two-hundred-grain.

'We may just have found your murder weapon.'

54

Stark wasn't sure he should go, but *was* sure he could not sit around the empty flat. When the morning news wasn't rehashing the ongoing manhunt for Simon Kirsch it was eulogizing Private Nathan Lovelace. They'd connected the latter to Stark. How nuts would they go once they connected the former too? There was no sign yet of Gwen Maddox's 'Personal Piece', but it was surely only a matter of time.

Knowing she would be about her business early, he'd called Pierson for intel. Such things were confidential, she'd reminded him severely, then called back ten minutes later with what he needed. That was the thing about Major Wendy Pierson; for all her bluster, she knew what mattered.

Taking the cane down from its hook by the door, he'd set off. He might have borrowed a pool car from the station, but not with honesty. Today was a day for cold, hard honesty. The journey by foot, train, tube, train and bus had taken over three hours and given him ample time to think cold, hard thoughts. There was no comfort in them.

The bus deposited him in Wootton Bassett high street well after midday, stiff from sitting and the kicking he'd taken the night before. The bruising was setting in, and his ribs ached and stabbed as he moved. Hairline fractures, bound tight. Penance for his wilful half-truth to Fran. He found his mind lingering on the OxyContin he'd not taken, back in the bathroom cabinet. He should really throw them out. Their reminder of where not to go was only of value if he didn't go there, and this morning he'd come perilously close. He'd actually taken them out and held them in his hand, for a full minute or so, before putting them back with a snarl.

He leant on his cane and waited. He wore a baseball cap to hide his shaven head and stiches, and gloves and scarf covered the worst of the rest. The sunglasses felt over the top, but it was sunny today and a few punches had made it through. Stark did not want to draw attention to himself. This wasn't easy; loitering on a sleepy high street while people around you got on with things drew glances. He wasn't alone, though. He spotted one or two elderly veterans in blazers and regimental ties and berets, tipped off via their own sources.

Fran stamped her feet and took another sip of scalding coffee, praying some might reach her frozen toes as she watched the police dive team impatiently. SOCO had confirmed blood traces on the doorway. But what else had been disposed of this way?

To preserve the crime scene they were accessing the river from the back of an upstream building opposite. This had the added advantage of holding the divers in place on taut steel cables in the moving water. The two burly guys had cheerfully donned their orange and black drysuits and been winched out into the currents of the recent rain surge, and now they sounded like jovially whingeing Darth Vaders through their full-face mask intercoms, complaining about the 'zero vis', knacker-shrinking cold and the delights of conducting a blind fingertip search in thick gloves when you can't feel your numb fingers in the wicked current.

'They'll whinge about the pay next,' the Dive Marshall predicted.

Fran checked her phone. If this turned out to be a waste of precious resources, she was in the shit. A detective sergeant didn't really have the clout to order this, but Groombridge was busy and Harper hadn't answered her call.

'Don't worry,' grinned the Marshall, reading her thoughts. 'If anyone gets shirty I'll say we had an exercise booked for this morning anyway. Never too far from the truth.'

There came a high-pitched electronic whirr over the radio: the underwater metal detectors the two men were using. 'Got something, boss . . .' One of the divers stood up in the river ten metres or so past the door to the lock-up, the water cutting a wake around his chest as he fought to keep his feet. He held up an orange mesh goody-bag with something colourful inside.

The Marshall and two others winched the diver in and helped him out of the water.

A pair of be-gloved SOCOs opened the lanyard and tipped the goodies out on a pristine tarp, one of the crew photographing everything for the evidence trail.

A plastic bin bag, water running out through several tears.

They peeled open the bag. Inside were a set of keys and the smashed remains of a portable hard drive.

Over two hours a crowd formed around Stark and swelled to hundreds. The old veterans stood chatting in the cold air, their breath catching the low sun, several now holding black-tipped regimental and British Legion standards. The mayor joined them in his ceremonial gold chain. Cameras too. TV and press. Stark kept his cap peak low.

The bell in the small clock tower began a slow-beat chime. All activity on the high street stopped. Customers and shopkeepers alike filed out to join the crowd lining the road. A small boy leant out, peering along the street impatiently before his mother reined him in.

Then, at the far end of the street, a funeral mourner in black top-hat, tails and cane appeared on foot, leading a solitary black hearse with glass sides displaying the coffin draped in the Union flag, followed by an unmarked police four-by-four with blacked-out windows and a patrol car.

The hearse was on its way from RAF Lyneham, where its cargo had just been repatriated from Helmand, to the John Radcliffe Hospital and the Oxfordshire city coroner. The forty-six mile route took them through Wootton Bassett. The mayor and local members of the Royal British Legion had started standing by as a mark of respect and it had snowballed from there. Now half the town turned out each time, and visitors, answering the tolling of the bell.

The cortège crawled up the street to whispered quiet, and a soft ripple of applause.

Across the street a woman burst into tears, Lovelace's mother. And another, younger, the fiancée Pierson had told Stark about, comforted by family and friends. Opposite, representatives from the regiment called to attention and saluted. Among the crowd, those that had served did likewise.

The little boy waved a small plastic Union flag with uncertain aplomb.

Stark removed his shades and cap and pulled on his beret, regimental badge gleaming, and saluted the passing of a comrade. It was only much later after their brief service together that Stark even learned his first name, but a comrade all the same.

Corporal Nathan Lovelace, survivor of the deadly day

that saw Stark honoured with the VC he now wore under his jacket, killed on his second tour trying to rescue injured comrades as he had once watched Stark do. Stark shouldn't feel responsibility for this. In such moments each does what he or she thinks right; that's soldiering. But he did feel it all the same. For Lovelace; for all of them still fighting, still dying.

The standards lowered to horizontal as the hearse drew up and stopped in front of the memorial. Family and friends stepped forward to place flowers on its roof, pausing to look in at the coffin, retreating in tears and hugs. A regimental bugler struck up the Last Post.

Stark had not expected to hear it again so soon.

As the last note faded into the still air, another ripple of applause rose and faded.

The cortège passed.

The bell stopped.

The weeping did not.

Stark changed hats again and waited at the bus stop as the crowd broke up, watching the old vets chatting and shaking their heads. One of them looked his way, catching his eye, and nodded, recognizing him for what he was, if not who.

A while later the bus arrived and Stark sat on it with deep relief to be off his feet. He would not attend Lovelace's funeral, he had no place there, but he had paid his respects at least.

Now it was time to pay the piper.

He pulled out his phone and dialled.

55

'So . . .' Fran pointed to the newest photos. A second board had been 'borrowed' from CID and placed next to the first.

'The lock-up is tucked away on its own. Uniform are canvassing, but so far no reported sightings of anyone coming and going. But here's the kicker – Land Registry say it belongs to T&C Security Ltd.'

'Thomas Chase and Clive Tilly's old company?' asked Dixon.

'Now owned outright by Chase Security. It's where they started up. And someone there used it to register a PO Box to run a fake invoice. And that's not all . . . Inside we found a list of addresses; with those crossed off matching burglaries going back three years. A hoard of moody-looking goods, we're cross-checking against items stolen. Boxes of disposable overalls, disposable overshoes and disposable gloves. Partial prints found on three items so far match Carlton Savage. Blood splatter type O, matches Savage. And Savage is a self-confessed burglar and falsifier of alibis. But if there's one thing we know for sure, someone else was in that lock-up with him. Some SOCO nerd calculated from the bullet impact height that if Savage was the victim, then the killer was probably between five-foot nine and six-foot one, for what that's worth.' Fran's blood was up. Finally it felt like they were getting somewhere.

'The van is on fake plates. More fakes found inside. All

the VIN numbers removed so we can assume it's stolen, probably used exclusively for the burglaries. Carlton Savage's pimped Honda was found two streets away.

'The wood-burning stove in the lock-up was recently used. SOCO are analysing the contents, but doubt they'll find much. Handy way of *disposing* of disposable overalls and gloves, et cetera. Not to mention identifiable goods. But whoever did got careless.' She pointed to the photo of the black glove. 'Size large. Same brand issued to Chase Security staff. Gunshot residue confirmed. Sent to lab for DNA testing – should be plenty of hand sweat.'

'Anyone willing to bet against Simon Kirsch?' said Harper darkly. The edge in his voice said he was still hissy at not being in on the find, but if he wanted to waste time playing the big man at Scotland Yard, then too bad.

'I've asked my contact in Forensics to lean on the testing team.' Fran pointed to the next photo. 'Ballistics have confirmed the weapon recovered was a Webley – Mark Four, loaded with the same thirty-eight-calibre, two-hundred-grain, wartime bullets that killed Thomas and Mary Chase. Bullet comparison shouldn't take long. The serial number's been filed off the gun. Geeks have techniques but even if they recover it, this mark was manufactured for British and Commonwealth forces from 1932 to 1963, approximately half a million made and the CSM said they can be hard to trace.'

'Thomas Chase had an old revolver, his grandfather's,' said Dixon.

'Yes.' Fran nodded. 'If only there was someone here with army connections to help check . . .'

Harper ignored the jibe, but she shouldn't push her luck. 'What about the keys?'

'Confirmed as copies of the Chases' house keys.'

Harper nodded. 'Easy enough for a trusted employee to snaffle.'

'The killer just let themselves in,' said Williams.

'Looks like . . .' agreed Fran. Stark would be looking insufferably un-smug if he was here. He never had believed in a break-in. 'And then there's this . . .' She pointed at the last photo – the smashed computer hard drive. 'Size and make match the empty cases found near the Chases' safe and later in their garage, but I'm willing to bet this one was from the safe. Forensics aren't very chatty on the chances of retrieving anything from it, but there's a second one out there somewhere.'

'And Simon Kirsch, aka Mark White, took it and killed a copper in the process,' added Harper, as if it needed repeating. 'Whatever's on that drive is key to this, and that puts Kirsch slap bang in the frame.'

'Maybe they were back-ups of each other,' suggested Williams. 'The killer needed both to be sure?'

'Kirsch,' said Harper firmly. 'And once he had them he did away with Savage.'

Fran wasn't certain. 'Not sure who I'd put as alpha dog.'

'But Savage was in on it after all,' said Harper, pleased. 'He and Kirsch were partners.'

'There didn't seem to be much love lost between them,' said Williams.

'An act,' said Harper. 'Or a falling-out after burglary-gone-bad.'

Fran bit her lip rather than point out that assumptions were dangerous. 'There's nothing linking Simon Kirsch to the lock-up.'

'You haven't found anything yet, you mean,' said Harper.

Fran let that go. 'We should ask Clive Tilly about the place. The Chases were skimming the taxman's share off the business. Maybe they were part of all this. Maybe he was too. This wasn't Revenue and Customs exacting revenge. Someone wanted us to think the Chases' murder was a burglary. There was something on those hard drives someone wished there wasn't.'

'Agreed. *Simon Kirsch*. And the sooner we collar him, the sooner we can bang him up and piss off down the pub.'

Fran rolled her eyes but said nothing. Much as she disliked his bombastic certainty, and everything else about him, he was right about one thing: if they wanted to know what really happened, getting Simon Kirsch safely off the streets would be a fair start. But uniform were getting nowhere. Kirsch had disappeared. If he had one false identity he might have others. A change of appearance and he could be sunning himself in Rio by now.

56

Hazel watched Stark settle stiffly on to her consulting room chair. His call asking to see her was unprecedented, troubling enough in itself for her to give up a late Sunday afternoon to meet with him.

Patients rarely unnerved her; she'd seen all sorts. But sometimes she found it hard to look at Stark. He was like a fixed point in space; you knew you were in orbit around him and not the other way around. She didn't understand him. It was that simple. She'd prodded and poked, provoked and tricked him. She'd worked with him, laughed with him, helped him ... yes, helped him, that wasn't pride. But, deep down, he unnerved her.

Physician, heal thyself, she thought.

His call had come out of the blue. Never before had he *requested* an appointment. His work colleagues were worried about him, and now Hazel was too.

He looked pale and gaunt, his head shaved to stubble around a rippled line of sutured skin with black fishing-line stitches, a split lip, bruising around one cheek and eye; split knuckles on both hands.

She'd read his A&E chart. He'd been prescribed pain-killers. She didn't know whether to hope he'd taken them or not.

Opposing forces had been stretching him thinner and thinner for two years now, perhaps longer. Duty and Guilt. Two powerful locomotives in a tug of war, not realizing they were on a circular track and that if the couplings ever let go they'd hurtle round and meet head on. She'd watched the darkness rise and be squashed down, rise and fall; listened to his justifications, obfuscations, frustrations; waiting, slipping in observations where she hoped they'd best help. Hoped. Such an inexact science, sometimes she wondered whether psychology was closer to faith. No, not faith. Philosophy, though.

It wasn't her fault. He'd come to her damaged. Among other things, Combat PTSD was a moral injury. It impaired the capacity to trust. He'd come a long way; been coaxed kicking and screaming from denial to engagement, but he'd always held something back, something she had not understood. Now that thing was slowly pulling him under. No, that wasn't quite right. It was holding him fixed while the waters rose about him. That was one of the key differences between military PTSD and civilian. The more the patient reintegrated, the more they reawakened to the complexities of civilian life, the stresses, the higher the tide rose about them. The patient had to rise with it. You had to help them swim. Stark was stubbornly holding his breath. Unless she could untangle the knot, this depression would engulf him and Christ knows where he'd wash up, if he ever did.

He was watching her too.

He never spoke first.

'How are you?' she asked genially.

'Operational.'

He typically answered direct questions directly, so she typically avoided them. But today was different. Today *he'd* asked to see *her*. 'How are you sleeping?'

'Not well.'

Sleep deprivation was the killer. It dulled rationale, undermined ethical self-restraint and impulse control, gave credence to dark thoughts. 'When did you last eat?'

He frowned impatiently. 'I don't know. Yesterday.'

He didn't sound sure. 'Are you in pain?'

'Physical or mental?'

'Either.'

'Yes.'

'Which?'

'Both.'

'It's going to be that kind of session today,' she commented, making a note because she knew it annoyed him.

'My head hurts. My ribs hurt.'

'Your fists?'

'Them too.'

No. This wasn't one of 'those sessions'. He was on edge, on a brink. Of another breakdown perhaps; the signs were similar, yet . . . 'Is there something you want to tell me, Joe?'

The hard stare. Not threatening, not deliberate, just deliberating. What whirled behind those eyes? If only she knew what thoughts were forming in his mind right now she would have the key, she could save him. The perennial shrink wish – and conceit.

'Is there something you want to ask me?' he countered.

'Many things.'

'What stops you?'

'I'm afraid.'

'Afraid?' His eyes softened. One thing she did know was that he did not like causing harm, causing fear. 'Of me?'

'No. I have back-up.' She chuckled, fingering the big panic button around her neck. She suspected he could kill her with the damn thing before she could press it, if he chose. She wasn't afraid that he would. It was nothing new; a determined man could always overpower and kill her if he chose, when she worked in prisons, here in her office, out in the street, at home in her bed – that was the vulnerability of her sex. Her work was strange insulation against that. 'I'm afraid of asking the wrong questions.'

He frowned. 'I thought there was no such thing as a stupid question.'

'In my line of work the wrong question can shatter trust.'

'Ask it.'

'Ask what? Why you requested this appointment?'

'Ask me –' he began, but could or would not continue.

Hazel forced herself to sit still. There *was* something he wanted to say, wanted desperately, but couldn't. What was the question? 'What hurts *mentally*?' she asked.

'No. Not that,' he shook his head chidingly. 'That's the effect. The *cause*; you have to understand the cause.'

'I'd like to, Joe. Perhaps you could help me?' His fists were flexing and his jaw was tight. From him, those two small signs were akin to screaming. Anger. With her?

'I'm not angry with you,' he said. She was not the only observer in the room.

'Who, then? At the men who attacked you last night?'

He chuckled, shaking his head sadly. The tension in him was beginning to give, to give up. He was giving up. She was losing him, losing the moment, asking the *wrong* questions. 'With yourself, then?' she asked desperately.

'Obviously.'

'Why obviously, Joe? You fought to protect yourself.'

'Didn't I just.'

Hazel frowned. 'You're saying . . . you enjoyed it? Is that it?'

He said nothing, just closed his eyes.

So that *was* it? After all this time? The moment hummed like a taut wire but now, at last, she could guess. 'How did it make you feel? Is that the question?'

Stark breathed out a barely audible sigh. 'Bingo. The clumsy, ham-fisted, clichéd prodding of the snake-oil head-shrink,' he said softly. 'Tell me; how did that make you feel?' His eyes opened, shining with life. 'It made me feel wild, free, unleashed, *righteous*. I despised them for their cowardice, their callous stupidity, but I loved them for it too, for letting me hate them, for the outlet. And I thanked them in kind. How did it make me feel? It made me feel *alive*.'

Hazel thought quickly. He was not the first man to feel this, nor the first to confess it to her. This was not the problem. Finally it began to fall into place. How long since she'd thought they'd passed this point? More than a year. 'Guilt, Joe? Again?'

'The difference between you and I,' he said softly, 'is that you believe guilt can be faced, packaged and put away whether justified or not, while I believe that justified guilt is rational, honest and that subsuming it is a crime.'

'But we talked about this, so many times. You never felt remorse for the lives you took. You explained eloquently. And you've always understood survivor-guilt, faced that there was little more you should or could have done, I thought we'd made progress on that?'

'Progress . . .'

'So what is it? What is it that's hurting you, Joe?'

'You've always come at this from the wrong direction,'

he said kindly, but wearily. 'You've always assumed you are treating someone haunted by war.'

'You're *not* haunted by war?'

'Of course I am.' He smiled, a parent coaxing a child towards the conclusion. 'But . . .'

'You also miss it. But that's nothing unusual, Joe, many veterans —'

'I don't miss the institution,' he interrupted firmly. 'I don't pray for the order of military routine to save me from the chaos of civilian irrationality. I don't miss the safety, the camaraderie, the bond of friends laying their lives on the line for each other daily. I don't miss the uniform, or knowing my place in the ranks of life. I miss the *violence*. I miss the cold, hard fury. Knowing that I must kill or be killed, kill or risk the lives of comrades, kill in the name of right, principle, justice, democracy, family, country. And the guilt I feel for actions past is nothing to the fear I feel that people will see me for what I really am, red in tooth and claw, knowing that I must never reach across the gap between me and people I love, or might love.'

Another person delivering such a conclusion might weep. Stark merely stared, as if daring her to contradict him.

Hazel sat back and placed her pen on her pad. 'Well,' she sighed. 'We've come a long way, you and I. And yet you can still surprise me.'

'I'm glad I still cause amusement.'

Hazel tilted her head. 'I'm not surprised at what you've told me, Joe. I'm surprised that it's taken this long to come out. You're far from the first person to feel this way.'

'Sharing a psychosis doesn't lessen it.'

'Joe . . .'

'Don't look at me like that. I'm not here for sympathy.'

'Perish the thought.' Hazel pondered for a moment. 'You once told me off sharply for asking about an ex of yours – Julie, wasn't it?'

'Yes.'

'You insisted it wasn't relevant that you pushed her away after you were injured. You were probably wrong, of course.'

'Probably.'

'And Kelly . . . You explained what happened, calmly, rationally. Are you going to bite my head off if I ask about it again?'

'That depends on whether you ask the wrong question,' he said, watching her carefully.

'Kelly is effect, not cause,' agreed Hazel. 'Then, tell me, Joe, how does that make you feel?'

57

Stark emerged from Hazel's torture chamber, drained. He'd said his piece, she hers. She might note it down as a milestone. He just saw another hurdle crashed into.

With another due any moment. He'd told her about the reporter, Gwen. She'd hinted before that he should consider telling his side, drawing a line under the story under his own terms. Her suggestion implied a faith in the press that Stark didn't share. It was out of his hands now anyway. Bullets flew where they would.

Standing up to leave had been like lifting twice his weight, like wounded man exercise, but instead of running with a man over his shoulder he was barely carrying his own weight. His ribs stabbed. His legs were like lead and everything hurt. He needed to take on fuel, but was struggling to find anything appetizing in the cafeteria downstairs when his phone rang.

For some reason he thought it might be Selena, but it wasn't.

'Major? I thought you were off me,' he said.

'You're an idiot,' said Pierson.

Stark sighed silently. 'I've spent the last hour being told just that. Perhaps you could narrow it down?'

'First you waste my time on a spurious question and then don't follow up with the pertinent one.'

'Which is?'

'You're supposed to be the detective, think . . .'

Then it hit him; he'd asked her about Mark White. 'Was there ever a Simon Kirsch in the FFL?'

'No.'

'Meaning yes?'

'Meaning no.'

'So he used a different name? His mother's maiden name is Larson.'

'No and no. He had his passport. Simon Kirsch.'

'Hang on, you said . . .' Stark paused. 'He was rejected?'

'Failed the medical,' confirmed Pierson. 'Heart murmur.'

So Simon Kirsch had fled his past in the UK for the romantic dream of serving in the Foreign Legion, only to be knocked back. 'Do they have any idea what he did after? Did he stay in France?'

'Getting them to cough up *that* much was like asking them to drink red wine with fish. And on a Sunday . . . You would've thought I was asking them for the crown-bloody-jewels.'

Stark decided now was not the best time to point out that the French had toppled their crown, beheaded their royalty and presumably flogged the jewels to fund their bloody republic. Pierson was chalking up the IOU and enjoying it. The French had not volunteered this information. For all her declared irritation, Pierson had called them of her own volition and doggedly worn them down. 'Thank you.'

'Talking of which, pay your respects?'

'Yes.'

She was silent on the line. Stark wondered if she had further bad news to impart. 'Good man,' she said, ringing off. Stark shrugged in bemusement. He stared at the rations on offer but couldn't face them. He just wanted to go home to bed but now he had one more stop to make.

Fran gripped the TV remote in her hand, trying not to hurl it at the screen in disgust.

Harper, bullishly proclaiming that further evidence had come to light linking the death of Carlton Savage to that of Thomas and Mary Chase, that the police now believed Mark White and Simon Kirsch were indeed one and the same and that it was only a matter of time before he was found.

He'd wasted no time getting back in front of the cameras, taking credit. Compensation for biological insufficiency, thought Fran uncharitably. She was getting heartily sick of seeing him on TV. Somehow it was worse than seeing him in person. It had never, not even once, occurred to her that he would make inspector before her. She wasn't jealous; not really. She was a sergeant and a bloody good one; better than Harper ever was. She'd be a better inspector too, when the time came, but she'd hoped that would be years away. Too many distractions from real police-work, too much politics and media. But finding herself working under Harper hadn't featured in her plans.

He was a prime example of how it wasn't only cream that floated. The police force, like any large organization, failed to achieve meritocracy. As a woman of colour, she was acutely aware of that. And in her experience, those with a burning desire to move on up were as often motivated by a fear of being exposed for incompetence at their current level as they were by overconfidence, and too often, like Harper, a twisted combination of both.

Temporary; she just had to remember it was temporary.

Ballistics had test-fired the Webley revolver and ammunition. The resulting bullet markings were a match for those recovered from Thomas and Mary Chase. The NABIS database still offered no matches from other crime scenes. They had no bullet from Savage's body. It was probably in the Quaggy, but the divers had just laughed at the hope of finding it unless the river miraculously dried up overnight. Using X-ray first, and then acid to expose the metal fatigue shadow of the stamping, they'd recovered a nearly complete serial number from the revolver, but without the whole number they had little or no chance of tracing it.

More significant: Marcus had come up trumps with the lab geeks. Professional courtesy, which had been notably absent all the times *she'd* begged them to get a bloody move on. They'd verbally confirmed a preliminary match between the DNA in the glove to the sample submitted by Kirsch when he was still pretending to be Mark White.

Harper didn't go into detail, of course, confirming only that police had searched a property and an area of the Quaggy River, and a weapon had been recovered. He looked straight into camera, grave and commanding. 'If you're listening, Simon, the net is closing in. You *will* be brought to justice, one way or another. Turn yourself in before it's too late.'

'Before my big head crushes me,' added Fran in a mock-Harper voice.

'Did I miss anything?' said someone behind her.

Fran jumped so hard that her feet, hitherto resting up on her desk, slipped off and kicked the contents of her bin all over the floor. 'Jeeezus!' she hissed, angrily scooping up the detritus to cover her shock.

'Sorry,' said Stark.

'What the hell are you doing here? You look like crap.'

'Always good to hear,' he replied, limping to his desk and sitting, hooking his cane on the lip of the photocopier. 'So what's been happening?'

Fran gave him a summary. 'And you?'

'Sightseeing,' he lied.

'Not resting, then.'

'It's a zen thing.'

'So what brings you here this sunny evening?' she asked, indicating the chilly darkness outside.

He explained Pierson's findings. 'I thought maybe Interpol might have something.'

Fran doubted that. They'd already tried the aliases they knew. 'Any chance you could call in another favour with Major Pierson?'

'I'm in debt.'

'A little more won't hurt then.'

'Tell that to the economists.'

She explained about the gun, and he nodded with little enthusiasm. 'Worth asking, I suppose,' he said, dialling.

'You'd better be calling to reiterate your eternal gratitude, and not to ask another favour,' said Pierson.

'Put this one on Fran's tab. She's here on speakerphone.'

Neither woman said hello. 'DS Millhaven's credit has limits too,' said Pierson.

'More or less than mine?'

'Out with it.'

'Clive Tilly believed one of Thomas Chase's grandfathers had a World War Two revolver, but we only have a partial serial number . . .'

'And you want me to trawl through the archives to see

if it was his?' She sounded far from keen. If the records had been kept in any semblance of order at all it would be a miracle, and God knows what damp or dusty basement they languished in.

Fran held up a piece of paper and Stark read out the details.

'Have you any idea how laborious this might be?' asked Pierson irritably.

'You have underlings, I presume.'

'I list you in that number, *Sergeant* Stark. Though the world seems to have turned on its head.'

'The world is no respecter of rank. Justice even less so.'

'Don't appeal to my better nature. I don't have one.'

'We both know you're all fluffy kittens inside.'

'Fuck off.' She hung up.

Fran blinked, wondering if all their conversations went that well. 'She'll do it?'

Stark nodded.

She grinned. 'She'll put it on your tab.'

He nodded again. 'Talking of which . . . fancy a drink?'

He looked like he needed one. Fran bit her lip. She hated the idea of him drinking alone, especially in his current state, but she had plans. 'Sorry . . .'

He shrugged, plucked up his cane and stood with a suppressed grunt. Christ, he looked terrible. She was about to change her mind when her phone beeped to announce a text. She read the ID with a smile and when she looked up moments later, Stark was gone.

58

Sometimes drinking alone was fine, sometimes not. Most times it was simple necessity.

Chopsticks protruded from the plastic Chinese take-away containers on the coffee table in front of him, half-eaten and abandoned. Stark sipped his beer without tasting it, staring at the large manila envelope he'd found waiting on the mat. Hand delivered. Hand addressed.

Stark
For when you change your mind . . .

He'd almost binned it.

Like he'd almost binned the business card, but hadn't.

Ripping it open, he'd pulled out printed photos with a sinking heart.

Selena on his arm, then frozen mid-scream. The fight in the street; grainy, street-lit, damning.

And Wootton Bassett. The cortège, the weeping, his form in the crowd, leaning on his distinctive cane in cap and shades. And a zoom shot of him saluting in those brief moments he'd exposed his battered face. Gwen had invested in a better camera. And hidden in plain sight among the others. His foolish threats had clearly caused the opposite effect to that he'd hoped for, and exactly the effect he'd feared.

There was a note.

You've got my number . . .

I certainly have, he thought, grinding his teeth. He should've been politer. But if she thought she could leverage him with this shit he'd enjoy telling her to fuck off even more the second time.

He wondered where Selena was right now. Scared off for sure, he thought, looking at her frozen face. Just as well.

His mobile made him jump.

Unknown caller.

He ignored it on principle. The caller declined to leave a message, but then rang again. Surely Gwen hadn't got his number. If there was one thing more aggravating than a cold caller, it was a persistent one. Stark snatched up the phone. '*What?*'

Silence. Then, 'I'm sorry . . . I should've called.'

'*Kelly?*'

'Yes. I'm sorry. I . . .' More silence. 'Just to check you were okay.'

'I'm fine,' Stark lied automatically.

A pause. It hurt her the worst when she knew he was lying. 'A physio I know saw you in A&E last night. Said you were covered in blood.'

'It's a long story.'

She waited for him to say more, but what could he say? He had deleted her number from his phone and asked her not to call.

'I heard about Nathan Lovelace,' she said hesitantly. 'I'm *so* sorry . . .'

The choke in her voice rent his heart. 'I can't do this.'

'Joe, please . . .'

'Thanks for calling –'

'I love you, Joe . . .'

'I know.' He hung up. 'I love you too,' he said to the silence, where the cruelty of the words could harm none but him.

The phone rang again, before he could even put it down. 'Please,' he said desperately. 'Just leave me alone.'

Silence again. 'I might, should you return the courtesy,' said Pierson.

'I'm sorry,' sighed Stark. 'I thought you were someone else.'

'I guessed.' She didn't ask who. 'Let's make this quick then . . . I'm halfway through pasta, Chianti and packing –'

'Packing?'

There was a momentary hesitation. 'Even shiny arses need to get out of the basement into sunshine occasionally. Now, I've news on our gun if you've a mind to listen?'

'*Our* gun?'

'Property of the Ministry, technically.'

'Good luck asking for it back.'

'Don't be trite. Now, my army of underlings have come up with two possible names.'

'Already?'

'I believe speed is of the essence, in such matters?'

'Indeed.'

'So, of the two grandfathers you named, one was too young to serve and the other was an RAF mechanic at Biggin Hill. So no match to your pistol. However, I am emailing a list based on the serial number variables. Eyes only, Sergeant. You may find number eight interesting. And should you need anything else . . . please don't hesitate to piss off.'

'I love you too,' muttered Stark to the sudden dial tone, wondering how many ways there were to mean those words.

He opened the email. A list of ten names – zero to nine variables of the unclear serial number digit. The X-ray and acid-etching photos made it look like a three, six or eight. He scanned down. And stopped at eight: Lieutenant Eugene Tilly, London Rifles.

He dialled Fran.

'We really must have a word about the meaning of time off,' she said.

'Are you still in the office?'

'I've got my coat on.'

'Perfect.'

'I've got plans, remember?'

'That gun didn't belong to Tom Chase's grandfather. It belonged to Clive Tilly's.'

59

Fran glanced at Stark as she drove. He looked tired but alert. Pretty much normal, aside from the stitches in his head and countless scrapes and bruises. Given his history he probably thought they *were* normal. She sounded the horn at a van that had the temerity to pull into her lane, altered course and squeezed the car between two buses, sensing Stark flinch.

'The keys,' he said suddenly. 'From the river . . .'

'What about them?'

'If we search Tom's office or home again, will we find a set of keys to Clive Tilly's house?'

Fran thought this through. 'A reciprocal arrangement?'

Stark nodded. 'Best friends.'

'Best friends water your plants and feed the cat . . .'

'And lie about guns . . . ?'

It was as simple to believe as Simon Kirsch stealing the keys but, although she loathed to think it, Fran hoped Harper was right. One killer was better than two.

Tilly wasn't at home, so they were heading to his office. They could have called ahead but they wanted to make this informal, amiable, and above all lawyer-free. She yawned. Under the circumstances cancelling her 'plans' was for the best, but she still felt a pang of regret.

This development had her head muddled. It just didn't feel like they had unravelled the knot. It came down to who at Chase Security knew about the operation running out of the old lock-up. As well as using it as a base for the burglaries, someone had run at least one parallel company scam, possibly diverting customer orders to the different address. Was that Simon Kirsch and Carlton Savage too, or was someone higher in on it all? It could have been another side-scam instigated by Thomas and Mary Chase. Burglary seemed a little blunt, a little blue-collar compared to their white-collar frauds.

Or was it Tilly? He'd lied; or at the very least omitted to mention that if Tom's grandfather had brought a revolver back from the war, it wasn't the only one.

Her stomach growled loudly as they sat idle at the lights, protesting missed dinner. As if in reply, Stark's growled too. A smile crept over both their faces, and they broke into chuckles, shaking their heads. Probably wondering what it was that drove them to eschew sustenance and rest to go chasing down a single anomaly on a Sunday evening.

God, it felt good to laugh, to let the absurdity of it all out. Better still to see Stark laugh, to know he hadn't forgotten how.

The radio crackled into life: *All cars – shots fired at Stone Lake Industrial Park – business premises – Chase Security Ltd. Staff hiding on site report armed suspect motorcyclist still on premises. ARV and ambulance inbound. Repeat, all –*

The radio message rattled on but Fran had already flicked on the siren and concealed lights and booted the car into the oncoming lane and across the red lights. Stark called in their proximity as other cars did likewise.

Only three streets away, they arrived first, with other cars still minutes away. Fran cut the siren and lights and pulled up short of the gate to wait for the armed response vehicle.

'Wait here,' Stark ordered. But at that moment a motorbike shot out of the gates, turned their way, wavered and then skidded to a halt ten metres away, headlight glaring straight into their eyes.

'Fuck!' hissed Fran. She couldn't see anything but the glare, but it had to be Kirsch. What was he doing?

'Get down!' barked Stark, grabbing Fran's jacket and dragging her towards him.

Fran's head clipped the wheel on its way down and she yelled a curse at Stark just as the windscreen imploded to the sound of five deafening gunshots.

Gasping, choking, heart in her mouth, Fran was only distantly aware of the revving engine and squeal of the bike racing away into the night.

PART THREE

60

'This is *your fault*,' growled Harper at Stark, his bitter expression stuttering in the blue flashing lights like some twisted stop-frame animation. He looked tired, the strain telling. 'You and your army girlfriend. We could've had Tilly in *custody*!'

'He was dead before we got here,' said Fran wearily. Adrenaline had lasted a full ten minutes before it pulled off its mask to reveal the grinning face of shock. That had eventually given way to bone-numbing weariness. The lights tore at her eyes like sandpaper and she had to stop herself barking at one of the uniforms to turn the bloody things off. She was still finding glass in her hair. Her car squatted beneath plastic tarp like a fat corpse. A work car, of course, but it felt like hers. Her second-best hair comb was still in the glove compartment; now a crime scene. She'd be stuck with a pool car now, or Stark's driving.

'You didn't get here soon enough, then, did you?' said Harper. 'We've got a dead cop and now a dead suspect. We'll be a laughing stock!'

Stark cleared his throat.

Harper's eyes narrowed. 'Something to say, Constable?'

'Not a thing,' said Stark evenly.

Harper bristled. 'When told to speak, you will address me as Detective Inspector, or Guv. Is that clear?'

'Crystal.' Everyone waited for a Detective Inspector or

Guv, but neither were forthcoming. Fran nearly laughed. Stark had a far subtler impatience than her, but he was pushing his luck.

There was a polite cough from behind them. Marcus Turner stood in his anti-contamination gear, the mask pulled down around his neck.

'What've we got?' demanded Harper.

'Five bullets: one to the face, four to the chest after the body fell. Thorough but messy. First took the back off the skull and lodged in the wall. No shell cases.'

'So a revolver again,' said Harper. 'Thirty-eight?'

'Forty-five,' said Stark quietly.

'You saw it?' asked Marcus, interested.

Stark shook his head. 'Too loud for a thirty-eight.'

Marcus nodded, seeming to accept this. 'We'll know for sure soon enough. The SOCO chaps will pull it out once the photographer's finished. Sorry about your car,' he said to Fran sincerely. 'Looks like your biker left you a nice tyre track, though; perhaps you'll have some luck there. And then there's this . . .' He held up an evidence bag containing the bloody envelope found placed on the body. Scrawled on the front was one word – *Police*.

'What's inside?' asked Fran. Stark had insisted she leave it for the bomb squad and SOCO.

'Hard drive,' muttered Stark, looking down as eyes turned on him.

'Feels about right,' agreed Marcus. Fran was reaching for it but he pulled it to himself. 'I'll make sure Forensics process it at something other than their standard glacial pace, of course. Get you a copy of the content asap.'

Fran cursed. If it was indeed the twin of the smashed

one from the river, she needed to see what was on it now, not tomorrow!

Marcus looked apologetic, but unmoved. 'So . . . Any notion who perpetrated this dark act?'

'We had better hope it was Simon Kirsch,' said a new voice behind Fran. 'Or Superintendent Cox is going to blow an aneurysm.'

Groombridge, lurking in earshot as was his wont. How long had he been here?

'Not to mention the damn press,' growled Harper.

Groombridge patted him on the shoulder reassuringly. 'I'm sure you can handle them.'

No doubt, thought Fran, and welcome to it.

Harper nodded to her and Stark. 'Right, I want a full report on my desk before either of you thinks of swanning off home.'

Dixon and Williams had been called in and were in the CCTV suite helping scan traffic-cam footage for the bike, but the rider had either got lucky or knew to stick to side roads to avoid cameras.

Stark wrote the report. Fran hated doing them, and had even less patience for collaborative writing, especially with Stark. She made some calls, got overtly bored and wandered off to the canteen, leaving him alone.

Tired, he took less care than normal. However he couched it, Harper would find fault or ammunition. Eschewing his usual verbosity, he stuck with dispassionate accuracy, adding nothing of his burning frustration or scalding rage, all now ghostly and beyond description anyway.

He closed his eyes, and rolled his shoulder where he'd

wrenched it pulling Fran down. The old bullet damage still ached in the mornings; tomorrow morning wasn't going to be fun; if it ever came.

'Some people just can't help getting shot at,' said Ptolemy, materializing to place a steaming mug of coffee on Stark's desk. 'Milk and two, I'm told.' He looked dog-tired.

'Have you been home?' asked Stark.

'Double shift,' replied Ptolemy, rubbing his eyes. 'You lot keep screwing up our roster. Here,' he said, glancing around and furtively sliding a piece of paper to Stark.

Five names: two sergeants, three constables.

'I'm not saying it's one of them,' added Ptolemy in a low voice. 'But if things went official, I'd start there.'

'What does Sergeant Clark think?' asked Stark. They hadn't discussed sharing this problem with anyone else, but the two were friends and both nurtured their status as station confidants.

'He reckons it's one of your lot.'

'And you?'

'I don't know. There's a lot of resentment below stairs. Voluntary lay-offs, recruitment cuts, everyone wondering whether involuntary lay-offs are next. Add in overtime restrictions and yet another pay freeze . . . It's getting harder and harder to do our job, harder to motivate people to care, and harder to keep the ones who do. I have three constables trained up for Trainee Investigator slots only for brass to cut their funding, and that's just the start. I've had three more leave because they can't keep a roof over their family's heads on a basic forty hours.

'The politicians lean on the brass who lean on the coppers, but the public still expects . . . This station is running on duty and goodwill, and both have limits. I'm not condoning it, and if I find out one of my lot has been sell-ing out to the press they'll know about it, but it's getting harder to blame them. How about you? Any names?'

'Just one.'

'Begin with an H?'

Stark nodded. 'But I think the leaks started before he got here.' He was in the hospital when the press linked White to Kirsch, but that was as much opportunity as alibi.

'You're assuming there's only one hole in the boat.'

Stark sighed. 'Just hoping.'

Ptolemy nodded. 'And what can good men do but act and hope?' He patted Stark on his unharmed shoulder and left.

Act and hope? Stark looked at the report in front of him. If only there were some fact he could tweak, some detail he could plant for Harper's eyes only, which were it to turn up on the news would incriminate him . . . Stark shook his head. Woolly fantasy. Unconscionable. Any wrong detail might impede the search. Anger, not logic. It couldn't be Harper, not even him.

Speculation, spying and suspicion within – the whole business left a bitter taste in the mouth.

And this pernicious breakdown in trust was just the internal damage. One individual's casual betrayal, their grubby pieces of silver, would cause this station a cata-strophic loss of credibility. What member of the public would help them, what informant would trust them when they couldn't trust each other? The cost of these leaks was incalculable. He wished Groombridge had never set him on this trail. Surely he'd known Stark could achieve little alone. Ptolemy, Peters and now Clark . . . Who else had been enlisted into Groombridge's growing band of Royal

Hill Irregulars? Maggie for one; Groombridge's perfectly placed spy.

Stark sat up. Maggie. The centre of all information. He got up and wandered down to her throne room and knocked.

'*Sweetie* . . .' She smiled, though it was a touch forced. She looked tired too. 'What can I do for you?'

Stark wondered how to start. Maggie was above suspicion, but her little empire . . . 'It's delicate,' he replied awkwardly.

'Ooh,' she grinned theatrically. 'Better close the door then, sweetie. Let Maggie take a look.'

Fran took her time over coffee. No sense rushing back and spoiling Stark's flow. He seemed to like writing reports, and much as she liked spoiling his fun, in this instance she was prepared to take the higher road.

She wasn't in the least surprised to find him still at it when she came back. Peering over his shoulder, she gave his efforts a withering scan. 'A bit dry, even for you.' *We took cover in the front seats as the assailant discharged his weapon into the car*. Nothing about probably saving her life. Nothing about his cool-headedness afterwards, or her near hysteria.

Stark tried to ignore her as he typed on. For someone who'd blatantly delegated a duty, she was aware that resorting to every impatient tut, huff and fidget in her arsenal was shameless even by her standards, but it *was* fun. 'Come *on*,' she complained eventually. 'I need a bloody drink. It's nearly closing!'

'Thought you had plans?'

'Postponed.'

'You buying?' he asked.

'Don't be facetious.'

A cleared throat behind them announced Marcus Turner.

'Marcus?' said Fran.

The forensic pathologist looked a little flustered. 'Thought you should see this.' He held up an evidence photo – of a hard drive. 'From the envelope, as suspected. Exactly the same make and model as the smashed one from Old Man Quaggy, but this one's functional. I've made you a copy. There's a lot of financial records and accounting that our chaps are translating into English, but there's more . . .'

61

'Okay, what's so urgent?' said Harper, irritable after Fran had pulled him away from throwing his weight around on the uniform floor, where the manhunt was in full swing again.

Stark clicked play on the audio file.

'Make this quick, some of us have work to do.' A man's voice, terse, irritable.

'Take a seat, Clive,' replied a female voice.

'I don't have time for your games, Mary.'

'You'll have time for this . . .' A sound, paper.

'What's this?'

'Every little ghost-company scam you've pulled, every penny you've stolen from this company.'

Tilly laughed scornfully. 'Get off your high horse, Mary. You've been quietly bleeding this company dry ever since you got your feet under that desk.'

'Really? This is my proof. Where's yours?' Silence. 'You can keep that copy. I have it all backed up safe and sound.'

'What do you want?'

'I want you out of my way.'

'And what makes you think that's likely?'

'I know what happened with Billy Forester.'

A pause. 'Bullshit.'

'I overheard you and Tom arguing about it in his office. You thought you were the last ones here but I'd come back for my purse.'

Silence from Tilly.

'I heard everything,' Mary's voice continued evenly. 'You all lied to the police that night. I suppose none of you realized the other driver was hurt, but even so . . . Conspiracy to pervert the course of justice, they call it. I looked it up. The courts take a very dim view.'

'And who's going to believe you?' scoffed Tilly. 'That was . . . over thirty years ago.'

'Luckily I videoed your whole conversation on my phone.'

There was a momentary pause. 'Give me that.'

'As if I don't have this backed up too. Suddenly I understood why Tom kept you on here all these years.'

'He's my best friend!'

'That didn't stop you fucking me, though, did it, Clive?' Mary's voice was sneering now. 'How would Tom feel about that?'

'Who's going to tell him? You?'

'Oh, Tom knows I fool around. He knows it doesn't mean anything. I'm not sure he'd forgive you, though . . .'

'You . . . threw yourself at me,' spluttered Tilly. 'You practically begged!'

'That's not how I remember it.' Stark had never seen Mary alive, but he could picture her now, smiling sweetly. 'Still, don't feel bad. It's only fair you screw his wife since he spent so much time screwing yours.'

Silence.

'Oh dear,' cooed Mary. 'Sandra didn't tell you?'

'You *liar*!'

'Ask her yourself. She came to see me when I got engaged to Tom, tried to warn me off him. So sweet. Still, if it's any consolation, I have all the leverage I need now to take Tom to the cleaners in a divorce.'

'You gold-digging bitch!' spat Tilly.

'Get back in your box, Clive,' snapped Mary, all sweetness abandoned. 'There's nothing left for you here. I'll give you one week to clear your desk and go. And if you breathe a word to Tom I'll drop you both in the shit with the police.'

Another pause. 'You've no idea what you're doing,' said Tilly, a hard, cold edge to his voice.

'I'm winning, Clive,' replied Mary glibly. 'And guess where that leaves you.'

The recording ended with scornful laughter and the sound of a door slamming.

A collective silence pervaded the MIT office.

'Far be it from me to say,' said Marcus, 'but isn't that what you people call motive?'

'His grandfather's pistol gives means,' added Fran, trying to read Harper's blank expression. 'And his hour's "nap" in a petrol station car park half a mile away gives opportunity.'

'This isn't proof,' said Harper. 'All we know for sure is that Simon Kirsch killed him, *and* Carlton Savage.'

'I'm afraid I've news on that score too,' said Marcus. 'The written report came back on the glove you found. Gunshot residue outside. DNA from sweat inside match for your Mark White aka Simon Kirsch, of course, but they also found powdered corn-starch inside – commonly used as surface lubricant on surgical gloves, such as the ones found in the lock-up.'

'Someone wore gloves inside the gloves?' asked Fran.

'Quite neat, when you think about it,' added Marcus. 'Steal gloves belonging to your chosen patsy, pull them on over your surgical gloves, fire the weapon, then burn all the evidence whilst "accidentally" dropping one glove under the stove . . . Pure conjecture, of course.'

'Tilly had access to Kirsch's locker,' said Williams.

'And Savage's,' added Dixon. 'Maybe he put that necklace in Savage's jacket after all.'

Fran made a face. 'Nothing puts Tilly at the lock-up, though.'

Stark rubbed the scar on his right temple, deep in thought. 'What's the betting that if we check the list of burglaries you found in the lock-up we'll find a corresponding list of rejected Chase Security quotes for domestic alarms? Tilly's intel, Savage's skills.'

'Team burglary?' said Williams. 'Makes sense.'

'If so, why would Tilly try framing his partner in crime with that necklace and risk it all spilling out?' Fran objected.

'Pressure from us?' suggested Stark. 'Who better than a burglar to take the rap for a burglary-gone-bad?'

'But Savage comes up with an alibi . . .' added Williams.

'And the pressure doubles,' said Stark. 'Now Savage is a liability. After the necklace, he knows someone is trying to set him up. Maybe he guessed it was Tilly and tried a spot of blackmail. Tilly kills him and frames our next best suspect, White aka Kirsch, for everything. Two birds. One bullet.'

Fran nodded, slowly. 'We've been chasing the wrong man all along.'

'Simon Kirsch shot me with a fucking Taser!' Harper blurted out angrily. 'And killed a traffic cop!'

'Accidentally,' said Stark, shaking his head at the enormity of their error. 'After we drove him into hiding. We did this.'

'*We?*' said Harper. 'You mean *me*.'

'I –'

'You're forgetting that Simon Kirsch killed an innocent schoolgirl twenty years ago, fled abroad, assumed an illegal identity and has lied through his backside every day since. And three hours ago he gunned down Clive Tilly – *deliberately*. So you'd all better get on with finding him before he does it again.'

62

A tap on Stark's shoulder brought him round. He didn't recall falling asleep and blinked, disoriented, in the harsh fluorescent lighting. The archivist waved a file at him impatiently. 'William Forester.'

Two birds with one stone – curiosity and impatience to get out of the same space as Harper. Stark had struggled to summon the requisite charm to endear the archivist to his cause at one in the morning, but name-dropping Fran procured the man's keen cooperation.

Stark got to his feet with a series of aches protesting, and signed for the file. It was thicker than expected, but neat and chronological.

The tale began with the fatal car collision in 1975 – Clive Tilly and Thomas Chase were named as passengers but faced no charges. They spent a night in the cells, sleeping off the shandies. Owner of the car, William Forester, hadn't been drinking but was later prosecuted for causing death by dangerous driving and jailed for four years.

But Billy's brushes with the law hadn't ended with his release from prison. At the time of the crash his girlfriend was pregnant. A daughter, born shortly before his trial, and incarceration: Belinda, shortened to Billie. Unfortunately for Billy senior, shortly before his release the girlfriend shacked up with someone new, restricted visitation, then moved away taking little Billie beyond reach or hope.

So began Billy's descent. Drunk and disorderly more than once, affray, suspected of mugging. Stints of employment for T&C Security ... So he'd come out of jail and worked for his old mates' firm, on and off at least, until his second spell inside in 1982 for burglary. Released after two years only to be killed in a suspected mugging one week later. Not a lucky man. Shot dead on the way home from the pub, wallet stolen.

Stark's eyes scanned through the investigating officer's notes until one section caught his interest. The officer had logged a call from a warden in the prison where Forester had spent his second spell. A former cellmate had attempted to buy favour with information, alleging that Billy had claimed to have taken the dangerous driving rap of another man.

It was Billy's car, his pride and joy, but he claimed Tom Chase had begged a go one night, and it was he who'd caused the crash. Drunk and frightened, Tom then persuaded the sober Billy to take the blame. The other driver had looked relatively unhurt, and the roads were wet; Tom and Clive persuaded him that it would pass as a simple accident. But the next day the other driver had fallen ill and died, brain haemorrhage, and the police had taken a dimmer view of things. Billy shouldered the blame, served the time and kept quiet, all for friendship. But afterwards he had to beg a job from Tom and Clive – his old mates were making their way in the world, and Billy grew increasingly resentful to the point where he somehow blamed Tom for his decline into debt and criminality and consequent second incarceration. The investigating officer had dutifully written it all down, but Billy's prison records charted a decline into volatility and illicit drunkenness, no one else had heard the claim, and the cellmate was dismissed as a time-waster.

The weapon was never found, there were no leads, no suspects, and Billy's family had long washed their hands of him. The officer stamped the case unsolved and moved on.

Stark sat back and let it sink in. So this was what Mary had heard her husband and Tilly arguing about. Perverting the course of justice.

He began to close the file, but something else caught his eye. The weapon wasn't found . . . but a bullet was recovered from the body. There was a close-up photo of the deformed lead. Stark could imagine all too well the damage it had done Billy. It was thirty-eight calibre, two-hundred-grain . . . the same as the one found with the Webley revolver used to kill the Chases.

Coincidence was perfectly feasible, but there was a second. Time of death had been impossible to pin down accurately because the body had been found in water. In Deptford Creek, mouth of the River Ravensbourne into the Thames. Point of entry had never been identified . . . but the Ravensbourne was fed upstream by the River Quaggy.

Coincidence squared.

Alternatively, after his second release from jail, the bitter, desperate Billy Forester had gone looking to his oldest friends for help, or making demands of the men he blamed for his train-wreck of a life, and Tilly had silenced him. Maybe Billy's brief burglary career had been directed by Tilly, just like Carlton Savage later; and with the same fatal conclusion. Mary thought she was threatening Tilly with a short jail term, but Tilly was more frightened that revisiting the case might have led the police to an altogether bigger conclusion.

*

'But there was no bullet match?' Fran yawned.

'I spoke with ballistics from the car,' said Stark. 'In old cases, bullets weren't uniformly scanned. If a case was low priority, the bullet was deformed or there was no weapon found to compare . . .'

'And . . . ?'

'I need your signature to get them to test the old bullet.'

'You're making friends tonight.'

'I'm affable.'

'So you think Clive Tilly killed his oldest pal?'

'Families fall out,' replied Stark. Her words.

Fran signed and Stark scanned the document and emailed it to ballistics. She looked at the clock. Two in the morning. She'd already sent Williams and Dixon home. 'Right. Let's get some sleep. Next briefing is at eight. I need you fit.'

'No need for that,' said Harper. 'You're off for the rest of the week, Stark. And don't give me any guff about being off this weekend. You hit your forty hours for the week long before your extra-curricular jaunts with DS Millhaven over the weekend. And I note that you have six weeks' leave accrued. Take this week off or I'll see to it that you can't carry a single day over in January. HQ have ratified my request for additional manpower. We've got two DCs joining us from DI Graham's team, and three more from outside.' He smiled thinly. 'No need to thank me. I want your timesheet for this week before you go. Not one minute over your forty.'

'Sir,' said Stark, returning Harper's gaze without the contempt he felt. He would not gift Harper the reaction he sought, however tempting. He'd endured far worse

362

during military training, but that had a purpose, to teach you the need to play along, to put personal discomfort aside and do as you were told. You knew the only time being wasted was yours and it didn't matter. But *this* mattered. Brian Bates deserved answers, Susan Watts deserved peace, Mary and Thomas Chase, Carlton Savage and even Clive Tilly deserved their measure of justice. Stark was not so conceited as to believe any of that depended on him, but he should play his part. Otherwise, what was the point in the oath he'd taken?

Harper had taken that oath too, of course. But this smacked of trying to get Stark out of the way, paranoia that he'd somehow snatch the glory again.

Stark risked a glance at Fran and saw her staring at Harper, aghast. Better for everyone if he packed up and left without delay. The last thing the team needed was Fran backed into a corner, though judging from her face it may already be too late.

'Go on then . . .' smiled Harper brightly. 'Off you fuck.'

63

Fran watched Stark meekly pull on his coat and leave. She wanted to say something to him. She wanted *him* to say something. But what she wanted most was to say something to Harper. Instead she bit her tongue. But as Harper turned towards his office she saw him smirk.

He closed the door behind him but was barely in his chair before he looked up to see her closing it behind *her*. He looked at her with enquiring innocence, inviting her rant. He wanted her to crack.

'That's enough,' she said quietly.

'What?'

'You heard.'

'I think you're forgetting yourself, Detective Sergeant.'

'No,' she replied calmly, determined not to lose her temper. 'I'm remembering myself. It's my job to help you get the best out of this team, even when that means telling you you're wrong.'

'Wrong? For managing the load evenly between resources? For hurting your little favourite's feelings?' mocked Harper.

'We need him at his desk.'

'You should be thanking me. It's *my* job to get the best out of this team, and that includes dealing with the resentment created by DCI Groombridge and *you* invariably favouring your little war hero over more experienced constables.'

Fran stared at him, incredulous. 'The other constables *respect* Stark for his obvious talents and commitment and his respect for theirs. The only resentment here is yours; it always has been. Stark is worth ten extra bodies and you know it.'

His eyes flashed with anger. 'Constable Stark is a conniving, contemptuous prick, living off his celebrity –'

'*Celebrity?*' Fran interrupted. 'He got the Victoria Cross, for God's sake!'

'For what? Surviving while others died?'

'You're insane! They don't give them out for nothing.'

'They give them out whenever they need a new hero to gloss over failing public support for their pointless wars, so people like you will lap it up. Well, I don't. I saw through Stark from the start. And this whole conversation only underlines your poor judgement. He's a liability and I want him gone.' It was clear he meant for more than just a week. Harper was finally showing his true colours.

He stood now, leaning forward with his fists planted on the desk, intent on bullying her with his size. 'And don't think I don't see through you too. You've worked to undermine me ever since you got here. I was the DCI's right-hand man. Well, I'm wearing the pips now, *Sergeant*, and you'll come to heel like a good little doggy or I'll have you out of here with so many black marks on your sheet you couldn't get a job investigating lost pets!'

Fran stood her ground, but any hope of keeping her cool had evaporated. 'No one has ever undermined you but yourself. I used to think you were just sad and lazy, but ever since you got back you've been lording it around like a complete tosser. I don't care whether it's your lack of ability, tiny dick or the knowledge that Stark can twist your arm out of its socket any time he pleases, but yours must go down as the most justified inferiority complex of all time. And while you're indulging your childish vendetta, you're not doing your fucking job!'

Harper's face grew darker by the syllable, but Fran wasn't about to let him get a word in. 'I've stood by and kept my mouth shut too long. You're fucking my team and you're fucking these investigations, and if you don't grow up and grow a pair I'll make sure you come out of all this smelling of shit, and the last thing you ever see of this office will be the super throwing your bullshit belongings out the fucking window!'

She was half out the door before he got his first word out – '*Sergeant* . . .' – and slammed the door on the rest, striding out of the office before he could emerge and order her back.

* * *

Hope you're okay. Sorry I ran away. Call me. Selena x

Stark stared at the text. It had arrived hours earlier but he'd only just noticed it. There might still be time to salvage something there but he was no longer in any mood to think about that. Such things were best attended with one's tanks full anyway, not at two in the morning, running on fumes and fury.

He filed Selena away with the rest: Kelly, Fran, Major Pierson and Gwen *sodding* Maddox; each wanting a different piece of him.

Nothing stayed filed away, of course.

Grimacing, he limped into the bathroom and opened the cabinet to stare at the pills.

His life was a daily form of rationing. Yes, he could

walk to work, climb stairs, cycle, run if he had to, perhaps even chase villains over fences, but it all came at cumulative cost. The more he used his damaged body, the more it hurt. So he rationed the pain and, when he had to, mortgaged it with painkillers. Meagre over-the-counter crap these days.

Doc Hazel was always interested in this aspect of his 'coping mechanisms' because she believed he did the same emotionally – rationing heart to avoid hurt, and paying the overdraft with whisky. When he'd first re-entered the world, fighting on both fronts with prescription opiates and whisky had left him teetering on the brink of the abyss.

Next to the forbidden OxyContin sat the sleeping pills, to which he still sometimes turned in dire need, when the nightmares got their claws in. But too often death stalked his waking mind too. The irony of a man who was trying to leave death behind working in the murder investigation team of a central London borough was never far from his mind, but tonight felt worse. Tonight he knew that not only was the job affecting him, he was affecting the job. However blown out of proportion, Harper's resentment of him had grounds. And now Stark's very presence was diverting attention from what really mattered. Worst of all, it was putting Fran in an impossible position.

Stark actually pitied the man. Harper's current domestic status hadn't been mentioned since his return, but when Stark first joined the station all the gossip was of the wife's drunken assaults, Harper's sudden illnesses manifesting more often in cuts and bruises than sniffles and coughs. What no one ever discussed was Harper's restraint. A big man, powerfully built and cocksure, the alpha male; yet there was never any hint of him returning the violence, even in self-defence. Harper needed a different outlet and Stark had turned up just in time. But deep down, he'd stuck by his wife.

It wasn't just Harper, or the day-to-day grind of death – there would always be idiots to contend with or human depravity to confront – in the end it came down to him, Joseph Peter Stark.

He didn't fit. Never had. Never would.

He slowly closed the cabinet door and stared at himself in its mirror, daring himself to give in, to open it again and leave the pain behind, for the next few hours at least. The problem with knowing you could push pain aside was that you started wanting to. A few hours might turn into a few days, and the coward's way out might look more appealing from gutter level. This was the unspoken side of Hazel's interest; watchful concern that a depressed war veteran and a lethal stockpile of opiates and sleeping pills was a risky combination.

He opened the door, popped two OxyContins into his hand and stared at them. Innocent-looking little pills, no different from those you'd take for a regular ache.

His hand shook.

He popped two more, tossed all four into his mouth and lifted the glass to his lips. The good stuff. Royal Lochnagar, Special Reserve. The pale amber glinted green in the harsh bathroom halogen, the golden aroma brutalized by the sickening tang of the pills on his tongue.

A life-long second passed.

Stark spat the pills into the sink with a vicious string of curses, running the tap and forcing them furiously down the plughole with his fingers.

He slammed the cabinet door, shattering the glass.

His fractured reflection glared back. Accusing. Mocking. Pushing himself away, he retreated out to the balcony.

Cold, wet air reached into his lungs like cadaverous fingers. A thick fog had closed in, haloing lights and haunting sounds, shrouding the world beyond, even the hard ground below. If he were to jump, he might fall forever.

The crystal rattled against his teeth as he sipped. He rolled the whisky round the glass, relieved that its true colour and flavour hadn't burned away for good.

Perhaps that was the answer, he thought, savouring with slow, deliberate appreciation. A week off wasn't going to solve things, but Harper had unwittingly shown him what might. Perhaps it finally was time to sample a better life, a calmer life . . . a normal life.

64

Groombridge counted to ten in his head, hiding his dismay in the ever-expanding corner of his mind where he squeezed such things for later consideration. This probably wouldn't go down as the worst Monday morning of his life, but it was building its case. The last thing he needed was a disintegrating team. He glanced around his home from home, reminding himself that the definite advantage of having no windows was that it obviated the temptation to throw yourself out of one.

'Are you sure this is what you want?'

'We worked together for years,' said Harper. 'You had my respect and support. Should I expect less from my sergeant?'

Respect works both ways, thought Groombridge. Harper had been a decent sergeant, but he'd accepted Groombridge as king because it granted him lordship over the constables in turn and placed him first in line to the throne. Fran's appearance had divided both fiefdom and claim. But the Harper he knew back then was better than this. Deep down, he still must be. Groombridge had done some checking. Harper had stood by his wife through her drinking, turning the other cheek time after time. But then, he loved his wife . . . 'Fran is hot-headed, I know, but a formal reprimand?'

'Would you have let her speak to you like that?'

Groombridge noted Harper's use of past tense. 'I have,

and expect to again. It was well after midnight. Tempers were frayed.' And there were no witnesses, he didn't add.

'Will you take her side in this?' said Harper curtly.

Groombridge disliked the inference. 'I trust you're not accusing me of favouritism?'

'Will you issue a reprimand or not?'

Groombridge took a deep breath. Fran had offered her resignation on several occasions in the past but never with such conviction as when she'd confronted him first thing this morning. She would not, could not, work with Harper one more minute, she'd said flatly. It had taken patience and perseverance to talk her down, playing every loyalty card in his arsenal, all the while knowing that Harper would darken his door within the hour and undo all his efforts. 'I will,' he conceded.

Harper couldn't conceal a faint smile of satisfaction.

'But,' continued Groombridge, 'only after the current investigations are concluded.'

Harper's face darkened with anger and Groombridge held up a hand. 'I'm not fobbing you off, Owen. If, when the dust settles, you still insist, I will formally reprimand DS Millhaven and enter it on her file. But for now I cannot, *will* not let this spat undermine what we have to do. We have a duty, under oath.' Not to mention how precariously they stood with HQ. 'So in the meantime I know I can trust you to take the lead. Find a way to work together for all our sakes.'

Harper could not mask his dissatisfaction, but he had little choice. 'I have your word?' he said coldly.

'You have my word.'

Stark raised his hand to knock but the door swung away from his fist. Harper came up short in surprise, then displeasure. 'I thought I made myself clear last night, Constable.'

'I'm off the clock,' Stark replied stiffly.

Harper glanced down at Stark's casual attire, then brushed wordlessly past and stalked away down the corridor.

'Is there something I can do for you?' asked Groombridge.

Stark hesitated, but he'd made his decision. 'Guv.'

'Well . . . ? Come in.'

Stark closed the door behind him, and noted the significance register on his boss's face.

'This an unofficial visit?' asked the DCI, nodding to Stark's clothing.

'I'm not here, Guv.'

'Too late to convince DI Harper of that, I fear,' Groombridge observed. 'Sit.' Two years out of the military and Stark still needed to be told. 'Well?'

Stark slid a sheet of paper across the desk.

'Not your resignation, I hope,' sighed Groombridge. 'You'd have to get in line.'

Stark glanced back at the door. 'DI Harper?'

Groombridge shook his head. 'I wouldn't pin your hopes on that.' He scanned the page and frowned. 'Is this correct?'

Stark had filled in the leave request form with great thought. 'I have the time saved, Guv.'

'*Six weeks?*'

'DS Millhaven has been on my case to take the backlog.'

'I doubt she meant now.'

'She might, if she thought about it.'

'But you didn't risk asking her.'

Stark shrugged.

Groombridge smiled sadly. 'DI Harper told me you'd "requested" *one* week, though that's not the way DS Mill-haven tells it.'

'Guv.'

'How the hell did you end up with so much un-taken leave, anyway?'

'There never seemed to be a good time,' said Stark. To begin with, he and Kelly hadn't known each other well enough to plan holidays, and towards the end it was too late.

'But now? Seriously?'

Groombridge looked like this was somehow the last straw. Stark wondered what Harper had been doing in here – nothing good, that much was certain. 'I know it seems like bad timing, Guv, but there's new bodies due today, DC Hammed will be back at some point and . . .' He trailed off.

'And what?'

Stark gave it his best I'd-rather-not-say face, but he could tell Groombridge was in no mood. 'I'm tired, Guv. And my presence in the team at this time is . . . disruptive.'

'Disruptive.' Groombridge stared at him. He could fill in the blanks well enough. 'Is this about that, or about you? You said you didn't need any time.'

'To be honest, Guv, I'm not sure what I need. But it's not this. I'm . . . not contributing.'

'Is that what you really think?'

'Yes.'

Groombridge leant back in his chair, deep in thought. 'Where would you go?' He didn't just mean for six weeks.

He had always seen through Stark better than most. He knew they stood at a fork in the road.

'I don't know.'

Did he care? That was the question in Groombridge's eyes. Had Stark already chosen a path?

All Stark knew was that he needed time to think, and somewhere else to do it. Some secluded beach bar where he could sink a few beers, eat what the locals ate, sleep under the stars, swim in the ocean and read all day; a place where his decisions would matter as little to others as to himself, and his day-to-day life wouldn't be constrained by a constant fight not to scream.

And if he never came back, so be it.

The DCI's eyes narrowed slightly, as if reading Stark's thoughts. 'What about our other problem?'

Which one? thought Stark bitterly. 'A shortlist, nothing we're confident in.' He rattled off the names from Ptolemy's list.

Groombridge stared at him. 'You've left someone off.' More statement than question. 'DI Harper?'

It was shocking to hear it from Groombridge's lips. 'I never said that.'

'Neither should you. Owen is a lot of things, but not that, I hope.'

'Hope.' Stark didn't mean to say it so flatly.

A stern look from Groombridge was worth ten of Fran's withering glances. 'Owen Harper, I've learned, has mortgaged himself to the hilt to put his wife through rehab. But he would die before he took a penny in charity and he'd arrest any press hack waving a bribe. You may not like each other, but there are more similarities than either of you might care to admit.'

Stark strongly doubted that, but the rest . . . ?

Groombridge drum-rolled his fingertips on his desk, twice. 'It'll be out of our hands soon anyway: HQ are getting pressure from the Home Affairs Select Committee. Hacking, leak or both; they're sending specialists to investigate. I'll arrange for you and Ptolemy to sit with them on the quiet.'

He slid the leave request slowly back across the desk. 'Denied.' He held up a hand to silence Stark's protest. 'I can't spare you, Joe. Not right now. Get through this mess and we'll talk. You need a break, I can see that, and lord knows I understand your other motivation all too well. But whatever you think, this team would be worse for your absence. I'll let DI Harper know I refused your request for a *week* off until after Kirsch is caught. Was there anything else?'

Dismissed. 'No, sir, thank you.'

'Good. Close the door on your way out.'

'And I'll try to resist the temptation to wedge a chair under the sodding handle,' muttered Groombridge after Stark had closed the door.

He pulled open his desk drawer and withdrew an envelope with no name on the front, and wandered up the corridor to Cox's office. The superintendent's PA waved him though.

Cox acknowledged his entry but kept his attention on the TV. The press were reporting the latest killing and the ongoing hunt for Simon Kirsch, but not yet the suspicion that he might be innocent of the first murders.

The item finished and Cox muted the idiot box. 'Long night. Get any sleep?'

'A few hours, sir.'

'Alice giving you a hard time?'

'Our wives are saints to our sins.'

Cox nodded. They were probably in a minority; coppers whose wives hadn't divorced them. 'Ballistics have confirmed?'

'They pulled the old bullet from stores last night. Perfect match. The old thirty-eight Webley revolver found in the lock-up, used to kill the Chases two weeks ago, was also used on Billy Forester back in 1984.'

'By Clive Tilly, to prevent Billy blabbing about the miscarriage of justice,' said Cox, making sure he had it straight. 'And decades later Tilly kills Mary Chase to get a hard drive he believed contained recordings that might lead us to reopen the Forester case. And maybe burglaries too.'

'It's the only theory we have that fits, sir.'

'And Thomas Chase was just in the wrong place at the wrong time. And Mary had a back-up anyway. It all rather backfired on Tilly.'

'And us.'

Cox eyed him warily. 'But that's not why you're here.'

'No. Things have come to a head.'

Cox sighed and turned the television off altogether. 'How bad?'

Groombridge slid the envelope across the desk. 'We need a decision, sir.'

Cox didn't pick it up. He knew what it contained. 'An ultimatum?'

'An inducement.'

'More stick than carrot, wouldn't you say?'

'Whatever works . . . I made my proposals weeks ago. Brass need to make up their minds.'

'In the middle of an investigation?'

'A wise man once told me that we don't know where we are in an investigation until we reach the end.'

Cox smiled at his mistake. 'A wiser man would remember never to throw out aphorisms when he knows he's not the smartest person in the room.' He slid the envelope into his desk drawer and closed it. 'I'm meeting the committee later this morning. I'll see what I can do.'

65

Stark couldn't face the office quite yet. The last thing he needed was another face-full of Harper's petulant aggression. The more tired he got the harder it was to override the urge to plant his fist in it.

He sat in the canteen over coffee and full English, but neither stirred his spirits, or appetite.

It had seemed so obvious. He had expected Groombridge to see the merit of his proposal, the necessity, but until now he himself had not fully grasped how much he desperately *wanted* to go, to leave all this behind. Perhaps that unacknowledged desire had blinded him to the possibility that Groombridge might say no. Or Groombridge had seen it and that was *why* he'd said no.

'Are you wearing some kind of ankle bracelet that electrocutes you if you leave the building?' Fran stood over him looking even more tired than the night before.

'I could ask you the same thing.'

'I had an early meeting with the guv'nor.'

'Me too. He denied my "request" for a week off.'

Fran sat down. 'Our mutual admirer won't be happy about that.'

'No.'

'Did you ever hear from your date?'

'She texted.'

'To apologize for running off?'

'She'd every right to be scared.'

'Seeing her again?'

Stark shrugged. 'She may have seen too much.'

Fran didn't contradict him. 'There's another of your admirers downstairs. Major Pierson. I said you were at home but she seemed to know better.'

Stark huffed. 'Her bracelet's on my *other* ankle.'

'I've never seen her out of uniform. She almost looks human.'

Stark abandoned breakfast and wandered down to reception, curious to see for himself.

Standing with her back to him, perusing the notice-board in slim jeans and a fashion hoodie, Pierson was almost unrecognizable. She turned and noted his questioning look. 'Twenty-four-hour pass,' she explained, taking in his injuries. 'What happened to you?'

'Walked into a door.'

She frowned, disapproving. 'Spare five?'

He nodded and followed her out into the dry, cold morning. On the corner opposite the station was Burney Street Gardens, a tiny public space with a few benches.

The Major didn't sit, so neither did Stark. Old habits. 'Does it get any easier?' she asked. 'Looking back?'

Stark frowned, unsure if she meant what he thought. 'Watching from the sidelines?'

'You know I'd never accuse you of that,' she replied. 'Though I might wear the accusation.'

'No one could say that.'

'I could,' she replied flatly. For the first time in their relationship, for want of a better word, Stark sensed a crack in her façade. She looked up at the high, wispy clouds, silent for a few seconds. 'My regiment is deploying to Helmand in a month. I put in for transfer back as soon as I heard.'

Packing, thought Stark, and all the other odd remarks she'd let slip in recent weeks. 'They said yes?'

A tight smile. 'I've been shining my arse on MoD secondment too long. It's high time I did some soldiering.'

He nodded, uncertain what reaction she needed from him, but could not help his heart sinking a little. Something of his own family's pain, perhaps, the pride and fear of waving a loved one off to war. 'You've deployed before?' He'd never actually asked her.

'Telic Six,' – sixth roulement of the British operation in Iraq – '2005, as a fresh-faced lieutenant.'

Stark was there in the first half of 2006 with Telic Seven as a fresh-faced lance-corporal. How faces changed.

'I'm rejoining the regiment for pre-deployment on Wednesday,' she explained. 'I thought you should know. I'm not sure why.'

'You should've said sooner. I've been pestering you with problems.'

She shook her head and smiled. 'A friend has shown me that the good fight doesn't stop at the edge of some foreign field.'

More than friend, thought Stark; family. 'Then while I am still technically a reservist . . .' He pulled his broken form into something resembling attention, and saluted her. 'Good luck, Major.'

She smiled and saluted back, for the first time entirely without irony. 'Thank you, Sergeant.'

'Hope your arse isn't *too* shiny,' he smirked, 'they'll make you take the CFT again.' The dreaded Combat Fitness Test, a gruelling eight-mile all-terrain march in full combat gear, in less than one hour fifty-five – or else.

'My arse is in fine shape, thank you very much.'

'Indeed it is, Major,' replied Stark, deadpan. If their relationship hadn't begun on such a bad note he might have considered its merits with more than casual appreciation himself. 'I look forward to seeing it safe home.'

'I really must look into what's holding up your discharge,' she said evenly. 'I think perhaps the army could do without you and your cheek.'

'Just so long as it takes good care of your cheeks, Major.'

Stark watched the cheeks in question march away.

'I'm starting to lose count of the women in your life,' said a voice behind him.

His smile faded. Gwen Maddox. At least she didn't have a phone or camera in her hand. 'One more than I'd like,' he replied coldly.

Gwen made a moue. 'I'm crushed.'

'If wishing made it so . . .'

Gwen sighed. 'You didn't call.'

'I've been busy.'

'Care to elaborate?' Hazel's favourite question. Stark's least. 'The slaying of Clive Tilly?' Gwen pressed. 'Shots fired at officers. At you?'

'I told you to stop following me.'

'I have.'

Stark opened his hands to indicate their location, and contemporary proximity within it, hoping his face displayed the appropriate level of scorn.

Gwen shrugged. 'Your reception told me you were out here.'

'And Wootton Bassett?'

'I got there first.'

'A lucky guess?'

'A smart one.'

Stark didn't have the patience for this. 'Leave me alone.'

'We need to talk.'

'Seriously? You want to do this here?'

'Not a good time to be seen talking with a reporter?' she asked pointedly. Another smart guess.

'Not a good location to try blackmailing a police officer.'

She sighed again. 'I'm sorry. The envelope was a bit cloak and dagger.' She gave an odd smile and placed a memory stick on the brick wall in front of her. 'This is all of it. Photos, video, times, dates, notes. No copies.'

Stark stared at it and her with suspicion. 'Why?'

'Your life is yours,' she replied simply.

'What about your big scoop?'

'There's always the next one.'

'Wasn't this going to be your break-through story, your chance to impress?'

'Sometimes it's worth taking a look at who it is you're trying to impress.'

'Or whether you're in the wrong game?'

She shook her head. 'The wrong team, perhaps.'

Stark watched her carefully. She seemed sincere, but his ingrained distrust of her kind was hard to shake. 'Won't you starve?'

She smiled wryly. 'There'll never be a shortage of slime and decay.'

He picked up the stick. 'Was I wrong about you?'

'Probably not.'

'What changed your mind?'

She nodded to the memory stick in his hand. 'Call it cumulative. You should think about hanging on to that. There's good material there. A story worth telling.'

'Still holding out for that exclusive?'

'When you're ready.'

'What if I'm never ready?'

'Everyone talks, in the end.'

The counter-interrogation mantra that Stark liked least. He frowned. In daylight she was older than he'd originally thought. His age or close, in years at least. But there was something in her eyes suggesting she'd covered her share of miles too. There was something else behind this decision, behind those eyes. The same thing he'd seen in eight thousand-plus faces lining up at the Cenotaph two weeks earlier. 'Who did you lose?'

Her face tightened. 'My brother, Rhys. Captain. Welsh Guards.'

'Where?'

'Helmand, last year.'

Stark nearly said *tell his story, not mine*, but perhaps that was what she'd been trying to do in a roundabout way. Until now. 'A story doesn't end when you tell it.'

'I should hope not.' She forced a smile, dabbing her eyes with her sleeve. 'Where would be the adventure?'

'I'm done with adventure.'

Gwen shook her head, with a touch of sadness. 'Somehow, I doubt that.'

Stark made himself useful in the CCTV suite, helping scan recordings, but black motorbikes with riders all in black were almost as common on London streets as white vans. All Stark had really seen himself was the headlight. CCTV at Chase Security couldn't pick out a badge or markings, but blacked-out plates helped narrow down potential sightings.

They thought they'd found it on two cameras inbound and outbound, but no further. Last sighted north of Abbey Wood, there were a hundred ways it could have disappeared in the darkness, not least across the woods themselves. If he'd uncovered the plate or otherwise altered appearance whilst out of shot, it could be any one of dozens of bikes they were now tracing, all of which had proved innocent so far. The longer it went on the greater the temptation to fast-forward too quickly and miss something.

Thankfully Harper had taken himself off to HQ and Stark could relax in the canteen for lunch with his colleagues and the new faces. He ignored the latter's sideways glances. His current appearance would do little to dismiss whatever preconceptions of him they'd arrived with.

On the TV high on the wall Harper made an uncharacteristically bland statement to the press, that the investigation had 'shifted focus'. It was odd watching him mouth off in silence, his words flowing late on the stilted subtitles. News wasn't yet out that Clive Tilly was both latest victim and prime suspect in the Chase killings as well as a killing from the eighties. But too many people in the station knew for that to narrow the source if it leaked.

A few hours more of the world's most boring TV show and Stark was wishing more than ever that he was at home looking for flights online. The phone rang and one of the new faces passed it to him.

'Hello, this is DC Stark.'

'Hi . . . It's Jenny Stubbs.' A tremulous voice. 'Mary Chase's sister?'

'Yes, of course. How can I help?'

'Is it true?' she asked, voice a little hoarse. 'Terry is telling us that Clive Tilly killed Mary.'

Terry had to be the Family Liaison officer. 'That's what we believe.'

'But is it true?'

The FLO would, or should, have included the word *probably*. Mary and Tom Chase were dead. Billy Forester was long dead. And now Tilly was dead. No witnesses and no confession. Certainty died with them. But that wasn't what Jenny needed to hear. They didn't teach this, as Groombridge had said. Meaning you had to learn it by yourself. 'Yes.'

Jenny was silent. Summoning her questions, no doubt. It took several seconds for Stark to realize she was simply crying. Hard enough to deal with in person, impossible over the phone. 'I'm very sorry for your loss.' How people must hate those words.

She sniffed, pulling herself together, clearing her throat, taking a deep breath and letting it out. 'Thank you. For caring. It matters.'

Stark had no response. He'd been thanked before, in uniform; for matters of life, not death. Nathan Lovelace's mother had visited Stark in hospital to thank him, believing he'd saved her son's life. What would she say to him now?

He stared into the past, listening to the dialling tone long after Jenny had hung up; then slowly replaced the receiver.

Fran stuck her head round the door and picked out Stark. 'Come on. We're summoned.'

66

Stark was told to wait outside. Fran took a seat in Groombridge's excuse for an office, wary as a cat ready to hiss.
With Harper out all day she'd probably had time to be
grateful her resignation hadn't been accepted, not that
Groombridge would hold his breath for her to voice it,
given their recent run-ins.

'Right. Well, as you've probably guessed, DI Harper
has made a formal complaint against you and –'

'Arsehole!' spat Fran. 'I told you he would –'

'But . . .' interrupted Groombridge, pointedly. Not getting through his first sentence without interruption wasn't
without precedent, but today she needed to shut up and
listen. 'I have persuaded him to let me park it for now. I
strongly suggest you do likewise, and I'll try to talk him out
of it later.'

Fran looked utterly indignant. Not a good start. 'But that's
not why you're here,' he continued before she could marshal
her thoughts. 'I'll get straight to the point. As I may have
mentioned, I've been trying to get agreement to a permanent
solution to our staffing shortfall. Our problem is that the
super is under considerable pressure to make further cuts.'

Now she looked alarmed. 'Guv, we can't –'

'I know,' Groombridge held up a hand. 'And I've dug
my heels in so far, but you've probably heard the
rumours . . . He's in line for promotion and he needs to
show that he has his house in order.'

'We're barely staying afloat as it is,' protested Fran. 'We need another DS and a DI that's in it for more than his ego.'

Groombridge nodded. 'I agree completely. But Cox needs a saving. I've been forced to compromise.'

Her eyes narrowed. 'You've struck some kind of deal I'm not going to like, haven't you?'

And Cox had just delivered the go-ahead from brass. 'The team gets a permanent Detective Inspector –'

'Not Harper,' interrupted Fran, jaw set. 'Over my dead body.'

Groombridge swallowed his irritation. Everyone was run ragged, himself included, but Fran was leaning right over the line with her arms flailing. 'Superintendent Cox is eternally grateful to DI Harper, and once this investigation is concluded will be happy to propose a commendation and personally thank Owen's super for the loan.' Fran clearly would rather Harper be dispatched to some Hebridean outpost in disgrace, but he'd done nothing to deserve it. Removed from this place, Owen's ego might fare better. 'We get a second Detective Sergeant too, but . . . we lose one DCI –'

'No,' Fran blurted out. 'No, no, no, you can't!'

'I have no choice. Cox wants me in his chair as acting super pending promotion. If he can't swing that, I get transferred –' He held up his hand again to cut off further protest. 'It's the only way, Fran.'

She was still shaking her head violently. 'Leaving us with some unknown DI to run the team?'

Groombridge shook his head slowly. 'I'm not proposing a new face.'

He couldn't help but enjoy watching the implications

registering in her expression. Now she looked positively alarmed. 'No. No, no, no . . . come on, Guv, this is going too far.'

'You've been dragging your heels on this and you know it.'

'I'm not ready.'

'Yes, you are. Long since ready. I've told Cox that unless you take the DI slot the whole deal is off. He approved your application for the inspectors exam this morning. It's congratulations all round,' he concluded wryly.

Fran's mouth opened and closed several times, but nothing came out. Ignoring the irony of his own unwanted prospects, Groombridge savoured this rarity.

'Which brings me on to the other bitter pill . . .' he continued. Fran's look asked what could possibly be worse. 'The money only works if we give up one Detective Constable position –'

'*What?*' she hissed, glancing at the door and lowering her voice. 'So that's why you've been asking about Stark; he was last in! You can't be serious! I know he's not at his best right now but he's still head and shoulders above the rest and you know it . . . and you know how it kills me to *say* it.'

Groombridge held up his hands in desperation. 'Let me *finish*. For God's sake, Fran, just let me finish before you go off on one.'

Her nostrils flared with indignation. 'I do not –'

'Yes, you do,' Groombridge interrupted irritably. 'Often, and with vigour! Now please stop interrupting and listen. The numbers cannot be fudged on this and Stark will have to adapt like the rest of us.'

*

Stark had found a plastic chair from somewhere to await his turn in the lion's den, or in his case . . . catch forty.

Fran rolled her eyes. He confessed to insomnia yet could nap at the drop of a hat, mostly in cars while she was still talking at him. One of his most irritating 'soldier's habits'. And while she knew he couldn't leave a puzzle alone, he could blithely slip off to la-la-land when she'd have had her ear pressed anxiously to the door.

Just so long as he didn't wake up screaming, she thought.

He was in for a shock all the same. And how would the others react?

Fran still felt utterly lost for words. The thing about being a sergeant was that you had people below you to boss about and people above you to ask the hard questions, face the hard decisions. She really did *not* want to be an inspector. Just the thought of sitting the exam gave her the shivers. She hated change. Relocating from Croydon three years ago had been enough upheaval for a lifetime. And Groombridge was too good a detective to turn brass. This was wrong!

She stared down at Stark, sleeping. He looked innocent and unafraid; it seemed a shame to wake him.

'Wake up,' she barked loudly, kicking his chair. 'Your turn.'

67

'Take a seat. You're not in trouble,' said Groombridge, but Stark didn't smile. 'Here.' He slid a paper across the table.

Stark took a breath and picked it up. Perhaps the DCI had had second thoughts since this morning too. He frowned as he comprehended what he was reading.

'Sign at the bottom,' said Groombridge.

Stark continued to stare at the form: an application to sit the sergeants exam, already completed and counter-signed by Cox. 'But, Guv –'

'No buts. I'm in a corner and if I'm going to hold this team together we're all going to have to swallow our medicine.' Groombridge explained the deal he'd struck. Fran had to step up, and so must Stark.

Stark looked like he'd have preferred a dressing-down.

'We don't have any choice,' said Groombridge. 'Super-intendent Cox included; this isn't his fault. It's this or they tear the heart out of this team.'

'But they *are* tearing the heart out of this team. *You* are this team. We're floundering without you.'

Groombridge shook his head. 'There's no standing in the path of progress,' he said wryly. 'Or cutbacks. Sign the form, Detective Constable.'

Stark shook his head, clearly struggling to accept this. 'But the others, Guv . . . I don't have seniority.'

'I said no buts. My only consolation in this Faustian negotiation is that I get to reward merit over blind seniority. We'll keep all this under our hats until things have settled down,' – until Harper's power to sabotage it was removed, in other words – 'then I'll speak with the others. If they take issue, they can take it up with me. Now sign the damn form, try to stay out of trouble till this is all over, study your arse off for that exam and do your best to keep your *future* DI's temper focused on catching bad people – that's an order.'

'Guv.' Stark signed and left.

So be it, thought Groombridge, rubbing his eyes; the die was cast. How much sleep had he lost over all this? No one got fired, that was the main thing, and he had positioned the best people as well as he could. And it had taken his threat of resignation to win that. Cox still had it in his drawer. Committee approval was conditional on all the pieces slotting into place without costing a bean. Exams could be failed, Harper could refuse to go quietly and the case might still explode.

It was endearing that they both seemed as upset at Groombridge's potential move as their own, accepting advancement that would effectively tear him away from the investigative branch for good. But one couldn't dwell.

Fran of course had protested volubly over Stark's advancement. He wasn't ready, the others had seniority, et cetera. But Stark had over seven years as constable. Take away his military service and injury and he still had five; the same as Dixon and only slightly fewer than Hammed. Williams had eight, but he'd stay career constable if he possibly could. They all had the years, but only Stark was ready. The army considered him sergeant material and the others already looked to him. They'd have to find the second DS from outside; low pay-grade, of course, but therefore fresh, mouldable, and on a level playing field with Stark.

Fran might have questioned Stark's long-term commitment, but she'd left that card unplayed and Groombridge had neglected to mention Stark's loaded leave request that morning.

She needed to be able to say this had been forced past her, but her objections were hollow. Stark got under her skin because she couldn't get a complete handle on him, but perhaps for that same reason a bond had formed that she didn't have with the others. And when she went out banging on doors she took Stark along more than the rest, for obvious reasons. For all her bluster, he was the obvious choice. They made a good team.

And it was in that team that Groombridge had to place his faith and future hopes. God help them.

What Fran's expression told Dixon and Williams as she wandered back into the office was anyone's guess. They knew nothing of last night's fireworks, but a summoning to the guv'nor's office would have anxious minds racing.

Her sullen silence didn't help. They watched her as they might a suspicious package, tiptoeing around in case she started ticking, or worse. No one was about to ask what had transpired. Stark arrived twenty minutes later and placed a coffee and Danish in front of her, taking his own to his desk without a word.

'Thanks,' she said numbly, earning even more worried glances from the two DCs and studious ignoring from the visitors who'd probably been warned to avoid her wrath.

The phone broke the silence. 'DS Millhaven,' said Fran, savouring the prefix in a way she hadn't since it was new.

'Control. We're getting multiple reports of shots fired, Rawlings Luxury Cars, Blackheath. ARU and ambulance en route. Suspect fled on black motorcycle.'

68

'If a hundred bankers at the bottom of the sea is a good start, what should we call one used-car salesman full of bullets?' asked Fran, standing over the body.

'A cautionary note to estate agents?' suggested Marcus Turner without looking up from the corpse. Jim Rawlings, forty-one, owner and manager, buying and selling in the luxury marques, Beamers, Mercs, Jags and the odd Porsche, from classics to nearly-new via pimped rides and heaps, polished up and sold on. The place looked as though it was doing well enough, but independents like this always lacked the big-money gloss and uniformity of brand dealerships. 'Someone certainly had a point to make with this one. First shot to the face. Bullet left the skull and fled through that window; no sign of it yet. Death would've been instantaneous, but the killer paused to put four more in the chest all the same. Thorough, messy, and now familiar.'

'Shit.' Fran sighed. 'Forty-five again?'

'Actually, the bullets from Clive Tilly were point four-five-four, three-hundred-grain. Unusually large. Not many revolvers can carry the load.'

'How about a Taurus Raging Judge Magnum?' said Stark, beckoning them into the showroom office, and pointing at the CCTV monitor with the remote. The image he'd paused was the killer, arm outstretched, gun aiming directly at the victim's terrified face. '*Five* shots.

Into Tilly. Into your car. I should've guessed. Very unusual for a revolver. I saw some idiot jar-heads at Camp Bastion waving prototypes around thinking five rounds from "the most powerful handgun in the world" was more impressive than fifteen from a nine-mil auto you could reliably keep the sand out of.'

'I thought the *Dirty Harry* gun famously had *six* bullets,' said Fran, trying to appear knowledgeable and immediately feeling foolish.

The two men shook their heads in sync. 'That was a Smith & Wesson,' said Marcus.

'The Taurus stole its crown,' explained Stark, without any condescension she could justifiably take offence to.

'The bullets were jacketed hollow point, severely domed,' added Marcus.

'The Yanks love overkill.'

'What is it with boys and guns?' she muttered. All she could tell was that it looked big, even in the hands of Simon Kirsch. Assuming it was Kirsch. Right build and height.

'Don't look at me,' said Marcus. 'Can't stand them. I see too much of this sort of thing.' He glanced at Stark in case he'd offended, but Stark just nodded.

There was sometimes a perverse camaraderie between the two that made Fran feel left out. Ludicrous, of course. As a younger man, Marcus had done a spell in the reserves as a doctor. She had no idea whether Stark knew – likely he did. They probably had a secret handshake or code word.

Side by side they could hardly have been more different, yet both seemed perfectly at home, even in these wretched ball gowns. The SOCOs had overalls that fitted, disposable or not, but the blue visitors' suits came in small, medium or large. Stark made everything look like it was made for him. Fran did not fit in a small and the medium made her look like a sack of spuds, gathered at the ankles and wrists like a clown.

'So an American gun, with American bullets?' she mused. 'Illegal import – like an over-sized Taser.'

'Internet shopping is a mixed blessing,' agreed Marcus.

And the dark web was a curse. Stark rewound the footage and pressed play.

It was colour CCTV, reasonable quality, taken from the camera up in the corner of the showroom. A salesman stood talking with a man and woman. They all looked around as a figure entered. The newcomer wore a black motorcycle helmet and leathers, and was holding a pistol. He raised his arm to aim it at the salesman.

The two customers ducked, falling to the floor and scrambling desperately behind the car they'd just been admiring.

The biker ignored them, following the salesman as he backed up against one of his cars, arms out, pleading.

The biker flipped up the front of the helmet, which was like the ones worn by cops and bike couriers, with the chin being part of the visor so they could communicate. He fired, stepped over to the body and fired again downwards four times, then turned and walked away. It was over in seconds.

The two witnesses were being treated for shock in the ambulance outside. Fran would need to speak with them before shock, shame and horror twisted their memories, but the paramedics would have to clear them first.

Stark rewound and played it again and paused as the killer turned to leave, visor still up, glancing into the camera. The beard was gone but there was no mistaking him. 'Kirsch.'

'Doesn't seem to care that we know.'

'He wanted the victim to know,' said Stark. 'He's shouting, jabbing the gun in punctuation before he shoots.' He plucked a business card from the shiny dispenser on the shiny desk, and held it out.

Fran stared at the name. 'Wait a minute . . . James Rawlings?'

'The kid who'd bullied Kirsch at school. And who Kimberly Bates was allegedly seeing behind Kirsch's back.'

'Revenge? After twenty years?' Fran stared at the bloodied corpse as Marcus directed his people to bag it up. Was this them? Had they driven Kirsch over the edge?

'Sarge.' Dixon hovered in his anti-contamination gear, just his eyes visible, trying to look anywhere but at the body. 'DI Harper's here.'

She clicked her tongue in irritation. 'Anything else I need to see?' she asked Marcus.

Marcus's eyes wrinkled. Fran could tell he was smiling with amusement, as he so often did at her impatience. 'I'll call you when I'm back in my evil laboratory.'

Stark was still staring at Kirsch on screen. 'He doesn't care that we know who he is, but he waited till dark again. The gear and blacked-out bike help him come and go. And he went, into the night . . .'

Fran had reached the same conclusion. 'He's not finished.'

69

Harper was good at winning trust, better than Fran, but the witnesses proved to be every bit as shaken up and useless as she'd feared. They had not seen the killer's face and disagreed about what he'd said. The girl said he'd bellowed out a name, the victim's, she assumed, and then something like, *I've come for you. You can't hurt me.* Her boyfriend agreed the killer shouted something on arrival but wasn't sure what, and thought the killer had added something like, *Remember me?* or *I remember you.* Their recollection would grow more certain or less, as the fear faded, but the whole truth was already lost.

Fran kept Stark out of Harper's way, then volunteered to get back to the office to begin putting together a timeline, and took Stark with her.

Nothing had been said of Groombridge's deal on the way, and nothing was said on the way back. She'd glanced at Stark from time to time but he had nothing to offer. What was done was done. Mutual congratulations were hardly appropriate. He was a good choice for DS, inevitable really, there was little use denying it. But DS to her DI? Assuming she passed her sodding exam. He'd ace his, like he had the national investigators' exam. Much as she didn't want to be an inspector, the ignominy of sharing rank with Stark should be incentive enough to panic her into revision.

At least she'd get a new car. She sniffed, certain that

whoever had booked this shitheap out before her had been smoking in it. One thing for sure, she wouldn't let Stark drive her around, whatever the convention.

'Constable Butler's death was the trigger,' said Stark suddenly. 'Up until that point he was still trying to prove his innocence.'

'Of killing the Chases and Carlton Savage, perhaps,' said Fran. 'But what about Kimberly Bates?'

Stark nodded, conceding the point. 'He escaped justice, but not persecution; press and police. And with a bit of help from Clive Tilly, we've tipped him over the edge.'

'He had the gun, the Taser and an unregistered black motorbike hidden away. Maybe we turned up the heat, but he's been simmering a long time.'

Harper made a statement from the scene. An employee had already told them Rawlings was twice divorced and estranged from three children, but that didn't stop Harper ladling on the syrup. Good TV. More importantly, a chance for Fran to get the ball rolling without his interference; though it soon became apparent they had little more to go on than before. Traffic cameras had the bike coming and going, but again lost it within half a mile of the scene. If Kirsch had been simmering for a long while, perhaps he'd planned his route to avoid detection, made practice runs, even. So Stark found himself staring at CCTV from near the showroom going back days, with no success. At midnight Fran enforced a shift change and Stark went home with nothing to show for his efforts but a headache and a belly full of bad coffee and cold pizza, none of which settled well as he installed himself on the sofa. Other issues churned his stomach too.

The long-feared reorientation of the Murder Investigation Team had finally descended, and Stark's would not be the only discomfort. A friend was shipping out into harm's way. An enemy with Stark in her sights had suddenly ceased hostilities. And all this while a known killer was freely pursuing a murderous vendetta twenty years in the making. Because they couldn't find him. Because they kicked over his rock with their suspicions, and worse . . . The fact that Stark still hadn't told Fran about Harper's whispered threat to Kirsch gnawed at him too.

A day with nothing left up its sleeves. What the hell would tomorrow have in store?

One blink and five hours later, his phone woke him to say. *Unknown number.*

He didn't know why he answered it. If it was Kelly, now was not a good time. If it was a cold caller, he was going to say something very rude indeed.

It was neither.

'This had better be good,' snapped Fran, despite her drowse, and ignoring the number of times she'd woken him with calls.

'Where are you?' asked Stark.

'Don't take the piss.'

'How soon can you get here?'

She could almost hear him grinning. 'I'm warning you.'

'I just got a call from Denise Albright.'

Fran didn't ask if this was some conquest of his because she didn't believe Stark was crazy enough to wake her with news of his so-called love life. 'Who?'

'It's a long story.'

'I can feel it lulling me back to sleep already.'

'She lives next door to the old boarded-up house Simon Kirsch grew up in. I told you about her.'

'You know my brain shuts down when you talk, right?'

'She was just letting the dog out,' Stark continued doggedly, 'and noticed the back gate and door of the Kirsch house are open.'

Fran sat up in bed, wincing as the night-before's hastily consumed wine took its toll on the morning-after skull. 'But it's still dark.'

'When a dog's gotta pee . . .'

She blinked at the blurry numbers on her clock. 'At . . . six in the morning?'

'And justice never sleeps, I'm often told.'

'I hate you.'

'I hear that a lot too.'

'All right,' she sighed. 'I'm on my way.' The shape in the covers beside her groaned loudly in protest and pulled the pillow over its head.

The silence coming down the line from Stark took on a loaded quality. Fran swore, and rang off.

'How is it possible for you to look even more tired now than when I sent you home to sleep?' asked Fran, as they sat in the car awaiting the all-clear.

Stark had already let uniform know. This was their show. Specialist Firearms Officers had conducted a plain-clothes drive by and seeing no light from within, had closed the cordon cautiously, edged up, cut the front door padlock and barrelled in as noisily as they could, with more at the rear. All clear. Nobody home, and no body to add to the tally. Another training day. But whatever they'd found was sufficient for SOCO to be called.

Harper turned up in time to be told Kirsch was not there.

'Another waste of time?' he'd announced impatiently and stalked off talking on his phone as SOCO arrived and went in.

A short while later a crime scene manager Stark didn't know emerged and beckoned all three of them inside with a solemn expression on her face.

The house was dim, the early-morning light barely creeping through the perforated metal shutters. The windows inside were dusty. Everything was dusty. The house was stripped bare, carpet, lights, boiler, pipes and radiators. The squatters had been thorough. She showed them footprints on the bare boards, fresh mud. 'Size twelve bootprints, heavy tread, army style. We're taking a cast outside. Latch and bolt on the back gate were oiled. And the padlock on the rear door shutter doesn't match the others,' she said, holding out a heavy combination in an evidence bag.

It was identical to the one on Kirsch's gym locker. Stark cursed silently, berating himself for not checking three days ago . . . but the back door was in a side return, sideways to the back fence.

'Nothing much upstairs,' she said, giving Harper an odd sideways glance. 'The real interest is here . . .' She showed them the cupboard under the stairs, floored with an ancient piece of cracked linoleum too wretched even for the squatters to take. She gripped its curling edge and slid it out into the hallway. On first glance the exposed floor looked innocuous enough but then Stark noticed a knot-hole, and hinges. Slipping his gloved finger into the hole, he lifted a trapdoor. Stairs led into the darkness. The

CSM handed him a torch. 'Careful as you go. Not much headroom.'

The wooden stairs creaked alarmingly. The air inside seemed musty, but with a familiar, metallic tang that triggered something in Stark's memory. There was a workbench with a PC, printer and modem. Someone had been paying for power and data to a dead house. No prizes for guessing who. There was a camera on a nearby shelf, a digital SLR with a long lens. There were tools too, a pair of heavy-duty bolt cutters, a stack of American gun enthusiast magazines and . . .

Stark suddenly placed the smell – gun grease. The familiar scent of stripping down, cleaning, lubricating and reassembling; meticulous, repetitive, reassuring. The smell and fine grey residue stayed ingrained in the lines of your fingerprints and nails. This gun-cleaning set looked freshly used. And there were boxes of ammunition. Stark picked one up. Point four-five-four, three-hundred-grain; the same as the bullets pulled out of Clive Tilly, and probably James Rawlings.

But that wasn't the most disturbing thing . . .

Printouts adorned the wall above the workbench – news and historical accounts – Dunblane, Columbine and Austin, Texas. Spree killings. There was a glossy picture of Charles Whitman. And a centrefold ad for a sniper rifle removed from one of the magazines.

'Oh crap . . .' said Stark, picking up a larger box of ammunition and showing it to the others. 'Rifle rounds . . . Subsonics.'

Fran looked at him.

'For additional quiet, when used with a suppressor,' he explained.

Another blank stare.

Stark pointed to the ad – *Order your Nemesis Vanquish breakdown sniper rifle with silencer and receive this robust waterproof case free!* 'Quiet bullets with a quiet rifle. Not good.'

She winced.

'Here . . .' Stark pointed at some printouts on the bench. 'Mercedes fuse system schematics. Mary's car.'

Fran indicated a folder. 'Susan Watts' school personnel file.'

Two notable absences were Simon Kirsch, and any guns.

'The back door and gate,' said Stark. 'He's obviously been coming and going here for a while, but this time he doesn't bother closing up behind him.'

Fran nodded grimly. 'He's not coming back.'

'Shit . . .' hissed Harper, behind them.

They turned to the wall beneath the stairs.

'Oh my God,' breathed Fran, squinting in the light.

Stark felt a chill down his spine. 'What the hell have we started?'

70

Photos. A lot of them.

'That's Rawlings,' said Fran. A dozen or more, from across the street, showing cars to customers, crisp suit, wide tie, beaming smile, shaking hands.

'And Mary Chase,' added Harper. 'In her garden, and house. *Jesus* . . .' There were shots through windows of Mary and Carlton Savage in flagrante in the kitchen and living room. 'I said he was jealous, but . . .' Even Harper couldn't summon smugness in the face of all this.

It wasn't just people. There were newspaper cuttings, from the Kimberly Bates case, dozens, yellowed and torn, her smiling face in school uniform which had been the staple press image. Kirsch too, the trial . . . everything. Even photos of young Kirsch's battered face and body, presumably from the beating he'd taken from the police.

Every spare inch of wall was covered, except one patch. Stark blinked. 'Sir . . .'

The others looked where he was pointing.

An area of wall was blank. Pinholes suggested something large and rectangular had been removed. In the centre, a solitary photo had been pinned. Harper, leaving his house, a thin, pretty woman waving farewell . . . His wife.

Harper stared at the image, swallowing, stricken. 'Are nineteen still here?' he asked quietly. Turning and catching his head on a beam, with a curse, he ran up the stairs and began barking orders.

'Owen!' Fran called after him but he was already out of earshot. She was crouching to stare at another small cluster of photos.

Stark followed her eyes. More of DI Harper. Outside the front of the station on his phone. In his car. Outside his home.

'Why the hell is he stalking *Harper*?' asked Fran.

Stark grimaced. 'Ahh . . .'

Fran fixed him with one of her best stares, and he reluctantly confessed about Pensol's lip-reading, and Harper's whispered threat to fit Kirsch up.

She wasn't pleased. 'And you're just telling me this now?'

'Pensol couldn't swear to it, and . . .'

'And what? Loyalty? To Harper? Who hates you?'

Stark shrugged apologetically.

'Christ . . . As if Kirsch needed his fuse lit,' muttered Fran, looking all around.

She was right. This room was a persecution complex laid bare. Twenty years of pain, twisted into revenge fantasies. Beneath the benign construct of Mark White, Simon Kirsch had squatted in torment, an unexploded bomb waiting to be kicked.

'Wait a minute . . .' Fran craned in on one photo. Harper in a car park. Handing a file to . . . the DAC Stark had seen entering the station the other night. 'That's Deputy Assistant Commissioner Stevens,' said Fran. 'What's a lowly DI doing talking with a DAC?'

More to the point, thought Stark, why is Stevens out of uniform, in a car park somewhere, being handed a file by a lowly DI? The photo proved nothing but two people talking. Cameras didn't lie, but they froze time, omitting context. But everything about the image screamed *clandestine*.

Fran pulled out her phone and photographed that area of wall, capturing the damning image in position. 'In case this gets lost between here and the evidence locker.'

'Seriously?'

'Crazier things have happened. Owen has friends . . . Funny handshakes and all that.'

Another unwelcome revelation. Not because Stark had strong feelings against Freemasonry. In general he disliked prejudging things he knew little about, but extrapolating from first principles – any system of reciprocal favours must be viewed with scepticism at best. What perturbed him was the thought that there might be more to Harper's secondment than met the eye, and that his shortcomings might therefore not prevent him taking Groombridge's office long-term.

Two-way street . . . Stark suddenly placed the memory . . . Harper on the phone . . . to Stevens?

Now *there* was a thought that would keep him awake.

But for now, he needed to focus. There were maps on the wall too: Abbey Woods – Kirsch's likely escape route after killing Rawlings; Oxleas Woods outside, as well as the town centre and half the borough in chunks. Stark crouched to look in the bottom right-hand corner of the space cleared to make space for the photo of Harper. Still pinned was a corner scrap of paper – the partial title block of a map or architectural drawing with an imperial scale bar and the end of two words above one another, *–all* and *–ans*; something *plans*?

'Oh shit,' said Fran, pointing at another cluster. 'Susan Watts.' On the doorstep of the friend's house they'd moved her to.

*

Harper had already left with CO19 towards his home in Sidcup.

Fran and Stark headed towards Susan Watts' school.

'She hasn't shown up for work,' said Stark, hanging up his phone. 'No answer on her mobile or the landline.'

Fran changed direction and stepped on the gas. Harper had refused to spare manpower to babysit the house. Uniform had prioritized the manhunt, offering drive-past patrols only.

Stark clung on to the door handle, twitching and squirming at every blared horn or cutting up. One advantage of the shitheap, she cared even less if she dinged it.

They were still a mile or so away when the radio crackled.

Suspect motorcycle matching description spotted in vicinity of Brownlee Road, Sidcup. Harper's address. ARV intercepting.

A flurry of calls, checks, ETAs, and then, minutes later – *Suspect apprehended.*

Fran eased off the accelerator.

Stark let out a breath, imagining Harper's impotent panic and relief, listening to all this en route.

Minutes later they were knocking on Susan Watts' door. No answer.

Louder banging, and calling out her name. Still nothing.

Stark looked around. Susan's little red Nissan wasn't in sight, but it could be parked in the next street. Still, something felt wrong. The curtains were closed.

'Excuse me, Sarge,' he said, gently moving Fran aside and peering in through the spyhole. The elongated hallway looked clear. 'I'll check round the back,' he said. 'Stay away from the windows and door.'

Fran raised her eyebrows impatiently, but complied.

A shared footpath ran behind the tiny back gardens, Stark remembered, open at both ends of the street. As soon as he turned into it he saw he was right, and that whoever had been apprehended in the vicinity of Harper's house, it wasn't Kirsch.

It was narrow and overgrown, but heavy off-road tyre tracks cut through it, to where the bike, with blacked-out plates, stood parked beside an open gate.

Stark took out his phone and called Fran. 'Get clear and call it in.' He didn't wait for her response.

Large, heavy-treaded bootprints led into the garden. The back curtains were closed. The back door had been forced. Muddy bootprints led inside.

Stark flicked out the ASP baton he'd borrowed from the car and crept inside.

There were dregs of coffee in a mug on the side in the tiny rear kitchen, evidence of a fried breakfast. The pan was cold. The house, silent. He crept along the hall, testing every floorboard to avoid creaks. The living room was empty. The bootprints led up the stairs carpet. Climbing silently, he checked rooms one by one, all empty, until just the main bedroom was left. Stark thought he heard a noise.

The main bedroom door was open. Peeping through the gap by the hinges, he knew Kirsch was gone.

Susan Watts lay on the bed, unmoving.

71

The first thing Stark did after reassuring her, finding some scissors to remove her duct-tape bindings and gag and letting Fran in, was check for the car keys.

Missing.

He called in the description of Susan's little red Nissan and let it be known that Kirsch was still at large. There was no news from Harper yet. The suspect motorcyclist was being given a cup of tea and a fulsome apology.

'He said he just wanted to talk,' said Susan, her quiet voice flat with shock.

'What did he say?'

'He was just there,' she continued, eyes staring into the distance. 'On the edge of the bed, talking. He only tied me up when he went to get something to eat. He made me breakfast in bed.' The evidence sat congealed on a tray, untouched.

'But what did he say?' So far they'd established only that Kirsch had broken in around midnight and left before it got light.

'He took my phone.' Susan frowned distractedly, as if that was the most perplexing thing. 'I woke up and he was sitting on the bed . . . You said you'd protect me,' her voice rose, and then she broke down into sobs.

Stark waited, but when it was clear the crying wasn't going to stop on its own, Fran jerked her head for him to press on.

'Did he say where he was going next?' he asked.

Changing vehicles was a smart move but Kirsch had to know they'd find Susan. Like the gate at his old house, he didn't care. This was the endgame. They had to know where he was heading next. Harper's house, or somewhere else . . .

Susan shook her head, face buried in her hands.

'What did he say?'

Susan waved her hand, still sobbing, wishing them away.

'What did he *say*, Susan?' demanded Fran impatiently.

'I don't know . . .' wailed Susan. 'Rubbish, just rubbish . . . about knowing we weren't meant to be together, that he understood now. He was raving. He said it wasn't my fault. That it was all someone called Tilly's fault. That he couldn't trust anyone, especially you, the police. He kept cursing someone called Harper. He said everything was ruined. And that he was going to punish everyone.'

'Did he say who? Or where?'

Susan was shaking her head, wiping snot from her nose with the back of her hand, oblivious to how she looked. 'He mentioned his mum. He'd been to see her, I think.'

News was in that Harper's wife was safely surrounded by armed cops. Harper was packing her off to a friend's house until this was over. Grudgingly relieved, Fran jabbed irritably at the doorbell for a second time, though someone was clearly visible through the obscured glass, shuffling towards them. Miriam Kirsch unlocked the door painfully slowly and peered cautiously round the chain at them. Her eyes were ringed red and bloodshot. 'You again,' she muttered. 'Figured you'd be back. He's not here.'

'Good. May we come in?'

Miriam grunted, slid out the chain and shuffled back

down her hall into the living room without looking back. No *close the door* or *wipe your feet* this time.

Stark went first without asking. Instinct, Fran assumed, in case Miriam was lying. Protect your officer or some presumptuous mantra. Miriam was already slumped in her armchair when they caught up. She looked as if years had descended on her since their last call, and like she'd been up all night crying. Fran sat opposite. Stark hovered by the door, half an eye on the hallway.

'Are you well, Mrs Kirsch?' asked Fran, deliberately deploying her married name.

The old woman stared back but didn't protest. No fire, no feisty old bat. Stark caught Fran's eye and nodded to the sideboard. The photo of Simon was lying face down. Fran glanced around the room. Nothing much else seemed out of place . . . except. 'Where is the medal, Mrs Kirsch? Simon's medal?'

Miriam shifted in her seat but didn't look at her. 'He was good at losing himself in running,' she said absently. 'He could keep going and going.'

'Where is it now?'

'Away,' she said, coming back into focus. 'He's . . . sinned.' A mother facing the awful truth – of her little boy lost.

Stark shifted his weight and Miriam jumped. Not just tired and tearful, but fearful. Fran nodded to the picture and Stark stepped over.

'Do you mind?' he asked, picking it up. Miriam flinched, looking away. Stark made a thing of looking closely at the picture then carefully placed it back, upright. Miriam couldn't look at it.

'Has Simon been here?' asked Stark, standing over her. Miriam shuddered, and shrank. Unable to look up at

412

Stark, her eyes met Fran's almost by default and in the briefest exchange Fran saw her confession. It was true. 'Last night?' she demanded. Miriam shrank further but said nothing. 'When was he here, Mrs Kirsch?'

'Larson,' she croaked. 'My name is Larson.' Fresh tears were forming.

'No, it's not. Not for many years. Your son is wanted for murder, Mrs Kirsch. Tell me everything you know or I'll haul you down the station and let my DCI ask you. He's not as polite as me,' Fran lied.

Stark picked up the photo again and held it for Miriam to see. She jerked her head away but he followed, keeping it in her vision. She closed her eyes. 'Look at it, Miriam,' he said firmly. 'Look at it.' She did so, and tears streaked down her cheeks. 'Your son is a very dangerous man.'

Miriam pushed the picture away violently. 'You think I don't know that?' she cried. 'You think I don't know what he's capable of? That I haven't known for years? Since that girl . . .'

'What girl?' Fran seized on the slip.

Miriam shook her head, dropping her chin as if trying to retreat within herself.

'She had a name, Mrs Kirsch . . .' Still nothing. 'Kimberly Bates. Sixteen, feisty, her whole life ahead of her, Mrs Kirsch.'

'Whore.'

Fran blinked. But even this twenty-year-old hatred sounded . . . exhausted. 'Tell me what you know, Miriam. Now.'

'He'll kill me.' A quiet statement, said with absolute certainty. Her eyes darted this way and that, alighting on the old crucifix on the wall.

'Is that what he told you?' asked Stark.

Miriam managed a jerky nod, tears rolling down her cheeks unheeded.

'When?' demanded Fran.

'Last night.'

'What time?'

'Elevenish, I don't know.'

'That was hours ago,' said Fran hotly. 'Why haven't you reported this?'

Miriam pointed to the phone. Its cord was cut. 'He took my mobile.'

'You could've got off your arse and used a neighbour's!'

Miriam just shrugged.

'What did he say? What did he want?'

'He wanted . . .' She cast another glance at Jesus, as if asking permission, or absolution. 'He made me make him toast. With a ketchup smiley face, like when he was young. We never had much money after his father died. I couldn't even afford baked beans for his tea . . .' She broke down sobbing.

'His father didn't *die*, Miriam,' said Fran coldly. 'He *left*. And if you utter one more lie to me I swear to your precious God I'll arrest you for conspiracy. Tell us everything you know about Kimberly Bates, right now. And if you hold anything back . . .' She paused for effect, letting her anger show. 'You knew at the time, didn't you?'

Miriam nodded, looking up, eyes awash with desolation. 'I'm his mother, his only family. Who else would he turn to? Who else was going to help him?'

'Help him what?'

'He was frightened.' A spark of the old defiance now. 'My little boy.'

'Help him *what*?'

Miriam looked up at the crucifix. 'Jesus knows . . . Isn't that enough?'

'Help him *what*?'

'*Get rid of her!*' wailed Miriam, making the sign of the cross again as another wave of sobbing crashed through her.

Help him get rid of her.

Of the body.

Stark met Fran's glance, but with nothing of triumph, only anger. Anger she shared. This woman had helped dispose of the body and left Kimberly Bates' family to weep over a *plaque*.

'Where?' said Fran, trying to control her temper. 'Where is she?' Miriam wept on. This wretched woman, with no right to weep. Fran grabbed her arms and shook her. '*Where is Kimberly?*'

Miriam opened her bloodshot eyes and stared back, defiance gone, misery victorious. Her voice came in a hoarse whisper. 'In the woods. Where else?'

72

The low sun strobed between buildings as the car streaked along, and shone straight in their eyes as they hung a right by the old Shooter's Hill nick, now 'fashionable flats'.

Oxleas Woods, Stark informed her, was part of the woodland just north of the old Kirsch home. Protected woodland, popular with dog walkers. No-man's land as far as Fran was concerned. Walking in the woods – or anywhere else for that matter – for fun, was anathema to her, as were dogs, cats or any of the parasitic vermin people chose to call pets.

'Here?' she asked, pulling over in Crookston Road, well short of the old house now taped off with a uniform car and SOCO van still parked outside.

Stark was pointing to an opening between the houses, a path leading up towards greenery. The woods, Fran figured.

Miriam looked around as they got her out, still cuffed, shamed perhaps at being seen by someone in her old neighbourhood, even if most people here would be unlikely to know her or care.

Stark removed her cuffs. 'You'll need your hands in the woods.'

Fran didn't like the sound of that. Miriam seemed indifferent. Tears dried, face haggard, eyes distant; she'd shut down.

Walking into the park Fran could see high up the hill,

a narrow castle-like tower projecting up through the leafless trees. Severndroog Castle, she assumed. Simon and Kimberly's love-nest. A folly or monument of some kind; Fran neither knew nor cared. History was of even less interest to her than nature.

Miriam stared at it too, and muttered something under her breath before turning right to trudge along a muddy path lining the back of the houses. Stark seemed to know where he was going. Fran followed hindmost in order and enthusiasm, picking her way through the mud with a face on.

The back of the old house was taped off too. Miriam peered over the fence, dead-eyed, then looked about, getting her bearings. 'This way.'

She led them along a way then turned uphill into the woods.

Fran stared at the barely distinguishable path, then down at her shoes. However much she complained, she cared about crime. But what about the crime of picking her way through the quagmire of black, rotting leaves in her everyday shoes? It was a good job she wasn't built for heels, but even so, these were good shoes. And good trousers . . . damn! She pinched the thigh material to hoick up the legs but the hems were already splattered.

Miriam's shoes were if anything less suitable, as were her tights, old dress and woollen coat, but she gave little sign of caring. She steadied herself with trunks and twigs as they made their way along the path, without really seeming to notice. Fran tried her best to touch nothing.

Nature was so . . . *dirty*. People harped on about the 'clean air' but it stank. Woods stank of decay and fields stank of dung or oilseed rape. Give her city air any day.

The only place Fran liked to be outdoors was the Caribbean. Barbados smelled of spicy barbecue, ripe ackee, rum and people, not cowshit and mouldy leaves. It was too long since she'd visited her relatives there. She found it amazing that places like this even existed, that they hadn't been swallowed up, bulldozed in the path of progress. A few soggy steps from the road and the only thing telling you that civilization hadn't been rendered away was the buzz of traffic and the whine of an airliner.

They crossed a main path but plunged back into the wood's twists and turns.

'There was another path further up,' said Miriam, sounding far from sure.

Twenty or more years ago, thought Fran. How was anyone supposed to remember? Every tree looked the same to her. They turned a few more corners and Fran's impatience and doubt began to coalesce.

But then Miriam paused, staring right at two large trees which had sprouted close together and grown apart, in disgust. 'This way, I think.'

Fran frowned. It wasn't even a path. 'Are you sure?'

Miriam swallowed. 'There was a clearing, a way in, with a fallen tree.'

Stark led the way, stamping down thorns and nettles for their impertinence and holding aside twigs like he was holding open a door for the ladies. Of course he would be loving this. His shoes had treads, not flat leather like civilized people wore, people in offices and cars, and coffee shops.

Miriam steadied herself clumsily with every available twig as they made their way. Fran kept her arms raised to avoid the undergrowth, until she slipped over and came up caked and cross. 'How much further?' she demanded, not caring if she sounded like a whining child.

Miriam stopped and looked forward and backward. 'I'm . . . I don't know. I don't remember it being this far . . .'

Fran's temper threatened to boil over.

'Wait . . .' said Stark, who'd crested a small ridge. 'This it?'

There was a large fallen tree in their way. Time and the elements were eating into the massive trunk and nature was taking over. A tall mass to one side marked its base, earth and roots torn vertical as it toppled, other smaller trees taken with it. What made big trees fall over? Wind, she supposed, old age? Or just suicidal boredom?

'This isn't a clearing,' she pointed out, barely keeping a lid on her patience.

'It was,' said Stark, looking around, and up. 'Twenty years ago.'

Fran had to admit the nearest trees were thinner, and less tall. Though there were no leaves it was just about possible to tell that their tops – or canopies, or whatever people who cared about these things called them – left more space to the sky. Stark probably knew the right name. He could probably tell you the bloody species, thought Fran, gloomily rubbing mud from her hands on to her trousers.

'I couldn't go any further,' Miriam said, voice dull. 'Even with Simon carrying . . .' She trailed off, eyes lost in time, and perhaps horror. 'I've tried to forget this place. But it creeps back, in my dreams. It never lets go.'

Stark was nodding. Equating it with his morbid recollections, no doubt. 'There?' he said, pointing to the nettle-filled depression where the tree had torn itself out of the earth. The rounded mass of the roots stood taller than Stark and would have torn a deep hole at the time. A handy head-start for a shallow grave, but filling it in after must've been a sod in all this root-riddled ground. No shortage of fallen leaves to cover your handiwork. And rain. Fran really hated nature.

'Should I dig?' asked Stark, unfolding the collapsible spade he'd pulled from the boot of the pool car as if he'd known it would be there. Perhaps they all had one.

Fran considered letting him have a go, clearing the nettles at least. He could use a sting or two for dragging her out here. 'Best leave it to Forensics. Tape off the area.'

He jabbed the spade into the ground and began tying blue-and-white police tape around a nearby tree. Miriam watched impassively as he looped it from trunk to trunk to begin forming an irregular circle around them. Everything was irregular out here. Fran shifted her feet, the mud sucking at her shoes. Her socks were definitely wet now. This was intolerable. If there wasn't a body buried here she would hit Miriam over the head with the spade and make Stark bury her.

A snapping crack off in the woods made her jump. A branch falling, or some little furry animal doing whatever little furry animals did. There was a sudden, sharp, demonic birdcall and black wings clattered skyward overhead.

At least it seemed to have startled Stark too. He looked round sharply, suddenly tense, rigid, like a cat at a nearby dog bark.

Miriam looked round too, only slower. When she looked back at Stark her eyes looked lifeless as a shark's. 'That's right,' she nodded, smiling wanly.

Stark's eyes widened.

'He'll be furious,' continued Miriam, looking out into the woods again. 'I've tried to guess what he'll do, but I just can't. Jesus knows . . .'

'*Get down!*' yelled Stark. He barrelled across the clearing towards Fran as she stared at him dumbly.

He crashed into her, sending them both crashing down into the mud and nettles just as something hit a tree behind her.

With the breath knocked out of her and Stark's crushing weight, the curses that queued in Fran's throat at the cold, wet, stinging indignation, came out as a strangled gasp.

'Stay down,' he hissed, rolling off and peering away through the nettles. And brambles! Fran felt thorn scrapes and torn trousers.

Thwack! Something whipped past, slapping through foliage into the distance behind her.

Fran tried sitting up but Stark shoved her flat. '*Stay the fuck down!*'

The truth hit her, like a *bullet* . . .

She flattened herself against the ground, cold mud plastering her cheek, ice choking her veins. Through the undergrowth she watched Miriam staring around blankly. The stone-cold bitch had led them out here like lambs to the slaughter! Miriam stepped awkwardly over to the base of the fallen tree, staring into the depression. Was there even a grave there at all? Or would there soon be one, a shallow grave for two? Would Fran's parents cry over an empty coffin, or a plaque in the cemetery, like Mr and Mrs Bates? Would Stark's mother? Miriam was a mother too, of a monster maybe, but . . . how could she do this? Fran wanted to shout at her but she could hardly breathe. She could only watch as the so-called mother knelt in the nettles, clasped her hands in front of her and bowed her head to pray.

For forgiveness? Fran cursed her to fiery eternity.

Miriam's head knocked sideways in a spray of red, and she slumped down, limbs twitching briefly and then still.

73

Fran gaped, comprehension forcing its way into her like emetic through a tube.

She vomited.

She'd never seen death. She'd seen bodies, but she'd never witnessed death swoop down and snatch a life away before her very eyes.

She was too stunned to move. Too stunned even to blink, or spit away the acid in her mouth. Was this what terror felt like?

'*Stay down!*' growled Stark, then pressed her flat with both hands, using her to push himself up . . . and with barely a glance at Miriam he took off into the woods, not towards where the bullets were coming from but sideways over a slight ridge, lost from sight in seconds. Sideways. His army nickname, probably for things just like this . . .

Stay down? *Bloody right!* Her laugh escaped as a strangled sob.

But she couldn't stay here.

Kirsch could walk right over and shoot her where she lay. This wouldn't do. Forcing herself, she crawled on elbows and belly through the stinging, tearing fingers of Mother Nature to the base of the fallen tree. Then she crawled right down into the hole and lay there panting deep among the nettles, hoping she was hidden, trying to ignore the stings covering her hands and face, trying not to tremble, trying to stay silent as the grave. Not a happy turn of phrase considering where she lay. Her heart felt like it had either stopped or was rattling so fast as to make individual beats indiscernible.

Stark barrelled through the autumn foliage, ducking under or leaping over obstacles. Blood pumping, lungs straining against bandaged ribs, pain quashed.

He hit a trail and stopped.

He could hear the gunman crashing through the woods ahead, moving away, traversing the hill. Kirsch knew these woods. Stark took the path uphill, trusting the map in his head. Kirsch hadn't followed them here; Stark would have noticed. He was already here, watching, from the castle most likely. The upper windows of the triple-turreted tower offered clear lines of sight through the leaf-denuded winter trees. That meant Susan's little red car was up there too, in the car park, out of sight from passing police cars. Stark had this one chance to out-flank him.

But the trail he was on curved the wrong way and he was forced to cut left through thick woods, and by the time he broke cover again Kirsch had already passed, rifle in his hands, taking the stone steps towards the castle two at a time.

Stark accelerated, pounding up the steps and rounding the tower only to hear the sound he'd feared . . . A car revving to life and tyres skidding away. A flash of departing red.

Cursing, clutching his side, he took out his phone to call it in.

He needed to get back to Fran, so she could begin the vital process of blaming everything on him. For once, he was way ahead of her. If only he'd inspected the old house more closely, maybe he'd have spotted that Kirsch had been using it all along, could even have been inside at the time. But as he rounded the tower again something caught his eye.

Tracks. The same heavy off-road bike tyres from the alley earlier, the same pattern left behind outside Chase Security the night before last. Leading right up to the door . . . and up the steps.

The triple-turreted tower was boarded up with steel shutters . . . but the door wasn't padlocked. It swung open easily. Oiled. Inside a padlock lay on the floor; a study combination, identical to the gym locker and house back door. And someone had fitted a hasp and staple inside so it could be padlocked from within. There was another padlock nearby, weathered, cut through with bolt cutters. The original. Uniform had reported the place safely locked up – with Kirsch's lock, evidently.

The muddy tracks inside were preserved from the weather along with large bootprints. Size twelve, no doubt. There were drips of oil on the floor, scuffs from the bike stand. Smart again – hiding the bike's heat signature from the infra-red eye of police helicopters just a short walk from the house, his HQ.

The interior was in poor condition. The rear turret had been boarded up but a panel had been prised off, exposing the winding stair. Stark climbed, careful to keep his feet to the edge to avoid trampling evidence.

On the second floor he found Kirsch's home-from-home: roll mat, bivvy bag, camping stove, supplies. Stark had hoped he was wrong; hoped his failure to inspect the tower himself on Saturday wasn't the catastrophic mistake it clearly was. Whitewash had been scratched from some windowpanes. Peepholes. One offered a distant view of the alley through which they'd entered the park.

On the next floor up it got worse. Shell casings. Dozens. There was a pane cut out from one window. Kirsch may have failed his army medical but he knew how to read. The bullets in the house were subsonics, but even with no sonic boom and a silencer fitted, a rifle still made a noise, however small. Shooting from well inside the window made the whole room an additional suppressor.

Peering out, estimating trajectory, Stark doubled back outside and a quick search of the treeline revealed vivid orange splatter and the nearby disposal of a dozen or more exploded Halloween pumpkins.

Target practice.

Fran lay still for an age. The forest came alive with noise; every knock, snap, flutter, tweet and gust of wind amplified by her straining eardrums. Wet cold seeped into her but she could hardly feel it against the stings and scrapes, the ever-increasing, almost agonizing urge to move, and the oppressive, crushing fear.

At any moment she expected to hear his footsteps tramping through the mulch towards her, and to see Kirsch rear up.

Or perhaps Stark had caught him? Or was Stark dead on the ground not far away and Kirsch was waiting for her to show herself as foolishly as her possibly-erstwhile detective constable? Fran felt like crying. And also like shouting very loudly at Stark. At six this morning she'd been asleep next to what she may soon have to admit might just possibly be her boyfriend. Now she was lying in freezing mud, nettles and brambles, about to be killed by a psychopath. And it wasn't even lunchtime.

This wasn't supposed to happen. You joined the murder squad to catch killers, not to get killed. Her job began where someone *else* died.

Then, in the far distance, faint . . . footsteps. Coming closer, slowing, searching. Fran stared through the thick nettles but saw nothing. Her heart was ready to explode.

'Fran!' The footsteps came nearer. *'Fran!* Where are you? It's me, Stark.'

She almost wept. She tried to get to her feet but the cold had stiffened her like premature rigor mortis. The footsteps raced towards her and suddenly he was there, helping her up. Dragging her up.

'Are you okay?' he asked to her silence.

'Kirsch?' she managed.

'Gone. I tried to get round behind him but he must have scarpered as soon as he saw me go.' There were a number of scratches on his face – from twigs? And he was out of breath. How far had he run? His eyes shone. 'Made it to his car before I could cut him off. Here,' he held out a fistful of leaves.

Fran stared at them, confused.

Stark rolled his eyes. 'Dock leaves. For the nettle stings.'

'Does that work? I always assumed it was mumbo jumbo.'

'I could talk to you about formic acid neutralized by alkaline secretion or astringent properties, or about finite pain gateway theory and the benefit of rubbing with any soothingly cool material,' he said, crushing a handful and rubbing the veiny side against her left hand. 'Or you could shut up and do this yourself.'

'You're loving this, aren't you?' said Fran.

'*Don't be so bloody stupid!*'

Fran couldn't recall Stark ever raising his voice to her. His jaw clenched in anger. He wasn't about to take it back. Nor should he. They both glanced at the corpse sprawled a few feet away. Fran took a breath and released it slowly. It felt jerky, as if the sustained pounding of her heart had set up a systemic percussion wave that would take time to dissipate. Her hands still trembled. 'Sorry. That was . . .'

He softened. 'It's okay.'

Fran took the leaves and rubbed them on her hands and face, trying to mask the trembling.

'I was scared too,' said Stark, watching her intently. 'If that helps.'

'Really? Only it looked like it was only me huddled in a hole like a quivering rabbit.'

Stark's mouth twisted. 'You did what you were told,' he said soberly. 'The right thing. I had to split his attention. Once his targets separated his best option was to withdraw or be outflanked.'

'Yep, that's just what I thought too,' she said. 'Make sure you tell everyone how bravely I hid.'

74

Stark offered to drive. Fran told him what she thought. He took the passenger seat.

She hit the lights and siren, stomped on the accelerator and gripped the wheel tight to stop her hands shaking.

Scratched, stung, shot at, filthy, cold and pissed-the-fuck-off, she gunned the car through the traffic, taking her irritation out on the London masses. Making sure he wasn't looking, she furiously wiped at a stray tear and sniffed. He kept his eyes the other way.

Blaring the horn, she cut it fine past a van, weaved between lanes and ran a red light. Stark twitched in alarm.

'Oh for Christ's sake, stop flinching!' she cried. 'It's like driving with my mum in the car, only she's got more balls.'

'I'm not flinching at your driving,' he said, sounding exasperated. 'I'm . . .' He fell silent.

'You're what?'

'Nothing. Forget it.'

'You're forgetting who you're talking to,' she replied pointedly. She glanced across, hoping to catch his expression, but he was staring out the window. The muscles in his jaw were twitching as if he were biting down, trying to keep words in. 'You're *what*?'

He hissed a tight sigh, clearly frustrated. 'Look . . .' He paused as if not certain how best to explain. 'On combat patrol . . . the driver drives, the passenger does threat assessment.'

It took Fran a moment to comprehend this. 'You're . . . looking for *bombs*?'

Stark shifted in his seat uncomfortably. 'Bombs . . . ambush pinch-points, nervous locals, suspicious activity, approaching vehicles –'

'Approaching vehicles?' she interrupted, incredulous. 'In London?' Stark looked to be shrinking with embarrassment. 'You've been sitting next to me for nearly two years flinching every time a car passes? And all this time you've let me think it was my driving?'

'You're right. I'm sorry. Your driving's just a secondary factor.'

Fran punched him in the arm.

He rubbed it in silent admonishment and returned to looking out the window. 'I try to switch it off, but . . .' He sighed. 'It's worse when I'm tired. More like . . .'

'Like you're back there?' He hated letting these things out; saw it as weakness. Fran tried to imagine what it must be like to go through life expecting attack, suspecting everything. It must be exhausting. Now she thought about it, even the way he walked down the street hinted at it; his eyes were always peeled. What did they call it, hyper-vigilance? Ever since she'd realized he had PTSD her ears pricked up at every mention of it on the news. Was Stark literally still living the war? No wonder he looked like shit. He'd been fine for so long, while he was with Kelly, but since then . . .

'Did you know that the plural for crows is a murder?' he asked quietly.

Even Fran's insatiable curiosity wasn't going near that one. 'I've had quite enough nature for one day. Tell me why we're doing this?' They were heading back to

Miriam's flat. The uniforms guarding the place had been notified to be wary, but Stark still hadn't explained himself.

'Jesus knows.'

'What?'

'Just something I want to check.'

'We should be out chasing down Kirsch.'

'Where?' he asked flatly. 'How?'

Fran had no answer. She drove the car past a line of vehicles that had pulled over at the wailing siren and lights, suddenly blinking back another threat of tears. 'You died,' she said quietly.

'What?'

'It said in the papers – on the operating table in Camp Bastion. Is that true?'

Stark glanced at her. She gripped the wheel, willing her face expressionless. 'So they say.'

'You don't remember?'

'I was on an operating table.'

'Do you remember losing consciousness, then?'

'Is now really the time for this?' he asked.

'It's the perfect time.'

He thought for a moment. 'Yes, sort of; it's hazy. I was in and out for a while on the medevac chopper.' Perhaps he sensed her need for direct answers rather than his usual dodges. It must be obvious where this was coming from, so she pressed on.

'Did you think you were dying?'

'Yes.'

'What did you feel?'

'Are you asking if I saw a warm welcoming light and heard the choir of angels?'

'Don't take the piss. I'm asking, seriously.'

'Seriously?' Stark sighed, thinking. 'Pain. Utter weariness. Encroaching darkness and an overwhelming sense of relief.'

Fran took a moment to absorb this. 'Well, aren't you just the little ray of sunshine.'

They screeched to a halt outside Miriam's flats. A uniform car was already there. 'No sign of him,' said one of the constables.

Fran looked both relieved and disappointed. Stark marched silently up the stairs and she followed in silence. SOCO hadn't arrived yet. He wiped his feet, pulled on gloves and unlocked the door with Miriam's keys.

'All right, smartarse. Why are we here?' she asked impatiently.

Stark took down the wooden crucifix from the wall and gave it a gentle shake. It rattled. 'Jesus knows.'

The two detectives locked eyes.

Fran took out her phone and began photographing.

'She kept looking at it,' said Stark. 'I only remembered after . . . my gran had one similar that opened into a candle holder.' As he held it in two hands, applying pressure with his thumbs, the front of the cross with its icon slid down to reveal the hollow interior.

It wasn't a candle inside.

It was a scroll of yellowing paper. Stark unrolled it, scanned it, and sighed. Handwritten in a pin-neat copperplate, in biro. 'The one thing she couldn't confess to her priest.'

But the scroll hadn't made the rattling. There was

another object inside. A golden pendant necklace spelling a name.

Kimberly.

SOCO arrived ten minutes later.

Outside the two constables were looking agitated. 'We've had a shout. Abbey Woods. Two separate reports of IC1 male with a rifle. Shots heard. Everyone and their dog is heading there now. All three choppers are up. Armed response vehicles inbound and Specialist Firearms are on their way. Should we go?'

Fran looked up at the flats. 'No, stay here with SOCO.'

'No,' said Stark. Everyone looked at him, thinking he was contradicting her. 'Sorry, no, not you; Kirsch . . .' His mind was racing. 'He stole their phones . . .'

'What are you talking about?' demanded Fran.

'Misdirection. Abbey Woods . . .' Stark winced, trying to think it through, searching for the links. 'Kirsch took Susan's and Miriam's phones. Two calls. Shots heard. But Kirsch's rifle is *silenced*.' Kirsch had that big pistol too, but the reports hadn't mentioned that.

He looked at Fran and saw the idea take seed. She still had mud on her face. Did she know?

Stark blinked as the links lined up. The photo of Harper on his phone outside Royal Hill station – taken on a long lens, from an angle, from *above*. Not much, but definitely. There was only one place that photo could have been taken from. The rectangle removed from the basement wall and the torn corner of paper with *–all* and *–ans* printed on it . . . a drawing – Greenwich Town *Hall Plans*. Now the Greenwich School of Management, who'd kicked Simon Kirsch out for his disruptive post-trial notoriety. 'Charles Whitman,' hissed Stark, the certainty settling into him like icicles elongating through his heart.

Fran frowned. 'Who?'

'The original spree killer.' Austin, Texas, University – ex-US Marine up a tower with a rifle. Dunblane and Columbine. All school shootings . . .

'You do know that only some of your thoughts reach your mouth?' said Fran, exasperated.

'I'll explain on the way,' said Stark, turning to the car. 'Abbey Woods?'

Stark shook his head. 'Royal Hill.'

Fran felt the colour draining from her face as she drove. 'What if you're wrong?'

'Then we end up miles from our gun-toting madman. It's if I'm right we should worry,' replied Stark, tapping the radio handset impatiently.

Unmarked forty-two – control – please respond, crackled the radio.

Stark thumbed the handset. 'This is unmarked forty-two – receiving, over.'

Unmarked forty-two – control – The two public reports from Abbey Woods originated from the two phone numbers you gave us – Confirm positive match.

Bogus calls. Kirsch using the phones he'd taken from his mother and Susan Watts. Stark would have given anything to be wrong. 'Control – car forty-two, DC Stark. Reason to believe armed suspect, Simon Kirsch, may be targeting Greenwich School of Management and Royal Hill Police Station. Imperative – have school evacuated

434

and dispersed asap – and initiate station lock-down protocols. Over.' Nothing happened for a few seconds. 'Control – confirm receipt, over?'

That protocol requires authorization from an inspector or above, said the disembodied voice, uncertainly.

Stark explained why they should take his word for it in terms so terse that even Fran winced.

She was less impressed with the sodding traffic, which seemed to have trebled in the last hour. Nose-to-nose vehicles made the usual token attempts to move aside, but it was hopeless. The car's angry siren barely represented Fran's impatience as she turned the air inside the car bluer than the lights outside it.

Switching to side streets and back-doubles gave little relief. After an age of fighting through gaps and snaking around cars pulled over or frozen in indecision, they eventually broke free across Blackheath.

All cars. Shots fired, Royal Hill station, barked control over the radio. *Repeat. Shots fired, Royal Hill Police Station. All cars respond.*

PART FOUR

75

Fran's heart caught in her throat.

Stark snatched up the radio. 'Control, unmarked forty-two inbound. ETA one minute. Where's the shooter? Repeat, where is the shooter?'

Stand by, called the voice. With the siren on it was hard to tell, but it sounded like Maggie had taken over. The radio clogged with calls, cars reporting in, people demanding information.

Then Maggie's voice cut in abruptly. *Stand by . . . Stand by . . . All units, officer down. Code Zero. Repeat, Code Zero, officer down in the street outside. Be advised, shooter is not in the building, shots coming in from outside.*

'Take Burney Street,' said Stark. 'Westbound. He shouldn't see us coming.'

'Shouldn't?'

'If he's putting shots into the station from outside he'll be low in the tower, one of the windows on the lower staircase.' Where the photo of Harper had been taken from. How, was a question for later.

'*If . . .*' Fran glanced at Stark. His jaw was set, eyes peeled as if staring could clear the road ahead.

They screeched to a halt as an aggregate lorry tried to get out of their way by turning into the street they wanted to take. Fran sounded the horn repeatedly, shouting, as if either could be heard over the siren. Futile. She thumped the steering wheel with her palms, uttering a vicious curse, then mounted the kerb, beeping furiously at startled pedestrians.

They tore down Crooms Hill with the park on their right, and left into Burney Street with the station at the far end. There was a uniform car abandoned in the middle of the junction with Royal Hill, right outside the Old Town Hall college building. The clock tower loomed to the right. If Kirsch was up top with his rifle, instead of low as Stark thought, they were sitting ducks.

'Stop there.' Stark pointed to the car park entrance on the right. 'Med-kit,' he barked, already half out of his door and off up the street, leaving her to fetch the medical kit from the boot like his lackey. Two uniforms were sheltering off to the right by the gardens opposite the station. There was a prone figure in the street by the abandoned car.

A sound drew her eye, a puff of dust from the station. Not dust, glass. Several of the windows were pocked with bullet holes. They weren't bulletproof, or even mirrored. Those inside must feel like goldfish in a bowl with a cat's claws dipping in.

Stark edged up the street towards the sheltering uniforms and crouched to talk with them, gesticulating towards the tower, looking around. He called out to the casualty but got no response. And then he stood and walked into the road, looking towards the tower and all around as if he had all the time in the world, before retreating casually back into cover. A spout of black erupted from the road behind him. But no gunshot. Stark's 'quiet rifle'.

Fran had a sinking feeling.

He said something to the uniforms, then darted out

across to the prone figure, gripped the back of their collar and dragged them unceremoniously into the shelter of the car.

Seconds later part of the light atop the car exploded.

Stark knelt over the figure, checking them out.

Fran could see it was police. Male, she thought. She could also see blood on Stark's hands. Another rending explosion as the rear windscreen shattered.

If there was one difference between real life and the movies Fran was confident in, it was that cars were not bulletproof. Get behind the front wheels and engine block, they were told. Stark had done so, but concentrating on the victim, his head was in the air.

Nothing happened for about twenty seconds; an eerie quiet, and then a door panel puckered out as a bullet buried itself in the road beyond.

Stark looked around, at her, at the med-kit in her hand, both of his applying downward pressure to a wound.

She saw his mouth move in a curse. He undid the man's utility belt and then tugged out the trouser belt beneath, looped it round the man's thigh and pulled it tight. Then he pulled out the man's ASP, slid it into the tourniquet, gave it two twists and tied the belt slack around it. But then he began looking at the man's head. Was he shot twice?

Fran considered sliding the case to him but it was too far. She'd fluff it and leave the sodding thing stranded in the middle of the road. She'd have to make a dash for it.

She stood and dashed.

'Fran, *no!*'

An eruption of tarmac just in front of her brought her up short, freezing her in a flinching half-crouch, arms up over her head like a fool. There was a deep-looking gash torn up, about five inches long, widening from the angular impact.

'*Fran, take cover!*'

Fran blinked at Stark. For the second time in days she saw fear written across his face.

Realization dawned that she was just standing there in the open like a damn bunny transfixed in headlights, *again*. She looked up at the brick edifice expecting to see Kirsch, expecting the next bullet to bear down on her like a juggernaut.

76

'*FRAN!*' bellowed Stark. '*Get back!*' He jumped out into the open again, waving his arms frantically up at the tower to create a distraction. Fran tore her eyes from the tower to him, realization slapping her in the face. Ducking beneath her hands, she back-pedalled into cover just as another strip of macadam tore out of the road where she'd been standing.

'Three,' said Stark under his breath.

Another car screeched to a halt behind hers. Sergeant Clark and Constable Barclay climbed out and ran towards Fran.

Stark peered over the bonnet of the car towards the tower. The uppermost of four small square windows, third floor of the tower's lower staircase, was smashed open. Muzzle-flash and another section of the bodywork rent upward in a shower of dust and noise.

'Four,' hissed Stark. Four shots since the brief hiatus that Stark hoped was Kirsch reloading. 'Come on . . .'

And then another.

'Five!' He jumped to his feet, hoisted up the limp man into a fireman's lift and set off towards Fran, accelerating painfully slowly through the grinding protest from his ribs, and the protest from his brain that his bullet count could be wrong.

'*Run!*' he heard Fran shout. '*RUN!*'

I am bloody running, he thought. But it was more

yomp than jog, and if his hip gave out now he'd be in big trouble. Nearly there, *come on*! Breath-clouds bursting from him like a steam train. Another eruption of macadam, a yard from his feet; Kirsch had changed magazines quickly. Stark barrelled across the pavement, bumped off the opposite wall and dropped to one knee to roll his burden unceremoniously on to the ground.

Fran was beside him. 'Are you hit? Are you all right?'

'Ambulance . . .' he gasped, rolling the man over and pressing his bloody hands on to the wound in the top of the shoulder where it met the neck. The bleeding had slowed; either good news or very bad. 'Dressing . . . *Quick!*'

Fran opened the med-kit and tore open a dressing. Stark snatched it from her hand and pressed it against the wound. He looked up at Barclay and Clark who was already on his radio. 'Here, take over!' he ordered fiercely, grabbing Barclay's arm and dragging him down. He pressed Barclay's hands where his had been. 'Keep the pressure on, both sides, front and back, like this . . . When it's saturated press another over it. Don't ease up till the paramedics take over. Understand?'

Nodding, Barclay looked panicky but did as he was told.

Another smack indicated a shot ripping into the street nearby. A shot at nothing. Frustration.

'Two,' Stark hissed, climbing to his feet with a grimace. His suit was torn at the left knee, the kneecap bloodied. He was covered in blood, hands and arms, chest where the casualty had bled while being carried.

'What the *hell* do you think you were doing?' demanded Fran, the concern on her face boiling off in fury. 'Are you trying to get yourself killed?'

'I wasn't standing there with a *fucking* target painted on me!' he growled, straightening up with a wince. Hardly a cross word to her in two years and now twice in one day.

He could see she was trembling.

There'd be time for soft words later.

Another spurt of tarmac. Short on targets, if not on ammo. 'Three,' he muttered.

'Three *what*?' demanded Fran angrily.

Ignoring her, Stark called to Clark, who'd just come off his radio. 'The college evac?'

'All the students are out, we think. But the caretaker, principal, three teaching staff and two unarmed officers locked themselves in the cash office when Kirsch marched in. Shots were fired inside and we have one officer unaccounted for.'

Stark swore. 'Other casualties?'

'Unknown.'

'Firearms?'

Clark shook his head. 'Every armed response vehicle for miles is still in Abbey Woods or stuck in traffic. Specialist Firearms too.'

'ETA?'

'Fifteen minutes minimum,' confirmed Clark unhappily.

Too long. Kirsch had sold the perfect dummy. Stark bit his lip, looking up at the top of the clock tower high overhead. 'We have to clear the streets.'

'We've got uniforms in the high road. Public are being shepherded away or into shops. Streets cordoned off. But with everyone else holed up in the station, we don't have the bodies . . .' Clark explained.

The lock-down. Stark's doing. Time for a rethink. He turned and walked out into the road to peer at the tower and slipped back into cover as a bullet ricocheted off the kerbstone and across the road. 'Four.'

'*Four* . . . *?*' Fran lost it. '*What the* . . . *living* fuck *are you doing? Have you got a fucking death wish?*'

Stark waved away her distraction, shaking his head as he tried to concentrate, to assess the distances. 'The picture on the basement wall said the rifle has a five-shot magazine, bolt action,' he explained. 'Force him to hurry and he fumbles, rushes his next shot. And he's inaccurate; he's practised for elevation and range, but not tracking.' A glance told him she didn't comprehend. 'Pumpkins don't move. At least with subsonic ammunition he's limited his range.' Her frown returned. 'He's using slow ammo. Greater parabola to distance . . . ?' Still nothing. 'If he retreats up the tower he can put accurate shots through any window within a quarter-mile, inaccurate up to a mile.'

Fran's face paled. Siren noise mercifully drowned out her reply. An ambulance cornered into the street and stopped behind the uniformed car. Stark beckoned urgently to the paramedics.

'Shot through and through, left calf,' he called as they came running up. 'No fracture. Then again through the deltoid muscle, back to front. Heavy blood loss, pulse thready.'

The paramedics were already moving Barclay aside. The young constable stood over them, face ashen, his bloody hands shaking. Stark knew that look.

'Right,' he said, turning to the others. 'We can't wait. Start getting officers out the back of the station but keep them away from Royal Hill, Kirsch will see them. Get them over the rear blocks and out through Gloucester Gardens, and get on to Lewisham for help clearing streets and windows. Get eyes on every exit from the school at safe distance until Firearms take over. We have to keep Kirsch contained. Tell the officers in the cash office to stay put, and direct the SFO team to the rear courtyard for ingress. Give me your ASP, CS and radio.'

'What are you going to do?' asked Clark.

'Be a distraction.'

Fran stared into the eyes of a stranger. Or perhaps she had seen this face once before, when he'd taken a knife from their attacker outside a rancid squat. Fran recalled that instant of murderous fury in his eyes. This was like that, but a colder, distilled, icy fury, hardly less frightening; his face scratched, splattered with mud and smeared with blood.

Clark complied. A sergeant with what . . . twenty-five years on the job? Nodding to a constable. Fran shook her head, disbelieving; but she was no better. Stark had assumed command without hesitation, and those that lead are followed.

So much so, that the reality of his words only sank in as he was stuffing the items into his jacket.

'No!' she barked, grabbing for his arm . . .

Too late. He'd already turned and sprinted away through the gardens and towards the open street.

'*Stark!*' she shouted, but it was futile. The bloody fool!

Something splintered off a tree just after he passed but Stark didn't miss a step, bursting from the garden opposite the college entrance steps and out into the road, right in front of the tower's windows. No showy zig-zagging, just a full-out sprint, or the best he could manage favouring one leg.

'*RUN!*' Fran screamed, as if that would help, as if he might not already think it prudent, as if he could go any quicker on his stupid *bloody* hip. How long did it take to change a rifle magazine, anyway? It was only thirty metres or so but it looked like Stark was in slow motion, wading through water. Any second now he was going to die, she knew it like it had already happened, like some horrible déjà vu. He was going to die and she was going to watch it happen.

But then he bounded up the steps into the darkness, as a chunk of stonework shattered off the modern portico.

'*Shit!*' she breathed, exhaling where she'd not known she was holding her breath. 'Shit! *SHIT!*' She turned to Barclay whose eyes were like saucers.

Fran was still trembling and nauseous. If her mother ever found out what her only daughter had done today she'd have a coronary out of spite. Worse, her dad would give her that look he always produced when she'd tried to do something one of her elder brothers had done and hurt herself in the process; the look that said she was his precious little girl.

She shook that off.

She had work to do . . .

'Barclay,' barked Clark, startling the young officer out of his thousand-yard stare. 'Go the long way round to the back of the station and find Inspector Cartwright. Anyone hurt gets help, anyone not helps us. Roadblocks every junction. Megaphones, door to door, any building with a view of the tower – warn everyone to keep down and away from windows. *Now!*'

Fran already had her mobile out, dialling Groombridge. They had to get this out on the news too. 'Come on, *COME ON!*'

*

Stark's eyes struggled to adjust from daylight to gloom but there was no mistaking the shape on the floor, or the glazed expression staring across the marble. Blood from a chest wound, centre-mass, pooled dark and tacky around the corpse. Stark checked for a pulse all the same. The skin already felt cool.

PC Steve Lamont. The name came to Stark, unbidden.

Chirpy, professional, often the centre of a pocket of laughter in the canteen or locker room. Unmarried, no kids, as if that were solace. Wouldn't have been standing here were it not for Stark's call. Probably the first person Kirsch saw, walking in expecting a building full of targets. Ornate marble steps led up to the main reception through glass doors, crazed with four bullet holes. Five spent cartridges littered the floor. Kirsch had reloaded his revolver here.

Stark closed Lamont's eyelids with a silent agnostic prayer for the fallen – remembrance, and vengeance.

He considered not broadcasting the news, but intel was king and morale the padre's problem. He thumbed the radio. 'Officer down. School of Management foyer. Officer RG-762,' he read from Lamont's collar number. 'Fatal shooting. DC Stark in pursuit of suspect.'

Peering round he picked out the floor plans inside the front door; next to the fire alarm panel for the brigade's use. Wrenching the frame from the wall he studied them, turned right through doors, running along a corridor . . .

A dull thud echoed to meet him. The sound of the suppressed rifle amplified within the larger suppressor of the stair-tower.

'Two.'

77

The car slewed to a halt, thumping up a kerb, the driver ducking down behind the wheel. Groombridge dropped his phone into the footwell with a curse, then blinked at the neat, frosted circular hole through the centre of the windscreen. Peering round he saw where the bullet had disappeared through the rear seat, leaving another hole, less neat, with seating foam feathered out of it. A cloud of dust motes floated in the sunlight. The driver – Groombridge realized he couldn't think of the girl's name . . . bright girl, potential – was trembling. He reached out a hand to comfort her, but the windscreen shattered into thousands of pieces and fell over her, over them.

She screamed.

Looking over his shoulder again he stared at the second hole in the back seat, not ten inches from the first. A second bullet. He'd not realized; he'd thought the screen had just given way from the first. Stupid.

No more stupid than sitting here waiting for a third.

Reality snapped home with stomach-clenching nausea. '*Stay down!*' he shouted, pushing the sobbing girl lower. She was panicking, wildly thrashing at her hair to shake off the myriad glass cubes as if each were a biting creepy-crawly. '*Constable! Stay down! Get as low as you can!*'

He was already thrusting the door open with one foot and pulling himself out of the car. The siren's wail was deafening outside the car, and the lights . . . Stupid! What had they been thinking?

The radio messages were garbled and contradicting. They'd tried to reach the station's side gate down Royal Hill, but it had brought them face on to the clock tower.

As if his own glare were responsible, part of the lights exploded right in front of his face. Something bit his cheek. He felt at it. Blood. A piece of the light. He staggered back, away from the car, tripping on the kerb into pots arranged outside the florist.

The constable was screaming again, sitting up in plain view, taking deep breaths between screams. Groombridge felt himself step forward, but she was opening her door on the far side and climbing out.

'*Stay down*,' he bellowed.

She shot sideways, knocked aside like a doll.

Another five. Fresh target, thought Stark, cursing. Who was on the other end of those shots? Had someone else just been knocked to the ground by an unprovoked bullet they never heard coming?

He peeped round the corner up to his right. A generous, four-sided stair with corner landings; the base of the tower. The crunch of a magazine snapping into place, bolt action, a thump, another bolt action and the sound of an ejected shell casing bouncing down hard stairs.

One.

Stark took the steps two at a time, ignoring an early warning from his hip and a pointed reminder from his ribs.

Groombridge ran round the back of the car and saw her sprawled across the bloody pavement. He reached out for her epaulette and dragged. She was a slim girl, but as dead weight . . . dead weight . . .

He leant out further and dragged with all his might. Friction gave way to his desperation and she slid behind the car with him.

Staying low, he rolled her over. Her eyes were closed. He'd expected the glassy stare of death, but they were closed. He tried to find a pulse.

The car rocked ever so slightly as the rear windscreen shattered above his head. No gunshot, he realized, remembering the report from the old house basement; silenced rifle. It was only then he noticed the number plate was smashed. There were two jagged exit holes in the metal panelling of the boot, each a little Mount Fuji shape tipped with bare metal for snow, level with his head where the first two bullets had gone right through the car. Level with his head. He stared at them dumbly . . . then blinked. Grabbing the girl under her arms he dragged her across the road towards the florist, expecting any second to be knocked sideways himself.

Something whipped through the air and smacked the road away to his right.

He barged the florist's door expecting it to open, but it rattled on its lock. Through the glass he glimpsed the florist peering terrified over her counter.

'*Police, emergency! Open up!*'

He dragged the girl sideways so not even her feet were visible from the tower around the slight curve in the road.

Another bullet tore into the car, then, several seconds later, yet another. Potshots. Vexation, perhaps. There was blood on the road, dragged in a ragged line towards them.

Growling a vicious curse, Groombridge felt for his phone, but it was still in the damn car.

Twisting, he banged on the florist's door. *'Police! Call an ambulance!'*

Five, in quick succession. Oil-blue gun-smoke hung around the fourth level.

Stark closed the distance as fast as possible, but turning the corner into the third-floor landing he heard a change above . . . no mag change . . . but activity . . . *footsteps!* He accelerated, but heard a door slam shut.

Moments later he was on the final flight, the carpet giving way to bare steps, littered with rifle shell casings. The stairwell stopped. This whole last landing obviously hadn't been decorated in years. Kirsch had been able to walk in and ensconce himself up here out of sight with a perfect view of the station. The photo of Harper from here was probably recon as much as stalking. There was a set of small lift doors and a sign across them announcing the lift defunct, itself decrepit. Adjacent, a plain door . . . to more stairs. No handle, lock broken . . . barred from the other side.

He couldn't hope to kick it down with his unreliable hip, or shoulder it open with cracked ribs. His primary objective, after stopping Kirsch getting off shots into the street, had been to prevent him from retreating upwards.

'Suspect heading up tower,' he barked into the radio. 'DC Stark in pursuit.' Cursing his slowness, he cast around and snatched up a fire extinguisher, took a step back and rammed the latch with all his might, bursting the door open with a splintering of wood.

Footsteps echoed down the bare concrete stairwell.

Stark growled, and ran.

78

Fran turned to Clark, whose cohort had swollen by three. They'd all heard it. 'We should head inside.'

Clark shook his head. 'Not without armed support.'

He was right, but she wasn't much for rules right now.

Officer down! crackled Clark's radio for the second time in the space of a minute. Not Stark's voice, but familiar.

Faces already shocked with grief and anger, paled once more. No bullets had hit the station in the last minute, but they'd all heard the screech of tyres round the corner up Royal Hill, and faint sounds of smashing or impacts, achingly out of sight.

Garbled messages overlapped, but Fran picked out a name – Groombridge.

Her heart froze in her chest.

It was several seconds before news emerged that it wasn't him who was injured, but an officer with him, though how badly no one knew. Another ambulance was inbound and one of Clark's uniforms was speaking with them on his radio, directing them down Royal Hill with caution.

'He's stopped firing,' said Clark.

'What the . . . ?' exclaimed another, peering over Fran's shoulder.

She turned to see a news channel satellite van pulling up. Out climbed two guys with cameras and lighting and a woman with platinum-blonde hair in a long, fitted red coat.

*

Straight flights of ten, dog-legging, two flights per floor. Each level had a narrow single-glazed window facing west away from the station and a high, bare windowless cavern in the main body of the tower, the first stacked with old desks and chairs and assorted forgotten items, thereafter empty with the concrete cross-bracing visible. The unbroken noise of Kirsch above allowed Stark to pass each ambush point without caution, but he could feel himself slowing.

Always too slow.

To join the dots and clear this building before anyone got killed. To see through Clive Tilly. To see through Mark White in time to prevent the murder of James Rawlings and the fresh terrorization of Susan Watts. To recognize the ambush that claimed Miriam Kirsch and could just have easily have claimed Fran . . .

The nausea rose up. Seeing his fears confirmed in Miriam's eyes; that he'd let them be led into a kill zone. He fought down the urge to stop and vomit.

Weakness. Always weakness.

Now PC Lamont, and how many more outside? *How many more lives?* He cursed his useless body, cursed the sodding bandages restricting his breathing, cursed his stupidity and cursed Simon Kirsch.

Suddenly he registered a cessation in Kirsch's footfalls above.

Looking up, he saw Kirsch peering down, gasping too, ruddy face twisted in what might have been a snarl or a grin as he started up again. Stark did likewise, but the pause had allowed lactic acid to pool in his legs like hot lead.

Four more flights and his steps were all but drowned out by his ragged breath and thumping pulse. His thighs burned and his ribs stabbed, each step telling him it must be the last, screaming at him to rest. *No, no, NO!*

Madness rolled through Stark, an intensity of fury that almost brought tears. *If that fucker kills one more person today I'll throw him from the fucking roof, even if I have to drag him over myself!*

'If you want to be useful,' Fran barked, 'tell everyone within sight of the clock tower to stay away from their windows.'

'Excuse me?' asked the reporter, turning away from the camera, mid declaratory utterance.

Fran plucked the microphone from her hand, pushed the polished parasite aside and stared into the lens, trying not to think about her dishevelled, muddy, half-crazed appearance.

She'd lost it; she could see that, as if she were trapped inside some separate irrational being, and the only thing preventing her from screaming was the tiny rational Fran inside that was far too cross to blow it now.

Some idiots liked this sort of thing, living off the 'buzz' or whatever moronic jargon they used to justify their self-indulgence. It just made Fran feel like vomiting. Stark was one of those idiots, dashing off as if death hadn't just blown several kisses in his direction. This was his fault! Some people fought and some froze. She hated being the latter and hated him for not. She hated him so much right now.

'This is Detective Sergeant Millhaven of Greenwich Police. A dangerous suspect has been cornered in the Greenwich clock tower armed with a rifle. He has proven himself willing to kill with it. Anyone within sight of

Greenwich clock tower should get as far away as possible and keep away from windows until we give the all-clear.'

'Sergeant, can you confirm the suspect is Simon Kirsch?' demanded the reporter.

Fran flicked the microphone switch off and handed it back. 'Repeat my warning every thirty seconds or I'll arrest you.'

'For what?' asked the woman imperiously.

Fran rounded on her angrily, thrusting her hand over the camera lens. 'For your part in whipping this madman into a killing spree.'

'And what about your part?' demanded the woman. 'What about police blame?'

'*My people are risking their lives to stop this,*' roared Fran, forcing the woman to take a step back. '*What are you and yours doing?*'

The concrete stairs finally gave out to a cast-iron tight spiral stair with daylight glaring through a door. The glazed observation deck, below the roof level. Kirsch had ignored it, going for the roof, another level up.

Stark's baseline fitness had narrowed the gap but injuries old and new meant there still was one. He attacked the spiral steps, but the combination of climbing and turning sent a jolt through his hip. *Not now*, he railed inside. Not today; he'd pay double tomorrow, gladly, if he could just have today for free.

Kirsch disappeared from sight above.

Stark made it to the top of the second spiral, gasping. *Two hundred and sixty steps*, the military OCD announced unbidden. Why did they call it a spiral anyway, when it was a sodding helix?

A doorway with no door opened into another bare antechamber, containing an ancient lift winch. On the far side Kirsch was struggling to pull a heavy rucksack after him through a two-foot-square crawl door – to the lower balcony, thought Stark. The only way out. If Kirsch barricaded it Stark would have to try climbing from the observation deck windows below – a low probability option with a steep downside.

He delved in his pocket, flicked out the ASP baton and jammed it in the door just as Kirsch tried to kick it closed.

With a growl of frustration, Kirsch stamped on the offending article, but Stark had already let go of it to retrieve the CS spray. As the door bounced open he crouched and sprayed upward at the silhouetted figure.

He was rewarded with a choking howl and kept his finger down as Kirsch twisted aside, shielding his face, but a panicky kick sent the little door crashing into Stark's arm and the spray bouncing across the roof.

With deep regret, he ditched the radio too. Intel was king, but, much as he'd wanted to hear of the cavalry's approach, Kirsch mustn't. Crawling through was also a poor option, but all Stark had left. If Kirsch made it to the roof . . .

Fortunately, Kirsch decided a face-full of CS solvent was enough to be going along with, and a free kick at Stark's head wasn't worth waiting around to see what other tricks he might produce. Slinging rifle and backpack over his shoulder with a grunt, he fumbled for the external ladder and began climbing.

Dragging himself through the small opening, Stark creaked upright and reached for the rungs, hoping Kirsch would pause to stamp down and give him something to grab, but the big man seemed more interested in building a lead; in buying time to clear his vision, and ready a weapon. He disappeared over the top.

Gritting his teeth, Stark followed, topped the ladder and peeked over the parapet. Kirsch was on the far side of the little roof, frantically pulling something from his backpack.

Stark recognized the pistol shape, weighed the variables, climbed and leapt.

The pistol came up, and the world turned white.

79

The Taser crackled its vicious, pitiless laughter, clamping Stark's teeth as his convulsing body travelled through the air towards Kirsch.

The impact barely registered but, as he'd hoped, the Taser shorted between their two bodies with a loud *POP* and a grunt from Kirsch as they crashed to the roof.

The relief was instant, but incomplete. Stark's plan, such as it was, was based on his experience of being Tasered during Special Forces selection. But where legal Tasers deliver a short burst of oscillating shock with no lingering effect, the illegal thing in Kirsch's hand had more dangerous frequency and power. Stark could hardly breathe as he fought to regain command of his body. Misjudgements were common in combat. The critical thing was to make sure they didn't kill you.

Cursing, Kirsch shoved Stark off and kicked him away, getting to his feet. Stark did likewise, rolling, practised, fast despite the lingering spasms, and lunged – and this was where luck finally failed him; his foot snagged on the strap of the backpack, robbing him of impetus. Kirsch tripped backwards, swinging his arm defensively, and the stock of the discharged Taser caught Stark a back-handed blow across the cranium.

Concussion-thump like a truck side-swipe. Stark hit the ground without seeing it coming, brain exploding like a fireworks finale . . . Like the whining scream of an

RPG . . . Blackness. Stars . . . Above the deafening shower of debris, the distant sound of a chopper, an Apache? Too quiet for a Chinook. His stomach heaved but didn't vomit, not quite. Vision swimming, he caught a glimpse of camouflage, legs, body, arms, face . . . Soldiers crowding round, mouths moving . . . or was it just one?

MAN DOWN! MEDIC!

The medic rummaged in his backpack and pulled out a massive revolver.

'Deb!'

The reporter's techie was beckoning her frantically to the van's side door. Inside were banks of tech crap and several TV monitors. On one was footage of the clock tower roof. Where one figure stood over another, waving . . . a pistol.

The flashing red word read *LIVE*.

'Shit,' breathed Fran. 'Where is this coming from?'

'Our chopper.'

Fran glanced up, registering the faint chopper noise for the first time.

'Tell them to back away, for Christ's sake. The gunman has a rifle. And he hates you lot almost as much as us.'

'They're a mile out,' said the techie, 'gyro-stable camera.'

Fran stared at the screen, trying to make out who was who, desperately hoping it was Stark standing over Kirsch and not the other way around, desperately wishing the sodding news helicopter would do what all despicable hacks did, and go closer.

Stark raised his hands to ward off danger, confused; dry-swallowing the nausea and panic.

The medic stared down the barrel, grinning.

But it wasn't a medic . . . it was Simon Kirsch, sneering, eyes red and streaming from CS but wild with victory . . . wheezing, coughing, saying something . . . but Stark's head was still ringing.

Keep talking, thought Stark. He rolled over and threw up, retching painfully, waiting for the explosions to subside, for his vision to clear, for something better to happen. Blood ran down the side of his face.

Rushing in headlong might already have cost him his life, but the longer he could distract Kirsch the fewer other lives might be lost. Every second was precious, keeping Kirsch from picking up that rifle again, bringing armed officers closer. *Recklessness.* Hazel's word. But Stark knew hesitation was the greater killer. Luck decided the difference. He owed his life to the Lady, several times over, but he would never bow to her. Her gaze was the cold snake-eyes of the dice, the unblinking barrel of the gun, beyond care or reason. Hope was as futile as prayer. You did what needed doing and accepted the cost; making damn sure it cost the enemy more.

He'd prevented Kirsch from barricading the little door below. Kirsch might kill him any second, but every moment he didn't added to Stark's victory; time for SFOs to scale the tower, lob flash-bangs up over this parapet and storm the roof without Kirsch pinning them down from above. That was Plan B.

Stark had yet to formulate Plan A.

Even if he could force himself up he wouldn't stand much chance. He needed another distraction. '*It's over, Kirsch.*' Hollow words; they rang inside his skull like a bell hammer but came out like a croak.

Kirsch shook his head, hate filling his eyes, raised the pistol and fired.

'*No!*' Fran slammed her palm against the van door, adding to the echo of the gunshot around the abandoned streets, brutal in contrast to the silenced rifle.

But the prone man on screen peered over his raised arm, alive.

The aggressor wore green, she could see that now. Camouflage. Kirsch.

He fired again, and again Stark flinched but didn't die.

'*Bastard*,' hissed Clark, beside her.

Kirsch was toying with Stark. They could see him shouting, or laughing.

'What was Stark thinking?' she said, to herself.

'Buying us time,' said Clark, checking his watch.

Then where the bloody hell were the firearm goons? Fran ground her teeth. For the first time in her career she wished for an armed police force. Not just specialists; everyone. It went against everything she believed, but if she could have it today she would. If she had a gun she'd be legging it up that tower herself. Every bone in her body ached to do so anyway. If Stark had a gun this would've been over two nights ago outside Chase Security.

Instead she was reduced to standing here, watching it play out on TV of all things; useless, helpless, hopeless in the cold certainty that it was about to end in the worst possible way. 'Right, I'm not waiting a moment longer . . .'

She turned towards the tower but at a nod from Clark, the recently arrived Sergeant Dearing blocked her path with his giant frame, a one-man roadblock, calm, polite and immovable.

'Yes, thank you, Jim ... As you can see, events have taken a dramatic turn here, with what is believed to be a police officer at the mercy of the gunman.'

Fran whirled round to see the reporter spouting her smug summary to camera, her face appearing in the corner of the screen in the van with the main image still displaying the unfolding nightmare.

'With exclusive live footage from our own eye in the sky we are the only channel with up-to-the-second live coverage. Sources tell us the gunman is believed to be Simon Kirsch, though police are still refusing to confirm so at this stage . . .'

Fran thought about *confirming* the microphone between the woman's perfect, pearly teeth and scrawling the word VULTURE across her botoxed forehead in scarlet lipstick.

'There are believed to be casualties in the police station itself,' continued the reporter, 'and up to six people still trapped inside the college building . . .'

Where are they getting this from? Fran wondered, before another gunshot tore her attention back to the screens.

80

'Oops . . . *Missed again.*' Kirsch gave a braying, scornful laugh at the rents in the roofing bitumen by Stark's feet.

Three. Stark winced, each shot splitting his head and twisting his stomach. But another not fired into the street, another moment stolen from Kirsch's plan and given to the SFOs. If Kirsch wanted to string this out, Stark would try to oblige. 'What do you want?' he managed, wiping blood from his brow before it gummed up one eye. 'What can you possibly hope to achieve?'

'*Want?*' spat Kirsch. '*Hope?*' His expression twisted with fury. '*I want to forget!*' he shouted. 'I want every memory wiped. But there's no hope of that, is there? You ruined my life! Police, press, you're all the same – filling in the gaps with lies and threats . . . like your precious Detective Inspector Harper! I never stood a chance, then or now. So I want everyone who betrayed me to know what they did. That this is all *their* fault!' The words tumbled out of him like a confession long withheld, finally bursting free on a wave of bilious self-pity. 'They have to *remember!*'

'Remember what?'

'*Remember me!*'

Stark shook his head but regretted it as fresh stars detonated. '*Christ* . . . why not save everyone the bother and just blow your tiny brains out?' Kirsch's face darkened, but Stark pressed on. 'Leave a note if you want some sap to *feel your pain*, but this? You think people will remember you for this? You're a moron.'

The pistol fired into the roof between Stark's knees, the terrible percussion of it tangible. A handgun so ridiculously powerful it only had space for five rounds. One left now. If Kirsch could be provoked into wasting it, Stark's odds would even up. 'People won't even remember your name. There's been too many of these sick sprees now. If anyone does, it will just be to remember what a colossal arsehole you were. Just another narcissistic prick with no feelings in him but selfish rage – hiding behind his rifle like a coward.'

Kirsch looked fit to explode.

The gun shook . . . but didn't fire.

His eyes narrowed. Then his fury warped into dark amusement, lips parting into a vicious sneer. 'I can count too, shithead,' he chuckled darkly, slowly raising the gun from pointing at the roof, to pointing at Stark's face.

So much for that idea, thought Stark bitterly. More seconds, though. Every exchange used up more seconds. Back to Plan B. You couldn't play for time if you were dead. 'There's still time to walk this back a little. I know what Harper whispered to you. God knows you've endured provocation –'

'*Don't talk to me about GOD!*' shouted Kirsch, spittle on his lips. 'I had my fill of that shit from my lying *bitch* of a mother.'

A sore spot, thought Stark, picturing the yellowing scroll of paper, Miriam's brief, neatly written confession. 'Told you, did she? Or did you know all along?'

'*I loved her!*'

Not his mother, clearly. Kirsch was thinking of

Kimberly now. Misery welled in his chemically afflicted eyes. 'We met in the castle as usual . . . our *special* place. I brought candles, and flowers. It was beautiful. *She* was beautiful . . . But after, walking her home . . . it was raining and I lent her my coat, but she just *said* it . . .' His face twisted with anguish as if he still couldn't comprehend it. 'That it was *over*. Like it didn't matter.'

His eyes looked almost pleading, as if Stark could explain it to him. Stark could, unequivocally, but first needed to keep Kirsch talking.

'The things she said to me!' Kirsch said bitterly. 'Everything she'd done behind my back! I slapped her . . . and she fell and hit her head and I couldn't wake her up . . . It was an *accident*!'

And he'd carried her to his mum, the nurse, and begged for her help; and she'd sent him into the house to pray and then held his defiler's nose and lips closed until her heart stopped.

Maybe Kimberly would have died from a cracked skull, who knew? Miriam only cared that the filthy whore who'd stolen her child's innocence, his immortal soul, now threatened to steal him bodily by sending him to prison for murder and probably rape too. *A mother's soul for her son's*, her confession concluded bluntly; her penance for letting him stray, rolled up and hidden away for only Jesus to know. And Simon's penance – twenty years to repent for a killing he didn't commit. And in the end he'd chosen sin over repentance and she'd punished him with the truth, suspecting what might follow, consigning herself to the hell she'd had one foot in all along.

What a waste.

Kirsch's eyes were crazed now, the gun wavering. Stark

weighed his chances, but even moving his head still made it spin.

Kirsch shook his head, as if dispelling the memory, shaking it off. 'Get on your knees,' he snarled.

Stark sighed. 'What for?'

'Get on your knees and *beg*.'

Stark rolled his eyes and rolled up to sitting with his back against the parapet, blinking away the dizziness, taking his time. 'No.'

An execution, thought Fran. We're about to watch an execution live on British TV. This image would be on the front of every newspaper in the country tomorrow.

Behind her the reporter chirped on, barely pausing for breath between the crushingly obvious and rabid hyperbole. This was her Pulitzer moment and she was seizing it.

A screech of tyres announced the arrival of two armed response vehicles. About time, thought Fran bitterly. But what the hell was keeping Specialist Firearms?

Out of one car climbed Detective Inspector Owen *bloody* Harper, square jaw set, wife presumably tucked safely away, ready to take command.

'Right,' he barked. 'Someone tell me what the fuck is going on.'

Clark waved him towards the monitors, then turned to speak hurriedly with the firearms officers, who quickly looked up at the tower, swearing crossly, probably at Stark's disregard for protocol.

'Who the hell . . . ?' Harper stared at the screens in horror. 'Tell me that's not . . . *Stark*? What the hell does he think he's doing?'

'Buying us time,' said Fran, dull-voiced. *But at what cost?*

Harper looked stricken, a wild glare in his eye, almost demented, glancing this way and that as if searching for a better reality. But for him that was just one where Stark wasn't stealing the glory, and to hell with any other considerations . . .

Disgusted, Fran turned away to watch her friend die.

81

'Beg!' sneered Kirsch.

Stark stared down the quivering barrel. 'No.'

'I'll kill you.'

'You'll kill me anyway.'

'Maybe I'll let you live to tell my story.'

'Great idea,' scoffed Stark. 'Shouldn't take too long to tell the world what a loser you were right to the end.'

Kirsch thrust the pistol forward again. 'You think you're *funny*?'

'I'm not the one standing there in surplus camouflage with guns you had to buy online; pretending to be a soldier when everyone knows you're *defective*. Real men earn their ink,' sneered Stark scornfully. 'The Légion Étrangère threw you back like a minnow and that tornado on your arm might as well be a steaming turd. Soldiering, biker gangs, cage fighting, your gypsy mother, it's all bullshit. The best thing I could say about you is that you're a lousy fucking shot.'

Kirsch's anger flared visibly. 'Couldn't catch me in the woods, though, could you, *war hero*? I know who you are. Who's the better soldier now, eh? Get up on your knees, war hero. It's time to beg for my mercy.'

'Mercy?' Stark laughed bitterly, creaking up on to one knee. 'You don't have the heart.'

'I'M ALL FUCKING HEART!' Kirsch exploded, waving the gun like a lunatic. *'I'm all fucking heart! And they*

took it! They crushed it and laughed! Pretending to care as they crushed and stamped and laughed behind my back!'

'*Oh boo*-fucking-*hoo!*' mocked Stark, disgusted. Bloke Rule One – no sympathy. But Simon wasn't a man; he was an amoral, selfish child. Instead of taking his pain he'd pushed it on to others, inflicting exponential horror on strangers to eclipse his own humiliation. 'Look at you. Headline for a day; the fetid arsehole with a gun and nothing to say. You're *pathetic*. Just another snivelling shit failing to compensate for life without love. The only person who *ever* loved you was your mother, and only because that's what mothers do.' Stark was pushing every button he could think of. 'And even she turned on you in the end.'

'Leave my mother out of it!' Kirsch growled threateningly.

'She knew you'd kill her for it. I saw it in her eyes. She knew that bullet was coming, but she was just too tired of being scared of you, too tired of hating you.'

'*I said shut up!*'

'You blew her brains out and left her cooling in the woods for the bugs and crows.' Stark braced himself. 'Right where you left Kimberly for the worms.'

With a guttural growl Kirsch took a stride forward, thrusting the oversized pistol in Stark's face.

Stark jerked his head aside, reaching for the gun and twisting. His posture was all wrong for a disarm, he stood no chance of taking the gun, but he had the satisfaction of hearing a snap and Kirsch's howl of pain.

Let's see how good your rifle aim is with a broken trigger finger, arsehole, he thought with vicious triumph. Short-lived, of course. Victories, however small, always came at a price. Overbalanced on hands and knees, he was wide open.

Kirsch's howl moved seamlessly from pain into fury as he lifted a boot and kicked Stark in the side, sending him over on to his back, gasping, berating himself for offering cracked ribs as a target.

Gritting his teeth, with almost maniacal determination, Kirsch straightened his index finger enough to extract it from the trigger guard and replace it with his middle finger.

His next kick landed on Stark's left hip, right where the titanium plate held him together.

Stark curled up in pain.

'Oh dear . . . still tender there, war hero?' taunted Kirsch. 'Who's *defective* now?'

Stark could only flinch as the big man followed up. He cried out in pain but this time half-faked. He'd twisted enough to take both blows in the meat of his upper thigh rather than his pelvis. He had to eke this out, anything to distract Kirsch from picking up his rifle once more. But he couldn't afford to be knocked senseless. He needed to remain alive, alert, ready. *Give 'em what they want*, hissed his instructor. *Let them know it hurts. Let their satisfaction distract them. Let 'em gloat. Everyone breaks in the end, but make 'em wait.*

The final kick didn't miss.

Kirsch laughed maniacally as Stark writhed on the floor hoping none of the nuts and bolts had given way. 'Not so funny now, are you? No more jokes, no more insults? It's time to beg, *war hero*.

'*Up!*' he screamed. '*Up on your knees!*'

'Tell me that's not who I think it is,' said Groombridge, staring at the banked monitors in disbelief.

Fran turned, her eyes widening in relief and horror at the dried blood he was caked in, not dissimilar in coverage to the mud caking her. 'You're okay?'

He didn't have any bullet holes, but other than that the jury was out.

The paramedics had shoved him aside and gone to work on the girl. PC Marianne Pensol; her name had come to him. Away in the ambulance, status unknown. Unpromising, from the terse vocab of the medics. They hadn't asked if he wanted to ride along, just rushed away, wordless and grim. He'd run across the open street to the back of the station without incident, where Barclay had directed him here to what was rapidly becoming the nerve centre for their collective impotence. 'Never mind me,' he snapped. 'Who's *that*?'

On screen the hostage got slowly to his knees, the gunman aiming the pistol at his head. Groombridge had already glanced around and done the maths. The look on Fran's face confirmed his fears.

'Stupid prick,' muttered Harper.

Groombridge hadn't the time to spare on Owen's pride or prejudice. But if the damn fool was here, Specialist Firearms should be too.

'Mickey!' Tony Clark greeted him with a grim smile and a grimmer update.

Behind him, a huddle of armed response car officers broke apart, checked weapons, chambered rounds, and ran.

82

He should be grateful to be spitting blood and not teeth, Stark supposed, but if this carried on he'd be breathing blood from imploded ribs. Genuine dizziness washed through him again and he made the most of it, putting one hand down and raising a foot so he was on one knee as if he was about to be sick again. Kirsch grinned down in triumph.

That's ten more seconds, arsehole. Give me another ten, I dare you. 'Let me die on my feet.'

'No.' Kirsch laughed. 'On your knees!'

Stark was out of time. He made a show of trying to get up and slumping back down, playing beaten; not much acting required. Every second was precious. He began again, as slowly as he dared, but unless the SFOs showed up any second now he was on his own.

'Up!' Kirsch ordered. 'Get up on your knees and beg, war hero.'

'Not in a million years, you spineless shit!' hissed Stark.

'Beg!'

He could play along, but it might be the last thing he ever did. *Everyone breaks in the end* . . . but not today. Stark shifted his weight, and muttered, 'No wonder Kimberly despised you.'

With an animal scream of rage, Kirsch extended his pistol arm to shoot.

Stark leapt up. He'd surreptitiously positioned his hand

and foot to give him all the thrust he could and he lunged for Kirsch, knocking the weapon aside. But as he did the last bullet fired with a sickening retort. His leg gave way, lost all strength beneath him, and he fell grasping at Kirsch's bandoliers in a desperate effort, dragging Kirsch down on top of him.

Stark clung on but knew it was futile. His leg felt like it was swelling to bursting with a deep, dull agony front to back. Shot through. And whatever strength that left him would not be enough. Cursing, Kirsch kicked himself free, booting Stark in the face, rattling his brain and teeth. It may even have broken his jaw, he couldn't tell. It hardly mattered.

Kirsch scrambled up and levelled the pistol at Stark's head and pulled the trigger.

The satisfaction of finally hearing the hammer strike a spent cartridge and seeing Kirsch's frantic confusion came too late. Stark was all out of tricks, strength and time. Lady Luck smiled with cold indifference. He could only watch as the pistol was clumsily reloaded. There was nothing left to try.

So be it, he thought. He'd done what he could. Bought time. In the end that was all he could do. He let out a deep sigh as the barrel levelled with his head for the last time.

Kirsch spun round and a distant shot rang out.

The church, thought Stark. The bell tower of St Alfege's was the only nearby location high enough. Hell of a one-shot for range and elevation. God bless CO19 for all that sodding practice!

It took a second, but when Kirsch's scream came it was a pig squeal of agony and disbelief as he clutched his side, looking around madly for the shooter. Starting to crumple, he tripped over his bag, staggering back towards the edge of the roof.

Stark made it to one knee, blood gushing from his other thigh. Pain twisting his vision, he launched himself and got a hand to Kirsch as the big man struck the low stone coping and toppled backwards. Stark got a second hand on, just as his own hips and waist slammed up against hard stone. Before he could think he found himself bent over the parapet holding Kirsch by his bandoliers over the hundred-foot drop to the main roof below.

His feet began to lift and he instinctively tensed every muscle in his body, trying to somehow grip the parapet with his midriff, to stop his legs rising and tipping them both into thin air.

Over Kirsch's shoulder the Magnum spun silently down, seeming to take more time than it should, missed the main roof and smashed itself to bits on the unforgiving ground.

83

Kirsch stared up at him, face a mask of pure terror, mouth working open and closed like a fish out of water. 'Up,' he managed. '*Pull me up! PULL ME UP!*' His voice rose to a shriek.

Stark just held on, frozen by his own fear.

Kirsch's hands gripped Stark's wrists desperately, but his left was covered with blood and slippery. Stark couldn't see the man's wound but it seemed there was little Kirsch could do to help himself.

'*PULL ME UP!*'

Stark was pretty sure he couldn't, and unsure if he wanted to try. Just around the corner was the narrow ledge-parapet of the tower's lower roof ten feet below, but there was no hope of him swinging Kirsch on to it, or of Kirsch staying on it if he did. 'Just wait,' he gasped. 'Cavalry on the way.'

With a slow ripping sound the left bandolier started to part slightly. How ironic it would be if Kirsch were to fall to his death because of a cheap military fake.

Kirsch's hand slipped off Stark's wrist, snatched back on, but slipped off again.

Panicking, he began frantically fumbling inside his coat, pulled out a small pistol and pointed it at Stark's face.

Another gun, thought Stark distractedly. This is getting farcical. If the Magnum had looked ridiculously large in Kirsch's hand, this looked ridiculously small. One of those baby Berettas so popular in the States now, where the addiction to concealed gun permits was growing fast. Trust a fantasist like Kirsch to crave the quietest, the biggest and the smallest.

'PULL. ME. UP!'

Stark stared blankly down the barrel. At the back of his brain he could feel the pain in his leg, but his arms and shoulders were burning now too, his hips and stomach were agony against the unrelenting stone, his ribcage was splitting, every muscle in his legs was at snapping point trying to keep his toes in friction with the roof and he was bleeding from a bullet hole.

He began to laugh. That hurt even more but he couldn't stop himself.

Kirsch stared up in disbelief. Thrusting the gun higher, inches from Stark's eyes, he hissed, '*Pull me up now!*'

'Or what?' laughed Stark. Every chuckle lessened his breath, lessened his strength, but he couldn't see past the absurdity. 'Or you'll shoot me?'

Kirsch nodded frantically. 'Pull me up or both of us die!'

'Do it then.' The words came out cold, the laughter fading. They locked eyes and Stark felt a chill. 'Do it, you pointless loser.'

'*I mean it!*'

'So do I.' And he did. He should probably let go before Kirsch realized that. No one would ever know. Kirsch had made his choice the moment he opened fire on a stranger. Before that it was just twenty years in prison, twenty years to explain, the rest of his life to be a man. Now no one would listen. Whether he came down from the tower dead ,or alive, no one would care. He'd chosen wrong.

Stark suddenly recalled his conversation with Groombridge, about dangling Kirsch from the roof. Here he was after all. But he hadn't the breath in him to ask whether Kimberly Bates really was buried in those woods where Miriam Kirsch now lay dead . . . Or to laugh. Truth and laughter were for others now.

Twisting with desperate effort Kirsch managed to raise the pistol higher, barrel pressed hard against the centre of Stark's forehead. 'I *will* do it,' he gasped.

The finger tightened on the trigger in front of Stark's eyes . . . but a strange peace was descending. Did Kirsch feel it too or was it just Stark? Perhaps the blood loss was beginning to tell. If the bullet had severed his femoral artery he'd be dead already, but it might've nicked it. There was a discernible dimming at the edge of his vision. It could equally be that with his diaphragm crushed into the stone the physical effort was slowly suffocating him. Either way, his strength was fading fast. Any second now his toes would lose contact with the roof and their combined weight would carry them both over.

He dragged in one last breath. '*I . . . don't . . . care.*'

Kirsch's panic was overwritten with blind fury.

The command formed in Stark's mind but his hands wouldn't listen. He willed them to open, to give in to their agony, to let go, but nothing . . .

The trigger finger tensed.

The shot rang out.

Both men looked at each other, at the cold, un-smoking gun. Blood bubbled up from Kirsch's mouth, and fear in his eyes. He choked. The little pistol fell away and tumbled over and over as his hand gripped at his ribs, trying to stem the gushing blood. He was a dead man, he just didn't know it yet.

And still Stark couldn't make his fists open.

Second shooter? he puzzled. They were dangling over the rear corner of the tower, away from the church, he thought idly as he watched the pistol turn all the way down and slam into the pavement near the first. His toes slipped an inch and bit again. Try as he might he could not draw breath. He could feel his face swelling, passing red into purple.

He stared at the dying Kirsch. This was what history would remember. Spree killers turn their guns on themselves, but Kirsch didn't have the balls. It was never about going out in a blaze of infamy; it was about ego, spite, the fantasy of revenge. Kirsch wasn't just an arsehole, he was a coward, thought Stark, wishing he had breath to say it aloud. Instead he rolled his tongue round his dry mouth, summoning what saliva he could, and with the final air in his body and every ounce of disdain in his soul, he spat in Kirsch's face.

Kirsch's panic turned to horror, and he slipped from Stark's failing grip just as Stark's toes lost their battle with physics and tipped him up and almost over.

Balanced atop the stone parapet, arms and legs flailing at thin air, Stark watched Kirsch fall; not toppling as the pistols had, just arcing slowly backward with that look on his face: fear, panic and the knowledge that the very last thing anyone thought of him in this world was to spit in his face.

He clipped the edge of the main roof and spun into the ground like a rag doll.

*

Stark's limbs clamped down on stone. He clung there limpet-like, gasping, staring at the body far below. Then movement to his right caught his eye. On the far end of the main building roof ... A marksman in black police combats stood up and stared at him, rifle in hand. The second shooter. A much easier shot than the guy from the church, technically. And infinitely harder. Kirsch's final victim. Condemned to remembering the squeezing of a trigger. The man was shouting something but Stark couldn't hear it.

Releasing his grip, he fell back on to the roof, his diaphragm imploding to suck air into his lungs.

He rolled up into a sitting position, back propped against the parapet.

Blood seeped from his thigh in time with his slowing heartbeat, not gushing but not stopping, pooling on the roof. He should do something about it ... but the effort was daunting.

Maybe he was already too weak. Or maybe it was something else; like his hands refusing to drop Kirsch, refusing to do what they should, the seemingly endless mutiny of soul against mind, between instinct and rational action.

His head was swimming now, vision dimming, lids getting heavy.

So it *was* blood loss.

And here he was again; much the same. Pain, dull in the background somewhere behind nausea and growing chill, utter weariness and willing capitulation to immobility, encroaching darkness and the overwhelming sense of relief. That peaceful feeling. That you'd done all you could and now it was up to someone else.

This time he was alone, though. No faces crowding

round, soldiers talking, reassuring; no medic. People would be on their way, charging up the endless stairs, but they'd be too late. No one to decide for him. Pity.

But faces did flit in his tunnelling vision . . .

Fran, livid with him, of course.

Groombridge's penetrating gaze, his unspoken disappointment.

Lovelace, looking on in embarrassment as his mother tearfully thanked Stark over and over in the hospital; then mother and fiancée weeping at the passing of his flag-draped coffin.

Major Collins' widow, Margaret, defiant morning-yellow dress bleeding to mourning black. He tried to bring her husband's face to mind, but couldn't . . . Couldn't see any of them any more. He ran through the names instead, roll-call of the dead, culminating with Miriam Kirsch and Steve Lamont. Of course he didn't know how many lay in the street below, or in ambulances. He tried to remember how many shots Kirsch had made but it was too many. Too many.

Promise you'll never do anything so bloody stupid ever again! chided his mother's voice, tearily.

Sorry, Mum, he thought.

The sun broke the clouds, turning its beady yellow stare on him with carrion care from the fluttering sheen of death-black feathers. The darkness was closing in. He should do something about that . . . But in the end, what was the point? If it came down to him, Joseph Peter Stark; who didn't fit, never had, never would, not here, not anywhere . . . He'd lived two years past his allotted time already and given all he could give. Not enough.

Never enough. Regret was the only feeling one could never outwait.

But he'd not broken faith. He hadn't.

Head drooping, he stared down at numbing fingers, white as stone crosses, tainted with poppy-red blood, and the deepening darkness between them.

So be it.

'Pillock,' tutted Pierson.

Leave me alone, he pleaded silently. *I never broke faith. Leave me alone.*

The last voice he heard was Kelly's. 'I love you, Joe . . .'

EPILOGUE

84

Groombridge watched the coffin being lowered into the ground. Funerals never sat easy with him. He'd attended too many, hovering at a discreet distance, letting the families know you were there but staying out of the way. So many of them said thanks. Too many.

Like Brian Bates.

As a murder detective, the moment you strived for was always bittersweet.

Groombridge had sat quietly and let Neville Darlington deliver the news. Bates had listened and nodded and stared at the golden necklace in the evidence bag, his trembling fingers hovering over it as if uncertain whether he was allowed to touch it, or if he dared. Dared believe it was over.

The bones had lain buried in Oxleas Woods all this time. Dental records and preliminary DNA confirmed the following morning. Kimberly Bates. Miriam Kirsch's one act of truth, right there in the resting place of her greatest lie. Two empty plastic bleach bottles and an empty jar of chilli powder went some way to explaining why the dogs never found her. The weather, manpower and bad luck probably played more part.

Kimberly's father listened to it all, and then thanked them . . . That his girl would at last, at least, have a funeral. That he could lay her in the ground beside his wife. Thanked them. And then, slowly, put his face in his hands and wept twenty years of tears.

Inspector Cartwright had joined them for the phone call to Billy Forester's daughter, Billie, now Linda, married with a child on the way. Neville explained finding her father's body in Deptford Creek all those years ago and wanted her to know, for what it was worth, that the man most likely responsible had paid for it in the end. Odd that a woman who barely remembered her natural father should cry for him all the same. *She'd* thanked them too.

Kimberly Bates' funeral would be in the coming weeks, once the coroner released the remains. Groombridge would be there, and Neville, fate willing. The old DI looked sallow and shrunken in the coat, scarf and hat his wife had swaddled him in. His own appointment with the earth could hardly be far from his mind right now. Deputy Assistant Commissioner Stevens would be there too. He'd put himself in front of every camera he could in the last week, trying to prevent his career following his reputation down the toilet.

Stark had been right. There *had* been more than one leak. Acting on his supposition, Maggie had apprehended one mole busy texting updates throughout the whole ordeal, right from the control room where he was primary uniform liaison with Maggie's civilians. Groombridge was quite sure that disarmingly cheerful Maggie would cheerfully de-arm the culprit if she ever clapped eyes on him again. Hell had no fury like an old softie betrayed. But the man wasn't facing charges. Caught red-handed, he'd confessed to spilling confidential information, not to the press, but to DAC Stevens. Rumour had it he was a Freemason candidate trying to curry favour, but he claimed he was just following orders and was now parked firmly behind a union lawyer. He'd be moved to a different station. Stevens hadn't denied the texts, dismissing them as merely 'judicious oversight'.

The second leak was worse, but harder to prove. The photo on Kirsch's basement wall-of-hate showed Harper, recent masonic initiate, passing a file to Stevens. Both men had dismissed it as an innocent progress update, but that sort of flannel never washed with the rank and file and would be hard for the brass to overlook. Too many snippets of information had found their way to the press.

That was the crux.

While Cox had been edging for promotion, someone up-chain had been agitating for change, for power. The illicit paper Cox had shown Groombridge proposed a number of mergers, consolidating boroughs to cut costs. The name on the proposal – Deputy Assistant Commissioner Stevens. The 'Super Boroughs' would each be led by Chief Superintendents, no doubt supporters of Stevens and any bid he planned for Commissioner. Greenwich and Lewisham had been identified as the ideal trial subject. Both Cox and the young Super of Lewisham were 'acquaintances' of Stevens' and both were in line for promotion to Chief, but Stevens was more likely to garner support from a new-broom climber than old-school copper.

As well as his spy in Maggie's team, Stevens had foisted Harper on them not as a salve but as a puppet, extracted information and leaked it at key moments to destabilize and discredit the borough. All it took was a pay-as-you-go phone and the number of a friendly reporter. In this case, Groombridge suspected, a bottle-blonde with a penchant for red, working for a satellite news station with affiliate newspapers. Utterly deniable, of course. Stevens could blame the whole thing on phone hacking, where lack of proof was cover enough. No amount of public enquiries or prosecutions would drag a confession out of the press.

The best that could be hoped for was that opponents to Stevens' plan now had the ammunition to quietly see him off.

Little compensation for the terrible loss.

The threat of internal changes had lifted too. Cox wouldn't be moving on up any time soon; this was his patch, his mess. So Groombridge would not be taking his chair, acting or otherwise, and 'austerity' therefore dictated that Harper's secondment 'not be extended'. That was the outward message, at least. Harper could brazen out his collusion with Stevens, but not the interview footage. So far, knowledge of his incendiary threat to Kirsch remained hidden in the silence of the interview recording. Public knowledge might end his career, but it was wider knowledge inside the station that Harper feared more. Officers had died.

Fran shifted on her feet beside him, her impatience with the world never far from the surface.

The vicar concluded his ministrations and one by one coppers began filing past to pitch a pinch of earth into the hole.

Fran would never forget seeing Stark lowered down the side of the tower on a thread-thin black rope; dangling limp, lifeless.

It had taken an age to get to that point and, apart from the two paramedics who'd raced up the tower to relieve the firearms officers, no one knew whether he was alive or dead. Groombridge had ordered Sergeant Dearing to deter Fran from charging up there and getting in the way.

She still hadn't forgiven him, and the fact that he was right wasn't going to change that any time soon.

There was no easy way to get Stark down the winding stairs, apparently, and the air ambulance didn't have winch capability. The coastguard offered but the firearms boys got their ropes together and heaved Stark over the side instead.

So ignominious. So cold. The news channels ran the footage over and over. Video excerpts were all over the internet.

Fran shuddered, unable to forget the skin, where it wasn't livid with bruising or caked with blood – corpse white. The paramedics' haste gave hope. Their grave expressions stole it back. They slammed the doors and rushed him away to hospital.

When Fran finally got there the doctors were unwilling to speculate and only Groombridge's arrival averted her ejection into the street. One of the paramedics had thoughtlessly told her that he'd never felt a pulse so weak in a patient that lived. Stark had lost about as much blood as a body can lose. If he hadn't thought to use his belt as a tourniquet he'd have been dead before anyone reached him.

Surgeons operated to stop the bleeding, closed the wound temporarily, topped up his blood, slapped on an oxygen mask and hoped for the best.

Marcus Turner had stopped by the hospital to offer some authoritative medical translation and, when Groombridge wasn't looking, to squeeze Fran's hand. Bloody man – nearly made her cry. But he couldn't linger. His own grisly vigil called; to assist SOCO in the exhumation of the shallow grave in Oxleas Woods and subsequent identification work. Marcus had driven the DNA samples to the lab himself.

Fran stamped her feet on the cold ground, and hunkered down in her coat collar. Shallow graves, in her opinion, were as lazy as they were insulting.

That first night in the hospital had been torture. Kelly had shown up, hesitant and stiff-faced with worry; Major Pierson decked out in desert fatigues, cap and boots, on her way somewhere, unhesitant, short on time and temper. And the mother, terrified and tearful. Same hospital, same patient. None of them smiled at the déjà vu. Nor at the blunt-faced head-shrink, Doctor Hazel *bloody* McDonald; so *infuriatingly* calm and compassionate, worse even than the police counsellors.

Extras had been drafted in to begin the arse-covering clean-up. The cheek to suggest she take 'personal time'! To ask how she *felt*.

Incan-*bloody*-descent!

Ready to slit her throat just for the chance of marching into hell and giving Simon Kirsch the slap he so richly deserved.

Or at least that's how she'd feel tomorrow, or the day after. Right now she still felt . . . numb; the anger hovering just out of reach, forcing her to fumble elsewhere for an outlet. But in the meantime she had a team to hold together, and a mountain of work to delegate to keep their heads busy. Later, a week from now, a month, she'd go home, get royally pissed, cry and probably break something; but not yet.

How *dare* they?

'I'm not confident of funeral etiquette, Sergeant,' said Groombridge quietly, 'but I think unconscious tutting is probably poor form.'

'Guv,' muttered Fran, only just stopping herself from tutting again.

Their turn came and she shivered in the freezing air, shuffled forward and threw dirt on a wooden box. She could summon no words to say or think, other than she hoped he'd died knowing he'd made a difference.

She'd gone with Groombridge right after Kimberly's father had been told. Striding past the receptionist's odd protestations in his hurry to share the news with his old Sergeant, his stride only breaking at the sight of the stripped bed, sanitized room and the commiserating eyes of the nurse.

Ronald Cooper had passed away in his sleep the night before.

85

Hazel waited while the consultant scribbled something on Stark's notes.

She felt anxious. Not an inappropriate state. Their first session, as the doctors brought him round, had begun and ended with one croaky word. 'No.'

Not the most auspicious start.

Since then he'd refused to see anyone except his mother.

DS Millhaven wasn't taking that well. But it was hardest on Kelly. Finding her hovering, distressed, Hazel had sat with her over a coffee. Things were complicated there, perhaps too complicated for hope; but letting go was easier to think than do.

The nurses said he was a model patient, if quiet. Hazel would expect nothing else. The pain was troubling him, they thought, confused that the morphine wasn't suppressing it. But Hazel knew that previous experience had somehow taught him to see around it. 'Smoke and mirrors', he'd called it. Morphine didn't remove pain, merely hid it.

The second operation, to review the stitching on the femoral artery and assess the muscle and nerve damage, had gone well. He was young and would recover quickly, they said, though quickly was a relative term. He was looking at weeks of rehab and physio, perhaps months. They seemed to think his previous experience would stand him in good stead in that regard. Hazel was less sure. He mended quickly but loathed hospital, loathed incapacity, loathed reliance on others and was apt to attack recovery with too much impatience, leading to inevitable frustration.

No broken jaw, but a stupid amount of bruising. More had radiated out across much of his torso, she'd been told. Ribs now broken, but not displaced. No fracture to his skull but another dozen stitches. More to his tally, she thought. Did he even keep count any more?

Stubbly hair and chin, he looked more gaunt than ever, almost cadaver-like.

He'd grown leaner over the last few months, harder, throwing himself into exercise to plug a Kelly-shaped gap; but it was more than that. Indeed the signs had been there earlier, visible with the twenty-twenty clarity of professional hindsight. As with most things he'd pushed too far, too fast, too hard. Penance, and not just for Kelly. Ever conscious of his previous decline, Hazel had witnessed this calcification with growing alarm, her subtle interventions ignored, her unsubtle ones rebuffed.

And now this . . .

He may have shut himself off from colleagues, but he'd been watching the news to satisfy his inevitable first question – How many?

In that respect alone the news had been better than feared, but not good. No one in the police station was seriously hurt. Some cuts from flying glass, a few knocks from panic and plenty of emotional trauma to keep *her* ilk busy for a while. But the officer Stark had rescued from the street looked to have pulled through. PC Chris Woods. PC Steve Lamont hadn't been so fortunate. Not someone Stark knew above a nod, DCI Groombridge said. Along with the traffic cop, PC Greg Butler, from the previous week. The funerals would be held after the coroner was done with the bodies but before the doctors here were done with Stark's. And today, someone called Sergeant Cooper was being buried.

Stark had talked in the past of missing funerals. Those flown home while he fought on. Those killed that fateful day that ended his war. Others while he recovered. More since. He knew shame was illogical but couldn't shake it. Hence his pilgrimage to Wootton Bassett to watch Private Lovelace's cortège.

And then there was the shame in his injury, knowing that he could never go back, never do what he'd trained for, never be the soldier inside, while his comrades went into battle without him. Soldiers from his old TA company had deployed since. Some had died. Dear God, how did any of them cope, coming home? Even the ones who came through outwardly unscathed?

Her fingers tightened around the book in her hands; a beautiful leather-bound anthology of war poetry that Stark had given her after that first partial breakthrough, suggesting some might explain what he could not, and in his way gently mocking the shelves of vocational tomes lining her office. The poems made her weep. What did they do to Stark? Never once a tear let fall, in all their sessions. Nor even in the lonely dark, she suspected. What did it cost him to hold them in? How much more did he think he needed to give? Or atone for?

The media were already clamouring for him to be awarded the George Cross, the non-combat equivalent of his Victoria Cross. He would be the first person ever to receive both, to 'do the double' as they blithely declared it, with no inkling . . . Another weight to his chest, another pressing to his mute endurance.

A pushy young reporter had sweet-talked her way in, claiming acquaintance, but been ejected before she made it into Stark's room. She'd be back, in that form or another. Hazel had once probed the possibility of Stark telling his story. *Selling*, he'd countered. The pressure would be all the greater now, but she wouldn't raise it again.

The other injured officer, Stark *had* known personally. Constable Marianne Pensol. Shot but survived through the quick actions of DCI Groombridge. A ricochet, the bullet was removed from her right lung and she was expected to make a full recovery. That ought to be good news, but Stark would likely look past her survival to her trauma and stack yet another stone upon his chest.

Remembrance, thought Hazel, recalling where this had all started. Conscious memorial or guilty conscience, wounded soldier or haunted killer, it all came down to what you did with it. How you channelled it. Construction, or destruction. Good versus bad. Hope over despair. The difference, she hoped, between Joseph Stark and Simon Kirsch.

Hazel sighed. There was no telling how this would go. People would say that it was her job to know, but she wasn't a mind-reader. Sometimes – often, in fact – she was glad of it. More often than not with Stark. God knew which of his torments was going through his mind at any one time.

But today was different. For only the second time, he had asked to see her. And today, she held the joker. So much of her job was about timing. Careful listening, observation, patience, and timing. Choosing when to speak was as critical as deciding what to say or how.

He had all but died, again. *All but.* That was her winning card.

He was never likely to wash down a fistful of pills with a bottle of whisky, whatever his past abuse of the two. He couldn't. He was trapped by his debt to the dead and the living. He subsumed despair, accepting the manifest hardening in sentiment that cut him off further. Thoughts of blissful oblivion were dismissed as indulgence. Self-murder was not an option. But, presented with peril, he consistently marched forward. Though it always appeared to be the right thing to do, the 'heroic' thing even, he would argue something darker; anger most often. He described a kind of cold clarity descending, that even to Hazel's professional ears sounded chillingly clear-headed. Anger made him logical, he said. It made him do what he must. But it also made him question his motivation afterwards and devalue his victories. He seemed only ever to see what he'd failed to do, never what he'd done.

It was a perverse kind of conceit. He placed himself firmly at the centre of his own universe, but not in a narcissistic way. If a tree fell in the woods it was his to hear and his fault it had fallen. He thought, therefore he was responsible. Perhaps he really did think everything else was a metaphysical uncertainty?

Hazel would argue that in his experiences anger was just, and his logic both faultless and all the more remarkable for it, the clarity to choose the lesser of evils. It was going to be a long argument, long overdue. He had a number of arguments ahead, if his list of rejected visitors was any measure.

She sighed again. So many variables.

The transition from depression to acceptance was never clear and never quick.

But a joker did no good in your hand. Sooner or later you had to play it. She could draw this out, try to get *him* to say it, but he would see through it and dig his heels in. Sometimes that was worth it for the sheer provocation, but not today. *She* would have to say it:

The tourniquet.

Instinct might have prevented him simply toppling from the roof, giving in to gravity; but instinct had nothing to do with the tourniquet. Bleeding to death didn't require a decision, merely inaction; a blameless slide into the welcoming darkness. No one would ever have known. But in that final moment, some voice in his head had persuaded him otherwise. He'd chosen life. And for the first time in their relationship Hazel had something to work with, a fulcrum with which she might eventually lever him free.

He stirred, eyes fluttering open, lips smacking, working his dry mouth, moving his neck stiffly to look around. His squint came to rest on Hazel.

The consultant retracted his pen point with a click and nodded. 'Ready?'

Hazel took a deep breath and let it out. 'Ready.'

Acknowledgements

The completion of any book owes as much to the forbearance, enthusiasm and effort of others, as to the author. None more so than this. The delight with which I explored this second Joseph Stark novel was augmented by all those who read, reviewed or shared the first, and in some cases let me know they were looking forward to more. If, reading this, you are one of them – thank you. Nothing gives a debut author greater encouragement than to hear their book is being read with appreciation.

Particular thanks must go to Gwen and Wendy, their countless helpers and all the wonderful people of Waverton, for their kindness and hospitality, hard work in promotion of reading and debut authorship, and for voting *If I Should Die* their *Waverton Good Read – British Debut Novel of the Year 2014–15*. I could not have hoped for any finer accolade, nor a more invigorating boost to my efforts with this sequel.

Finally, I offer profound thanks to all my loving family for their unstinting faith, to firm friends and warm acquaintances who never tired of asking how it was going, to my agent and editor for their elastic patience and discerning input, my copy editor for her keen-eyed care, everyone busy on my behalf at Penguin Books (Michael Joseph imprint) for affording me this chance, but most of all, as ever, to my darling wife and sons, for the joy.

He just wanted a decent book to read ...

Not too much to ask, is it? It was in 1935 when Allen Lane, Managing Director of Bodley Head Publishers, stood on a platform at Exeter railway station looking for something good to read on his journey back to London. His choice was limited to popular magazines and poor-quality paperbacks – the same choice faced every day by the vast majority of readers, few of whom could afford hardbacks. Lane's disappointment and subsequent anger at the range of books generally available led him to found a company – and change the world.

'We believed in the existence in this country of a vast reading public for intelligent books at a low price, and staked everything on it'
Sir Allen Lane, 1902–1970, founder of Penguin Books

The quality paperback had arrived – and not just in bookshops. Lane was adamant that his Penguins should appear in chain stores and tobacconists, and should cost no more than a packet of cigarettes.

Reading habits (and cigarette prices) have changed since 1935, but Penguin still believes in publishing the best books for everybody to enjoy. We still believe that good design costs no more than bad design, and we still believe that quality books published passionately and responsibly make the world a better place.

So wherever you see the little bird – whether it's on a piece of prize-winning literary fiction or a celebrity autobiography, political tour de force or historical masterpiece, a serial-killer thriller, reference book, world classic or a piece of pure escapism – you can bet that it represents the very best that the genre has to offer.

Whatever you like to read – trust Penguin.